Long Time *Coming*

 Published in the United States of America. ISBN: 978-1-962626-41-5

FOLLOW ME

To keep up to date with her writing and more, visit S.L. Scott's website: www.slscottauthor.com

To receive the newsletter about all of her publishing adventures, free books, giveaways, steals and more:

https://geni.us/SLScottNL

Follow me on TikTok: https://geni.us/SLTikTok
Follow on IG: https://geni.us/IGSLS
Follow on Bookbub: https://geni.us/SLScottBB

ALSO BY S.L. SCOTT

To keep up to date with her writing and more, visit her website:
www.slscottauthor.com

To receive the scoop about all of her publishing adventures, free books, giveaways, steals and more:

Visit www.slscottauthor.com

Join S.L.'s Facebook group: S.L. Scott Books

Read the Bestselling Book that's been called **"The Most Romantic Book Ever"** by readers and have them raving. We Were Once is now available and FREE in Kindle Unlimited.

We Were Once

You do not want to miss the international sensation, **Best I Ever Had.** This book has won readers over with its emotion and soul deep love. **Best I Ever Had** is now available in ebook, audio, and paperback, and is Free in Kindle Unlimited.

Best I Ever Had

Audiobooks on Audible - CLICK HERE

Peachtree Pass Series (Stand-alones)

Long Time Coming

Lead Me Knot

TBD

The Westcott Series (Stand-alones)

Swear on My Life

Never Saw You Coming

Forgot to Say Goodbye

When I Had You

Never Have I Ever - Faris Family Series

Speak of the Devil - Faris Family Series

Hard to Resist Series (Stand-Alones)

The Resistance

The Reckoning

The Redemption

The Revolution

The Rebellion

The Crow Brothers (Stand-Alones)

Spark

Tulsa

Rivers

Ridge

The Crow Brothers Box Set

DARE - A Rock Star Hero (Stand-Alone)

New York Love Stories (Stand-Alones)

Never Got Over You

The One I Want

Crazy in Love

Head Over Feels

It Started with a Kiss

The Everest Brothers (Stand-Alones)

Everest - Ethan Everest

Bad Reputation - Hutton Everest

Force of Nature - Bennett Everest

The Everest Brothers Box Set

The Kingwood Series

SAVAGE

SAVIOR

SACRED

FINDING SOLACE

The Kingwood Series Box Set

Playboy in Paradise Series

Falling for the Playboy

Redeeming the Playboy

Loving the Playboy

Playboy in Paradise Box Set

Stand-Alone Books

Best I Ever Had

We Were Once

Along Came Charlie

Missing Grace

Finding Solace

Until I Met You

Drunk on Love

Lost in Translation

Sleeping with Mr. Sexy

Morning Glory

LONG TIME COMING

S.L. SCOTT

1

Christine "Pris" Greene

Fridays are the best day of the week.

I practically shoulder the door open to Peaches' Sundries & More in my rush to get inside. If I'm even five minutes late, I'll end up empty-handed. The smell of fresh bread escapes through the door as the bell chimes above my head.

Coming from the bright outdoors, I take a quick second for my eyes to adjust to the indoor lighting. And when they do, I'm not disappointed. One remains. One glorious cheddar biscuit sits inside the bakery display.

"Lauralee?" I call, walking toward the glass-and-brass-trimmed display. I'm used to my best friend greeting me when I walk in. When she doesn't, I peer above the counter and toward the ice cream on the right side of the register. "Lauralee?"

"In the back with some cookies," she says, her voice slipping through the crack of the swinging door to the back. "I'll be right out."

"I'm getting the last biscuit, okay?"

"It's all yours."

I lean over the counter to slide the case open from the back, but I can't wedge it open far enough. My stubborn side sends me toward choosing the more difficult route in everything I do, and since I have no intention of climbing over the counter, I prop my knees on a stool and try again. I just about have the buttery, cheesy bread of the heavens in my hand when someone says, "Pris?"

Startled, I slip forward, sending my ass into the air as I slide toward a face-plant on the linoleum floor. Big hands catch me, grabbing my hips as the strength of fingers dig into the plush of my lower waist.

The voice . . .

The nickname . . .

The butterflies awakened from the dead now fluttering in my stomach . . .

I'm brought to safety on the stool again and swirl around to come face-to-face with the same man I just dreamed about rather recently. Though I'll keep that tidbit to myself instead of giving him the pleasure. I smirk. "I haven't been called that in a long time."

His smile just about knocks me right off this stool again. I'd forgotten how potent it was. Although, judging by my heart's rapid pace, it didn't. I'm right back to that sweet sixteen little girl who righteously earned the nickname. "It's been a long time all around."

I can't help but notice his hands haven't left the curve of my hips, and it seems he notices at the same time. I'm released against my silent protests, leaving a chill where his warm palms once were. Regretfully, my brother's best friend never held me like that before. He didn't take the chance. The threat of death from the middle Greene sibling, my brother Baylor, might have played a part as well.

I set one foot down and then not so gracefully scuttle down until I'm solid on both, coming toe-to-toe with my childhood crush after eight years. A lot has changed.

His hair isn't as wild, though I wouldn't call those strands on top tame. The Pass's winds probably whipped through them when he arrived in town. A day or two worth of stubble only adds to the rugged good looks he was bestowed at birth. I have imagined a clean-shaven face from the last time I saw him. My memory didn't serve as well as the real thing does. I think he's even taller, if that's possible. *Damn him.*

"It sure has. Tagger Grange," I say, smiling like I still have a crush on the guy. I might. *Fine. I do.* The rolled-up sleeves and tailored pants aren't deterrents to scrambling my chemistry all over again for him. "What brings you back to Peachtree Pass?" Straightening the skirt of my dress after revealing a lot of leg in my almost tumble from the stool, I fuss about it. But when the hem anchors on the top of my boot, I leave it, not wanting to come off as nervous. This dress is the least of my concerns since the man in front of me is busy stealing my full attention.

A smile hasn't left his face, but it's not pure sunshine. The devil lies inside as he looks me over like my brothers wouldn't kick his ass if they caught him. Licking his lips, he takes a breath and slowly exhales. "It was time."

The way his green eyes hold my gaze, I start taking inventory of all the ways I could have made more effort today—a swipe of mascara and a coat of lip balm are all that I'm wearing on my face while I chose a dress I reserve when it's laundry day for everything else in my wardrobe. My cowgirl boots are scuffed and worn, broken in, and the most comfortable pair of shoes I own. I can't say I'd be wearing anything else other than these, but maybe something more feminine would have given me the confidence to stare into his eyes a little longer.

"Can I have these, Daddy?"

Daddy? I look down at the boy tugging on Tagger's hand. His eyes are green like his dad's, and his smile so sweet as he looks up at Tag like he's his hero.

Tagger squats down, getting eye level with him, and then eyes the bag of candy. "I think that's okay. Are you still wanting ice cream?"

But I'm still stuck on the daddy part. Seems Baylor has left a few details out of our conversations over the years. Still in a bit of shock by this news, I watch the interaction, utterly fascinated that Tag's a dad.

The blond-headed boy nods as his smile spans his face. "Yes, please."

Looking up at me, Tagger says, "This is my friend Pris—" Shaking his head, he blinks long and hard as if the habit was just too hard to break. "Miss Christine." He takes hold of his son's hand as he glances at his son and then at me again when he stands to his full height. "This is my son, Beckett Grange. Beck."

As if I wasn't already charmed by the past standing before me, my heart melts for this little cutie at his side. I kneel to shake his hand. "It's nice to meet you, Beck."

"You too, Miss Christine. How old are you?"

"Oh." My chin juts back in surprise. I start to laugh at Beck's bluntness. "I'm twenty-six. How old are you?"

"Six." His eyes flick up to his dad, and then back to me. "I turn seven soon. Dad said I can ride a horse while I'm here."

"How fun. I love horses. Have you ridden one before?" I can't imagine raising a kid without the wide-open spaces I grew up with. The animals, and farm, the striking sunsets, and diving into the river on hot days. It was fun to visit Baylor in New York once, but I was a fish out of water. Austin isn't too far of a drive from here, but it's not the same culture shock to my hill country system.

"No. We're not allowed to go near them at the park."

"The horse carriages at Central Park," Tag slips in.

"Ah." I nod. "Yeah, they're doing a job. It's probably best not to disturb them. I have lots of horses if you'd like to come out to our ranch and see them."

His face clenches in excitement. "Yes, please."

"Great. We'll make sure it happens while you're visiting."

The squeak of the door swinging open alerts us to Lauralee entering from the back. Stunned, she stops, and the door practically hits her in the face. "Um." As she wipes her hands down the apron, her eyes volley between the two of us, then dips to Beck. "This is unexpected."

"Hey there, Lauralee. How are you?" Tagger's voice is smoother than I remember as if he's grown into more of himself over the years. He was always confident, but now there's an ease to his words that makes me think he's more at peace.

With his eyes set on her, he smiles, causing my sweet friend's cheeks pink. *Girl, I know the feeling firsthand.* When she pushes her hair back from her face, flour dusts her dark brown bangs, which she's been growing out for a year and are too stubborn to stay in the elastic at the back of her head. She moves to the counter, resting her palms on the hard surface. "I'm good, Tag. How are you?"

"Fine and dandy," he replies, which has my gaze racing

to meet Lauralee's. We silently agree that, yes, he is, indeed, very fine. "Are you running the store these days?"

"Yeah, but my mom still comes in to work a few hours most days. Keeps her and my dad from getting on each other's nerves since they retired early. Also takes some of the load off my shoulders."

"Tell Peaches hello from me."

A tug on my skirt draws my attention down to Beck, who asks, "How do you know my daddy?"

"Oh, um." Another one of his little blindside questions causes me to laugh. I glance up at Tagger. "I've known your daddy all my life. He's best friends with my brother Baylor."

Tag's hand shags through his son's hair. "You know Baylor, buddy. That's Miss Christine's brother."

"He's my uncle," Beck replies proudly.

The sentiment warms my heart for many reasons, but maybe even more that my brother has family in the form of friends since he lives so far from Peachtree Pass, Texas. I stand again. "How's my brother doing?"

"He's . . . I don't think he'll ever change."

Smiling like we're both in on the joke, I reply, "I doubt it. It would take a miracle and the right woman to get that wild card back home."

He nods, seeming to know exactly what I mean. Baylor was never subtle in his pursuits, whether wrangling the cattle, pursuing his career in New York City, or catching women. They all fell into his golden boy hands without much effort.

I could say the same about the man standing here in Peaches, but it's best if I don't travel down unfamiliar roads. The four years that separated our birthdays felt like ten when we were young. Not so much now that we've grown up.

Tag encourages his son forward. "Go pick out your ice cream, and Miss Lauralee will get you what you want."

Lauralee grins. "Come on over. I have the best peach ice cream in the state, or if you like bubblegum, my personal favorite, you're in luck."

He runs toward her, dropping the bag of gummies on the counter, then presses his nose against the glass.

A tension that wasn't there sweeps between as if neither of us knows what to say or where to go from here. I don't let it build. "I—"

"I was thinking—"

We both laugh, letting the awkwardness fade. I ask, "You were thinking?"

He runs his fingers through his hair, something I watched him do a million times when we were younger. A shyness I don't recognize takes over his expression, and he lowers his gaze. "My parents sold the stables." He looks at me, this time with an intensity that makes me wish I had something to hold on to to steady me.

"I heard. A few years back, right?"

"Yes. It was a lot to handle without me or my brother being around. They always preferred a slower pace of the small farm to feed a family over housing the toys of ranchers who only visited every six months. They hated seeing them treated like prized possessions instead of animals that deserve care and respect." He shifts. "Anyway, I was going to pay Rollingwood Ranch a visit in hopes of introducing my son to one of your horses." The question isn't obvious in the words but is clear in his eyes.

"The invitation stands. Come out anytime."

"Thanks."

I find myself shifting in a way that makes me feel embarrassed. Am I flirting? Am I flirting with Tagger Grange? I smile. I sure am. "Maybe we'll even get you in some jeans and cowboy boots again, like old times."

"I might have left The Pass, but it never left me." He starts walking toward the counter, stopping even with me. With his hand brushed against mine, he lowers his head, and whispers, "It was good seeing you, Pris."

My breath stops in my chest, and before I have a chance to reply, he's already gone. I take a moment to myself and catch my breath again but fail to calm my racing heart before I turn around.

Lauralee hands him back his credit card and then shrugs. That's when I discover what the traitor has done to me. I clasp my lips closed because what am I going to do? Rip the last cheddar biscuit from Beck's sticky hands?

I'm supposed to be the grown-up here, but I'm feeling ready to stamp my foot in dismay and snatch it anyway. I won't, of course, but it's tempting, just like that biscuit.

Heading for the door, Tagger says, "Bye, ladies."

"Bye," we say in unison with a swoony sigh tainting our tone.

"Lordy, we're weak," I say to Lauralee as soon as the door closes behind them.

"Listen, we don't get much action in the middle of nowhere Texas. That it was *the* Tagger Grange . . . well, it's not the first time he's heard a woman swoon over him."

"True." Anchoring my elbows on the bakery display, I drop my head into my hands. "But why does seeing him make me feel like an insecure teen again?"

She rubs my shoulder. "Because we were when he lived here. Once he was gone, though, you flourished. You don't have to shrink just because your all-time crush is back in town. You could do the opposite and get him out of your system once and for all."

I pop back up, ideas filling my head . . . ideas I shouldn't even consider but suddenly am. "And by once and for all, you mean jump him?"

Laughing, she replies, "Or something a little more subtle like making love in the back of the Chevy."

Now I'm laughing. "Thank you for indulging me, but I think it's safest if we just stick to the platonic relationship we've always had as the younger sister of his best friend. No need to muddy the waters when he's only visiting for a few days." I push off and head toward the soda fountain. "I'm sure a week tops."

"Guess we'll see when he visits you out at the ranch."

"Guess so." I get a cola with light ice and two dashes of cherry cola and then cap it with a lid. Pushing the straw in, I return to the stool that had me almost meeting the floor in pursuit of warm bread and spin around once. "But I still need to keep my thoughts and intentions clean when it comes to him. His life is fifteen hundred miles away while I'm settled here like the previous seven-plus generations of Greenes." My chest deflates. "God, now I'm depressed."

"Don't be. You're a good daughter for coming home when you did. You've made a life for yourself." Smiling, she adds, "And you always have me. We can grow old together rocking on the front porch."

I pull a dollar from my pocket and lay it on the counter. "As appealing as that is, don't you miss having a guy look at you like you're prettier than a sunset could ever be?"

"I miss guys. Period." She rings up the soda and slides the money into the register. "You know you don't have to pay."

"But I always will," I singsong, walking backward toward the door. "I'll take you up on that front-porch-rocking-chairs offer when we're old and gray, though."

She laughs. "Deal."

"In the meantime, keep me posted if any hotties come to town."

Throwing her arm out to the side, she says, "One just did, and you already friend zoned him."

"Tagger Grange can never be more than a friend. First, my brother would kill me." Holding out two fingers, I continue, "Second, I'm not sure I ever got the details of where things stand with his son's mother."

"They're not together."

My feet come to an abrupt halt. "How do you know that?"

"Peaches. She knows everything, and she's on the Peach Festival committee with his mother. She gets all the gossip at meetings."

My mom used to be on that committee before she passed. Hearing about it so suddenly has my chest tightening, though I know Lauralee would never mention something to hurt me. But not all wounds heal. "Then how did we not know he had a son?"

"We did know. I told you back when you—" She looks down and then says, "It was around the time of your return. A lot was going on back then."

More doesn't have to be shared, and I'd prefer if we didn't. Hoping to move past this, I reply, "Yeah." Refocusing on the man who was just at hand, I feel a little lighter again—mind and soul. "That still doesn't mean he's single, my friend." I start backing toward the door until my back rests against the handlebar. "So third, I'm sure he has a stable of women waiting for him back in New York City. La de dah and fancy pants. I'm just a small-town girl with dirt under my nails. I think I'm safe from falling under his spell."

"Again."

"You don't let anything slide, do you?"

"That's what friends are for."

"So are enemies." I laugh as the bell chimes when I exit. "You also owe me a biscuit."

"Next Friday," she calls out before the door closes.

I head to the truck, still laughing, until I notice my nails while reaching for the door. Shaking my head, I try not to feel embarrassed. It's not a competition for Tagger Grange's attention. I have too much on my plate to worry about being perfect for a man who's basically passing through town.

It still might be time to have a girls' night again to get my nails done and a haircut. I might be a whiz at cutting split ends, but my nails need outside help.

I start the truck and back out, creating a plume of dust behind me. Needing to get back to the ranch, I shift into drive and leave my encounter with Tagger right where it should be—in the rearview mirror.

But why am I still thinking about him when I cross onto Rollingwood Ranch property fifteen minutes later? I know. I just hate to admit it.

It sure was good to see him again . . .

CHAPTER 2

Tagger

"YOU SEE THAT, BECKETT?" While slowing down, I drive steady and point across the interior of the rental car to direct his attention in the back seat to out the window. "When I was your age, only rows of crops were there."

"What happened to them?"

"It was a lot for Grammy and Pops to take care of, so they sold some land and now farm for their own food and sell the rest at a farmstand on the weekends."

"What does farming mean?"

The curiosity in his tone nearly undoes me. This was my whole world for eighteen years, yet six years into his life, my son only knows pavement and skyscrapers. It's tempting to bang my head against the steering wheel. Instead, I take in a deep breath and remind myself why we're back in Texas.

This is for him. *And me*. I need this trip more than I've let on to friends and family.

"You know Old MacDonald?" I ask as thoughts of Beck playing in the dirt roll through my mind.

"Had a farm! E-I-E-I-O," he sings excitedly. Poking the window, he's still singing but more to himself, but then stops and looks at me with his mouth twisted to the left side of his face. Our eyes connect in the mirror. I know that look; I'm about to be hit with a barrage of questions. He asks, "Do you farm?"

"I did. I used to while growing up here."

"Did you like it?"

I nod without needing time to think. I grin, the memories probably better than the hard work it took to keep things running back then. "I liked it a lot."

"Then why do you live in New York City?"

I stop the car just after entering the property past the rusted metal gate. Looking back at him, I reply, "Because you're there."

A smile grows just like my mom's prized cabbage always grew—big and showy, and worth every ribbon she ever won. Beck's smile has often been compared to mine. I'm always happy to take the compliment. "You ready to see Grammy and Pops?"

"Yeah!" He throws a little fist pump into the air.

I start down the dirt road that leads to the sage-green house with the front porch that wraps around three sides. The same rocking chairs are still there like I never left. The swing still hangs from chains I helped my dad attach when I was about Beck's age. The house hasn't been painted since I was in middle school, and it is well past time, judging by the strips of wood I can see running across the siding. But I needed to see this place again when I left the city.

Home.

My mom is already pushing through the screen door before I can park. Her hair is shorter, a mixture of blond and gray running through it. She's tan, as usual, though she typically wears a hat in the sun. She was a young mom, but years of working the farm can age anyone. Those green eyes that she passed down to Beckett and me shine like emeralds when the sunshine hits them. "Tagger!"

I cut the engine and open my door. She may be a lot smaller than me, but she still knows how to swallow me in a hug like I'm still her little boy. "I missed you, Mom."

Leaning back, she looks up at me. "I missed you so much." When we part, I move to the back seat and open the door to get Beck out. "Oh my grandson, come to Grammy."

Though they've only seen each other a few times in the past few years, Beck adores her. She's comfort in human form, good for the soul, and always my biggest cheerleader.

She's also hugging the life out of my son. He giggles, so I guess he's going to survive. "You have gotten so big, Beck. I thought you were your father at first."

He giggles again. "I'm big like you, Daddy."

"You sure are, buddy." I glance back at the house, "Where's Dad?"

"Down at the river fishing." She takes Beck's hand and says, "You should go see him. While you're gone, I can stuff this little monkey bear with homemade strawberry cobbler. I just took it out of the oven."

That reminds me. I grab the candy from the back seat before it has a chance to melt and hand it to her. "I always had great timing, but I think he's had enough sweets until after dinner. We stopped and got ice cream in town before heading out here."

"Ah! Well then." Looking down at him, she asks, "How about you and I go inside and start on the succotash together?"

"What's succotash?"

"I'll teach you all about succotash. It's one of your dad's favorites from when he was little."

I wouldn't go that far, but no need to burst any bubbles. I need a break from the life I just left, so I won't start any fights over vegetables while I'm here.

She starts leading him to the house. The two are peas in a pod, and it is like no time has passed since they were together last. "You should change clothes. You'll get your nice clothes dirty if you don't. You can find your boots and jeans upstairs in your room."

My room was never kept as an altar to my glory days of high school or college but as a soft place to land as if she knew I'd need it one day. I find myself breathing easier being back home again and from knowing he's in good hands.

My mom stops on the porch. "Your dad took the utility vehicle, but you can take the tractor if you want."

The heat isn't overbearing since it's only April. "I can walk."

"The fresh air always does us good." She turns but then stops to add, "I'm so glad you're home, Tag."

I leave the keys in the car and shut the door. "Me, too, Mom."

Shoving my hands in my pockets, I step forward. My Italian leather shoes contrast sharply against the green grass of spring, and I pay no mind to the dirt that already clings to the stitching and toes. Clothes can be replaced, but this feeling of freedom? It's priceless.

I feel like I take up more space in the city, but that could be my ego or reputation. This, though . . . *Amazing*. At the top of the hill, I stop to look up at the clear blue skies and green land that stretches for miles, in awe of what a small part of the universe I am.

Passing the stables that used to be full, I see they've gone into disrepair. I don't blame them. With the larger barn still intact and in use, I don't see the sense in keeping the stables up if they're never going to be used again. I start down the hill, spotting the tack shed. My dad will be tucked in a lawn chair on the other side in the shadows of the sun.

It's been too long since I walked around without the sound of car horns or someone shouting on the streets next to me. The hustle and bustle I've grown used to and annoyed by was left behind. I have the next five days to loosen the tension I've been carrying in my shoulders.

The quiet surrounds me—birds in the distance, the faintest water lapping the edge of the river, leaves on the nearby oaks blowing in the wind, and the crunch of weeds under my shoes. It's not quite the same sound that I remember from my childhood. Instead, it's lighter as if the weight of my boots made the crunch just a little more noticeable.

Boots . . . I grin, thinking about Pris. She looked so damn good in that dress, and equally just how I remembered, though so many years have passed us by. Windblown hair and boots so scuffed that I can still hear her getting a talking-to on Sunday mornings on the church steps. And those bluer-than-the-Texas-sky eyes were always a giveaway to what she was up to—no good or the pristine little angel that earned her the nickname. But so much has changed. I never looked at her twice when I lived here because the one time I did, Baylor knocked me down on my ass for it.

The memory has me chuckling like a fool to myself. It was one of the worst fights we ever got in. We weren't known to disagree much, except when it came to who had the better truck, scored more points at the rodeo and with the ladies in town for the big show, and his sister.

Back then, she was an annoying little squirt who bugged us while we were trying to come into our own. That dress with the little flowers flowing down the shape of her curves, with the dip at the front where the top button had slipped the hole, gave me another peek into how she's grown. I liked the swell of her hips when I held her, but it was her face that had me staring too long. She's fucking gorgeous and has come into her own alright. *Damn.*

Baylor hasn't shared photos in a long time. Who shows off photos of their sister anyway? But I could have used a warning. Instead, I was stuck there with a growing . . . I clear my throat, though I'm not sure what suddenly clogged it.

Nothing like having your kid wreck your game, as if I still have any. I laugh again as I approach the tack shed. I'm not looking to give my dad a heart attack, so as I come around the corner, I call out, "Hey, Dad?"

Busted. He's not fishing.

Asleep in a hammock under the trees, he's snoring loudly. I consider waking him but decide to give him a few more minutes to rest, figuring fishing was his cover so he could sneak in a nap before returning to his duties.

I always thought it would be hard to forget this place. Although it's embedded in my being, this river runs through my veins, and the air is the oxygen that I need to breathe. Nothing beats being here in person again.

I sit in the lawn chair at the river's edge, my shoulders easing and my body slumping into the worn fabric. This is the life.

"Catch anything?"

Whipping my gaze over my shoulder, I see my dad grumbling as he slips out of the hammock. "I thought I'd leave it to the professionals."

He grins as his eyes travel over the rocky bank and meet mine. "What brings you home, son?"

"A long flight and then just over an hour's drive." I stand and meet him halfway.

Turning a handshake into a hug, Dad pats me on the back. "Glad you made the trek. It's been too long."

"It has. Felt like a good time to make my way back."

We step apart, and both cross our arms over our chests as if we're a mirror with a time difference between his age and mine. "Where's my little man Beckett?" He's been trying to get my son here for years.

We only made the trip to Texas once when our son was barely one. Anna hated it here. She claimed it was too dusty, too in the middle of nowhere, too deserted, and the worst for her, was that not one shop served her overly complicated coffee drink. No barista ever got it right anyway, even in the city. We had one night in The Pass before she demanded we leave the next day.

"Beck is up at the house with Mom. I'm sure she's feeding him cobbler and smothering him in love."

"How it should be." He walks toward the river and picks up a rock, then taps it to his forehead. Then he skips it across the surface like magic. I always thought it was magic when I was young before he taught me his secrets. Angles and shapes of rocks matter, how fast the water flows, and a gentle tap to the forehead for luck. "Running from trouble or just need some fresh air in your lungs?"

My dad was never a man who talked to hear his own voice. He's more of a get to the heart of the matter kind of guy. It's a quality I've come to respect more as I've gotten older and dealt with assholes with their doublespeak to fuck everyone else at work for every lead, promotion, or opportunity presented.

Keeping my eyes forward, I reply, "A little of both."

He steps closer and squeezes my shoulder before turning to walk away. "You always have a place to come home, Tagger." He waves over his shoulder. "Come on. I want to see my grandson and get some cobbler before it's gone."

I pick up a rock and tap it on my forehead. I'm not sure if I have the same skills I once had, but I toss it anyway and hope for the best. I get two skips before it sinks. I'll take the win. I turn to catch up to him. "Coming."

"And you need to change clothes. I thought you were a tax collector when I saw you."

Chuckling, I run to join his side. "It's good to be home, Dad."

CHAPTER 3

Christine

THERE'S nothing like falling into bed clean after a long day of being covered in dirt.

I don't bother drying my hair, figuring I'll deal with the nest of tangles in the morning instead. Until I remember morning comes early on the ranch.

With a groan, I flip the covers off and push out of bed. The moonlight flooding my bedroom floor lights the way to my dresser. I'm not drying my hair, but I can at least brush it. I start at the ends, wanting to rush the process, but I know patience is a virtue, so I slow down. And just like every other time I stop rushing around and my mind has a moment to wander, Tagger invades my thoughts. Sort of like he did my whole life. The feelings of an innocent crush at eight differ from those I felt for him when I was sixteen.

I may have been invisible to him, but he made every fiber of my being tighten when he was around. I couldn't think straight, struggled to complete sentences without giggling, and, worst of all, I made a fool of myself, thinking he might be interested.

Why in hell would a twenty-year-old, who had every girl falling at his feet, find me something special?

My chest flames in embarrassment, remembering how I made a fool of myself trying to flirt with him. I didn't even know how to flirt back then. Asking him to help me onto my horse was ridiculous. He knew I could get on without help, but he still obliged. It was probably best he and Baylor returned to campus early that year. Otherwise, I might have done something else stupid to get his attention.

I can only hope he doesn't remember as vividly as I do.

God . . . so humiliating.

Setting the brush down, I return to bed, tucking myself back into the softness of the covers and mattress. I close my eyes and snuggle the covers under my chin. It's past eleven, but sleep doesn't seem to come like usual.

Tag looked good today. Too good for his own good.

I can only imagine the type of woman he dates back in New York. Classically pretty like Grace Kelly and a pert tip to their nose, fashion-forward blond hair much lighter than mine cut with precision by the fancy stylists, and ten minutes doing yoga gets their bodies back in perfect shape to draw in a man like Tagger Grange. They probably even dry their hair before they get in bed . . .

Dammit.

Not sure how I managed to guilt myself, but I get back up and go into the bathroom. Since I'm wide awake anyway, I spend the next fifteen minutes drying my unruly locks before brushing it again and adding a little product to tame the flyaway strands. It won't weather a hard night's sleep, but that doesn't seem to be in the cards for me tonight.

I don't fully style it, but I like my hair's natural shine and the way the light brown contrasts with the blond streaking through it. I even inherited a sprinkling of red strands from my mom.

A pang in my chest I'm all too familiar with returns. It's not fair she's gone. *No goodbye. No last I love you.* Nothing but my dad calling to tell me no one survived the car accident.

I tuck my hair behind my ears like she used to do, barely able to still hear her telling me I have such a pretty face. *Almost* . . . Her voice is fading from the memories I have so desperately tried to hold on to. I hate that she lives in videos and photos but not here with us anymore.

Swiping at the unexpected emotion sliding onto my face, I raise my chin and return to bed once more, determined to find sleep.

Of course, I didn't bargain on Tagger haunting me all night either. But here he is, plain as day in my head again. I guess some crushes never go away. I'm going to be rocking on that front porch with Lauralee and still thinking about him.

I clench my eyes, knowing he's at the forefront of my mind only because I saw him again today. But when I start accepting that thinking about him won't end until he flies back out of here, I realize today that he saw me as well.

At eighteen, I swear he noticed me for the first time, but he would never cross that line. Wonder what he thinks now that I'm eight years older?

Flipping over, I cover my face with the pillow, hoping to smother some sense into myself. Tagger Grange will be my undoing. I felt it back at the store. I lose my better judgment when he's in town. I need to keep my distance because he's nothing but trouble when hanging around.

The sun rose too early for my liking, but I still drag myself out of bed and stumble my way through getting dressed for the day. With some of the crew visiting family in Houston for a few days, I take over making sure the horses are fed and the irrigation system goes off as scheduled in the lower acres of crops.

Too busy for breakfast, I'm starving and finally head back toward the house. The crops aren't tall enough to hide the dust I spy in the air in the distance. I pick up the pace because I know that means we have visitors.

A gray sedan is parked near my truck when I reach the yard. I don't see anyone when I look around. Shielding my eyes from the sun with my hand, I turn back to see if they've climbed the fence.

"Hey, stranger."

My attention whips to the barn to find Tagger and Beck heading toward me. "Hey," I say, lowering my hand. "You're out and about early."

He checks his watch. With his brows narrowed, he replies, "It's almost eleven."

"Oh, it felt earlier to me."

Coming to a stop with a few feet remaining between us, he smiles. It's so genuine that I wish I had had time to prepare for it. Though admittedly, my heartbeat had already picked up speed from the very sight of him. "Time always did slip away out in these fields."

"Still does." Kneeling, I smile at his son who stands looking around. "Hi, Beck. Did you come out to see the horses?"

He jumps, stomping his feet back in the dirt to cause a little dust cloud to form. "Yes!" I love how everything sounds like such an adventure to him. He's the cutest kid. I remember Tag having that same color hair when he was young and eyes wide with possibility before life took hold.

I glance at his dad. It's easy to get caught in his looks.

He's the handsomest man I've ever seen, still after all these years. It's easy to be drawn to the charisma of his ways—easygoing, funny, and gives you his full attention when you're speaking. But it's his eyes that give him away. The charm doesn't quite reach them like it used to, and if I get the chance to stare into them for longer than a few seconds, I can see he brought some troubles back home with him.

It's not something I have a right to pry into with questions, and I would never do so in front of his kid, but it's noted.

To Beck, I smile again because he makes it hard not to, and say, "I like the enthusiasm. We can head over now or—"

"We don't want to get in the way if you're busy."

The scoff erupts before it can be stifled. "We're running a ranch . . ." I signal toward the hill that leads to the acres of crops we grow there. "And farm. When are we not busy out here?" His smile falters. I didn't intend to make him feel bad, so I say, "It's lunchtime. I was just coming to the house to eat something. Want to join me?" I start walking. Maybe the invite isn't only for him. I reap the benefits of his company as well. "It's not fancy. BLT sandwiches are on the menu today."

I hear the gravel under their feet just before Tag says, "It's been a long time since I had a BLT."

Turning back, I keep my feet moving. "I've been known to make a good one."

He rubs his stomach. "I'm suddenly hungry."

"I can eat, too, Daddy." Beck runs to me and slips his hand in mine like we're old friends. I like this kid.

Looking down at him, I ask, "Do you know what the B stands for?"

"Burger?"

I can't hold back a laugh. "Close. Bacon. Do you like bacon?"

"Does Beckett Grange like bacon?" Tag bellows behind us. "He's a bacon monster."

"Rawr," Beck roars, then dashes to the porch.

His place at my side isn't vacant for long, Tag sliding right into the space. "Sure you don't mind, Pris?"

I stop. Facing him, I tilt my head and arch an eyebrow. With a poke to the chest, his oh-so-hard chest, I caution, "Listen, I let you get away with it yesterday, but if you plan on hanging around and breaking bacon with me, the nickname needs to be left in the past."

Judging by how his brows knit together, he appears confused. "What's wrong with Pris?" There's such an innocence to his tone like I'm the one ruining the fun.

"You know what's wrong with it, so I don't know if you're trying to rile me up or you still see me as that same tag-along little sister, but I have news for you, buster."

"Oh yeah? What's that?" The confusion disappears from his face and is replaced with a growing smirk.

I swear he's the devil sent to tempt me into hell. And it's been so long since I was even near a man I wasn't related to or worked with, I'm ready to take the bait. I lean in, close enough to inhale the expensive aftershave that lightly coats his skin, and whisper, "I'm all grown up if you haven't noticed."

He moves in even closer, so close that my lips part in a desperate attempt for air to reach my lungs as my entire body stills. Our shoes bump together, his chest rests against my arm, and with the minutest of angles, the scruff on his cheek brushes against my temple. His eyes dip to my lips as he drags his tongue over the corner of his mouth, and then tilts his head until his breath reaches my ear, and whispers, "I've noticed, Pristine."

Pristine . . .

He's the devil alright.

Before I have a chance to poke him again, a cold front sweeps in when he leaves me standing there alone. The squeal of the screen door that needs oiling is swung open, and the two of them walk inside.

It's best he's gone, or he might find himself pinned to the wood planks of the porch.

I turn to face the property, resting my hands on the railing. I take a long moment not only to catch my breath but also to calm my racing heart. Dropping my head down and closing my eyes, I equally love and hate that he gets a reaction from me so easily.

He always did, even when it was annoying like that nickname.

But I suddenly feel alive in ways I haven't since I returned home, and if I'm to give credit where it's due, it's because of him.

God, I'm in so much trouble.

CHAPTER 4

Tagger

Even in April, shade is appreciated from the Texas sun.

Hanging back on the porch, I give Christine and Beck some time to explore on their own. Here, he can run free. In the city, he isn't allowed more than a few feet from me on the quieter residential streets. On the busier streets, his hand is always in mine.

He's in safekeeping as they explore the barn and meet each of the chickens by name. With him busy, I sit on the porch to catch up on emails, though anytime they come into view, my eyes are on them. *Especially him.*

I haven't seen his pure delight in a while. Probably Christmas, if I remember right. He's a happy kid by nature. His mom . . . not so much. But I'm not an innocent bystander. I contributed to both their dispositions. Custody of Beck is ever-evolving and seemingly never-ending. If I compromise, she makes a new demand. If I put my foot down, I hear from her lawyer the following morning. And if

I dare to make a request or add a stipulation of my own? All hell breaks loose, and we're back to square one.

Organizing this trip for his spring break took two rounds and a few thousand in attorney fees.

Looking up from my phone, I see Christine reach over and tickle Beck. She taps his nose as his giggles ring out across the yard before she turns in my direction. *Damn.* She's not the same Pris I remember. Even down to the nickname I promised not to use again. But calling her Christine just doesn't sit right. She's just as Pristine with my boy as she was all those years ago.

She swings by the house to grab some carrots from inside. "A little hot in the country for you?" she asks, grinning at me like I'm foreign to the outdoors.

"Not one bit."

I think I hear, "I beg to differ," but I could be wrong. I know Baylor's younger sister would never flirt with me. Though I'm still staring at the screen door as it slams closed like my ears didn't deceive me. *Would she?*

Nah.

She's got to have a line of guys waiting to take her out or hold her hand at the county fair. What would she see in some guy she's known her whole life? Considering how much I pestered her growing up, she probably sees me like a third brother.

Beck runs onto the porch, out of breath, and straight for me. "Dad?"

"Son?" I grin. I didn't think I'd failed my son until early last year when Anna and I broke up. The time apart gave me clarity of what we were both missing, and I realized I had never stopped climbing the corporate ladder to take in the view. That view will always pale compared to the one I have before me.

Seeing him now, it was worth every penny.

"Miss Christine said that I get to feed the horses." The anticipation zipping through his words has him smiling like a loon.

"Whoa, buddy!" I sit forward, just as enthused for him. "That's exciting."

There's a long exhale and even longer inhale before he adds, "They're big animals." There's no shake to his voice, but I can hear the change.

"They are. Are you nervous?"

He looks back at the field where two horses mosey their way toward the fence at the edge of the yard. When he turns back, he scrapes his hand across his sweaty forehead and then shakes his head. "No. I'm big and brave. She said so and that I'm old enough."

The squeak of the door alerts me to her presence again, though her proximity seems to be doing a solid job on its own.

With a cowboy hat now on her head, she hands him two carrots. "You ready to feed the horses?"

"Yes-sir-ree Bob."

Her laughter tickles a smile into place, which causes him to start giggling. I pat his back, though I know he's itching to run to the horses. "Seems like ranch life suits you, Beck."

"It's fun here."

"It is fun here." I add, "You go have fun, bud." He takes off before I finish the sentence.

Running the tips of her fingers over my shoulder as she passes by, she stops on the top step and looks back. "You're not coming, Daddy?"

Fuck. Me.

My brows shoot to the porch ceiling. I definitely did not mishear that. She's flirting . . . I think. Fuck. *Is she?*

I have no fucking clue. What I do know is I'm not getting up from this chair to show her how she affects me.

Chuckling, I look away.

Her laughter pulls me back to her. "You okay?"

"Yeah. Sure. Why wouldn't I be?"

"Because that was the most awkward laugh I've ever heard." She crosses the yard, not leaving any room for me to lie as if she already knew I would.

I'm not sure what that exchange was all about, but I'm letting it go. I don't know what to say anyway, so it's best if I keep my mouth shut.

I watch as Christine shows Beck how to balance on the lower fence rail. She hands him a carrot to hold out. He reaches forward with the safety of her behind him with her hand tucked under his. The horse is quick to take the carrot. And Beck looks back at her like she performed magic.

He looks over his shoulder. "Did you see that, Daddy?"

My mom was right. The fresh air is doing me good, but seeing my son experiencing things that were so natural to me at his age makes me feel like I'm doing something right. Like coming here to the ranch today. I might not have Greene as my last name, but it still feels like home. "I did," I reply, getting up and resting my hands on the porch railing.

I can't discount the woman beside him. She's got some sass under that hat, but she's doing me some good as well. Spending time together at lunch gave me insight into the woman she's become. Based on what I gathered, she's not fussy and is more than capable of anything she puts her mind to. The girl has grown up.

I allow my gaze to take her in. Her jeans aren't tight, but they can't hide the body beneath. The blue cotton of the T-shirt drapes over her, but that V at her chest keeps drawing my attention. I'm only human, and she's quite the sight to take in. I wasn't slick enough because I think she might have even caught me.

The hat shades her face, but I liked seeing her bare skin and the freckles dabbed across her nose earlier. *Twenty-six . . .* Old enough to get into some trouble with, but still young enough to get my ass kicked again by her brother. Of course, she could be fifty, and he'd still find a problem, so maybe I need to forget about the threat he once made and see her as her own woman now.

She's fucking gorgeous. I'm looking right at her when she anchors a hand on her hip and rolls her eyes at me. My lips wriggle sideways. She's cute, a little wild like an unbroken horse, doing things her way despite how it's always been done. Or maybe in spite of how it goes around this place. The ranch and farm are thriving, and I'd be willing to believe it's because she probably doesn't take shit from anyone. *I hope she doesn't.*

Beck feeds another carrot to a different horse coming to get a treat, then launches himself off the rail with no fear. If that doesn't sum up being a kid—flying free, feeling like the day never ends, and can't wait to wake up for the adventures to begin. He's playful but more reserved in the city.

Not wanting to miss out on the fun, I start toward them. I reach the fence and hold my hand out for the horse to smell before stroking the front of their head. "Girl?"

"Yes. Bluebelly. She's a sweetheart. She foaled for the first time last year."

Keeping my eyes on the horse, I admire her white and brown markings. "Colt or filly?"

"Colt," Christine says, sending her gaze to search the distance. "Hang around long enough, and Skyward will come for a carrot. He's our most curious horse of our stable, but he also loves a nap under the big peach tree closer to the gardens."

"That's a good spot. I may have napped there myself once or twice." Nudging my son, I ask, "Hey, Beck? Want to pet her?"

"Yeah."

I pick him up, holding him in front of me. "Gentle strokes like this."

He does as he's shown and smiles when Bluebelly leans in closer. I keep noting the simplest acts feel like a big deal when I'm with Beck. This is the first horse he's ever pet, and I have the privilege of becoming a part of a memory being made. Beats brokering deals worth millions. I'd trade pretty much anything to share more times like this with him.

She says, "She likes you." Reaching forward, Christine scratches along her neck. "They're incredible creatures."

"They are." When I catch her checking her watch, I say, "Let us know if we need to get out of your hair."

Looking at me from under the brim of her hat, she smiles. "You're a nice distraction."

I should take that at face value, but she's planted a seed I'll be watering the rest of the night and probably into tomorrow. It's becoming one of many growing larger the more time we spend together.

She adds, "Beck said you're coming for dinner." Giving his shoulder a little squeeze, she looks down at him. When he looks up at her, I'm starting to think they've hatched this plan together.

"Did he now?"

Beckett nods. Guilty little bugger.

"Well, we promised Grammy we'd be home for dinner."

"Ah man," Beck groans, crossing his arms over his chest and kicking some dirt up.

My gaze flicks to Christine and then to him again before kneeling and whispering in his ear so she can hear, "How about we invite Miss Christine over to ours for dinner?"

"Yes." He peers back at her. I catch the sweet smile growing on her face right before he asks, "Want to come to Grammy and Pops for dinner?"

Her gaze bounces from him to me, and then she rubs his head. "I'd like that. What time should I be there?"

"You can ride with us." I lean against the fence, propping my foot on the railing to play this off like it's no big deal, but nothing about this conversation feels natural. Glancing over at her, I realize I want her to say yes. *Not for Beck but for me.*

Being this close to her, I see a smudge of dirt streak across the bridge of her nose and her pretty blue eyes set on mine like she sees something interesting in me.

When our eyes meet, she shifts, looking down at her boot toeing the ground in front of her. "You'd be stuck driving me all the way back." Her eyes land on me again, posing a question her lips never asked.

"I don't mind." I shrug, angling my gaze toward the horse who's lost interest. "Unless you want your truck for a quick getaway." I look at her again, wanting to see her reaction.

A grin shapes her face, and she laughs. "Why would I need that?"

"I don't know. Maybe my mom serves lima beans, or I piss you off like I used to."

"First of all," she starts, watching Beck run around a few feet away from us. "Who hates lima beans? I love them."

"Unexpected. And second?"

"Second . . ." She picks up like she was never interrupted. "Don't piss me off then."

Bursting out in laughter, I joke, "Easier said than done."

"Ain't that the truth." She eyes Beck as if she's his guardian angel sent to look after him. "I think I'll take my chances."

When I tap the front of her hat, the brim lifts just enough for me to see her face again. I'm not disappointed. She's not the same pipsqueak anymore. She adds, "Don't make me regret it."

"I'll make sure you don't." I check my watch. "What time do you get off?"

The question seems to give her pause, and she quickly looks away as if it's taking her a second to digest. Then she grins. "I'll probably be done in an hour, but I'd love to freshen up after with a shower."

"Of course. Beck and I have plenty to do if you don't mind us roaming around."

Not wasting a minute, she's already backing away toward the barn, but I can still see that smile brightening her face. "You still know your way around the property?"

"Sure do."

"Then make yourself at home." She turns, giving me a good view of her backside and that walk that commands attention. And is owning mine right now.

The belt loop of my pants is tugged. "Can we go see the cows?"

I bring Beck to my side and pat his back. "Yeah, buddy, let's go see the cows." I look over at Christine once more before she disappears into the barn, wondering if it was saving her ass at the sundries shop that made me start to see her differently or when she teased me on the porch. Something has changed, though, for both of us.

An hour later, Beck and I have exhausted ourselves and head for the front porch where we find homemade lemonade waiting for us. I assume she's already upstairs, so we make ourselves comfortable in the rocking chairs, prepared to wait a while.

"We don't get the long days yet," Mr. Greene says, coming around from the side of the house. He plants his large hand on the top of the railing and pulls himself up the two steps onto the porch. "Chrissy told me you were out visiting."

I stand to move closer, not wanting him to have to travel the distance to shake hands. He's a larger man, always was, but age has grown on him as it should. "Good to see you, Mr. Greene."

"Mr. Greene? We're still doing that? Aren't you Baylor's age?"

"I am."

"Thomas will do then, Tagger." He looks at Beck, then at me again. "Spitting image. What's your name?"

"Beckett, but I like Beck best."

"Beck, it is." He looks ahead again. "You know, Tagger, I can still see you and Baylor out in that field right there messing around on the tractor, though you were told to stay off it."

I move aside so he can sit down. He starts rocking, eyeing me and the field as if the memories are being created right now instead of twenty-four years ago. "Your mom would drop you off at sunrise before heading back to tend to those horses." Leaning left toward Beck, he waits until he has his attention, then adds, "Your dad used to run around in his skivvies covered in a day's worth of play. Your grandmother would hose him off before letting him into her car."

"Grammy would?" You can see the mischievous plans forming in Beck's eyes. That's what I wanted, not him acting out, but him living life to the fullest instead of always being stuck in a suit and tie like his private school requires. And

Anna when they go out to dinner. Glancing at me, he laughs. "She'd spray you with a hose?"

"She would. The dirt comes right off, then you're as clean as a whistle and ready for the next day's adventures."

Thomas says, "That's before he and my son Baylor became big shots in New York City."

"What's a big shot?" Beck sits back in the chair again as if he has no plans on leaving anytime soon.

I'm trying to figure out the best way to explain it, but Thomas doesn't hesitate. "It means your dad does very important work. He's worked hard and been rewarded for it."

Success came fast. So did burnout. I could never work a day again, and I'd still be set for life. I have more money than I know what to do with, and that gives me a different outlook on how I should spend those hours.

My son matters. I plan to make up for the time I lost with Beck because of work to show him that life isn't only a concrete jungle. I want to broaden his horizons so he can chase his happiness when money isn't a concern.

I chuckle. "I don't know if managing other people's money is considered hard or important, but I appreciate the ego boost."

The chair protests under his weight, but he keeps rocking. With his eyes on me, he says, "I heard you paid off your parents' property?"

I glance at Beck. Money isn't something I talk about much around him. He's surrounded by it in the city. Keeping him grounded is something I strive for more. "I did. They paid most of it. I knew my mom was ready to retire from running the stables, so I thought I'd help get them there sooner."

He stands and comes toward me, patting me on the arm when he passes. "That's real nice, son."

"Can I get you some lemonade, Dad?" Her voice is a welcome melody to the gathering out here.

Thomas stops and looks at her. There's momentary silence, and then he says, "You look nice, Pris."

Pris? Her eyes immediately find mine. I don't even have to say anything because my lifted brows are already saying all that needs to be said.

Pointing her finger at me, she says, "Don't say a word."

I raise my hands in surrender. "Wasn't going to . . . *yet*. I was saving it for the ride over to my parents' place."

"Maybe I'll take my truck after all." She turns to go back inside.

"No. No. I'll zip it. Not a word. I promise. Unless you give me permission."

I'm gifted an eye roll with a grin she's trying to suppress. "Dad, a plate of spaghetti from last night is in the fridge. Is that alright?"

"Stop fussing over me. I'm a grown man. You go on. You look too nice to waste it out on the ranch."

Beck pops up from the chair and moves to Christine's side. "You look nice."

A tilt of her head in my direction gives me props when I'm left wondering when my six-year-old started stealing my lines.

Tapping his nose, she says, "Thank you, Beckett. Are you ready to go?"

"I'm hungry."

"Me too." She turns suddenly, pulling the screen door open again. "Hold on. I got your mom some flowers from the garden today. April has the prettiest blooms."

When she returns, she has a bouquet of pink, orange,

and yellow flowers wrapped in brown paper and tied with yellow string and a tote bag in the other hand. "Okay, I'm ready."

"Good to see you, Mr. . . . Thomas."

"Good to see you, too, kid. You've made us proud here in Peachtree Pass."

I pat Beck's back to encourage him in the right direction. "I appreciate it."

He comes to the top step and calls, "When are you bringing my daughter home?"

"Dad?" Christine snaps, looking back over her shoulder. "It's not a date. I'm going to see the Granges."

"Well, whatever you kids are calling it. She's an adult now, as she always reminds me, and can make her own decisions. So I won't be inside in my La-Z-Boy watching TV all hours of the night to make sure she gets home alright."

"He's totally going to be waiting up for me."

"The man's got jokes." I open the front door for her. "It won't be too late," I reply, hoping he doesn't stay up worrying about her.

"He always does." She slips into the car.

I'm standing there, suddenly realizing we might be going on a date. No. Beck is with us. There won't be any romance or alone time at all, except the drive home since he'll be in bed by then. Shit. *Is this a date?*

I load Beck into the back seat and then slowly walk around. I know what this looks like, what it feels like . . . walks like a duck. Quacks like a duck. It's a fucking duck.

Running my hand through my hair, I take a breath. It's not a duck.

She's coming over because Beck wanted her to. My mom was thrilled to hear she gets to host and see her again. I'm just the driver of the vehicle. Nothing more than a chauffeur. Yeah. That's good.

I pull open the door and slide into the driver's seat. When I start the car, I look at her. She whispers, "It's not a date."

"Old friends."

"Speak for yourself, old man. Just friends works better for me."

"Just friends it is, then." I put the car in drive and start for the house. Fifteen minutes. What's fifteen minutes between friends? "Do you want to listen to some music?"

She laughs but keeps her eyes out the window. "Whatever makes you comfortable."

Am I that obvious?

I don't know how I'm going to explain to my best friend that I accidentally took his sister out on a date, but I do know one thing. *Baylor's going to kill me.*

CHAPTER 5

Christine

"So pretty," Tagger's mom, Mary, says, taking my hands in hers as soon as we walk into the house. "You look so much like your mom."

Being told I remind everyone of my mom usually feels like a burden since I didn't want to carry the torch of her life alone. I wanted her to be here with me, and a part of me hasn't reconciled she's gone.

If I could have her braid my hair once more, to cradle my face in her hands as she tells me I'm more than she could have wished for, or even just to catch a glimpse of her watching me run my horse in that cloverleaf pattern around the barrels at the rodeo and to feel her comforting arms around me when I made a mistake that lost me the competition.

She was my loudest cheerleader and my broken heart's confidant. No, it's not fair she's gone, and I'm left with features that remind everyone of not only her life but also that she's gone too young.

"Thank you," I reply, accepting the compliment. It might still hurt to hear, but I'm glad I have some of her features.

I always saw Mary as someone's mom, but there's no pretense or vibe of hierarchy standing with her now. At some point, the kids grow up, and maybe it's because I have, but I see her as the woman she is as well.

She and Tagger share their grassier green eyes, and her smile is kind, her voice softer spoken, which makes me feel at home in her kitchen. The chill of Mary's hands after wiping them on a dish towel is in opposition to the warm welcome that lies in her eyes and greeting. Reminds me of my mom when she'd be cooking, washing her hands, and moving to the next task before they could warm up again. "It's so wonderful to spend time with you again, Christine."

Her words pull my mind out of the past and into the present.

"It's wonderful to see you again. It's been a while. Was it the church potluck or . . .?" My memory might not be serving me well. I thought I saw Mary around sometimes, but now I'm not sure, which makes me feel bad for not checking in on them or even inquiring. We may be a small town at heart, spread out over the county, but I'm usually better at knowing these things. "Last year's Peach Festival?"

"I think it was the farmers' market last fall."

"Oh, that's right. I don't work the Greene Farms stand often, but I covered last November when we were short-staffed."

Spying pots on the stove that appear to need attention, I ask, "Can I help you with dinner?"

"Actually," she starts with a grin that reminds me of Beck's when he's about to get into a little good trouble. "We're going to let Tag and Justin take over from here." She goes to the fridge and pulls out a bottle of white wine. "His dad will be out in a minute, and I'm confident my son can manage it until then. As for us, I thought we could catch up out on the porch. That sunset looks to be a beauty tonight." Looking at Tagger, she asks, "You can handle it, right?"

"Like a pro." Not a second of hesitation came with his response.

As soon as his mom shuffles Beck out the door with the bribe of a hopscotch, Tag says, "Hey, Pris?"

His eyes haven't left mine since he mentioned being a pro in the kitchen . . . leading my mind to wonder about the bedroom. The "Pris" doesn't even sidetrack my wicked thoughts. But then he says, "Come here."

My heart starts beating out of my chest from the dulcet tone of the request. I go without question, stopping just shy from the front of my leather sandal from touching his shoe. "Yes?" I reply all breathy, making it obvious that I don't get out of the house enough these days, and I've forgotten how to behave around men I find irredeemably attractive.

"The glasses are in the cabinet closest to the fridge."

Embarrassment lumps in my throat, dulling that vivid heartbeat as it drops to the pit of my stomach. "Right."

I turn, but the brush of his fingers against mine before he catches my hand has me looking between us at the connection instead of at the cabinet where he indicated. The teasing gives me whiplash, but the electricity between us is enough to light up a stadium.

Will I never grow out of this crush?

I'm starting to think it's futile to fight it.

I look into his eyes, which are set on mine so steadily that I shift under the intensity. And gulp, that lump finally clearing, hoping he doesn't hear it. I move away, needing to for self-preservation, and open the pale-yellow door to find two mismatched wineglasses inside the cabinet. The moment gives me a chance to right myself back into my better sensibilities. It's dinner with his family, not him. I need to remember that.

Anyway, I've known him my whole life. And in the short time he's been back, I've already gathered that Tagger Grange didn't come home for a good time. It seems he came home to reckon with his past. His son gave him a reason to reconsider a place that he hightailed away from as if being from here was marred in shame instead of his glory days.

Just another reason that attracts me to him. He left his all-star football days behind him and moved on with his life. He wasn't stuck in the past like so many guys around here still are, hanging onto their teen years like that was the best time of their lives. It probably was.

Not for Tagger or Baylor, though, not even for my older brother Griffin. They all went on to bigger and brighter futures while I landed back here to take care of things. Maybe I'm not any better than those guys from high school that I see hanging out at Whiskey's when Lauralee and I go out. Perhaps instead of fighting my fate, it's time to accept it. It might make meeting someone a lot easier if the standard isn't Tagger Grange anymore. The comparison will always fail to the real thing. Maybe I need to learn to make lemonade from the slim pickins' in The Pass. I never see myself settling for less. I'd rather be alone.

Although he's moved to lift the lids of the pots on the stove, Tag glances at me. "I didn't mean to make this awkward."

"It's not." I smile, but I can't hold it, not even for the sake of politeness.

With a little nudge of his elbow, he asks, "You sure about that?"

"No." This time, the corners of my mouth lift naturally. "It's awkward."

He laughs. "Honesty is always the best policy. Tell me how to turn this around."

"Wine will help."

"Speaking of . . ." He glances down at the glasses in my hands. "My mom's going to be drinking from the bottle if you don't get her that glass soon."

The reminder strikes, making me move toward the door, though the rest of me wasn't quite ready. I reach for the knob, about to pull the door open, when he adds, "It may not have felt like it, but I want you to know that I wasn't only Baylor's friend, Pris."

I don't look back, but I do nod, taking in the words and the implications of what he's said. It's a feeling more than words that rattle me awake to how our relationship is already evolving from kids to whatever stage this is. I open the door but feel compelled to look back just to see if the truth is embedded in his expression. *I'm not disappointed.*

Green eyes with softened lines at the sides and a smile that stays close to restraint but can't seem to hide an intention has me thinking of crossing some lines I shouldn't with my brother's best friend. Call me wild, but the flat-front pants and white button-up shirt he's wearing like that's all he owns isn't a deterrent. Images of him in faded jeans and T-shirts that got too tight around his biceps are still emblazoned into my memories. That he looks good in everything, even dressed like he's about to audit me, is quite annoying. I take a big breath and exhale slowly, knowing I need to walk out of here before my thoughts get away from me. Again. "Glad to hear it, but it would have been nice to know it, too."

He cuts the fire from the gas stove, but his eyes are quick to find mine. "You were four years younger—"

"And wanted to play with the big kids so badly."

"You ran around in dresses and boots—"

"Like yesterday," I volley.

A few long seconds tick by before he chuckles and rubs his hand along his jaw. "Yes, like yesterday."

"Yet, even dressed like a girl, I could climb a tree faster than most boys."

"I bet you could." He takes a deep breath, his chest noticeably filling before he exhales. "I can't turn back time, Pris, so how can I make it up to you?"

"See me as a whole person instead of only as Baylor's little sister."

His eyes dip down but are fast in their retreat to the floor as if he caught himself looking when he knew better. "I see you," he replies, his gaze finding mine again. But as if he can't help himself, it caresses my face and travels lower. Again. "I see who you are. I see you're not that little kid anymore." Maybe he shouldn't, but I can't lie that it's nice to have someone look at me like the woman I've become. He checks the roast in the oven before searching for oven mitts. "I appreciate you spending time with Beck today. He loved it."

I know it's best we don't delve deeper, but I'm still disappointed we've abandoned the topic so quickly. I ask, "And you?"

Should I be pushing him to the point of uncomfortable? *No.*

But do I like to watch him squirm? *Yes.*

With the roast pan in his hands, he sets it down and faces me. "I liked spending time with you today, too." There's a hint of rebellion in his tone, but his smile is genuine. Good to know I wasn't alone in feeling that way.

"And if it matters, it never bothered me when you hung around when we were kids."

"If that's the case, maybe we can be friends starting now. Equal footing as adults. What do you say?"

I tempt a lopsided grin right out of him. "I'd say that's fair. Forget about all the other stuff. Friends?" He holds out his hand. Just as I take it, we're startled by heavy footsteps.

"Christine Greene," his father says, coming from the hall near the stairs. "What brings you by?" Walking straight to the roast, he lowers to get a good whiff. "Man, I'm starving."

I reply, "I—"

"I'm glad you're here for dinner. I want to hear about your dad and how he's doing."

"Of course. Thank you for having me." I think that's my cue to leave. "I'm going to join Mrs. Grange on the porch."

He looks up and says, "Let Mary know dinner won't be long."

"I will." I walk outside, closing the door behind me. I bring the glasses to the table between a rocking chair where Mary sits holding Beck on her lap and the white wicker loveseat that's seen better days. The sun does a lot of damage to things left unattended too long. "Mr. Grange said dinner is almost ready. Is it okay if I open it?"

"Yes, please." After a kiss to Beck's head, she tells him, "Go and have fun." He takes off running as if freedom tastes too good to waste sitting around with the ladies on a porch.

Leaning forward toward me, she whispers, "Now let's gossip. Tell me everything."

I start to laugh. Twisting off the cap, I say, "I'm not sure there's much to tell these days. You know how it goes in Peachtree." I generously fill both glasses.

"I do, but there must be something the young people here

are up to or the latest church news. Who's been caught cheating or who was seen out at the bars when they shouldn't have been." She sips her wine. "This piece of paradise is a part of who I am, but the nights are a lot quieter these days." She looks at me as I settle onto the loveseat. The gentle tip at the corners of her lips can't conceal the sincerity in her expression. It's all laid bare for me. "I miss the bustling of the boys and the busyness of running the stables and seeing people, talking to others."

"I know that feeling. I mean, not the kids' part but the quiet part." Directing my gaze toward the sunset, I say, "I don't know that I'd trade these views for anything, but it would be nice to share them with someone."

She nods. "I met Justin in high school. He was a year older. We just clicked. Do you go on dates?" It's odd to be asked questions that the men in my life never do. Lauralee and I commiserate, but it feels good to have a different perspective, and it's comforting, like how it might have been with my mom.

"Truth be told," I start with a laugh, "the selection isn't great."

"I imagine it's not. And it's not like Prince Charming is going to show up on the ranch out of nowhere."

I grin. "Exactly." *She gets it.* "Lauralee and I go to the bar every so often, but it's no better there."

"And Dover County? Do they have any worthy prospects?"

"Define worthy." This time, we both laugh.

Although she's sitting back, her gaze volleying between watching Beck handle a stick like a wizard and me sharing how pathetic my dating life is, she reaches over and squeezes my hand. Looking only at me this time, she says, "It can't be easy running a ranch out here as a woman. You need a partner who respects your position and deserves all the love you have inside you. Don't settle, okay, Christine?"

My feelings wrap around my heart, giving it a little squeeze as tears form in the corners of my eyes. She's setting her glass down and moving next to me in seconds. With her arm around my back, she rubs and whispers, "I'm sorry. I didn't mean to make you cry."

I dip my head and swipe under my eyes, hoping I won't look like a raccoon from my mascara running. It feels good to be embraced in her arms like I'm one of her own.

My dad is a great go-get'em-tiger kind of man with a pat on the back. He's mastered the side hug and the occasional kiss to the head, but his upbringing taught him showing emotions is a sign of weakness. My mother was the opposite. She made him softer in the ways that a little girl needs. Once she was gone, he forgot how to feel anything.

Lifting my head from her shoulder, I laugh as embarrassment takes hold of me. "I'm sure I'm a mess now."

Using the soft side of her finger, she gently wipes under my eyes. "Beautiful as ever. I used to be so jealous of your mom. She was cheerful and optimistic, effortlessly beautiful, like you, and the kindest soul. I miss her visits. I miss hanging out on her porch drinking mimosas . . ." She eyes me like they were up to no good. "Because we thought that was fancy and catching up on the week while the boys played."

"I just miss her."

With a little rub of my knee, she nods and sits back again.

I don't know why I feel lighter. I would have thought humiliation for breaking down would be weighing on me, but it's the opposite. I exhale, letting a smile return to my face, and then sip my wine. Sitting with Mary is nice, so I say, "Mr. Gregors is sleeping with Iris Barker over in Dover."

Popping to the edge of her seat, she leans over. "Really?"

"Yep. She was widowed last year, but rumor has it this affair has been going on long before he died."

Her mouth hangs open. "How do you know this?"

"Lauralee gets all the juicy gossip up at Peaches."

When she's sitting back again, she laughs, holding out her glass to me. "It's good to have some girl time again."

"It is."

Opening the door, Tag pops his head outside. "Dinner is ready."

Mary stands, giving my wrist a little squeeze. "Perfect timing." She mouths to me, "Thank you." With a new glow about her, she takes the bottle of wine inside with her.

I stand with my glass as Tagger calls Beck inside. Turning to me, he says, "What did you two talk about?"

Facing him, I lean against the house, not a foot dividing us, and smirk. "Not you if that's what you're worried about."

"Disappointing." His smirk quirks into place. "Whoa," he says, jumping back to let Beckett fly past him. "Wash your hands, buddy." Tag is quick to return to his spot, smiling at me like there was no interruption. "Where were we?"

"You were expressing disappointment because your mom and I didn't make you the center of our conversation."

"Ah. Yes." His eyes look past me, and he takes in a breath. Standing this close to him has me taking in the finer details of his face—three lines from the corners of his eyes, the green is sager when reflecting the colors of the sunset, and the scruff covering the snow drift of his jaw has my mind wondering how it feels—against my fingertips and much lower. "Well, there's always tomorrow."

I don't know why that keeps my smile in place, but it does. "There's always tomorrow." I'm not sure I should be hoping he comes out to the ranch again, but I wouldn't be upset one bit if he did.

Back in my bedroom, I had convinced myself that my new little buddy had twisted Tagger's arm to invite me over. Now, standing here with him hanging out like we have nowhere to be or a dinner to eat, I'm rethinking that stance. Recent events would prove the case . . .

Large hands that covered my hips at the store.

The electrifying brush of our skin in the kitchen.

Even him offering to drive me was surprising.

I look down between us, giddiness threatening to zip up my spine. I shouldn't allow myself to feel things that might be one-sided, much less with a man I know will be gone in a few days. But when I look back up at him, I can't deny the signs of possibility coming from him as well.

Get a hold of yourself, Chris.

He's Baylor's best friend.

In some kind of situation with a woman back in New York City.

And has a son to focus on.

Tagger Grange was always nice when I remember the times we spent together. *He's just being a gentleman, so don't read too much into this.* It will only lead to my own disappointment. And when he leaves, like he already plans to do, I don't need to be healing another broken heart he's left behind.

Returning to what this really is—a friend having a friend over for dinner—I glimpse his family seated at the table, and ask, "Are you ready for me?"

His body still blocks my entry, and his eyes fix on mine. "I'm not sure, but I might be willing to take the risk."

And just like that, my heart is thrown into turmoil again.

CHAPTER 6

Tagger

My life in New York is quiet.

Too quiet. *And lonely.*

But here, around the family table in my childhood home, it's loud and filled with laughter. One story has led to another, memories shared, and I've not felt this content in longer than I can remember.

Seeing the smile on my son's face has me reaching over and tickling his side to watch him crack up. He's eating up all the attention he's been getting, which I love for him. He'll carry this visit with him for a long time. I hope forever.

Making these memories with him is the best thing I ever did.

I love my son, but Pris makes it hard to look away sometimes. She was a cute kid when she was a teen—a tiara wrapped around the crown of her pink hat, long hair tousled from blowing in the wind, and a chip on her shoulder I think she inherited from her brothers—leaving dust clouds in her wake of her arrival by horse. She loved to make an entrance and never cared if she got dirty doing it. But damn, she's gorgeous now, and a night-and-day difference from the women in New York.

Anna was a fish out of the water, or in terms of how she used it when we flew back after one night here—tuna was never going to pass for someone with caviar tastes.

I never looked at her the same. I couldn't. That cut deep, and she knew it. An apology was never given, but she did demand one from me months later for dragging her to the middle of Nowheresville.

It was the beginning of the end of us. However, if I were honest, we always moved in different directions. It just took the switch to be tripped to realize it.

Seeing how Pris and my mom have bonded . . . I don't know what it is. It just feels good. Natural. Nothing is forced between them. Their eyes shine with their every delight. They exchange glances, seeming to reference something they shared on the porch, and always start laughing right after. It's tempting to be let in on the inside joke, but I'm okay with them having their secrets. Also, I'm not wholly convinced it's not the wine kicking in after three glasses each.

Good thing I'm driving her home.

After dinner, my dad wants to take Beck out on the property for his last round of the night, and my mom practically shoves me out the door, promising to put Beck to bed. I give him a big hug and kiss his head. "Be good and get some sleep, okay?"

He grabs my face between his hands, and asks, "Will my face be rough like yours one day?"

Pretending to bite his hand sends him into another fit of giggles, but then I say, "Would it be so bad?"

"No. I want to be just like you, Daddy."

"You already are, little buddy." I hug him tight, then send him off to catch up with my dad.

Pris comes toward me after embracing my mom. The top of her dress is caught by the breeze we were lucky to get tonight. "Good night, Mary."

My mom waves. "Night, Chrissy."

Heading right for me, I ask, "Chrissy?" I cock a brow and grin. "I can't have Pris, but she can call you Chrissy?" Shaking my head, I spin the key ring around my finger. "The wound deepens."

She comes to where I'm leaning against the front of my dad's truck, choosing to drive it over the rental car. There's a little wine in her steps, an easygoing nature in her body that's loosened her shoulders and gives those hips some wiggle. With a smile that could win the Peach Festival planted on her face, she laughs.

Stopping right in front of me like we're on a friendlier basis, I'm greeted with a poke to the chest. "Mary asked, and you didn't."

"May I call you Pris, Pris?" I take her waggling finger and hold it between us.

Her eyes are glassy in the floodlight coming off the porch but have no trouble focusing on me—my eyes, mouth, and bite of her lips when her gaze goes lower. "No." The grin belies her response. But then she shakes her head. "Pris is a name to make fun of me, but I will let you call me Chrissy if you want."

"I'm partial to the original."

Tugging her finger free, she says, "Christine it is for you, then." She walks to the side of the truck and pulls the door open before I have a chance. "Come on, big boy. It's time to get me to bed."

If I weren't already standing still, my feet would have

come to a complete fucking stop after that request. I crack my neck to the side, then adjust the pants that have instantly tightened before I walk to the driver's side and climb into the cab of the truck.

This is going to be a long ride to her house.

Letting my mind wander is not something I do. I'm a focused-on-the-prize type of guy. But damn, if she's not putting images in my head that would lead me to take a detour with her that I shouldn't.

Baylor.

That's all I need to remind myself of my place in her life, and my thoughts clear. I start the engine, keeping my eyes forward as I turn us around. Pris keeps her cards tucked to her chest, making it nearly impossible to figure out her next move. I swear she's flirting one minute, then acting like Beck's the only one who wanted her here the next, as if I was humoring her.

The truth is, I should have been.

I know the golden rule when it comes to her. As tempting as she's become, she's more than off-limits. She's practically outlawed in this pocket of the state. I'm sure some bill has been filed at the courthouse after passing a Greene County council vote that clearly states that Christine Greene is out-of-bounds when it comes to looking at her, much less thinking about getting her to bed. *Even if it is at her invitation.*

The road from my place to hers is lit by the moon and stars and the occasional headlight from a passing truck. That's left us in the glow of the radio and a few lights on the dashboard. I steal some looks her way. She catches me once, but the others gave me enough time to take her in a bit more. The delicate features of her face, the slightest slope of the tip of her nose, and lips that have me trying to remember the last time I kissed someone. It's not something I do anymore on dates. Kissing has them thinking it's more than it is, and that gets messy real fast. I avoid messy at all costs. It's not worth the aftermath.

"What are you thinking about, Tag?"

I glance from the road to her eyes on me with her elbow on the door and head resting on her hand. So casual and comfortable. I feel it, too. There are no pretenses with her. She doesn't give a shit if I made a hundred K that day or if my suit was tailor-made.

When I give myself time to think about it, no one has asked me about my thoughts or well-being in years besides my mom.

One thing I'm damn sure of is there's no way in hell I'm telling her those soft pink lips of hers were consuming my thoughts when she busted me. "I forget nights are about the stars. I don't see them enough back in Manhattan. There's too much light pollution at all hours."

She glances out the window as if reminded the stars are there whenever she needs.

"Like the sun guides my day, the stars keep me company at night. I leave the blinds open so I can always find them if I wake before the sun." She laughs to herself. "I probably sound so country to you."

"No. I always did the same when I was growing up here." Wrenching my hands around the wheel, I look at her again. "Now I close every blind in the apartment with the push of a button. Life is weird."

"I can't say I wouldn't mind a button some days."

"Do you mind me asking you something, Pris?" I keep my eyes on the road ahead, giving her the freedom to say no.

"I'm an open book. Ask away."

This time, I turn my attention to her long enough to see

the slight upturn at the corners of her mouth. "I know why you came back, but why'd you stay? You had just graduated from college in Colorado, and Baylor said you had a job offer waiting in Denver."

Her eyes connect with mine only momentarily before water fills the inside corners, and she looks away toward the window. "That's not something I hide, but can we talk about it some other time?"

"Yeah, sure. Sorry if that's a sore subject."

"No," she says, her hand resting on my forearm. "It's okay. Really. I've been drinking and had too good of a time to drag up complicated answers." Her hand slides over my arm, leaving a path of warmth where her fingers once were. "You can ask me something else. Anything you want to know?"

So much more than I should be allowed. "I've been assuming you're single because I didn't think to ask."

"I'm so single." She sits back, and with a dramatic swing of the back of her hand to her forehead, she adds, "Painfully so." When her laughter fills the cab, I can't stop myself from soaking it in just to feel the same.

I'm rarely wrong, but now she has me questioning what I was assuming all along about her dating life. Could she really be out here without any prospects? "Painfully so, huh? There's no way you're telling me you don't have a regular roster of guys begging to take you out on a date."

"I appreciate the vote of confidence. I needed the ego boost." Her hands follow along in the air in front of her with every word she speaks. "As for guys, sure, some stop by with flowers, acting like fools, thinking that's what I'm into."

I chuckle. Listening to her is highly entertaining. I'm not sure I ever heard those words used together quite like it. "So you're not into fools? Or you don't like flowers?"

"I love flowers." *Noted.* Though I'm not sure why I need to know this tidbit of information. I'm not typically one to hold on to trivia that will never be used. "But flowers aren't going to make me fall in love."

I grin. "Oh yeah? What makes you fall in love with someone?"

"Their heart. Their intentions. The way . . ." she says as if she's known the answer her whole life.

She's fascinating, and when I glance over at her again, she's staring at the stars through the windshield with a smile on her face. Beautiful. "The way?"

Turning to me, she continues to smile. "The way he looks in a cowboy hat." She starts laughing. "Shallow, I know, but I was always a sucker for a hot cowboy."

"You know what you like. Nothing wrong with that."

She angles more in my direction. "What about you, Tagger? What tickles your fancy when it comes to women?"

"A great ass," I reply with a smirk. "Unoriginal, I suppose. But you know what really attracts me to a woman?"

Her lips part as her chest fills with the deep breath she's taking. With a slow blink, she whispers, "What?"

"A woman who knows who she is, what she wants, and has her own goals and ambitions." I run my palm down the thigh of my pants. That was heavier than even I expected. It's not how I want to end my night with her. "That, and a great ass." I chuckle.

Her laughter trails through the window she's cracked open. "Gotcha. Great ass, and a woman who can hold her own." Leaning her head back against the headrest, she asks, "Is that what made you fall for Beckett's mom?"

Anna. Not my choice of topics.

"Um." I scrape my hand over my head. "That was different."

"How so?"

The wind from my sails dies down, and with a rub of my temple, I sigh. "A lot of things led to our relationship." I can see the curiosity in her eyes, but why drag down a good night? "If you don't mind, that's not something I want to talk about tonight."

"I'm sorry." The sincerity in her voice has me reaching over and rubbing her shoulder. I don't know why I fucking do it, but now that I'm touching her—my palm against the soft fabric, the tips of my fingers against her soft skin—I don't want to stop. "I didn't mean to bring up—"

"No, it's fine." I return my hand to the steering wheel despite not wanting to. "I'm just enjoying my time with you too much to ruin it."

She reaches over and nudges me with her hand. "Careful, Grange, or I'm going to get the wrong impression."

"There could be worse things." I drive over the cattle guard and onto the ranch. Time seems to have sped up on the way back, making me wish I'd driven a little slower.

"Is this flirting?" Her pretty smile returns. "I'm so out of practice I might not recognize the signs."

"Trust me, babe, you'll know when I'm flirting." *Okay, that was fucking flirting.* I just flirted with Pris Greene.

Baylor's little sister . . .

Who's all grown up . . .

And looking at me like kissing might not be so out of the question . . .

Fuck.

Am I about to kiss her good night?

Do I want to kiss her? *I kind of do . . .*

"Oh my God!" she says, dropping her head behind a hand visoring her view.

"What is it?"

"My dad. I'm so embarrassed." She sighs heavily, staring through the window as I pull up to the house. "He waited up."

There goes that option.

CHAPTER 7

Christine

"Well, that was utterly mortifying!" I stomp right past my dad, tugging the screen door open like it personally offended me. I shoulder the wooden door open, only daring to look back in time to catch the taillights escaping into the night from this distance.

I don't blame Tag for taking off so fast. Who wants to deal with someone's dad at thirty? But I hate that I panicked and rushed our goodbye, jumping from the truck before he had time to shift into park. I caught a "good night" before I slammed the door closed.

But it wasn't the goodbye still playing on my mind. He called me babe, and I will never forget it as long as I live. Lauralee will never hear the end of it until my dying day. It's like Tag and I have come full circle, and he finally noticed I'm not a kid.

I smile, floating on air from my fantasy coming true. Though my fantasies go a lot deeper than babe, and his mouth always goes lower . . . *If I were being truthful with myself.*

My dad trails me inside, shutting the doors behind him. The crunch of the old lock set in place as I head for the stairs. He says, "Tagger Grange has known you since you were knee-high to a ladybug. He isn't someone to be mortified over."

I stop with my hand holding onto the oak newel at the foot of the stairs. With one foot resting on the bottom step, I look back. "I'm not mortified over anything Tag did. I'm mortified that at twenty-six years old, my dad waited up for me."

"A dad can't worry about his daughter?"

I step up and turn all the way around to face him. "You can worry about me, Dad, but scaring off my dates is a whole other story."

Toeing his boots off by the door, he says, "Good thing you weren't on a date, then." The long pause between us has him looking up at me with one boot still stuck on his foot. "You weren't on a date with Tagger Grange, were you?" The concern riddling his forehead is evident as it pinches.

I drag my teeth over my bottom lip, looking down, and then shake my head. "No. I was only making a point." Every part of that reply feels wrong, like a lie. "I'm going to bed."

"Sweet dreams, dear daughter."

"Sweet dreams, Dad." I drag myself upstairs, innately aware of every creak in the hardwoods and avoid those planks like I did in high school. I got busted once or twice and learned my lesson. I needed to be quieter. The hell to pay the next day, my chores doubling, might have also played a part.

I'm old enough not to get in trouble like that, but the stealthy path I climb comes naturally from memory.

In my room, I strip off my sandals and dress and slip on a roomy T-shirt I won years ago at the rodeo. It's too early to go to bed, though I could probably fall asleep after the long day and glasses of wine. I text Lauralee real quick:

He called me babe.

Who?

She's faster than I am.

I take a breath, my body relaxing as I perch on the end of the mattress.

Tagger.

That one word has my phone ringing the next second. I laugh when I answer, "I can die happy."

"No. No. Not yet. Before you die," my best friend says, rushing her words, "you need to hit rewind and tell me how you got from the *he never knew I existed* stage to *calling you babe*."

I grin because if the roles were reversed, I'd want the same. "It's not as salacious as you make it sound, Laur."

"Salacious? You're the one dying happy like you just jumped the man on top of the hood of his truck. *Whoa.*" She takes a deep breath. "That escalated quickly." Tipsy enough to think it was pretty dang funny, I giggle while she loops the mental track of her mind to get back in this race. "Anyway, stop beating around the bush and give me the good stuff, Chris."

My eyebrows shoot up from the demand, but I won't lie, I'm just as giddy to share with her. "My goodness." Of course, I still must give her a hard time. "Patience apparently isn't a virtue in your book—"

"We already know this," she says with a laugh. "Now go on."

I wave my free hand in front of me like a maestro, and say, "I shall continue now. His son invited me to dinner at the Granges, and I went. I also let him drive—"

"His six-year-old?" Her voice pitches.

"No, silly." I roll my eyes. "Tagger. Which means—"

"He had to drive you home? This story keeps getting better and better."

With a shrug, I reply, "I drank some wine—"

"Oh no." Her concern wavers through the line. "You and wine don't mix, Chris."

Slightly offended, I flip my hair over my shoulder. "I'll have you know that me and wine do just fine."

"Mm-hmm. Sure."

"I rhymed," I say, proud of myself.

"You sure did."

"*Anywho*, I had a great time. The food was great, the company even better. We laughed like we'd been friends forever. And it was good to catch up with his folks again."

"Good to hear. Good to hear. Now get to it, girl, because I know he wasn't calling you babe in front of his mother. So you're in a car at night with fifteen to twenty minutes to spend alone together. Sounds like the beginning of a fairy-tale ending if you ask me." She giggles, which causes my own laughter to bubble up.

"Which is why I'm not asking you." I drop my hand to the bed and huff. "I'm way too practical to get caught up in that business. It's as if you've forgotten we live in the middle of Texas with the slimmest selection of men in the entire universe."

"Are you going to let me live vicariously or ruin the illusion?"

She's too ridiculous to argue with. Closing my eyes, I can almost remember the feel of the air crackling between us. I suck in a slow and staggering breath, and then whisper, "We talked but didn't need to fill the silence. It felt good, easy, and a little zap sparked between us when I caught him looking at me. I can't explain it. It was no big deal, though I felt tension in the air."

"Sexual?"

"It's been far too long for me to know the difference." I lie back on the bed. "I had asked if we were flirting, and he said, "Trust me, babe. You'd know if I were flirting. Just like that, all sexy and deep tones that shot right through me."

"God, I can just imagine," she says, her tone as dreamy as mine. "He has the most amazing voice, deep with a slight rugged rasp. Did you have sex?"

"Lauralee?" The whiplash has me bolting to my feet again and pacing. "For Pete's sake, you think I'd only be telling you he called me babe if we had sex? I would have been texting you before I left that bed."

Her laughter fills the line. "You're a good friend, Chris."

"The best, in fact."

"Yes, I can't argue with that." I hear the crinkle of what I know must be a bag of gummy bears. The soft and pillowy kind. Only the best. We may not always make the best decisions with guys, but we have high standards when it comes to candy. "As for the babe," she says, with what sounds like a mouthful of deliciousness. I take a sip of water, waiting to hear what she's thinking. "It's a step in the right direction. But I'm rooting for sex next time."

"Pfffft." The water spews from my mouth, droplets showering my bare legs. "For you or me?"

"Both." She bursts out laughing, but the sound muffles like she's covered her mouth. Like me, she's stuck at home with her mom's bedroom beneath hers. "Well, it sounds like a good night."

I sigh after catching my breath, remembering how he rubbed my shoulder. It felt like we were friends. Not me, the little sister of his friend, but as my own being in his eyes. It felt good with him. "It was."

"Will you see him again before he leaves?"

"I'm not sure. We didn't have time to talk once he pulled onto the property." My face heats from humiliation just thinking about what thoughts were running through Tagger's mind when he saw my dad. We also now know where Baylor gets his overprotective nature. "I'm tired. I'll fill you in on that another time."

"You know where to find me." There's only a quick pause before she adds, "Hey Chris, I'm glad you can close that chapter on the crush you've always carried for him. Well done. Mission accomplished."

I'm not sure what to think about that. Was it all a game of getting him to notice me? Maybe when I was younger. Tonight, though, it was more. I know it, but only time will tell. "I still don't have any plans of getting tangled up with a guy who's leaving in three days."

"Tangled up or tied down. Either way, the countdown is on."

"There's no countdown, Laur." Before we get caught up in circles of what-ifs, I say, "Good night, friend."

"Good night."

I leave the phone on the bed and go to wrap up in the bathroom. I make sure to stop by the window and look up at the stars. "Good night, Mom." And then I climb under the covers and click on the TV. It's just gone ten, which isn't much earlier than I typically go to bed, but my mind is still reeling with the possibilities of how we would have ended the night if it weren't for my dad being there.

He was caught staring at my mouth. Call me evil, but I licked my lips involuntarily. It was innocent, but I saw how he shifted. I'm beginning to think I wasn't the only one with a fire lit inside me tonight.

I've always heard that the heart wants what the heart wants, but can a crush really turn into true love? I'm not so sure, and it doesn't seem like I'm going to find out either. So it's best if I watch TV and get my mind off him altogether.

I want the impossible.

Each hour that passes, dreams fill my head, and thoughts when I wake up are of one thing—*Tagger Grange*.

Damn him.

CHAPTER 8

Christine

IT WAS three glasses of wine, but it feels a lot like a Mack truck ran over my head this morning. Lauralee is right. Wine and I don't mix. *Or we shouldn't.*

I'll stick to beer and hard liquor instead. That makes me laugh until I wince from the pain in my throbbing brain. My mouth is as dry as a tumbleweed, but I can't be asked to move just yet. I lie there with my arms wide as the tip of the sun makes its debut for the day.

I don't have long, but I stay in bed until the last second, thinking about my night with Tagger and his family. It was fun and comfortable like with my own family because I've known them practically as long.

Reaching over to the nightstand, I take a few sips of water from the glass. I was smart enough to grab it before falling into bed, but I was too dumb to actually drink it to avoid a hangover. You can lead a horse to water, but apparently, I won't always drink it.

I get up and start getting ready—washing my face and

hoping to bring some life back into my skin, brushing my hair and teeth, popping an ibuprofen, and getting dressed. I may not feel my best, but today doesn't have to be a bad day. After all, not only did I catch Tagger staring at my mouth like he wanted to kiss me, but he called me babe.

It's probably careless to get excited over something so trivial, but I'll chalk it up to the lack of prospects. One hot guy comes along, and every part of my being has noticed.

After a few gulps of soda and some crackers in the kitchen to settle the headache threatening to rage, I head for the barn.

"Pris?"

I turn to the sound of my dad but don't see him. "Dad?"

"Christine?"

Walking around the barn, I look in the direction I believe his voice is coming from, but I still don't see him. Then he appears from behind a tractor at the edge of the cornfield. "Dad?" I go to him so he doesn't have to travel as far. I can tell his back is bothering him again by how he's redistributed his weight to the right to compensate. "What's going on?" I take him by the arm, hoping I can help the pain that's tensing his face.

He pats my hand and works up a grin. "Morning."

"Morning. Everything okay?"

Shaking his head, he replies, "Davey didn't make it in this morning. His wife went into labor just after four o'clock."

My chest squeezes in joy for them. We don't get many babies around here, and Davey and his wife have wanted this one for years. "That's wonderful news." But then the pieces fall together. "Oh no, were you trying to herd the cattle?" My heart drops, knowing that's not something he should be doing anymore.

"Someone has to, but as you can see, my herding days are over."

"You don't need to do that or anything else that requires a doctor to get fixed. I can cover for Davey if we can let the cows graze while I take care of a few of my other tasks this morning."

We finally reach the front porch, and I help him sit down. He winces but starts breathing normally again. "You're a good daughter, Pris."

"You're a good dad. Just stay here and rest. Enjoy the slower pace while I take care of what needs to get done." I touch his shoulder. "Can I get you anything? Water? Some orange juice for energy? Breakfast?"

"I ate earlier. Stop fussing over me and get on with your day."

He struggles to let anyone help. My brothers and I worked harder beyond our years than most kids, so I know what it takes to run this place. "Text me if you need anything. Okay?"

"Yes, ma'am."

Knowing my day just got a lot longer doesn't help stave the headache away. I think it made it worse. No use complaining. The animals depend on us, so I head for the barn again. After feeding the smaller animals on the farm, I saddle up my Palomino, Sunrise, and head to the back of the property to check on the cattle and see how far they've wandered from where Dad left them.

The sun is brutal today, and it's only mid-April, making me think this summer is going to be as hot as Hades. Another thing I take mental note of to make sure we're prepared.

Sunrise loves to run, so I let her loose on the way to the pastures. The stampede strap wasn't tightened, so when she really gets going, my hat is blown right off my head. The strap anchors against the front of my neck, but the wind blowing through my hair and whisking through the cotton of my shirt feels too good to wrestle it back onto my head.

Pulling the reins, I slow her to a trot until I stop her at the top of a hill on the lower pasture. The cows are fine and grazing through the wilder patches of grass that have arrived with spring. I do a quick count, not worrying too much about finite numbers but more a general sense for now. A breeze reaches this part of the property more often than the others. It's nice seeing the blades bend to the east under the cooling air.

Even nicer that it reaches up here where I'm sitting on my horse.

I take a deep breath and slowly release. As soon as a calm overcomes me, I find my head filling right back to the tip-top with a to-do list. With a gentle squeeze of my legs, I encourage Sunrise to walk, letting her go where she wants, which is a patch of the good grass she likes to eat.

I reach around to grab my hat and put it back on, tightening the strap under my chin and then adjusting in the saddle. I pull my phone from the holster at my hip and text my neighbor a few properties over:

> Hi Marjorie, it's Christine from Rollingwood Ranch. One of our hands out here and his wife welcomed their first baby. I wanted to see if you could send a pretty arrangement over to them? They're on the west side of Dover County.

Time moves slower out here in hill country. I may not hear from her for hours or even tomorrow, so I start to put my phone away when it buzzes.

Hi, good timing. I have some pretty daisies in orange, pink, and yellows. Out in the greenhouse, some heritage pink roses are blooming, and I usually have some carnations around. I can put something together in this new white milk glass vase I got in. I think this arrangement would be lovely to send them and perfect for the occasion.

Sounds great.

You know I love Rollingwood's ribeye steaks.

She's not subtle, but I prefer direct. I smile and reply:

How about four?

Neighbors around The Pass are always happy to exchange when they can. It's something I appreciate.

More than generous. Is it from you and your dad or from Rollingwood?

The ranch. Thank you! And we can get those steaks out to you later.

You're already short a hand. Since I'll be out delivering the flowers, I can stop by and pick them up. It's on the way anyway.

I'm covering his and my job today, so I appreciate it. They'll be in the fridge box to the left of the porch. Thanks again.

Always glad to help.

With another text for my dad to get the steaks ready, I tuck the phone back in and secure it before turning Sunrise around. I pet her neck and pat her body. She's always been good with commands and starts back to the farm. There's an irrigation system that needs to be put on the track. And then twenty thousand other things to do before I'll be able to end this day. At least my headache went away.

When I reach the peak of the edge of the farm where cornfields are lined with green stalks in the early stages of growth, I see a figure in the distance on horseback. It's definitely not my dad by the build, and the silhouette is unfamiliar to our staff and hands, whom I've worked with and known for years. I could pick them out in a lineup with my eyes closed. Broad shoulders. Wide-brimmed hat. Cut in at the midsection, where I can only imagine a devilish V of muscle leads to bigger and better things. I laugh, letting it drift behind me. A girl's got to entertain herself somehow.

We don't get a lot of visitors this time of year, so I ride into action. "C'mon, Sunrise. Go, girl." Riding fast enough to create our own breeze, I relish the cool air under the afternoon's hot sun. Not fifty yards ahead, the man stops, giving me a chance to realize that whoever it is, they're riding Nightfall, one of our biggest and stubbornest horses. Nightfall won't let anyone ride him, making me more curious about who it is.

I ride Sunrise full speed to see what this is about. Until I'm not thirty yards away, and it becomes clear. I gasp and hold my breath unwillingly in shock.

Oh.

My.

"Tagger?"

The hat.

The boots.

The jeans that look so good wrapped around his muscular legs.

The shirt that I remember him wearing in high school that the man he's become has outgrown.

Hot damn.

He looks better than I remembered he could, and I remember him fondly. *Very fondly.* But sitting on top of Nightfall like it's a horse he's known for years by the comfort level the two share, I might fall in love altogether. He pushes the brim of his hat up just enough to keep the sun out of his eyes, but those greens still blaze brightly underneath. "Hey there, Pris."

Riding up beside him, I can't hide the smile that insists on beaming just for him, even if he did call me that name. I pull the reins and squeeze my knees to come to a stop. "What brings you out to these parts, cowboy?"

"A little filly I wanted to spend more time with."

I smirk. "Bluebelly is up near the house."

He smirks this time. "Not her. Though she is quite a looker."

I playfully roll my eyes. "She gets all the studs."

Chuckling, he tilts his head, still staring right into my eyes. "I can see why."

My smile falters. This doesn't feel like a conversation over a horse. It feels more like an insinuation toward me. My lips part when I realize this is Tagger Grange flirting.

He said I'd know if he was, which was no lie. I most definitely recognize the charming smile beneath eyes that appear unable to look away from me. His shoulders are relaxed and his expression untroubled. Everything about him has me feeling like a teenager again.

I wish I could take a picture. He's my fantasy come to life, not only looking the part of how I remember him so clearly but owning the role in its entirety. But pulling out my phone to take a photo would be crossing a line, I'm sure. Though he still tempts me to do it anyway. "We're not talking about Bluebelly, are we?"

The corners of his mouth tilt up again as he hums. He leans forward and whispers, "No, we're not."

"Why'd you come to the ranch today?"

The left cheek tugs upward. "I came to see you, Pris."

"What about?"

He points into the distance, and replies, "The cost of a cart and horse to plow my field."

"What?" I try to soften the pinch of my brows, hoping not to do more damage than the sun already has to my skin.

He laughs from the gut and shakes his head. "Is it so shocking that I just came out to spend time with you?"

I'd love to play it cool, but I've never been one to hide my feelings. "You did?" But did I have to sound like I'm swooning over the man? Inwardly, I roll my eyes at myself this time.

"I did. I can help where you need me. Your dad told me one of the guys is out for a few days."

Mortification hits like a train. "He called you?" I knew it was too good to believe that he came just to see me.

"No. He just told me when I got here."

Okay, fine. That's the best of the scenarios it could have been. The giddiness returns and has me batting my eyelashes like a fool for him. "Oh. Right. Yes, they had a baby."

"That's nice."

"They're a sweet couple, so . . ." I let my words trail off, not sure I want to have a long conversation about this. Looking west, I think of the chores that need to get done.

He says, "I called my folks to let them know I'm helping

out. They're spending the day with Beckett, so put me to work, boss. I'm here to get my hands dirty."

My throat goes dry. Nothing about him wanting to get his hands dirty makes me think about chores around the ranch, but my thoughts do head straight for the bedroom. Good Lord, I really need to get some action. "Um . . ." Sunrise starts stomping, her go to when she's ready to get moving again. "I was heading up to get a bottle of water and then over to the equipment building on the far side of the ranch to work on an irrigation issue. That shouldn't take long, but it would be nice to have company if you want to come along."

"Lead the way."

Glancing at the shine that reflects off the black coat of the horse, I say, "I think Nightfall will lead the way. Though I love his spirit, he prefers being in front and struggles with being a team player. It's impressive that he let you saddle him. He's picky."

"So am I," he says, reaching down to rub the side of his neck. "Maybe he sensed we're the same."

Both are handsome. I'll give him that.

"We'll be racing the sunset if we don't get going. Five hours can fly when you're running behind."

"I'm ready," he says, rubbing his palms together with the leather rein trapped between them.

"Follow the cornfield and then past the lettuce and cabbages. You'll see the metal building."

We ride. Sunrise lets Nightfall take the lead since he was going to anyway. She doesn't need the glory. Never being a showy horse, she knows her worth. Gotta respect her for it.

When we reach the warehouse-style building, we dismount and lead the horses to the water, dropping their reigns around the hooks. I leave my hat on the horn of the saddle and stop at the opening to the building and turn back.

I make sure to catch Tagger drop to his feet. It's still quite the sight—his arms flexing every muscle as if they're in competition for most cut. His ass is hidden by denim, but that doesn't keep me from noticing the indention on the side I'm closest to. And when he lifts his hat, he swipes his fingers through his hair, sending droplets of sweat to roll down his neck.

Walking past him, I try to keep from ogling after the show he just put on for me. It's a struggle, so I switch gears. "How sore will you be tomorrow?"

"Unable to walk, I suspect." He chuckles, following close.

I glance back at him over my shoulder. "It's been a while."

"More than a while, but it felt good to ride again."

"That first time back is always a bitch, but you'll settle back in." I grab a wrench from the peg wall and head to the far side, where our tractor is hooked to the system trailer. "Maybe not before you leave, though." Ducking under the right side, I peer up at the bolt. An inkling of something twists in my chest. I have no right to concern myself with his visit, but seeing him around again has been nice.

"Probably not." Grabbing the top slider bar, he ducks underneath. "Where'd you learn to fix this thing?"

"Hands-on like everything else." I remove my phone from the holster again. "And technology helps." Lowering the wrench with the bolt in the same hand, I set them down, then search for a fix online. It doesn't take long before I find the blockage and reattach the feeder pipe and then the bolt again.

"I'm impressed, little Pris."

"Don't be. It's learning by necessity, not by choice."

He files around the tractor just as I duck out from under the irrigation system.

"Still." He nods. "Impressed."

Though I used to be intimidated to jump in, not wanting to screw up anything, but I don't really think about this type of thing anymore. It's just part of a day's work. As soon as I hang the wrench back up, I say, "You wanted to get your hands dirty. How do you feel about helping me herd the cattle from the lower field to the upper pasture? They've been in the lower field all night and today. We need to rotate them out."

"Sounds like my kind of job."

"You remember how to do it, right?" I ask as we walk back to the horses.

He shoots me a sideways glare and grabs my hat. "Don't worry about me, babe." He places my hat on my head, then zips the toggle up to secure the strap under my chin. "I know how to do it, alright."

I tease, "It will be like riding a bike or—"

"Or?"

I bite my lip as he latches his hands together to give me a lift onto my horse again. I can get up on my own, but I'll accept the offer. Swinging my leg over, I sit up straight in my saddle, then move my hips to adjust. "Making love. It's just not something you forget."

Tag's eyes haven't left my body where I've found the most comfortable spot on my saddle. I watch his Adam's apple dip and then rise again with his eyes. I thought it was fun teasing him, but his expression makes me wonder if I took it too far. "I . . . Not that." I release a heavy sigh. "Sorry. I thought we could joke about that, but—"

"We can." He leaves to get the reins from the hook and

hands them to me. Our hands meet, and neither of us moves. "This is new with you."

"Bad new?"

"Good new." He smiles, relieving me like the words. His gaze drops to my lips and back up again. "I like this new stage with you."

"Me too." I'm so quiet that I don't know if he heard me.

His gaze is fixated on the connection that has me tingling inside from his touch. Turning his palm up, he captures my hand and runs his thumb over my knuckles to my wrist and back again. I can't see his eyes, and his expression of indifference twists my belly.

Suddenly releasing me, he says, "The cattle aren't going to herd themselves." Walking to his horse, he gets on like an old pro and takes off on Nightfall, leaving me and Sunrise here wondering what went wrong when it felt like so much was going right.

CHAPTER 9

Tagger

*W*HAT THE FUCK *am I doing?*

Baylor is going to fucking kill me.

He was the ultimate player, still is, and I definitely learned my skills from him. I'm a little rusty in the area of chasing women since it's not something I have to do in the city. There, they drop like flies for any line I feed them. Not here. *Not with her...*

Hearing her boldly talk about making love has thrown my thoughts out of whack. With me, a guy she's known her whole life and probably despised for most of it. Why would she do that? *To taunt me? Tempt me?* Maybe we're buddies now and talk about these things without it being in reference to us. Maybe, but it didn't feel that way.

I think she was trying to get a rise out of me one way or the other, and it worked for both. I can't look at her now, but not because I don't want to. I want to stare at her and memorize every freckle on her face. I want to stare into those blue eyes to find the flash of gold that sparked for me the other day. I want to kiss those pink lips, and I don't kiss anyone these days, not in that way.

I'm so fucked.

I watch her racing toward me as if I'm a house on fire and she's the woman for the job. She might be. But if she wasn't distracting enough, being in the saddle again has messed with the rest of my head. Nightfall is powerful—long legs, solid muscle, and as dark as night. It's been too long since I've ridden, but we settled in together to get the work done. But I'm reminded of how good it feels to be outside for a job, breathing in the fresh air under blue skies without a skyscraper in sight.

The highest viewpoint is the ridge of our town's namesake, Peachtree Pass. Just below, the river flows even in times of drought. It's a constant in an ever-changing world. Even this property has changed so much since I was last out here years earlier. New equipment barn, more fields plowed, growing crops. It's become a bigger business than I realized. I wonder if Baylor knows since he doesn't frequent these parts that much anymore.

He's lucky he hasn't reached the burnout I have. Yet. He will. The city, the job in finance, the lifestyle. It will bury him eventually, like it did me. I'll be there for him as he has been for me. Except when it comes to his sister. He's managed to keep her under wraps for the most part.

Now I know why. Because he knows me too well.

But I didn't expect to discover that there's no hiding her beauty once you're in her presence. Her long hair flies behind her as she rides, the sun catching strands of gold and paler blond and streaks of light brown that tangle together and flow from underneath her hat. She looked cute at the store in her dress with little flowers, but I'm not minding the jeans and tees she wears either. Nothing has clung to her body, but the clothes fit enough to tell what's underneath. Still, I wouldn't be upset to see her naked.

I lift my hat and run my hand over my hair before setting it back in place where it feels more natural than the suits and Italian loafers I'm usually stuck wearing.

She and her horse slow on approach and shift to the side of us. "Hey, good workout here today," she says. "Once you wrangled the last calf inside the pasture, I closed the gate. Reggie is setting up the barn with fresh water for the night, so we're good to go."

"We can clock out?"

"Thank you for coming today. You helped make easy work of it. We're officially off the clock." Although a smile is there when she lowers her eyes to her fidgeting hands, it falls right after. Peeking up under her lashes, she adds, "So . . . guess you're free to go."

"I was free to go at any time. I stayed because I wanted to, Pris." I lean to my side and lift her chin until her eyes are set on me with the spirit of the woman who ran this ranch like a boss today. Sitting back, I say, "It's hot. I was thinking about the river and cooling off like we used to when we were kids. Any interest?"

"I have some interest." Her smile returns and brings out mine. "Do you want to go to the house and get bathing suits? I'm sure Baylor left one or two behind."

Looking in the distance at the ridge, I say, "I was hoping we could just go."

"Go, as in no suits?" I turn back to see the surprise in her eyes, though she hid it well in her tone. It's not all shock, though. Enticement dances in her eyes as she looks across the grassy land toward where the river flows. "Race you?" She takes off with a lift in her stirrups and a "Ya, let's go" to her horse. Sunrise runs as if the devil is chasing her.

Nightfall takes off, sending me back in the saddle, and I barely catch myself. *Shit.* This horse is fast. I tighten my grip on the reins and right myself, angling forward and keeping low just above the horse's mane. He's too fast, and I'm out of practice, but we find our rhythm and catch up to them.

Pris shines like the star she always was in the rodeo ring. Her happiness spreads across her features as her body is one with her horse. She glances over at me, and I see the fire in her eyes and the freedom that embodies her.

She's beautiful.

And when we slow near the trees where the river runs just beyond, she looks at me like I'm getting credit when it's not due. No credit needed. Only the freedom to leave the rest of the world out of our business for a short time, just the two of us alone together. "I don't ride like that anymore. It was amazing."

"Barrel racing, right?" Nightfall walks through a blanket of pine needles left over from winter. A tree comes between Pris and me, but her eyes find mine as soon as we pass.

"In another lifetime."

"And a beauty queen to boot."

"Rodeo queen," she corrects with a laugh, her spine relaxing on the easy walk. "Lauralee won the festival."

"They made a mistake." I don't mean to sound so serious. Is it normal to feel ill-will toward their bad decision eight years after the fact?

I notice how her eyebrows arch. It's subtle, but she caught the bitterness that kidnapped my tone. "How do you figure, cowboy?"

We pull in the reins when we reach the edge of the rocky creek. I take in our surroundings—isolated and in shadow on the bank atop a large limestone shelf overlooking the water. With a grin and some gumption, I speak my mind.

"From where I'm sitting, you're fucking fantastic." I could go on about the healthy, rosy cheeks and the pride in her eyes that comes with the exhilaration we both just felt, but I've already crossed one forbidden line. I probably shouldn't have said anything, but one line or ten, we're both adults here. And Baylor's nowhere to be found.

She laughs, directing her attention forward again before swinging her leg over and hopping down from the horse. "If only you had been one of the judges." She anchors the reins around the horn on the saddle, leaving Sunrise to decide to stay or walk away.

I dismount and follow her down large rocks that have fallen like large steps for the gods. A nice wide platform is a good place to take off our clothes. She's already one boot ahead of me, seeming to have no reservation about stripping down in front of me or jumping in the water that I remember being cold this time of year.

"It's probably like ice in there," I say, leaving my hat hanging on a branch next to hers. Starting on one boot and then the other, I begin to wonder how far she'll take it. Are we talking bra and underwear or nothing but the outfit we were born with? I'll let her lead and take the cue from there.

"I swear I have a fever after all that riding." Pulling a hand away from the top button of her jeans, she holds the back of it to her head. "Muscles burning and the heat getting the best of me out there today." Lowering her hand again, she pops the button and slides the zipper down without hesitation. "A cold shower was going to be my reward before dinner. Now, I can cool off here and take a hot shower later for my muscles."

Every word from her mouth is an invitation for my thoughts to go wild. I'd be happy to help her with those sore muscles. I have an aching one myself.

What the fuck am I doing? And thinking?

I've become a fucking pervert around her. *Get a hold of yourself, Grange.* It's a chick. It's not like I've never seen one or fucked plenty. In the city, I can send a text, and a woman will show up in high fucking heels and nothing else but a trench coat ready to fuck in less than an hour if I wanted. So why am I tripping over myself for this one?

I know.

Pris is the forbidden. And nothing will taste as sweet as this peach.

She's a delicacy I can't—*holy* . . . I start to pace, needing a moment with my back to her to get a fucking hold of myself. *Don't do this, Grange.* You're going to regret it.

You won't be able to look your best friend in the eyes ever again without guilt hanging over your head. *Fuck me.*

I turn back because I'm a weak sister-fucker and indulge myself.

Standing in nothing but a white cotton bra with lace wrapped around her ribs and pale pink bikini underwear with a white silk flower, drawing my attention straight to the top of her waistband, she asks, "Coming with me?"

Insinuation after invitation after every double entendre in the book. *She's good.* Very fucking good. "Yeah, I'm coming with you."

I tug off my shirt as she steps down into the water. I see her hesitate, but then she keeps going to the deeper part of the river. As I strip off my jeans, I watch her dip under, then come up with her hair slicked and even longer against her back when wet.

A streak of sunshine leaves that part of the river in the hottest part of the day, but I'm still leery. As a kid, it was nothing dealing with the icy river. I could have a heart attack now. Okay, a bit of a wuss response. *How bad can it be?* She's in there swimming in the current.

After my socks come off, I step to the edge. "How cold is it?"

"It feels great."

It only takes one step in the water to know she's lying. "Damn, it's cold. How are you out there and not shivering?" I keep wading out until my ass is under, then keep going.

"I was, but I wanted you to suffer with me."

"Gee, thanks, Pris. I owe you one."

She laughs and dips under again. When she comes back up, she says, "Just get in. It's not so bad once you're in the sun."

When the sun hits my face, maybe it's all in my head, but I appreciate the heat and try to soak it in. Reaching the same depth as her, I can still stand with my shoulders above the water. I dip under, though, because I have a big-as-fuck ego and feel the need to prove that I can at least match her in this arctic-temp water.

When I come up, I catch her bottom lip shiver and notice goose bumps covering the tops of her arms. "Come here. I'll warm you up."

She swims into my arms and, at first, tucks her head over my shoulder with her body pressed to mine. I rub the soft skin of her back and hold her in my arms. She's smaller with me wrapped around her, her elbows a little bony, but as I slide my hands lower and over the curve from her waist to her hips under the water, I nuzzle my nose along the shell of her ear, and whisper, "Better?"

Nodding, she dips her head back and then leans far enough to look into my eyes with her arms around my neck. Her gaze trails to my mouth before her eyes close, and she kisses me.

I wanted this just like she did, but having her take the lead is such a fucking turn-on. I take hold of the back of her head with one hand and keep her middle pressed to mine as I deepen the kiss.

Her lips are as soft as they looked in the truck last night. And the way they're embracing mine has me holding her as close as I can and memorizing the feel of her tongue to remember later. The grind of her hips has me craving more, so much more that I grab her by the ass, desperate to seek relief from the sweet torture.

That's when I realize the lines are too blurred to read anymore, and Pris Greene tastes too good not to kiss her like she should be.

So I do.

CHAPTER 10

Tagger

THERE'S no hiding my growing desire for her, even in frigid water.

Pris wraps her legs around me and lifts, rubbing herself against my erection. She feels so good, too good to be fucking her in a river. But I also know that once we get out, things will never be the same between us. I'm not sure how to feel about it.

I like her company.

I like looking at that pretty face of hers.

I like her.

I'm so fucked.

She pulls back and licks her glistening lips. Her chest swells with heavy breaths, the weight of them matching mine. Her eyes soften as her gaze drops back to my lips. "It was better than I ever imagined."

Those words, her soft blue eyes watching me with trust encircling the gold centers. It's like she's set off a reminder in my brain.

It's a compliment, nothing but an innocent remark . . .

The idealism rattles me back to reality. But it strikes a familiar chord that I don't want to revisit. I've been someone's fantasy of what they thought they wanted in life, only to turn me into a project that needed fixing. I won't be that guy again. *Not for anyone.*

"We should probably dry off before the sun heads below the trees." Looking back at where we left our clothes, I see the horses have gone. "Guess it would have been wise to tie them up." I release her and move back through the water in slow strides.

"They're used to roaming. They'll be up at the barn before we get there, ready to have their saddles taken off." As the water between us grows, she asks, "Why are you sneaking away?"

"I'm not sneaking," I reply, struggling to keep the defense out of my tone. "I'm right here." I shake my head. "I just think we should go."

"Because I kissed you?"

"No, because I kissed you." I turn around and paddle my hands through the shallower waters until I'm standing on the flat boulder again.

I hear the water rustle behind me as she works her way out, but I'm already drying off with my T-shirt before she's standing behind me. "What's wrong with kissing me?" I couldn't hide my defensiveness, and neither can she.

When I glance over my shoulder, she's shivering with her arms wrapped around her chest. Hard bud nipples push against the cotton, which is already see-through from being wet. I look down at her entire body because I'm an asshole, even if I pretended I wasn't this week. The pink of her panties is smooth against her pussy, revealing more than she's probably aware. I meet her gaze again, where I'm met with a tinge of anger she's not bothering to hide. "Nothing, that's the problem." I turn around and grab my jeans because I can't be showing up at the house with her daddy sitting there with a rifle at his side seeing us both soaking wet and basically naked together.

"That doesn't make sense, Tagger."

Of course it doesn't. None of this makes sense, even to me, other than I just played with fire and feel burned in the aftermath. I need to get out of here because she'll never understand. "Get dressed, Pris."

"And just drop it because you don't want to answer?"

"Exactly fucking that." I finally get the denim over my wet legs and button them up.

She finally reaches down and grabs her shirt to slip on over her head. Reaching underneath, she unfastens the bra and slips it off before it soaks through the fabric. "That's really weak, you know that?"

Grabbing my socks, I bend to put them on, not bothering to respond. We're only going to end up arguing, and that's not what I want despite being the instigator.

She pulls on her jeans and then walks to where she left her socks and boots. She says nothing more as she finishes getting dressed.

If she were most women, I'd probably be grateful they got the message. With her, though, I feel like shit. Standing tall in my boots again, I lower the temperature of my tone, and say, "Listen, Pris—"

"No. I don't care what you have to say, so save it for somebody else." She walks to the softer covering of the needles and then calls out, "Sunrise? Here, girl. Sunrise."

Sticks crack under her feet as she makes her way through the trees, taking her hat with her to the openness of the rest of the property. "Sunrise?"

Taking my hat off the branch, I start behind her but stop when her horse comes trotting into the woods. *Her saving grace from me.* Animals know these things. She gets on without any assistance needed and takes off toward the barn.

Hurting her feelings was the last thing I intended, much like her comment in the water. But I fucked up, and I'm not sure she's the forgiving type.

Guess I'll find out as soon as I get up to the house. To avoid the long walk back, I try her trick, and call out, "Nightfall?" Clapping my hands, I keep walking. "Come on, boy. Come, Nightfall."

Fifteen minutes later, I'm walking my ass up the last hill, finally spying the house ahead. When I pass the barn, I see Nightfall. His saddle is put away, and he's content eating just outside of the open doors. "Traitor," I mumble and keep walking. Not like he cares. The ornery thing didn't even bother looking in my direction.

I'm hoping to make it to the truck before Mr. Greene sees me and wants to have a sit-down. No such luck. *Fuck.*

He stands from the chair on the porch and rests his hands on the railing. "You sure have gone and done it, son."

I lift my hat to run my fingers through my hair. I stretch my neck to the side but keep walking, hoping to get out of here in one piece. "Sir, I, uh, I can explain—"

"You best be getting to it, and real fast now."

I stop at the front of the truck, not planning on going anywhere near that front porch. "I know I shouldn't—"

"Shouldn't? I feel betrayed, Tag."

The sweat beading at my hairline falls in buckets under the intensity of his eyes on me. "I'm sorry. I'll apologize to Pris right now."

"Your apology is no good here." He comes down the

steps steadier on his feet than he was yesterday. Guess anger does that to a man. "Why didn't you tell me?"

"There was no need to upset you. She handled it just fine on her own. You raised a fighter."

His forehead creases as he narrows his eyes at me. "Pris? She holds her own." He stops a few feet from me. "Are you okay? You look poorly."

The question stumps me. *Am I okay?* Is she okay? What's happening here? "Yeah, sure." Holding the hat to my chest, I graze over my head again, my nerves still on edge. "But I should check on *her*. I didn't mean to hurt any feelings."

"Pffft." He waves me off, crossing his arms over his chest and resting them on his belly. "She's not upset. Not even bothered."

My brow flattens over the top of my eyes. "Alright . . . I guess that's good."

"It's not like she expected you to drop your life in the Big Apple to come play cowboy here on the ranch." More salt is tossed on my wounded pride before he continues like nothing happened, "But you have a job if you ever want it."

"Huh?"

Moving in, he claps me on the shoulder. "Yeah, Pris said how you held more than your own out there today. It was a big help." He glances at the house, and then lowers his voice to add, "I'm not the same help as I used to be. She can do any task she's given, but I wish she didn't have to every time something arises." Stepping back, he crosses his arms like before. "So I really appreciate you stepping up to help herd today."

Too stunned to make sense of what just happened, I stumble to say, "I'm glad it worked out."

"I hear you're leaving Friday, but if you're looking for

work, Davey won't be back until next week. We sure could use the extra hands around here."

My eyes trail upward to see Pris duck from the window. She wouldn't let me fix my reaction today, so maybe I can fix it tomorrow. I reach my hand out. When he takes it to shake, I say, "I'll be here bright and early tomorrow morning. Is it okay if I bring Beckett with me?"

"Bring him. I can show him how to clean out the horse stalls." His chuckle bounces his belly before he turns, heading back to the house. "I'll see you in the morn."

Should I have said no? *Probably.*

Do I regret saying yes? *Not one bit.*

"See you tomorrow, Mr. Greene." I get in the truck and start the engine. I miss the convenience of leaving the keys in the vehicle and not having it stolen. I turn around and head for my parents before Pris gets wind of the offer her dad just made.

Pris will be pissed.

I get back before the sun finally sets and hop out, excited to see Beck. He runs from the house like a dust devil let loose, right into my arms. Lifting him, I kiss the top of his head. "Missed you, buddy."

"Missed you, too, Daddy."

I shift him to my back, where he holds on like a little monkey. "Tell me everything about your day."

My mom stands in the doorway with a smile on her face. "Did you work up an appetite?"

It's been a long time since I heard her ask that question. Hearing her now makes me homesick. "Sure did. What's for dinner?" I asked that every night growing up. It's weird how it's starting to feel like I never left home.

"Rollingwood Ranch steaks tonight, baked potatoes, and—"

"Broccoli," Beck snarks, and I'm already imagining his scrunched face. It's not his favorite vegetable, but he won't push it away. Even though Anna calls him picky, I've never seen it. He's a good eater like his dad when he's with me.

Rollingwood Ranch wasn't such a name back then. It was just steaks from the Greenes. They were always the best. I step up onto the porch. "What's the fancy occasion?"

"You and Beck being home."

She's about to walk inside, but I take her hand to stop her from leaving. Hugging her, I then kiss her cheek. "It's good to be here again." With her arms around both me and the monkey on my back, she sniffles. I release her and whisper, "Don't cry. It won't be so long next time."

"Promise?"

"I promise." And a promise is something I always keep . . . except when it comes to the one I made my best friend. Fuck. *Some friend I am.*

We move inside, where Dad is putting the food on the table. He takes one look at me. "Shower or dinner?"

"Dinner. I'm starved."

He sets a plate down on the table with cornbread squares and a bowl of broccoli next to it. "Sit. Eat. Looks like you've had a day."

My mom sets a plate of food in front of Beck, then makes one up for me, though she doesn't need to. I think part of her misses taking care of my brother and me. My dad is a good partner to her, but she's a mom through and through.

"Thanks, Mom." I dig into the steak, savoring how good it is. I've had the best steaks around the world, but nothing beats this one.

"You're welcome." She sits down with her own plate and asks, "What did Thomas have you do?"

"Not Mr. Greene. Pris had me herding with her today. Davey was out because his wife had a baby."

"Oh, that's great news," she replies, clasping her hands in front of her. "I think I'll deliver a meal out to them tomorrow."

"I think they'll appreciate that, Mary." Dad takes a big bite, then washes it down with water. "So you were herding? How'd that go? It's been a long time since you were driving a herd like that."

I can feel my shoulders slump forward, the adrenaline of the day wearing off as exhaustion replaces it. "I'm sure I'll feel it tomorrow."

"Looks like you're already feeling it," my mom says with concern running through her eyes. "You might want an early night."

"Yeah, I'll get Beck to bed and head up after that. I promised him Beck and I would help out tomorrow again."

Throwing his arms in the air, he says, "I want to herd cows."

"Do you know what that means?"

"No," he says so honestly. I miss this when we're apart. The openness, the trust he instills in me, the love that he gives without question. I'm not the bad guy Anna calls me. To him, I'm his hero, and I intend to live up to the title like my dad did.

Speaking of . . . my dad chuckles. "It means you need a good night's rest because tomorrow will be a busy day."

"You sure you don't need help around here?" I ask.

"No. You go ahead. I only have fishing on the schedule tomorrow."

I know his code now. Fishing means a nap during the day. I'll let him have it, especially because Beckett was probably a handful today. To my son, I say, "It also means you get to ride a horse with me."

"Yay! Tomorrow is going to be the best day ever."

That might be a warning before the storm, considering how Pris and I left things, but maybe it won't be so bad. She didn't tell her dad, so that's a good thing. And she said good things about me, to boot. I find her utterly unpredictable, though, so who knows what I should expect.

I spend time with Beckett after ushering him through the nighttime routine and settling him in bed. One book is the plan, but he talks me into two, then falls asleep before the end. I don't blame him. My eyes have grown heavy.

My legs feel like dead weight I'm dragging upstairs as I head to bed myself. Since I took a shower after dinner, I'm glad I can fall straight into bed. In the room, I fold up the pallet where Beck slept the first two nights. Tonight, he insisted he was a big boy and chose to sleep in the spare room downstairs all on his own.

He's comfortable here. It's good to see him acclimating, but I knew he would if given the chance. And it's great to see him expanding his wings.

I barely get the light turned off before I pass out.

CHAPTER 11

Tagger

My alarm startles me awake at five o'clock.

I have many regrets in my life, but promising Mr. Greene I'd be out there again today might be my biggest. I won't disappoint, though. I gave my word, so I get ready and wake Beckett from the dead. I don't remember him sleeping this heavy back in the city. Can't blame him with sirens going off throughout the night. Even twenty floors up, there's no avoiding the sounds of the city. And out here in the quiet countryside, the days are more physical, draining the body at night. So I get it.

"Hey buddy, good morning," I whisper, lifting him out of bed and setting him on his feet. "You still want to go with Daddy to the ranch today?"

"Mm-hmm." His eyes don't open, and I'm second-guessing if this is a good idea. I don't want to deal with a bad mood that could have been avoided. That won't be good for either of us. His arm comes around my back, and he rests his head in the crook of my neck. "I want to go with you."

"Okay. Let's get you ready, and we'll eat some breakfast before we head out."

Not twenty minutes later, he's wide awake and singing with his whole chest in the back seat of the truck like he's auditioning for Broadway. I try to keep my eyes from crossing. I love to hear the enthusiasm, but it's not even six in the morning.

Pris comes galloping down the porch steps as soon as we park. Going right for Beck, she opens the door and leans in to unlatch him. "I heard you were coming to visit today."

"Daddy said I can ride a horse, Miss Christine."

She restrains herself from glancing up at me, but I can tell ignoring me doesn't come easy. "Did your daddy? Well, we'll make sure that happens. But first, I wanted to see if you can help me collect the eggs as soon as the sun fully rises." When his feet land on the ground, she taps his nose. "What do you say, buddy?"

He looks at me. I can tell he wants to go with her but doesn't want to hurt my feelings. "You go, Beck. We have all day to spend together. Okay?"

Turning to her, he says, "Daddy said I could get eggs with you."

"And whatever Daddy says apparently goes." She slams the door closed before I can say anything.

Guess I'm not in her good graces like her dad led me to believe. I open the door and get out, ready to get on with it since it's going to be a long fucking day.

I wasn't wrong. I spent most of the day covering Davey's daily duties, herding being a part of it. Reggie didn't hold back on my duties. I even wondered at one point if Pris was behind the list. She'd make a great spy, considering how she managed to be out of my sight most of the day, to my disappointment.

So much for my plan of making it right.

I'm running out of time, and it might just have to be something I say on the way out later. I'm too busy to take a break in the meantime. At least my kid is having the time of his life riding Nightfall with me. There's no reason to complain.

By the time Reggie releases me for the day, Beckett is tired and cranky. His missing his nap means a rough evening ahead. I could bet a million bucks he won't make it past the cattle guard before falling asleep and would clean the house of their money.

Pris comes from the barn. She must have heard us cutting across the gravel of the drive to get in the truck. I toss my hat inside the cab, then duck back out when she says, "You leaving without saying goodbye?"

"I figured you didn't want to talk to me."

"I meant him." Deep cut to my ego. With her arms wide open, she squats down and says, "Come here, kid."

He runs to her, hugging her tight. They've built a bond that will only enhance his memories of this trip. And for her, I'm grateful. She took him in like he was one of her own.

They hug, and she kisses his head. "You be good for Daddy, alright?"

"I will."

When he shuffles back to the truck, she remains standing there looking at me like I'm a lost cause. I shove my hands in my front pockets, beginning to wonder if I am. I've lost myself over the past few years. It's been good here, but this is only temporary. But even so, I don't want to leave things on a bad note with her.

"I'm sorry, Christine."

"Christine? That was a fast-track change."

I can't seem to muster any defensive response because I already know that no one will get out of this mess unscathed. "I can't win, can I?"

"Not if you give up so easily."

I glance back at the truck. The doors were left open, and Beck sits in the front seat looking like he hopes I won't notice. I close some of the gap between Pris and me, hoping we can set down our weapons and be on the same team again. "I'm not giving up. I'm facing reality. We shouldn't have done that, and we both know it. Even though we started down a path, it's one that hits a dead end."

"Why?"

"Because I don't live here, and I'm not moving back. My kid's mother is in the city. Your brother will kill us. It's an impossible situation. So it's better to give us time and space, the distance needed to cool things between us."

"So you walk away despite what you felt yesterday?" She crosses her arms over her chest and angles away from me. "Yeah, that will solve the issues."

"We shouldn't even have any issues, so if we're being forced to solve them, then it's a disservice not to acknowledge that this can't happen between us."

She lowers her arms to her sides, and disappointment wrecks her expression, souring the look on her face. "You're probably right. There's no use in trying to make something happen when it's not meant to be."

That doesn't make me feel better. But I don't think it was supposed to.

I nod, taking one last good look at her. "Maybe I'll see you around next time I'm in town."

"Yeah, you and Beck are always welcome on the ranch." She shifts, and I think she senses this is goodbye like I do.

"And thanks for filling in for Davey the past two days. You were more help than I gave you credit for."

"I don't need any credit. It was good to be back in the saddle and put some physical work in. Saved me a couple of trips to the gym as well." I try to muster a smile but fail.

Her grin blooms like a flower for me. "There are no gyms in Peachtree Pass for a reason."

"Now I know why." I step up on the truck and steal one last lingering look. Her eyes latch onto mine like she knows what's coming. "I'll see you around, okay?"

She nods, shoving her hands in her pockets. "See you around, Tag."

I get in not feeling any better than how the day got started. I'm used to it, though. The demands of work make most days run into the next. Beck climbed over the seat and buckled himself up in the back. I start the engine and turn the truck around without looking in the rearview mirror. It's better for both of us if we leave things where they are instead of pretending we have more time to figure it out.

Heading toward the two-lane road that will lead me back to the house, I stop just on the other side of the cattle guard and look back at my son. I'd be a richer man if I'd made the bet. Beck's fallen asleep, leaving me with my thoughts on the way back to my parents' house.

We're back at the house earlier tonight, which might be the reason I'm not as tired. My dad cracks open a beer as I walk with him to do the final round before night comes. He says, "You're leaving tomorrow." Not asking much. He never did.

But I answer anyway. "Yes, sir."

"Joey stopped by to pick up some extra eggs from us."

"Joey from high school?" I haven't thought about him in

years. He played football with Baylor and me. Caused some trouble but was a good friend. "What's he up to?"

He takes one barn door while I take the other, and we close them at the same time. "He said he'll be down at Whiskey's later and said you should stop by."

"I think I'm good." I latch the barn doors closed and head back to the house with him.

"We're not doing anything but watching *Wheel of Fortune* and last week's episode of *Survivor*." On the porch, he says, "Can't say we'll be much fun."

"I don't mind. The days have gone fast."

Patting my back, he says, "He seemed like he really wanted to see you. Think about it once we head to bed. I know you kids start your nights late. Nothing exciting will be going on here other than my snoring."

"I'll think about it."

As soon as I walk in, my mom says, "Anna called to talk to Beckett."

I would have rather been here, but she's allowed to talk to her son. "How'd that go?"

"Seemed to go well. She talked to me before I handed over the phone."

That raises suspicion. I scratch the back of my neck. "Not to sound like a parrot, but how did that go?"

"She was cordial. She also asked about you and how you were doing?" I don't make things negative, but how I'm doing is the last thing she ever cared about. So yeah, that's odd. Mom continues, "I told her you were doing great and working out at Rollingwood the past two days."

I chuckle. "I can only imagine what she thought about that."

With us standing in the kitchen, keeping our voices down so little ears don't hear, she releases a sigh. "I may be reading too much into it, but she sounded like she missed you."

"We don't see each other except when we're picking up or dropping off Beckett, so I think you misread her tone." I rest my hand on the top of the chair because it seems my mom has more on her mind.

She moves closer and peeks down the hall before whispering, "Although I don't know what happened between you two, I know it's not been easy for you since. I hate to pry, but I still worry about you and Beckett."

"You're not prying. Ask what's on your mind."

"Is there a chance you and Anna could get back together? Many couples work it out for the kids—"

"No. There's no chance." I direct my attention down the hall where Beck fell asleep not long ago. "We weren't good before we found out about the baby, but I stuck out to support her during the pregnancy and after to be in my son's life. Now that the ties that bound us in the early years are severed, I'm not looking to fix them. I'm in his life equally, as much as I can be, but he's happy, and I'm happier. This trip helped."

"You found a piece of yourself again. I can see it in your eyes. That's what coming home does. It reminds you of who you were and the people who will always welcome you back." She embraces me around my middle.

I hug her, and say, "Thank you." It's quick, and the talk was over before it got too heavy. I'm glad we have the type of relationship where she doesn't mind that I don't tell her the gory details as long as she knows I'm okay. "I'm doing good."

"I'm glad to hear it and even happier to see it." Giving my arm a squeeze, she says, "I'm turning in. Night, son. Love you."

"Love you, Mom." The conversation replays in my mind

as I walk upstairs, and it stays on a loop as I take a hot shower. I washed my face and hands before dinner, but the water now pummeling my shoulders feels so good as the rest of the tension washes away.

I take my time, but even when I get out, it's not that late. It's just gone nine. So I sit on the end of the bed and flip the TV on. After a good twelve seconds of searching the few channels my parents pay for, I click it off, remembering what my dad said about Joey.

Am I up for driving over to Whiskey's?

It's been years since I've been there. I was barely legal that time, too. Now I'm a grown man with a child. I should be a responsible dad.

Since when does having a good time every now and again make me a bad father? *It doesn't.*

I still humor myself by looking around the small bedroom once more to see if anything remotely entertaining catches my eye. Nothing. I could go to sleep, but I'd be up at three in the morning wide awake. Our flight isn't until noon, so I don't need to go to bed early.

Pushing up, I grab my phone and text my dad:

> You okay watching Beck if I go meet Joey out at Whiskey's?

They go to bed early, but they're up watching TV and reading, so he doesn't take long to reply.

> We've got him covered. He's safe here. You have fun and drive safely.

> Thanks, Dad.

I could wear what I'd wear in New York or see if any shirts in the closet still fit. I go to the closet and start to flip through hangers until I find a black button-up. I pull on a pair of jeans that magically got washed today and then the shirt. The arms are tighter, so I wave my arms in front of me to stretch the cotton.

I'm missing a belt that will work with this attire, so I leave the shirt untucked, but I make sure to grab my boots and a felted black hat before I walk out the door. The clothes are foreign to my body, but it feels good to be in something different, something made to weather a bar fight, wear to a Texas wedding, and everything in between.

With the keys to the truck in hand and almost a full tank of gas, I take off across county lines and find my way back to the only bar worth visiting in a thirty-mile radius.

I grin when I see the flashing Y in the sign on the verge of going out. The metal exterior is rusted, neon beer signs hang in the windows, and the parking lot is full. I wasn't the only one with this idea.

Walking in, I quickly scope it out. The place has expanded, more pool tables are behind the bar to the left, and the dance floor is already crowded with couples dancing to a live band. This place has changed. It was nothing more than a dive bar when Baylor and I stopped in for a beer.

"Granger baby, you're back!" Joey comes up and slaps his hand in mine. "Good to see ya, man."

I almost don't recognize him. Tucked under a lighter straw cowboy hat, he used to wear a buzz cut, but his hair is shaggier around the ears now. His face is fuller to match the rest of his build, but his laid-back grin is still the same. "It's good to be back."

"Come on. Let's get you a beer and catch up."

We find some vacant stools and sit before ordering two draft beers. They're not so much as set down on the bar in front of us when the door opens. It draws the crowd's attention because everyone wants to see who walks in.

There's no denying who it is with her hair shining like silk free-falling over her shoulders, those eyes that remind me of sapphires, and a smile that just about knocks me on my ass because it's so gorgeous. The fitted green tank top clings to her tits and is tucked into a pair of denims that had to be painted on. She'll need the Jaws of Life to remove them later, or . . . *my teeth could do the job.*

I'm even privy to hearing her laugh from this distance. It's music to my ears. Finding her incredibly tantalizing, I empty the pint glass because I'm already well aware that I'm totally fucked in this situation. *Or will be if I'm lucky!*

CHAPTER 12

Christine

Two hours prior . . .

"Let's go out," I say as soon as Lauralee answers my call of anguish to take my mind off Tagger Grange. The *most* frustrating man I've ever met and the best kisser. *Damn him.*

I just don't know what to think about our relationship, though calling it a "relationship" might be getting about ten yards ahead of us still. "Okay, where? To Whiskey's?"

"I don't love that place, but it's familiar, and we get half-price beers, so that's a win."

She laughs. "That's because they're desperate to get women through the door. You'll have the pick of the litter in that place."

"*We'll* have the pick of the litter, Miss Peach Festival. Are you in for nine?"

"See you then."

I arrive five minutes early and wait beside her burnt-orange Mustang convertible. In Austin, you can find other cars this color in honor of the University of Texas, her alma mater. But out here, she's one in a million, so everyone knows it's her when they see this car coming.

She comes out with a small bag hanging from her elbow, her phone in hand, and keys in the other. "You're rarely on time. Anxious much?"

"Actually, I am."

The car beeps when she unlocks it. "Get in, hot stuff, and let's get to partying."

She peels out in a flurry of gravel crunching under her tires, and then turns up the music. The top is up tonight, but we've had many good times cruising with it down and singing at the top of our lungs over the years in this car. Just being with her lifts my spirits. "I'm not hooking up with anyone."

Glancing over at me, she asks, "You've already decided? Doesn't matter if Chris Hemsworth walks into Whiskey's, you'll say no, sorry, I made my best friend a promise she hopes I don't keep?"

How can I not laugh? "You're ridiculous, you know that? Anyway, he's married with a gaggle of kids. So no, I won't be hooking up with Chris Hemsworth if he walks into Whiskey's."

"*Ooh*, what about Brad Pitt? He's on the market."

"How many kids does he have again?" I'm already talking myself out of him before counting. "Nah, he's got that amazing face, but I'm looking to forget my troubles, not get into more with a celebrity."

"I'd get into trouble with him."

"You get first dibs then," I say, wondering why we're having to talk over the music. Turning the volume down, I add, "You're free to do as you please. I'll happily be your wingwoman."

"You say that now, but I know you get lonely." She smirks. "And horny. Not that I can blame you." When her eyes return to the road, she asks, "What's the latest with Tagger? He's still in town, right?"

"He's still here. He was back out at the ranch today filling in for Davey, but I only saw him from a distance."

"On purpose or?"

Lauralee has known me too long and doesn't let me get away with anything. "Do you have to see right through me every time?" Grinning, I laugh enough to be heard, but I can't say it goes deep. It's just all I can muster when thinking about Tag. His rejection still stings. "I wanted to go out to forget about him, quite honestly."

"We can do that right after you fill me in."

Here's the thing with my friend—she doesn't push to get the gossip. She keeps at it to make sure I'm okay. But getting into the weeds about what happened at the river doesn't sound like a fun way to kick off a night on the town. I angle toward her and rest my head back. "I promise to share the details soon, but I don't want to think about him at all tonight. Is that okay?"

She reaches over and rubs my arm. "Of course." Pulling into the lot, she parks in the field next to the bar since there are no closer spots. We do last-minute lip gloss touch-ups in the mirror before stepping out. Hooking her arm in mine, I walk with her toward the front door. She pulls it open but turns back to say, "And don't worry, we are Tagger Grange–free tonight."

"I appreciate it."

She's holding the door for me, so I walk in but stop just inside to wait for her. "Beer?" I ask. "It's on me."

“Shiner, please.”

I turn around, but I can’t force my feet to move forward the moment my eyes lock on those greens set on me from the other side of the bar. *Damn him . . .*

Why is the universe so cruel to me?

I turn in a rush to push Lauralee back out the door, but she’s been working out and holds her own against my tackle. “What the hell, Chris?”

Stepping back, I realize I just made a minor scene he most definitely caught. “Can we go?”

“We just got he—*oh!*” Her gaze hangs over my shoulder as her jaw drops open. “Wow. Um . . .”

My heart thumps, my breathing comes in rapid-fire from my chest, and my thoughts scramble as I try to figure out how to handle this situation. I freeze, pretending nothing is out of the norm.

She whispers, “He’s behind you.”

“Walking or standing?”

“He can hear everything you’re saying, Pris,” he says. *Crap.* His voice doesn’t hold the humor that he usually carries around me, but more the same tone by the river.

I lock eyes on Lauralee as panic overtakes me. She wraps her hands around mine. “I think you should talk to him,” she whispers, “and put whatever has you so twisted behind you.”

“Sure, why don’t I do that, Benedict Arnold.” Through clenched lips, I mouth, “What happened to us . . .” I signal behind me with a nod. “Being Tagger Grange–free tonight? That sure flew out the window fast.”

“I can still hear you,” he says, his dulcet tone slinking under the chip on my shoulder and begging me to turn around.

I cross my arms in defiance. "Maybe you should stop eavesdropping then?" I say loud enough for him to hear.

"I'm sorry, Pris."

Turning just slightly to the side, I steal a peek at him from my periphery. "For?"

"For hurting your feelings. It wasn't my intention."

Call me a sucker, but an apology gets me every time. I don't know why I find people who own their mistakes so heartening, but it's something I value in a person. So it would be hypocritical to hold Tagger to a different standard. I turn all the way around with my arms still crossed and question him under a perfectly styled arched eyebrow. I made the effort tonight before I knew I'd be running into him. I see Benedict has left me unsupervised, which could be bad for Tagger. "What was your intention, then?"

"Not to hurt you." He lifts his hat and holds it against his chest. "Not to rock the family dynamic. Your family means a lot to me. They feel like my own." *They*, as in my brothers and my parents. *Not me*. He says, "I don't want to piss off Baylor or your dad."

"Maybe they don't get a say in who I kiss in rivers or have sex in barns with or date at all. It's not their decision to make for me. I'm not a kid anymore. It's my decision. Mine alone."

His brow furrows, and he narrows his eyes at mine as he puts the hat back on his head. Staring at me, he seems to have lost the words on his tongue.

I ask, "What?"

"Who are you having sex in barns with?"

I thought it was when he called me babe the first time, but it wasn't. It was right now. Right here in Whiskey's. The jealousy seeped into his tone against his permission, and although he shed that expression for indifference, I caught it clear as a bell.

Tagger Grange has a jealousy streak when it comes to me.

And this time, I'm no fool. That random comment about sex in a barn bothered him.

I grin like an idiot because this victory tastes better than being called babe ever could. I straighten my shoulders and try not to strut, but yeah, it's impossible. I'm a freaking peacock with my feathers on full display as I walk past him. With a poke to the chest, I say, "Wouldn't you like to know?"

He catches up next to me, and replies, "I would actually."

"Why?" I work my way around the corner with barstools full of the regulars who are always here and toward Lauralee, who has beat me to the bar and is ordering.

"So I can kick their ass."

Stopping abruptly, I face him with my jaw hanging and my mouth ready to catch some flies. "Really?"

A smirk lifts steadily on the right side of his stupidly handsome face, and he shakes his head. "No. My fighting days are over, but I'm not opposed to having a word or two with them."

My gaze deviates from him to the long line of people sitting at the bar. "You're in luck. There's one now."

"Where?"

"Right there. Joey Melvin."

"What the fuck?" he mutters as he slowly turns to see him seated only a few stools away from us. A deep line cuts between his brows when he returns his eyes to mine. "Are you serious? You had sex with Joey?"

I playfully push him away and laugh. "God, no. That you believe I would is really disturbing. No way would I have sex with him." The relief that washes over him changes the tension engulfing us since I walked in. "He's old," I tease just to push a few more of Tag's buttons, hoping one day he'll be pushing mine . . . *God, so naughty.* And now I can't stop thinking about it.

"Old?" His voice clogs at the end. He clears his throat. "He's my age."

It was way too easy to rile him up. I laugh, grabbing his bicep. "I'm just kidding. I mean, not in the sense of he is your age because he is, but he's not old." I give him a wink. I feel someone like Tagger would appreciate that kind of detail to cap off this conversation.

"I need a beer. If I weren't driving, I'd drink something heavier. You're a handful." His gaze dips to my mouth when I lick my lips. He looks up to the heavens like he's asking for help before shaking his head. "Listen, Pris."

Why is it so hot when he seems like he's out of options and handling me like he probably shouldn't—not as careful as if I'll break like a dish?

"Yes?" I ask boldly, looking into his eyes as he searches for the words he wants to say.

A heavy sigh eases his chest, and his shoulders fall just enough to relax. "I don't know what's going on here—"

"What's going on here?" Lauralee asks, shoving a bottle of beer in my direction.

I take the beer and a quick sip before I answer, "I don't know. He was just getting to that part."

"Oh, perfect timing, then," she says with a laugh as we share a wicked exchange. Yep, she knows I got him riled up. Whether I can reel him in, though, is a whole other scenario. And more importantly, do I want to?

Should I really forgive him that quickly?

Make him pay a little longer?

Forget it ever happened, and we go on living our lives separately?

As much fun as it can be teasing him, I can tell by the regret in his eyes that this might not be the time to continue doing it. I touch Lauralee's arm. "Do you mind giving us a few minutes?"

She reads me like a book, always has. Her smile softens, and she nods. "Sure. I'll be over there at the bar talking to Joey." She takes my beer for me, then scowls at Tagger. "Play nice now."

I can see he's close to an eye roll, but the corners of his mouth lift. "I always do."

Now I'm about to roll my eyes, but like him, I can control when I want to.

As soon as we're alone, relatively speaking since we're standing in the middle of a crowded bar, he moves closer to me. "You know as well as I do, that something happening between us will only ruin the good thing we have going. So what do you suggest we do about this attraction between us?"

"Well damn, I didn't expect you to come right out and admit you're attracted to me."

"That's based on a mutual assumption that this attraction travels both ways."

Shifting my weight, I plant a hand on my hip. "Considering I'm the one who kissed you, I think you already know where I stand."

"I didn't think I was physically hiding any feelings between us, especially since you were grinding yourself against me."

"That's so vulgar," I say, "and so freaking hot." Should I have admitted that? Probably not, and I can't blame it on the alcohol since I haven't had any, but why hold back now? Let's just get it all out of our systems.

Staring at me like an equation he can't solve, he asks, "Are you always this honest?"

I sigh, then glance around the place, noticing a few eyeballs on us. We're giving quite the show to gossip about later. But if I ask him to go to the parking lot to finish this in private, the rumors will really fly around the county and probably get back to my dad or, worse, my brothers. I shrug. "I don't lie well, so it's better for me to tell the truth."

"What am I going to do with you, Pris?" The quandary continues in his expression, contorting it in ways he doesn't need to stress. I reach up and am just about to smooth the lines at his temple but stop myself, remembering we have an audience.

I tilt my head and smirk. "I have some ideas."

"Okay. That has to stop, or I might take you up on the offer."

Throwing my arms wide, I say, "Finally."

"Damn." He rubs the temple I wanted to. "Are you always like this? Were you like this in high school?"

I flip my hair over my shoulders and decide I'm ready to start drinking. "No, I couldn't live down that nickname you guys gave me. No guy within fifty miles of Peachtree Pass would come near me, thanks to Baylor and Griffin." I walk just past him and look back over my shoulder. "Now I'm just making up for lost time."

"Fucking hell, woman."

Beelining to Lauralee, I can see her already shaking her head. By the time I reach her, she hands me the bottle of beer again. "What did you do to that poor man?"

With the opening of the bottle pressed to my lips, I

glance back at him once more. I may be easy to read, but he most definitely is not.

From under the brim of that sexy black hat, his gaze pins me to the spot. And then he's storming toward me like hell-fire's cut loose.

My friend slips the beer from my hands, and I vaguely hear, "Let me take that for you."

And then my hand is grabbed and he's whisking me toward the dance floor in the back. "If you wanted to dance, all you had to do was ask."

"I'm starting to think you prefer if I don't ask and make the decision myself."

With a shrug, I confess, "I'm not opposed."

Pressed together, we two-step like we've been partners our whole lives. He looks down at me as we dance, not missing a step, and grins. "You're the kind of trouble I've tried to avoid, Pris Greene, but here you are like Eve, tempting me to take just one bite."

"Imagine how good it will taste."

Pulling me even closer, his cheek against mine, I hear him mumble though I can't catch what he said other than I distinctly heard a fuck in there.

He twirls me out from his body, then pulls me back against his chest with a thud. His arm is around my back, and by the grip he has on me, there's no escaping. Not like I would. *Nope.* Not when I finally have Tagger Grange right where I've always wanted.

CHAPTER 13

Christine

STAMPING the end of the pool stick to the floor in pride, I stand back so Tagger can attempt to save his dignity. Even though I'm a girl, he foolishly forgot I'm a Greene, and Greenes usually come out on top.

He also seems to have forgotten that my eldest brother taught me how to be a pool shark from a young age. I had to keep up with the big kids, and it's a gift he gave me that's still giving all these years later. The extra money came in handy as well back in high school.

I don't need the money now, but a bet is a bet, and when I win, I collect.

He sinks the eight ball, then tosses the stick in frustration on the table. Turning his back on the disgrace he left on that felt, he rests his hands on top of his hat. Annoyance shapes a tightened mouth, but then he seems to come to terms with the loss and grins. "Well played, Greene."

"Thank you very much," I say, holding out my hand. "Twenty bucks. Pay up, Grange."

He slides his hand into his back pocket, making his pecs stand out against his shirt. Digging through a few bills, he settles on one and sets it flat on my palm. "I thought we were playing for fun?"

"It was fun. For me." I grin up at him as I tuck the money in my front pocket. "And it's always a delight to win your money."

Chuckling, he says, "Yeah, just a fucking delight." He leans against the table and tips the beer back, drawing a long pull from the bottle. His gaze stays focused on me over the glass bottom. When he lowers it, he leans in as if he's going to tell me a secret. "You know, you sound a lot like Baylor right now."

Being so close to him has me wanting more. I draw a figure eight on his chest, then smile up at him. "I'll take that as the compliment I *know* you meant it as."

"Figured you would, babe." Tagger's getting mouthy as he gets more comfortable around me. I don't mind. I kind of like it. He shouldn't take anyone's crap, including mine. *I don't.* I learned that from working in the men's world of ranching. Stand up for yourself or get disrespected.

Whiskey's has more room to breathe with each passing hour. A few have slipped by without much notice until now while we're standing here in a brief patch of silence. Who knew everyone in The Pass had a midnight curfew? I scan once more for Lauralee. We're not attached at the hip, but we generally keep tabs. I saw her playing darts earlier, then dancing with a guy we've seen around before, but I don't see her now.

The band cleared out a while ago, but the pool tables are busy with people still waiting to play, so I step out of the way and pull my phone from my pocket.

Tagger asks, "Need another beer?"

"I don't *need* one," I reply, staring at my phone. No messages from her. "But I don't *want* one either." I glance up. "Thanks, though."

I text:

Hey, where are you? Did you take off, in the bathroom, or hiding somewhere at Whiskey's?

The three dots don't show up, so I wait a few seconds, still staring at the screen.

He sets his bottle on a table half empty. "I think it's time to go."

The phone vibrates in my hand drawing my attention to it again. She replies:

I was tired and didn't want to drink much since I was driving.

I would have gone with you.

Not a lie. I would have if she wanted me to. It's been fun with Tagger, though, so I'm glad she didn't.

I had no doubt you were in good hands.

I swing my gaze to his hands. They're very good hands indeed. Big, capable, and strong enough to grab my hips. He'd have no problem handling me in bed since he kept me from face-planting.

Another message pops up.

I just got home. You have fun and don't do anything I wouldn't.

With a giggle, I'm quick to reply.

That doesn't leave much.

Lauralee sends:

Precisely my point.

I laugh again before putting my phone away. When my eyes reach those shaded greens from the black hat he's wearing, I reach up to steal it from his head and set it on mine.

Something in his gaze darkens, and then, as if he's seen heaven, he smiles. "You look good." Glad he approves. The tip of the hat slips down over my brow, but instead of lifting it, he tilts his head sideways for a better view. "Want to get out of here?"

We've had some hot and cold moments the past few days, but smoothing through the misunderstandings has me thinking about the invisible lines he's drawn in the sand when it comes to where we go from here. Blurring them was fun down at the river, but now I have no idea where we stand other than back to being friends again. A few beers won't change that. A few bad decisions might, but that leads to other issues. And I don't want issues with him without a chance to fix them.

So where does that leave us?

Some guys I recognize from over in Dover start racking the balls, which makes it a good time to move anyway.

"I'm ready," I reply, unsure what exactly I'm agreeing to —a ride home or going somewhere else. That's the thing about Tagger Grange—I trust him. He's close enough to answer to my dad if he screws up, but not so close that the kiss we shared was weird. It was the opposite—what I always dreamed it would be.

He leads me by the small of my back toward the exit, and the heat penetrates the thin material of my shirt. I even slow down to get a better feel, and he doesn't disappoint. His entire hand flattens against my back, covering most of the acreage. So big.

As soon as we're outside, he switches it up and takes possession of my hand. *Okay. Okay, Mr. Grange.* You got my attention.

A roguish grin spreads across his face when we stop at the back of the truck. Clearly, he's trying to woo me and succeeding. I glance down at our still clasped hands, not anxious to release it just yet.

A storm brews in his eyes. I don't know if I should heed the warning or march right into it. My breathing picks up along with my heart rate, that intensity in our shared look has the pregnant pause between us inseminating me on the spot.

Reaching up, he tucks some of my hair behind my ear but leaves the hat right where it is on my head. "I should get you to bed." This man's deep voice, the scruff shadowing his jaw, and the way he drags the pad of his thumb over his bottom lip gets me worked up.

"I've heard that line before, cowboy. But last time, you didn't follow through."

"I got you to bed alright. I just didn't go with you." With a nod, he adds, "Which, you know, good and well, was best for both of us."

I huff and walk around to the passenger side of the truck. Looking back with a different kind of bed between us, I anchor my arm on the side of it and grin. "I actually don't know if that was best for both of us, but we could give it a go and see where we land this time." I know he catches the indirect question, the invitation I've given with a rolled-out red carpet for the man. I open the door and climb inside. I'm good leaving him hanging. If I've learned anything, it's that Tagger likes to play games. A little cat and mouse here, some tag there, and hide-and-seek in between.

He likes the mystery of me. The man's starving for a good time. Luckily for him, I am as well. But I really do start to wonder about the type of women he dates back in the city. Surely, I can't be offering him anything more than they can. And if I don't, why does he keep taking the bait?

Walking to the driver's side, he climbs in and silently buckles up. After starting the engine, his fingers flex a few times around the steering wheel before shifting into gear and gripping on tight.

We don't speak a word as he pulls out of the lot and onto the road that leads to the highway. Just as I'm about to break whatever barrier has sprung between us, he says, "You shouldn't come onto men like you do, Pris."

To hear what's been plaguing him the past few minutes has me smirking. Resting an elbow on the door, I casually lean my head on my hand. "Why not?"

"Because they might take you up on it."

"I don't see the problem." I look out the window when another car passes. They're few and far between, but the lights shine into the cab of the truck like we're on a Broadway stage. "If I'm saying it, I mean it."

"You're really impossible." Glancing over at me again, he says, "You're the kind of person who's given an inch but takes the whole damn mile."

"Only if they like it. If they don't, we can switch positions and try something new."

"Fuck me, Pris. Either you're the horniest woman I've ever met or you're all talk with that sweet little mouth of yours."

"It might not be as sweet as you think it is."

His grin grows with a shake of his head. "I swear your mind is in the gutter more than any guy I've ever known."

"That's saying something since you're best friends with my brother."

"I don't want to talk about your brother." His tone flips to firm, leaving no room for questions.

I push. "Why?"

He glances over with the tip of pain weaving lines into his forehead, a hint of confusion shaping the corners of his eyes, and a tinge of anger staring right at me. *He pulls.* "Because if I'm not careful, I won't be able to look him in the eyes the next time I see him."

Push. "Careful how?"

Pull. "With what I want to do to you." There's an edge to his tone that fills his words with caution. I'm thinking it's the same edge he's standing on when it comes to me. Will he jump or pull away again?

I angle the hat up in the front when the air thins between us and tensions thicken. "What do you want to do to me, Tagger?"

His eyes stay on the road ahead, his body stiff with restraint as he grips the wheel. "Did anyone ever tell you that you ask too many questions?"

"Everyone, but that doesn't answer the one I asked you."

This time, his eyes glide to the side to look at me. The slow and calculated movement keeps me on the edge of my seat in anticipation of what he'll say or do next.

"It's tempting to kiss you just to hear myself think."

I laugh, the vibration freeing to release the breath I was holding. "If you think that will keep me quiet, you have another thing coming."

His shoulders ease, and his elbows loosen as he steers.

"You might claim you're not so little anymore, but that's big-league talk, and you've only been playing with boys."

My heart hasn't stopped racing, but I'm not intimidated. I'm intrigued. Even though I know the answer because he's right, I still ask, "Let me guess, you're a real man?"

His hand dips to his jeans as he shifts on the seat. There appears to be a growing problem that needs solving down there, but I think it's best not to make the situation worse by pointing it out.

He shakes his head as if he's about ready to settle this argument once and for all. "I'm starting to think I'm the only man who can handle you."

When shots are fired, I fire right back. "And how would you do that exactly?"

"I'd start with that mouth of yours and keep it busy. Then . . ." he says, eyeing my chest without regard to the fact I can see him. Or maybe he doesn't care anymore. "Go lower. You were right earlier. You'd never be able to keep quiet once I have my way with you."

Oh . . . myyy!

Biting my lip, I sit up and grin like I just won the lottery. "Goodness, Mr. Grange, and here I thought you were a gentleman."

"Seems you've been outplayed, Ms. Greene."

"Or maybe you just played right into my hand."

I'm flung to the right from the sudden yank of the steering wheel as he pulls the truck off to the side of the deserted two-lane road.

With my hands anchoring me between the door and the dashboard, I hold strong until the truck comes to a skidding stop. "Oh my God!"

"This is what you wanted, right, Pris? You want a man to take charge so you don't have to carry that load all alone. I'm your guy." He flings his arms wide. "I'm right fucking here. Your message was loud and clear. You want me? You got me." He pops the lock on my seat belt and then rubs a finger under my chin as he raises it. When our eyes connect, he leans in. "Now . . . what are you going to do with me?"

Fine, sometimes I talk a big game but there's no intention behind it. This is not one of those times. *Tonight, I'm all action.*

CHAPTER 14

Christine

Tagger's seat belt flies back so hard that it hits the inside of the truck with a bang. His seat slides back so fast that I barely know what's happening before he grabs my hips and pulls me onto his lap to straddle him.

His hat tumbles between us, but he catches it on reflex, tossing it into the back seat. Then his hands reach up quickly, cupping my cheeks as he presses his lips to mine. My breath catches in the scuffle of hands and bodies, lips, hair tangling between fingers and lips.

I lean back against the steering wheel, my chest rising and falling again with each breath I take. "You kissed me?" I don't even know what I'm asking because my thoughts are so scrambled. But I know I wasn't the one instigating this time . . . though I'll admit I'm not innocent. But he kissed me. Tagger Grange kissed me all on his own.

I caress his face, the scruff like dull needles that need sharpening against my hands. He looks up with a lick to the corner of his mouth as if he doesn't want one taste of me to escape. "I want to do it again."

"No one's stopping you."

"You're so fucking naughty, Pris." With his hand holding the back of my neck, I'm pulled forward until our mouths crash together again. His lips are strong like his hands, embracing and owning my entire mouth. His tongue parts my lips and two-steps with mine as they explore every corner of our mouths together.

I'm high on the ecstasy of feeling his hard length for me. He reacts so quickly to me, his lips taking ownership of mine like this is long overdue, and he can't resist me. I'm already addicted to the headiness of it all and give in. I rub the seam that cuts right down the middle of my legs shamelessly over him. Again and again and harder and harder as the coiling begins deep in my center. The soft, thin material of my panties don't stand a chance against the thick roughness of the denim. "God, you feel so good."

The words seem to inspire him to dig his fingertips into the back of my ass. He holds me down while helping me grind against him. A moan escapes—his or mine is lost in the fogged-up space. "So good, babe." His lips find my neck, and his tongue flattens as it slides up to under my jaw. "Do you know how long I've thought about you?"

"Since Monday at Peaches?"

He stops and sits back, but the feigning of being upset doesn't stick, and he laughs. As soon as our eyes connect, he's right back to where he left off, and I start to lose my way again. Every gyrate a proposition for more, each moan comes throatier as I gasp for everything all at once—release, air, and more of him, all of him inside me.

It's not enough. "I want you. I want you so much."

He bucks into me, hitting the spot that I can't get enough

of and need his full attention on to get me off. Dropping my head back fills my desperately seeking lungs with air, but the coil begins unraveling, and as much as I try to stave it off, to revel in this feeling, the faster it spins inside. "Yes, babe. God yes. Right there." I lift and land, rub, and *take, take, take* as much as I can. But then his mouth finds my collarbone, one hand squeezing my breast while the other pops my jeans open and slips between my slickened lower lips.

One touch is all it takes, and I'm pushed right off the edge of the cliff where he placed me. Tremors rip through me, so I hold his shoulders, wanting to feel every last seismic shift. "Oh, Tagger. Yes. God, yes!"

The release hits quick, then my body slumps against him in the aftermath. Resting my head on his shoulder, I try to even my breaths and the beats of my heart.

As soon as I have the energy to lift my head, the adoring look in his eyes captures me. "So much for a Tagger-free night."

"It was free alright. I won't charge you a dime, not even that twenty you stole from me earlier."

"Winning fair and square isn't stealing anything except for your pride, but after that performance, you've earned every ounce right back." There's no smirk, just a smile I hold a fondness for. *Always have.* Maybe even more these days. "By the way, your hand is still in my pants."

"I know. I like it here." The wiggle of his fingers has me wanting more already.

A blue light blinds me even though the condensation on the windows obscures it. And then red. Blue. Red. "Oh no." The siren startles me before I've had a chance to recover.

Tagger lifts me and sets me back in the passenger seat.

"Fasten your pants." His voice is ragged, his breath heavy through the command.

I listen and lift to tug them up, doing as I'm told because my thoughts are still reeling from the bliss to think clearly on my own.

A knock on the window has Tagger wiping the condensation away to see a police officer on the other side of it. "Shit," he mumbles as if it hadn't looked like this would be happening. He pushes the button, and the window slowly rolls down. "How can I help you, Officer?"

Resting a hand against the hood, the officer says, "Tagger Grange?"

"Yeah?" I can tell Tagger doesn't recognize him.

I do. Too well but not on the wrong side of the law kind of way. "Dirk?"

He taps his name tag. "Deputy McCall."

Tagger eyes me and turns back to him. Dirk's toothy grin is brighter than the reflective lines on the street. "Oh hey there, Chrissy."

That earns me a hard glare after hearing him call me that name. I laugh but keep it under wraps as much as I can. I shrug, and whisper, "I can't control other people."

Turning back to Dirk, Tagger asks, "Do you two know each other?"

"We went to high school together. Of course, you were already gone, but I used to watch you play on Friday nights. It was the highlight of my week." Dirk has always been a little goofy, but he's a nice enough guy.

"Thanks. So it's Dirk?" Tagger begins to relax, reaching his hand out.

As Dirk shakes it, I can't stop thinking about that hand being in my pants not five minutes ago. "Deputy McCall. I'm Greene County's only deputy, actually."

I lean a bit closer so I'm not shouting across the cab. "How's your mom?"

"Recovering."

"Aw, that's good." I sit back again. "Tell her I'll bring her a peach cobbler when they're ripe."

"Sure will." His eyes return to Tagger. "I heard you were in town." But then he looks at me with concern squeezing his brow as if two and two are finally adding up for him.

"Yeah, I leave tomorrow."

I tried to save us by distracting him, but he's right back on the scent. Dirk says, "I see. Well, I'm still going to need to see your license and registration."

"Dirk?" I caution, "You're not serious right now?"

"I take my job very seriously. Sorry, Chrissy, but it's my duty to keep the roads safe. Unless you're broken down, this truck is an obstacle for oncoming traffic and could cause an accident."

I throw my hand out toward the windshield. "What oncoming traffic are we talking about here? No one has passed us the entire time we've been on this road. There's been no sight of anyone since we got off the highway." I sit back, crossing my arms over my chest.

He backs up with his hands on his sides, looking in one direction and then the other in consideration.

I continue, "You know as well as I do that this road leads to four ranches over a twenty-mile stretch. It's not a quick cut-through for the highway, which is the most direct way in and out of this county."

He lets out a sigh and then looks past Tagger at me instead. "You should have been a lawyer."

Tagger says, "She's a real ballbuster, but I think the ranch is lucky to have her."

I almost snapped back, but the big charmer came

around with flattery. If I weren't already caught up in the delicious aftermath of what we just did, I'd be all his now.

Tapping the side of the vehicle, Dirk says to Tagger, "Listen, I'm letting you go this time, but get on your way. And make sure to stay on the right side of the law when driving through our county."

The look on Tagger's face speaks volumes without saying a word. "Yes, sir. You got it."

When Dirk looks at me again, he smiles like we're at Sunday potluck and he scored the seat next to me. He always did have a crush on me. A lot like I had on Tagger. Full circle moment. "I'll see you around The Pass."

"Sure, Dirk. See you around."

As soon as he walks away, Tagger rolls up the window, then shoots a glare in my direction. "He wants to fuck you."

I snort. "I think he wants more than that." Waggling my ring finger, I say, "I think he wants to get married."

"He's quite the catch. Deputized and all." *There's that jealous streak.* "Solid job. Good provider. Works the night shift so I can come visit you in bed after hours."

My thighs rub together. The exhilaration of coming to life from an orgasm is the best feeling in the world. "*Well, well, well.* Who's the naughty one now?" I reach over and run my nails over the back of his head and down his neck.

He leans into it as if the touch itself is needed. Maybe it is. Maybe he needs the presence of someone as much as I am. Pulling his seat belt on again, he says, "Buckle up. Don't want Deputy Dirk to pull us over again."

"Technically, we didn't get pulled over. We were already here." I buckle up just before he shifts into drive. "Also, you should be thankful I was in the truck with you, or you might be spending the night in jail."

Holding a finger up, he says, "First off, you were

handling it just fine without any help from me. Second, you're the only reason I was pulled off to the side of the road in the first place. Something about wanting to kiss you again, and there you were, daring me to make bad decisions."

I mimic his finger in the air. "Well, first off, there was no dare involved. You came willingly—"

"Sadly, I didn't come at all."

The laughter is light, just enough to share at this hour. But he still has such sad eyes like his puppy was stolen. "I'll owe you one." That appears to appease him. I reach over, wanting to touch him again. I rub his shoulder, then slide my fingers into his hair. "And second, that was pretty great."

"Even though it was cut short?"

"Not for me," I whisper, suddenly feeling exposed in a new way. *Vulnerable*. I've lost my snapbacks to mushier feelings. "It was good and enough."

He rests his hand on my thigh and gently rubs. "I'm glad."

"As for your situation, it seems to have gone down because of the deputy. But I want to take care of you."

His hand returns to the steering wheel, and I already miss his warmth on my thigh. "You don't need to. I'll be fine." He pulls onto the property, and I start praying my dad is not on that front porch.

I think Tagger said a prayer as well, and it was answered. Nothing but a porch light is there to greet me. He puts it in park, and we sit, neither of us seemingly anxious to say good night. I'm content like this, which is something I can't typically admit. I have so much silence in my life—at night in my room, during the day doing my job—that I usually like some noise. Too much time with your own thoughts isn't always a good thing. He is the difference. With Tagger, the silence isn't filling my brain. I don't feel alone with him here, even if he is about to drive away. But I still savor his proximity.

Resting back on the seat, I roll my head to the side and look at him, taking him in. He stares ahead as if a part of him doesn't want to leave either.

A girl can dream.

But we can't sit here all night despite wanting to. Time is ticking, and I hate it.

Not wanting to rush through our ending, I whisper, "What time do you leave?"

"We need to be on the road to Austin by six o'clock for our flight." He rests his head back as well, his gaze dipping down to my hand before reaching over and taking it. Holding it in his, the comfort of his thumb runs over my knuckles. "We made a mess of things, huh?"

I'm not so sure he's asking more than stating the obvious. "I suppose we did." The high I was riding has faded, and my mood has turned somber. "And I still owe you one," I add with the softest of laughs, hoping the levity will clear the gray skies from between us.

Half a smirk is satisfying enough. "I'd say we're even. You're not the only one who enjoyed themselves. Watching you was . . . it was pretty incredible." He shifts and says, "Tell me you're not just lonely, Pris."

Reassurance wasn't on my bingo card when it came to Tagger, but maybe I previously overlooked a vulnerable side. Or maybe . . . this meant more to him than he'll admit. Is it wrong to hope for both?

He's always so strong, so if he lets his guard down around me, does that mean he feels safe to do so?

I can hope.

Turning my hand over, we weave our fingers together,

and I hold him like I have the strength to keep him here, even if for only one more day.

I won't lie to him, though, not about this. "I do get lonely. But not with you around."

He releases my hand to caress my cheek. "I don't know when I'll be back."

No promises can be made.

I catch his drift without the words being spoken. When his hand slides back to his side of the truck, I look down at my lap, my fingers fidgeting with the hem of my shirt. He's right about this being a mess, and I'm not sure it can be cleaned up without someone getting hurt, a.k.a. me. It might be too late to keep that from happening.

He's lived in my imagination for half my life. The real thing was even better. But that means it might be time for me to let him go, to free him from a situation he didn't create. I look back at him, knowing what's right and what's best for him. I hold my chin high and my gaze steady on him. "We'll always have the memories."

I unbuckle and open the door to avoid dragging this out longer than it needs to be. It was fun. He was great. I'll look back fondly one day, probably from that rocking chair next to Lauralee, and remember this all being worth it. The kisses, the orgasm, and that look in his eyes that, for one moment in time, I was his everything. *I was the prize.*

God, I think I just broke my own heart.

Swinging my legs out the opening, I'm just about to jump when he grabs my arm. When I look back, he says, "C'mere." Running his fingers into my hair, he leans across the divide and pulls me closer.

Our mouths meet, this time with care. There's no crashing of lips or frenzied kisses. No, he takes his time as if I'm being memorized. Slow strokes of his tongue around mine, lips that embrace every part of my mouth, and the hold he has on my head makes me think that he doesn't want this to end either. But I'll never ask. It's not fair when he was always planning on leaving. I knew the risk I was taking.

His eyes are closed when he leans his forehead against mine, and his breathing is staggered as if he feels the same as me. He lifts his head and searches my face once more before landing on my eyes. "Take care of yourself, okay?"

I nod since the words are stuck in my throat. I pull away and hop down to the ground. With my hand on the door, I look back once more. It's easy to find the will to smile when I'm greeted with one of his own. "See you around, Tagger."

"Here, take this." He tosses his black cowboy hat in the seat next to me. I take it, though I probably shouldn't. It's a nice hat, but now I have memories attached. I set it on my head, which makes him smile. "See you around, Pris."

I shut the door and walk toward the house, not even bothered by the name anymore. Now it would sound strange if he called me anything else. I'm quiet going up the wood steps and give my permission to turn back just in time to see him still there watching me. He raises a hand, then shifts into gear and turns around.

I stand there long enough to watch those taillights disappear, and then with his hat as a souvenir, I go to bed. *Alone again.*

CHAPTER 15

Tagger

Two hours is not enough sleep.

I scrub my hands over my face, knowing wrestling with my thoughts of Pris will keep me awake. So why fight it?

Opening my eyes, I stare at my bedroom ceiling as images of her populate my mind.

The curve of her jaw when her head tipped back against the steering wheel.

Her mouth hanging open, making me want to fuck it, kiss it, and do dirty fucking things to it.

And the feel of her soft tit that fit so perfectly in the palm of my hand.

My dick is hard just thinking about it. She drives me fucking wild.

Diving my hand under the blanket, I rub over the boxers I wore to bed and then take hold. I close my eyes, letting my head fill with images of her, the feel of her soft lips, my fingers sliding through the slick folds, and the taste of her skin. Two more minutes alone and I would have been licking my fingers.

Fuck the cotton barrier. I push them down and get a firm grip, pulling faster and sliding quicker. If I'd had five minutes more with her, I might have been fucking her. I bet that tight little pussy of hers feels like heaven.

It's not as good as the real thing, but the images of her are getting me there. I jerk faster, the pull deep down tightening.

Images flash as my orgasm builds.

Hard nipples pushed against wet and see-through fabric.

Faster.

There was no hiding. She wanted me to see her. She wanted me.

Harder.

I could have slipped right between her legs and buried myself deep in my desires for her. "Fuck," I groan, beginning to ache for release. I pump and thrust, imagining it's her I'm fucking instead.

She came with my fingers poised at her entrance. My touch was so potent that she couldn't hold on any longer. Fuck, that's sexy. The feel of her trembling over my hand, her body pulsing because of how my touch is an aphrodisiac. *And a mindfuck.*

Jerking becomes erratic with my thoughts. I should have fucked her . . .

"Oh fuck." My orgasm hits sideways, sending the back of my head to dig into the pillow in response. I come so hard that I lose myself in the darkness and the stars, the fireworks and her face. I moan as the last of my release escapes, and then my body lies in recovery. Arms limp at my sides, my legs are lifeless.

My breathing settles after I let the images go and return to reality. Opening my eyes again, I shift my arm across my forehead, resting it there, and stare at the ceiling. It's not the first time I've masturbated in this room. It was a regular occurrence back in high school, but I've been out of practice since. No need when I could get a woman just by saying hello to her. But there's something about Pris . . . *Shit.* I'm in so much trouble.

I don't know when emotions started factoring into the equation, but it's good to feel something again. She did that.

Fuck.

Sitting up, I know I can't leave with how we left it. I flip off the covers and rush to the bathroom. Being as quiet as I can, I move across the hall and shut the door. There's not much time, so the shower is cold because I can't wait for it to heat up. I dry off and slip on my New York clothes, already missing the feel of the jeans and the soft cotton against my skin.

After rushing through getting dressed, I walk down the stairs, keeping my shoes from echoing against the hardwoods. I don't quite reach the front door when someone says, "You don't have to sneak around, Tagger." My mom sits at the table with a glass of water in front of her.

"Did I wake you?"

"No, I can't sleep." Her hand covers her chest over her heart. "I'm going to miss you and Beckett so much."

"I miss you all the time. I know he will, too." I check the time on my watch before realizing how this must look. Shit. I hate that my patience has slipped when I should be here for my mom. "You can come visit. Anytime. First class."

"You know your dad is hard to get to travel. Then you put him in a big city, and he's a fish out of water."

"Then you come." I kneel in front of her. Covering her hand resting on the table with mine, I say, "Whenever you want, you just let me know. Okay?"

"You're a good son, Tagger. Don't let the world change who you are on the inside." It's a hope because she knows I've already changed, but being back this week was a good reminder. "Now you better get going, or you'll miss the opportunity."

I stand. "How do you know I'm going somewhere?"

She stands and rests her hand on my cheek. "Because I saw how you looked at her." She nods to the door. "Now go so you don't miss your flight later."

One more second won't keep me from my mission. I embrace her and whisper, "Thanks, Mom."

With her voice not much louder than a mouse, she says, "She's lovely."

She is lovely.

I take off in the truck, driving too fast to be legal and hoping I don't run into Deputy Dirk again. He won't let me off twice in one night, especially when I don't have Pris in the car to soften the blow. *Fuck it.* I only have this one chance to make it right.

I'm surprised to see headlights on this deserted part of the road. Farmers rise before dawn, but it's four thirty in the morning, and I know they also value sleep.

They're a little blinding as they near, but then they're lowered from the brightest setting. I look at the truck when it passes, my eyes locked on the driver's. The familiar blues unmistakable even at speeds over sixty miles an hour. Then my brain kicks in.

Oh shit.

I slam on my brakes and look over my shoulder. The other truck has stopped, so I do a U-turn and head back in that direction, stopping with twenty or so feet apart. I jump out of the truck to see Pris standing in the limelight of her headlights.

Carefree hair that refuses to be tamed.

Long T-shirt that covers everything to the very bottom of a pair of fitted shorts that kiss the middle of her thighs. *I've never been more jealous . . .*

Boots and those long athletic legs sprouting out of them.

And my hat on her head looking so beautiful that it'd be a crime to ever take it from her.

I start walking with the sole purpose of letting her know that she made me feel alive again. But she runs right into my arms, her body crashing into mine as she wraps her legs around my middle and arms encircling my neck. I'm kissed before I have the chance to kiss her first.

But I'm not passing this up. Standing in the middle of the road in the shine of our headlights, I hold her tightly to me, pushing her lips open and caressing her tongue with mine. I savor every second, so I remember everything and every moment I get to spend with her.

She pulls back with the most beautiful smile I've ever seen. "Did you miss me, cowboy?"

"I missed you, Pris." Setting her down on her boots, I push the front of the hat back, so I get the full exposure of that spectacular face. "But I also wanted to tell you something."

Her smile is still as bright as sunshine, and the rays reach her eyes as she stares into mine. "What is it?"

"A few days was not enough with you." I look up like I can blame the stars. "I just got here and now . . ."

"Leaving doesn't have to mean never talking again." I

redirect my gaze to her. She says, "Or even seeing each other again." I hear the hopeful lilt in her voice. "This is your home, Tagger, at minimum, in your heart even if you don't live here."

She's right, but it's not so minimal to me. Just four days here reminded me that Peachtree Pass is a bigger part of me than I acknowledged.

Taking her face between my hands, I kiss her again—slow and sweet—so if nothing ever comes of us, I know I gave her everything I had to give. Her hands wrap around my wrists as she lifts on her toes for more access. I'd give her anything she asked for, so this is easy. One more kiss and then she drops on her heels again, her gaze falling with her.

With the minutest of nods, she looks up once more, and a smile that seems forced at the corners appears. "Go on, cowboy, get going."

I lick my lips, studying everything about her pretty face, but it's this feeling I want to hold on to most—the feeling that I'm not failing anyone and the best is still yet to come. All I have to do is, well . . . take it.

She's given me hope again.

I kiss her once more, then we both turn our backs to walk in opposite directions. I get in one little ass pat before she gets too far and peer back over my shoulder. She doesn't turn back. Not once, because she's so much stronger than I ever was.

Climbing into the truck, I look at her in the driver's seat and can just make out her chest rising and then falling again before she drives forward.

Her window is down, and arm stretched out, so I do the same. One last look is exchanged along with our fingertips grazing as we roll past each other. I see her heading back to the ranch, keeping an eye on the taillights in the rearview mirror until the distance grows too much, and I'm left in the darkest part of the morning again, just before sunrise.

She planted a seed of hope in me that I'll tend to back in the city.

I left The Pass before sunrise this morning. Now, almost nine hours later, I should be home, but I'm stuck in traffic from the airport into Manhattan with a kid who was over it all, like his dad, five hours ago.

"But when, Daddy?"

I look around to see familiar landmarks and bridges, and how slow we're going. I think I could walk faster at this point. "Thirty minutes. Maybe forty-five, buddy."

"I'm hungry."

"I'll have food waiting. What do you want? Burger, pizza? Chinese food?"

"Roast and lima beans like at Grammy and Grandpa's," he replies with his full chest, looking me dead in the eye.

Ruffling his hair, I lean over, and say, "A kid after my own heart." Sitting back up, though, I have no clue where to get that in a city where I can have anything delivered at any hour. "Doubt it will be as good as Grammy and Grandpa's, but let me do some research."

No such luck on short notice, so pizza it is. Hot and waiting for us when we walk into the lobby with our suitcases. "How are you, Jeff?" I ask.

"Doing good, Mr. Grange." Leaning down, he asks Beck, "How are you, fine sir?"

"Hungry."

Jeff gives me a knowing look. He understands because he has kids. "That pizza is right here, little man. You carrying it or your dad?"

We've had a recent tripping incident that spilled the entire meal on the lobby floor. Accidents happen. No use in destroying his confidence. I take the handle of his suitcase and roll it next to me. "You carry it, Beckett."

Jeff carefully hands him the box.

Beckett grins like a Cheshire cat. "I promise I won't trip this time."

My parents believed in me and made me feel like I could do anything I put my mind to. I carried that faith with me through every stage of life, knowing failure was only temporary. I'll always do the same for my kid. "I believe in you. You got this, buddy."

I kick the door closed and leave the suitcases as I latch the locks behind me. Beck is already washing his hands, ready to chow down. I'm starving as well. But my phone vibrates in my pocket before I can sit down and eat.

Anna.

I swipe open the message and read:

Is he safe?

The insinuation that I would put our son in danger is annoying enough, but that I can't even walk in the apartment without the reminder that she needs to ask as she claims "just in case" hits a nerve. And I'm in no mood to deal with it.

But if I don't, she'll have the cops at my door.

He's safe and eating dinner.

It's like she has a reply locked and loaded it arrives so fast.

Hope there are proper vegetables involved.

Like everything else in her life, there's a ranking system with vegetable tiers and what she deems good and bad foods. The insult goes deep since she knows I grew up on a farm. She thought it was quaint for a while but then hokey ever since we broke up.

I don't owe her a response, but keeping things civil is a priority for me. I text her:

> Just walked in the door. We're wiped out. I'll bring Beckett over tomorrow as planned. Good night.

Maybe not subtle, but she didn't text back, so the message was received.

It's Friday night, and I wish I had booked our tickets back for tomorrow. It would have been nice to have an extra day, but Anna wanted him back at hers on Saturday, so he has the weekend to rest before school starts again after spring break on Monday.

I grab a bottle of water for me and a juice box for him. He carries the box to the coffee table like a professional. We both flop on the couch next to each other. I click on the TV to land on the Knicks playing, and we kick back for the night.

He doesn't make it to eight before he's asleep. Fortunately, he was ready for bed and in his jammies already. I carry him down the hall and cross his room to lay him in bed. He never budges as I tuck him in and even place a kiss on his head. It's not loud living in the sky, but I can hear the faintest sound of sirens in the distance.

We're not in the country anymore.

My chest tightens as my emotions twist.

I take one more look at him sleeping before closing the door and returning to the living room. To take my mind off the things I left in Texas, I do a quick cleanup, then turn off the TV and shut the blinds, making sure everything is secured for the night.

A shower sounds good, especially since my muscles have been sore in revolt of working the ranch again. From my legs to my arms and some of the linear muscles of my back. Guess running on a treadmill and a weekly pickup game of basketball down at the courts with Baylor aren't challenging me anymore.

Challenging . . .

The word alone makes me smile, thinking about Pris. That girl. She's going to do me in body and soul if I'm not careful.

Fuck.

That is, if her brother doesn't kill me first.

CHAPTER 16

Tagger

BECKETT HAS BEEN FUSSING with his tie since we left the apartment and most of the drive to Anna's building. He insisted he wear it because she likes it. I'm just wondering if he's allowed to be a kid when he's with her.

But I've learned that I can't control what happens at her house as long as it's legal, safe, and he's taken care of. Still sucks that me being a dad to my own kid ends at her doormat.

The doorman opens the door for us, but Anna is already walking out. She hits me with a glare. "You're late."

"I'm actually not late." Checking my watch, I add, "We're ten minutes early."

I spy the restrained grin on the doorman's face before he pretends he's not eavesdropping.

"We're late, then," she snaps, then bends down and straightens Beckett's tie before she gives him a quick hug and air kiss. She hates messing up her makeup. "Hi, honey. Did you have a good time with your father?"

"It was the best. We rode horses . . ."

She holds his hand and stands to face me as if her son wasn't just telling her about the past week of his life. "He has freckles," she whispers. "Did you use sunscreen?"

Be civil, my attorney always reminds me.

I kneel and wipe a smudge off his face. "I had a great time, buddy."

"Me, too, Daddy." I hate the sadness in his tone. These goodbyes are the worst. I want him to be strong, but I don't want him to hide his emotions from me. It's a tricky balance that I'm still learning.

I bring him to me and give him a solid hug. "Call me anytime, okay?"

His head nods against my shoulder. I ruffle his hair and then stand again. Anna's right in there fixing every hair that's out of place. "We're late," she says again. Looking down at Beckett, she smiles. "Want to go to a birthday party?"

His spirits are instantly brightened. I'm glad he'll have some fun to take his mind off the sadness of my departure. "Yes!"

"Bye, Beck. Love you."

"Love you, Daddy."

I slip into the back of the car, but before the door closes, I hear her say, "This is going to be so much fun. It's a work colleague of mine. His party is being hosted at the Waldorf."

"Will there be balloons?" he asks.

I shut the door and take a deep breath. She's a good mother to him. She just values different things, which is her right. Being a Manhattan socialite in her teens and twenties set her up for a life different from mine. Not bad. Just not the same.

The car pulls away from the curb, but I look out the back

window to see them getting into a cab. His hair is back in place, the tie straight, and the joy I saw in his eyes in Texas has disappeared.

I release a deep sigh, trying to figure out how soon I can get us both back to The Pass. Because if I'm honest, I feel the same.

Twenty blocks south, I'm dropped off in front of the bar. I walk into the sounds of a rousing crowd, TVs line the walls with every game in season being played, and a familiar face. I weave through the tables and duck so I don't block a Nuggets game that appears to have some viewers on edge.

Baylor stands out in a crowd. He's a big dude. Hair darker than his sister's. Eye-level to me but they grow'em bigger in Texas. He slaps his hand against mine and then pulls me into to bump shoulders like we always do. "Welcome back, fucker," he says with the signature smile of his that gets him laid on the regular.

We've known each other our entire lives and played on the same sports teams from Little League through football in college. Thick and thin, we've been through the good and bad and back again. We moved away to college together, both majored in finance, and afterward, we got jobs in the city. And somehow, I'm able to look him in the eyes like I didn't make his sister come on my hand last night.

Fuuuck.

"Tagger Grange is back in the house." He sits back down, oblivious to my deception. If I have my way, it will stay like that. "I got a pitcher just before you arrived."

"I can use a beer. This pitcher will do." I chuckle, but the humor isn't there.

"Anna?"

I scrub my hand over my forehead. "That and I'm tired from traveling."

He pours the beer, apparently not willing to sacrifice the pitcher to me, and asks, "Drop-off didn't go well?"

"It's fine. It is what it is for now."

"Sorry, man." He hands me the beer. "Maybe a night out with your best friend can cure it."

I clink my glass against his and grin. "Here's to the hops and friendship." The golden liquid is cold and too easy to drink, and I find myself refilling half the glass I just emptied before I set it down again.

The bar groans over a play I missed on the large screen hanging over the bar. It's not a game I care about, so I look around to see which one I want to watch instead.

Baylor points at a screen facing us, fifteen feet or so away. "I got here early to get a good view. Yankees are playing the Diamondbacks."

"Move over." I slide the chair to the same side where he's sitting and lean against the wall behind us. A basket of mozzarella sticks and some wings are dropped off without a word from the server. The place is packed, and she's running, so no offense is taken.

I grab a wing and catch up on the second inning of the game. When a commercial comes on, Baylor asks, "What's it like back there?"

"Where?" The game is back on, so we return our eyes to the screen.

The conversation doesn't miss a beat. "Back home."

I was kind of hoping to avoid the topic of my trip. No such luck. Guilt rattles me, so I take another long pull of beer before replying, "Same old."

He looks at me. "That place never changes." His tone tips toward disappointment, which I don't get.

"You haven't been back in years."

"Neither had you. And you found out firsthand." He

drinks, then sets the beer down and grabs a mozzarella stick. "It's like time stands still out there."

I don't know why this raises my defenses, but it does. "It's changed." Your sister has changed . . . "Maybe there aren't trendy restaurants or food delivery—"

"No rideshare, and nothing is open past nine."

"Whiskey's is."

He laughs, glancing over at me. "God. I haven't thought about that place in years. But it's exactly the same."

"I can vouch for that. Even the same regulars are parked at the bar, just older, a little drunker maybe."

He's on his feet and clapping. "Good play. Good play." He's focused on the game, which I don't mind. Maybe he'll forget what we were even talking about. But then he says, "Can't believe you went to that dive."

"It wasn't so bad." I shrug. "They've expanded. There was live music, and the crowd was good."

Baylor looks at me, really looks at me like he's seeing someone he doesn't recognize. "Okay. If I go back, I'll go to Whiskey's."

"Why do you say if?"

Shaking his head, he looks confused. "What do you mean?"

"You said *if* you go back. You never going home again? Not checking in on the ranch, or your dad, or your sister who's holding it all together while you pocket the quarterly checks?"

Lowering the glass that he was about to drink from, he furrows his forehead as he stares at me. "What the fuck are you talking about?" He attempts a smile to soften the blow, but I can tell he's annoyed under it. "Doesn't seem like most of that is any of your business." He scoffs, turning his attention back to the game. "Anyway, it took you, what, five years to go back, and now you're lecturing me?" He takes another swig, and then says, "I was there for my mom's funeral. Excuse me if I'm not in a rush to go relive that memory."

Now I feel like shit. "Sorry, man. I shouldn't have said anything."

"Did my sister put you up to guilting me to come back?" This is what happens when you mess with a hornet's nest. They bite back.

I turn my attention to the screen, keeping my eyes on the game. "No, she didn't say anything. It was me, just curious." I shove a mozzarella stick in my mouth to keep from saying more.

"You saw my sister?" *Shit*. Guess he's not ready to drop it. Figures.

I grab the last stick, ready to make it wait for me to eat it, but I don't have to lie about everything. "I ran into her at Peach's."

He glances at me, then redirects his eyes to the wings. "Was Lauralee working?"

"She was there. Friendly like always. Beckett liked her biscuits."

"Damn, I miss those," he says as if he can taste the memory. "The cheddar ones are the best."

"They're your sister's favorite, too." *Why can I not shut the fuck up?* "She was devastated when Beck got the last one."

"Ah. Yeah, I'd be devastated too." His gaze volleys to the TV and then to me. "How's Pristine? How'd she look?"

Five days ago, I wouldn't have hesitated to answer. Now I struggle to find words that aren't *she's so fucking sexy that I couldn't keep my hands off her*. "Good. Healthy."

"Did you see my dad?"

"Yeah. Older but holding his own like he always has." I don't hide behind food or drink this time. I look at him, and add, "I went to Rollingwood quite a bit with Beck. Found out Davey had a baby, so they asked me to help cover his duties."

"You worked the ranch? Damn, dude. That's not easy."

"Fucking hell," I gripe, watching the Yankees throw it away in the fourth inning.

Baylor runs his hand over his face, personally offended by the bad play we just witnessed. "If it's like this in the sixth, I'm going home."

"It's Saturday night. Since when do you ever have an early Saturday night?"

As if he had forgotten, he chuckles. "Right. Yeah, fine. I'll stay, but you'll be buying the rounds if they lose."

"Why am I stuck with the tab?"

Sitting back, he crosses his arms over his chest. "Because you're the one who got me into the Yankees, so you have to pay for making me suffer."

"There's not going to be any suffering. They're going to pull it out like we know they can."

They don't turn it around, and Baylor's now in a mood despite me picking up the entire check from tonight. We walk down the street, trying to decide where to go next, but I'm honestly not in the mood either. And it's not because of the Yankees.

"I think I'm going to head back and have an early night. The travel and dealing with Anna, the—"

"Working the ranch again? I bet your body's fucked up. That's hard work, and you've gotten soft in the city."

"Soft is the last word to describe me." I chuckle, then look down the street in both directions to see if any taxis are in the area before I order a car to drive me.

He shakes my hand. "You never said if there were any hot chicks around town or at Whiskey's?"

I walk backward to the curb. "Things have definitely changed." Throwing my arm in the air for an approaching cab, I add, "You should call your family. I know they miss you."

He seems to be taking that for what it's worth. "I will. See you on Thursday at the courts?"

"Wouldn't miss it." I get in the back of the taxi and give him my address. It was good to see Baylor, but I need to figure out what the hell is going on with me when it comes to his sister. I know full well that it can never work out with me here and her there.

CHAPTER 17

Christine

IT'S COMPLETELY unreasonable to be upset because Tagger left. It's not like I didn't see it coming. It was a four-day visit. *That's it.*

His life is in New York City.

Mine is here on the ranch.

We couldn't be more distant in miles, time zones, or even our way of life. I knew that before I kissed him. *So why does my heart still hurt?*

"Are you going to eat that, sweetie?" I look up from the counter to see Peaches smiling down at me. Sympathy shapes her brown eyes, pulling down the corners with the sides of her mouth. She's just like Lauralee and can see right through me.

Rubbing my stomach in a fake play to feign full, I try to change the emotion on her face. "I think that's all I can eat."

"Those biscuits are your favorite. Let me wrap up the last two for you to take home."

"I appreciate it." Lauralee's mom has always been the sweetest and brought me into her brood like I was one of her own.

She disappears into the back, leaving me with my thoughts again. Those thoughts are the reason I came up to the sundries store in the first place. It's been five days since he left, and I'm tired of being lost in my head over it. He owes me nothing. That's what he took with him. So why am I carrying around our time together like it's precious?

The man has always been popular with the ladies. He's more handsome than ever, so just chalk it up to what it was —nothing but a good time. *One time.* That's all.

The bell above the door chimes, and I look back like Tagger's going to walk through it. I need a major distraction from my life right now.

I'm being utterly ridiculous. Normally, I wouldn't mind indulging in my fantasies. It was a way to pass the time and gave me something to joke about with my best friend, and was completely harmless. I've done it for years without repercussions because they remained inside me. But Tagger and I made some come true last week, and now fantasies aren't the fairy tales I once thought they would be. They're reminders of what could have been, which hurts my heart.

I spin to the side on the chair, watching the kids bob and weave as they find the candy they want. The girls' laughter overshadows the soft music piped in overhead while he follows her around like he would follow her anywhere.

Lauralee walks out with flour on her temple and powder on the side of her neck. I laugh behind my hand. "Looks like you were caught in a battle of wills. Who won?"

"The mixer." She swipes across her forehead with the back of her arm. "It needs replacing."

The teens come to the counter to pay for their candy, so I stand and go to refill my soda to give them space. I hear the buttons of the old-fashioned register clacking and clanging, and then she says, "That will be three fifty-seven for the candy."

The kids pay and dash out the door, my attention grabbed when the chime sounds again. I've been trained like Pavlov's dog to respond to the sound of the bell because one time, that bell meant Tagger Grange was here.

I return to the counter. "What do I owe you?"

"For two eaten biscuits, one with nibbled edges, and two to go—"

"Don't forget the soda."

"Plus a small soda." The tap of the keys leaves us in suspense until she says, "Oh weird." Smacking the side of the metal register, she grunts. "It says on the house again. Lucky you."

I roll my eyes with a laugh. "You can't make it on the house all the time or your business will go under."

Leaning against the bakery display, she says, "Business is just fine. It's doing better than it's ever done. The added fountain drinks and morning coffee have turned it around."

I set down a ten-dollar bill anyway. "No change."

"Well, considering it was zero dollars, that's an outstanding tip. Hey, Mom," she calls to the back. "We've got a big tipper out here."

My cheeks heat from embarrassment. I grit my teeth, and whisper, "Do you have to make a scene every time?"

She nods, pleased with herself. "That's half the fun."

"What's the other half?"

"Pure delight."

I'll admit that she's funny when she wants to be.

Her mom pushes through the swing door, and Lauralee and I quickly straighten our shoulders as if she just caught us up to no good. When she sees the money on the counter, I swear I almost catch her about to roll her eyes, but she stops herself. Always being the prim and proper lady she is, it was refreshing to almost see her stoop to our level. She says, "I'm not taking that, Chrissy."

"Pocket it, put it in the register, or donate it, but it's staying right here on the counter."

She hands me a small white cardboard box. "I put some extra biscuits in there for your dad."

"Thank you." I take the box, knowing she won't let me leave without it even though they could make twice the money by selling it to someone else. And I don't have the willpower to walk away from their biscuits. They're comfort food, and right now, stewing in my vulnerability, I can use all the consolation I can get. "He loves your biscuits."

"Tell him to come by and see me sometime. It's been too long since we had a visit."

It's true. He doesn't leave the ranch much if he can help it. And other than the feed store, he really doesn't go anywhere. It's actually a good idea to bring him with me next Friday. "I will. Thank you again."

Lauralee is slipping off the apron. "I'm going to take a break and chat with Chris, okay, Mom?"

She replies, "You girls enjoy."

We walk outside together and start a short stroll down the small main street Peachtree Pass has maintained for the past one hundred-plus years. The stores have changed, but the bones are still here.

The sun is blasting today, but the covered sidewalk gives us a nice reprieve. I stop in front of the only clothing store in town to peer in. It's straight out of the nineties in style, but I score something good every once in a while.

"What's going on with you?" she asks, standing at my side and staring through the glass. "I held a whole conversation with you that you didn't hear. You didn't even realize when I left. You just sat there, staring . . . and eating a biscuit. What gives?"

"Nothing," I say effortlessly, but I'm certain the heavy sigh that escapes right after gives me away.

"That nothing sure is weighing on you." She shifts to face me, blocking my window shopping. "Chris? What is going on?" I'm given an arched brow and hands-on-hips stance. She means business. I'm not getting out of this easily, and if she has her way, she'll crack me open like she always does and know everything down to the soap I used this morning. "Is this about Tagger and him leaving?"

What can I say that won't involve information I'm not ready to share?

More importantly, why am I hiding this from her in the first place?

I tell her everything, but my lips feel locked when it comes to Tagger. He didn't ask me to keep a secret. I didn't think to say anything to him about it. I know neither of us is rushing to tell my brother anything, but Lauralee is different. She would never betray me. Or judge me for any good or bad decision I've made.

But I still say nothing.

Why am I protecting the time we spent together?

It's not like he will hop on a plane and surprise me just because we kissed in the middle of the road at four o'clock in the morning. I mean, maybe if this were the movies, a romance comedy or even a dramedy. But it's not. This is real, and my life doesn't work like that.

I once heard to never meet your idols. It will only disappoint you.

Is there a phrase about hooking up with crushes? I could really use the advice since it was better than I ever imagined, and now I'm expected to live life like it never happened.

Yeah, it's too soon. Too raw. My thoughts are unable to wrap around why my heart is so involved when it was only supposed to be a little fun.

This is too personal to talk about just yet, so I hook my arm with hers and redirect her down the sidewalk. Without pressuring me, she says, "There will be other men, better ones, the kind that call you babe and then stay." She stops and looks at me. "Forget him, Chris. It was a fluke that we even saw him. Lightning doesn't strike twice."

"You're probably right." I know she is. Tagger and I were lightning striking at the right time and place. We couldn't predict that sparks would fly in the aftermath. That he had the same idea, the same urge and craving, to drive over to see me one last time before leaving . . . Those sparks were fireworks. And then we left the door cracked open, inserting hope where it doesn't belong. The thing is, he's not here to walk through it. "I know you are," I add as we start walking again. "I need to get my head out of the clouds before I waste my life waiting for something that can never happen."

Her arm comes around my shoulders, and she hums. "Always here for you."

"Thanks." Starting now, I refuse to lose more time to a daydream. I put on a smile that feels more natural with each passing second. "As for you, who'd you go home with from Whiskey's?"

"It's a sad tale as old as time." She laughs. "I went home alone, crawled into my pajamas, and watched reruns of *The*

Golden Girls until I fell asleep. Exciting? Nah. But I needed the rest, so it's all good. You got home alright?"

"Got home safe and sound." Though the image of his taillights disappearing into the night still plagues me.

"I was hoping you'd have a good story to share. Like he kissed you because he couldn't resist you any longer. Or confessed under a full moon that he's always loved you." She shrugs. "A girl can dream for the big romantic gesture."

"A girl can dream, but this is real life. You know my family and what they're capable of. If they get their way, I'll never date anyone, much less get married." The realization that there is no winning in this situation with Tagger has me adding, "If they found out Tagger even glanced my way, we'd be attending his funeral."

"Stop living your life to please them."

I turn back to see her poised on the sidewalk with her brows cinched in irritation. "Trust me, Laur, it's not about pleasing them. It's about the first and only man I've ever felt connected to living an entirely separate life in another universe. We might as well be living on parallel timelines. I doubt we'll ever cross paths again, and if we do, it will be as friends and only friends."

With my truck parked nearby, I signal it. "I should get back to the ranch."

Kind enough to let things slide from here, she says, "Text me later."

"I will." I start backward, but ask, "Want to go to Austin this weekend and do some shopping, grab some lunch, and stuff?"

"I'll get my mom to cover for me."

She's the brunette to whatever mess of color I am, the brown eyes to my blue, the yin to my yang, and apparently my rocking chair companion. She deserves better than she gets, like I do. But we've become experts at playing the cards we've been dealt.

I hustle to the truck, get in, and set the box in the seat next to me. Would I prefer it be Tagger sitting there? I don't think I'll ever not want that, but I'll settle for the biscuits if I have to. *And clearly, I do.*

CHAPTER 18

Tagger

A MONTH LATER . . .

I LOOK AT MIKE, trying to read his expression as he stares across the table at the other attorney. He's a pro, so he gives nothing away. He says, "I'm going to consult with my client."

"We'll give you some privacy," the other attorney says before standing and pulling Anna's chair out for her.

The room remains silent until the door is closed behind them. Mike turns to me, breathing a sigh of relief, and says, "It's a fair offer, but if you want to fight for more time with Beckett or have more say when he's in her care, we can proceed with our previous plan."

"It's not about winning. It's about doing what's best for my son. I want it over. I'm tired. I'm sure she is as well." Still finding some humor after the hours this morning spent negotiating custody and related issues to his care, I crack a smile, and say, "I'm really tired of the legal bills."

He laughs. "I'm sure you are. Personally, I'll miss that monthly payment."

"I bet you will. My bank account will be thrilled."

"The judge has already approved the arrangement, so if you're ready to accept the deal, all you need to do is sign."

I was ready two years ago. It just took her that time and a lot of money to realize I'm not giving up custody, but I'll share. We ended right back where we started, what I offered in the beginning. Fifty-fifty and other arrangements can be discussed for special circumstances when they arise. I take the pen and sign the agreement, putting an end to the battle and saving us both a lot of damn money. "Done."

"I'll get copies to the other attorneys and get the paperwork filed for you to make it official." He stands. When I do, we shake hands. "It's been a pleasure."

"Is this about the money again?"

He laughs. "Sure is." Collecting the paperwork, he adds, "I'm glad it worked out, Tagger. Now you can move on with your life and enjoy time with your son."

"I intend to." I open the door to the conference room and start down the hall. Behind a wall of glass, I see Anna and her attorney deep in conversation. Her eyes track me as I walk by, and she jumps to her feet and rushes to the door. "Hey, Tagger?"

"I signed."

Relief washes through her expression, ending with half a smile. That's more than she typically offers since she claims happiness turns into wrinkles. "Thank you. It's not why I wanted to talk to you, though."

"What is it? Do I need a lawyer present?" The joke doesn't land, but I also don't know how much I was kidding.

She laughs. "Funny. You were always funny. Beckett

takes after you that way. He can be such a clown. It's cute and sweet."

"He's a little goose alright." The small talk is surprising. She hasn't had a taste for that when it comes to me in a long time. And as much as I could talk about our son all day, I don't have the same patience for her. "What did you want to talk to me about?"

"Um." She looks at a lady passing and then lowers her head and goes quiet until we're alone again. She looks up and says, "I just wanted to tell you that I'm glad this is settled, but I also wanted to apologize. I'm sorry for not agreeing sooner."

We were never a good match, but we have an amazing son from the relationship, so it's hard to have regrets. "Hey," I say, giving her an attagirl nudge to the arm to lighten the mood. "We got there in the end. Now we can focus on Beckett and what's best for him."

She clasps her hands in front of her. "Right. Well, thank you."

"Thank you, Anna. It's good to put this behind us." I start down the hall.

"He talks about Peachtree Pass all the time," she says behind me.

I stop and turn back. "Yeah?"

She tentatively comes a bit closer. "He talks about the horses and chickens, how you rode with him in the saddle with you." She smooths her hair over her ear, though I know that's a nervous tic of hers. It's always perfectly in place. Today, it's even pulled back, and not a hair dares to escape. "Sounds like I missed out on all the fun."

A memory of her making us leave because she felt dirty from being in the middle of Texas comes to mind. "It's dustier than ever."

"Right. Dirt." She laughs, but there's no humor in it. "Not my favorite." She glances away as if she's not sure what to say to keep me there a little longer, which is odd because she usually wants me to leave as soon as possible. But then she says, "But Beckett loved it, so if you're going back this summer and want to stay longer than a few days, we can work that out."

The walls I've held for years around her start to crumble, my shoulders already feeling lighter. "I appreciate that, Anna. I have some vacation time saved. It would be nice to go back for the festival in June and spend some time there."

"The peach festival?" After I confirm with a nod, she smiles, and it's the first genuine one I've seen in years. "I think I judged things too harshly. Sounds like a lot of fun. He'll love that." Releasing a breath that sounds like it's been locked in her chest for years, she asks, "One more thing, Tagger. Beckett keeps mentioning someone. Who's Miss Christine?"

Shit.

My gaze redirects to my attorney and his legal assistant coming out of the conference room and heading our way. "She owns one of the ranches out there."

"Ah." She's still smiling, so that's good. "He had a good time with her and still talks about feeding the horses carrots and how much she loves mushy lima beans."

"Yeah." It's all I can say. I've been thinking about Pris a lot since I left, but reaching out seemed to be crossing one of those lines we put in place without realizing it. For all I know, she could be dating someone. Though, I hope it's not that deputy.

I work, sleep, get Beck every other week, and repeat since being back in the city. Other women don't cross my mind. Since I was with Pris, I've lost interest in everyone else. I wonder if she has?

Mike stops and asks, "Everything okay?"

"Yes, we're good." I eye Anna, and say, "I'll see you on Sunday to pick up Beckett."

"See you then."

I walk out with Mike, and I'm glad to be putting this behind me as well before any more questions about Christine can be asked. I'm glad Beck liked her so much, but Anna won't be happy if she learns more.

When I return to the office, my assistant has a sandwich waiting on my desk. I hang my jacket on the hook behind the door, then sit to unwrap it. Turkey and Havarti. Kendra knows me well.

A knock draws my eyes up. With my mouth full, I wave her in. She comes closer but doesn't sit. "Figured you wouldn't eat."

"I appreciate it." I glance at the three screens on the far wall, which are updating the major markets. Habit. She didn't ask, but she's been a good support in the office and for me while dealing with this custody mess during the past few years. "It's settled. We both agree. Right down the center."

"That's great to hear."

"She's a good mom. I'm a good dad. He deserves equal time with us."

When she smiles, pride enters her eyes. Older than me with the patience of an angel, she's been with me for more than five years, and it's worked out well. She's almost like a second mom to me. She worries too much about me eating or hydrating, gets me to take deep breaths when my blood pressure shoots through the ceiling, and will stay long after it's time to leave until I force her out. I'm fortunate to have the support. "It's good to move on. My divorce was nasty.

The custody battle wiped me out. It's nice that you two can come to an agreement that you're both satisfied with. And having that negativity out of your life will benefit not only you and your health but also your time with your son." She walks toward the door. "Eat up. You have a meeting with the boss in fifteen."

"I also have a million calls and twice as many emails to deal with."

At the door, she says, "Boss meeting first. Calls second. The emails have been sorted by priority. Start on the red accounts first, yellow second, and green last."

"Thank you, Kendra. I owe you."

"In the form of a generous bonus check at the end of the year." She knows how to make an exit.

I wasn't needed in that meeting, but it still ate over an hour of my day. I return to my office to find Baylor staring out my window.

"What brings you by?" I ask, coming around the chairs to shake his hand.

"We haven't hung out in three weeks."

Maneuvering around my desk, I sit and roll forward. "I see you every week at basketball. We've run twice in Central Park, and you're seeing me now."

"That's not hanging out. That's meetups with a purpose, to exercise." He sits down. Leaning back in the chair, he kicks his feet up on my desk.

"Make yourself at home, why don't you?"

"Thanks. Don't mind if I do."

I steeple my fingers, my gaze darting to the screens to see the markets closing. No surprises are a great thing in finance. He's watching it, too, since his career is based in the same field. I work in the commercial sector. He's a whiz in personal finance. We've both done very well for ourselves as two kids from Peachtree Pass, Texas.

When he turns back, he asks, "So what gives?"

"Busy."

"Not that busy."

So fucking confident he knows everything. Always was. "How do you know how busy I am?"

"I don't but figured if you had a lot of shit going on, you'd tell me."

"Anna and I settled today."

He drops his feet and leans forward. "You serious?"

"Yep. It's signed."

It's the first real grin I've gotten from him. "I'm happy for you, man."

"Me, too." My phone screen lights up with another appointment added to my schedule. I push it to the side to ignore it. "You're right. I haven't been in the mood to go out much."

"Ever since you got back. Any correlation?"

Does appearing indifferent make me look guilty? I take the chance, not moving anything on my face but my mouth. "No," I lie. Pris has changed my perspective on a few things and had me reevaluating, figuring out how to be happy again. Today was a big step in the right direction. But I also find myself thinking about the woman more than I should, considering we've not been in touch once since I left. Why is that?

Is it me?

Or is this what she wants?

We're both to blame, but I've been wondering if I'm the only one who has struggled to reach out. *What would I say?*

Making you come was a highlight of my year? Kissing you made me regret waiting so long to do it? Being with you

. . . well, you're difficult in some ways, but so am I, so does that make us perfect together? *Or a ticking time bomb?*

Only one way to find out . . .

"No," I reply, lying through my teeth again. "Just been preoccupied."

He stands and bumps his hand against the desktop twice. "Okay. The Yankees are in town. I can get tickets for Saturday. You in?" He grins and points at me. "C'mon, Tag. Tell me you're in."

My mind might have been preoccupied with Pris, but I miss hanging out with my best friend. "I'm in."

"Good. I'll text the time." We slap our hands together before he heads for the door. "Wait until I tell you about this little honey I hooked up with from the gym." His hands fly from each other like an explosive went off. "Whew, pure fire."

As soon as he walks out, I grab the phone. "Kendra, can you book a flight back to Austin for a week from Saturday?"

"Sure can. Going to visit your folks again?"

"Yeah, that and catch up with some friends."

I hear the clacking of keys on her end. "Going solo, or should I book for Beckett as well?"

"Solo this time."

CHAPTER 19

Tagger

I GET out of the car and scan the area of Rollingwood Ranch. Although I'm not seeing any action, I know everyone who works here stays busy.

And who am I kidding? I'm not here to see anyone but one little firecracker I haven't stopped thinking about since I last saw her. Five weeks is too long to not kiss Pris.

Mr. Greene comes from the barn, and a noticeable limp on his right side seems to have gotten worse. "Hey there," I say, walking toward him.

"Hey there, Tagger. Back for another shift?"

"Tempting," I joke, stopping just shy of the utility task vehicle he drives around the property.

He thumbs over his shoulder. "The cattle were moved already, but I'm sure Christine can put you to work." He looks westward. "She's down with Julie."

Her name is said so casually, as if she's still here, that I'm not sure how to react. "I can wait."

"She might like to see a familiar face. She's usually stuck with me." He moves closer to the UTV and holds the back rack for support. "You know the high cliff due west of the equipment barn?"

"Sure." The property is big, thousands of acres. As much as Baylor and I explored when we were younger, there are parts I've never been to, but I'm familiar with the high cliff over the raging part of the river below. "I remember being stupid enough to stand on the edge a few times."

His expression falls, but he says, "Griff and Bay used to scare the heavens out of Julie by getting too close to the edge." Baylor and I need to talk. I think it's time he gets back home. "She's just south of the ledge." He glances at the barn and then back. "You can take a horse or utility truck."

The UTV will be faster but also louder. If Pris is visiting her mom, I don't want to ruin it with noise pollution. "I'll saddle Nightfall."

We part ways, but he calls to my back, "Staying for dinner?"

"If I'm welcome."

"You're always welcome, Tagger."

He says that now. If he knew what I did to his daughter in the cab of a truck, I have a feeling he'd be singing a different tune. It's just one of many things I need to discuss with her.

It feels good to be riding again. Realizing what I've been missing makes me wonder how I can get back more often.

I take off past the cornfields and gallop past the side of the equipment barn. I used to know the usual spots by heart, but things have changed. Trees have grown. Fences rearranged. But the trails remain from years before when we wore a path through the tall grasses.

The sun hangs low in the sky, and the clouds rolling in make me think a storm is coming. I ride until I spy her small frame sitting in a patch of wildflowers. I slow the horse and dismount, walking the rest of the way with the reins in my hand.

She looks up with her hair as wild as the flowers and cascading freely over her shoulders. Beautiful, even more so as if that was possible.

Considering the circumstances, I'm not sure if I can expect a smile or a frown. She gifts me with an eye roll and a gentle laugh that still manages to cover the distance. "Howdy, stranger." The usual strength in her tone is missing, which is concerning.

"Howdy, good-looking." Her cheeks still pink for me, and her smile blooms like the wildflowers surrounding her. Her white dress makes her look like an angel next to the red and yellow flowers, and the purples that bring out the blue in her eyes.

Her brown boots are scuffed to high heaven, but somehow, they work with it. Everything works on her.

Looking at the headstone next to her, I read the name of her mother and years of her life. Each of her children's names are lined up at the bottom just under her father's. No flowers are needed because they surround her.

Her gaze has fallen to a flower in her hands, a petal being slowly plucked from around the stem. I kneel with Nightfall at my back and only a few feet in front of me keeping me from her. "I'm sorry, Pris." She looks up at me, her smile almost vanished. The corners of her eyes are filled with unfallen tears, and she still manages to be the most stunning creature I've ever seen. "I should have been here for you and your family. I should have come back for the funeral." I glance at the carved granite that was probably quarried from the property somewhere. "I . . ." Out of excuses, I lower my head as shame comes over me.

"Beckett was young, probably barely one. No one expected you to drop your responsibilities to comfort us."

No one did. I never heard a peep about it. Not from Baylor. He was aware of my situation, but he still had a right to expect me to be here for him. Nothing from Mr. Greene, not from the pastor, or even my family. Not even Pris. Even now, she's making excuses for me. "She was like a mother to me."

"I used to tell my mom I couldn't wait to leave this place. I wanted to leave my boots in the closet and my hat on the hook, hide my raggedy work clothes and pretend I was from somewhere else." A tear falls, and she drops her head in her hands. "I was so mean at seventeen."

"You were never mean." I stand, noticing she doesn't have a horse out here. I settle the reins on him and let Nightfall go where he pleases. He'll return to the barn sooner or later. "You were a teen, though, and she'd gone through the same stage with two others at that point. We say shit we don't mean. Trust me, I was a complete asshole to my parents." That makes her smile. Figures. "Your mom was wise enough to love you through it."

"The last time I saw her was at my college graduation. She told me how proud she was." She takes a shaky breath. "And then she told me to follow my heart wherever it leads." I pat the horse before going to the grass and sitting next to her.

The long pause has me tilting to catch her eyes, but she's closed them. I wrap my arm around her and pull her to me. With her head on my shoulder and her wet cheek against my shirt, she whispers, "I had a job in Denver and an apartment downtown. I was living the high life. I was even dating a guy . . ." I shouldn't have tensed. I'm not surprised. Any guy would be lucky to have her. "Then I got the call."

Nothing more needs to be said.

I got the call from Baylor in the middle of the night. Anna told him to call back in the morning. A lot went wrong around that time. And he was already on a plane the following morning. I didn't get the news until a few days later and couldn't make it in time.

Pris doesn't need excuses. She needs answers, and no one can give those to her.

Her quiet sobs leave me feeling helpless, so I lift her to my lap and curl around her, holding her in my arms, and try to make up for all the time I wasn't here. I kiss her head and rub her leg. "I'm sorry."

This isn't how I saw our reunion going, but it means more.

Lifting her head, she then shakes it. "You don't owe me an apology. You're here now, and it's the first time I don't feel like I'm carrying the weight of what happened all alone." She exhales a long breath, then takes a deeper one before repeating. "You made me feel better." She kisses my cheek. "Thank you."

It's then I realize being here, being with her, and close to her mom frees me from the guilt and shame I've carried for years. We found healing together.

She sits up, her shoulders rising and her smile blooming again. "You're here."

"I came for you."

Straddling me, she wraps her arms around my neck, her pretty eyes staring into mine. God, I've missed this. *I missed her.* She asks, "How did you know I needed you here?"

I rub her back, and confess, "I took a chance."

She leans back, resting in my arms, her energy seeming lighter by that spark in her eyes. *Damn, I missed that spark.* "I didn't take you for the kind of guy who left anything to chance."

"My whole life and career were built on taking chances. Most have paid off. I can't wait to see how this one turns out."

"Careful, cowboy, or I might just think you're trying to charm me."

Pulling her close, her chest against mine, our mouths just inches apart, I whisper, "I am."

"Right here at my mother's grave?"

Oh shit. I glance next to her, feeling like the asshole I am. "I wasn't think—"

I'm playfully whacked on the shoulder. "I'm just giving you a hard time. She'd totally approve of this."

"What about me?" I always have to fucking push it . . . Pris and I are the same that way. Is it ego? For me, probably. For her, she's just holding her own.

Her grin softens again. "She adored you, Tagger."

When she caresses my cheek, I ask, "What about you, babe?"

"I adore you, too." There was no pause or question in her eyes. She spoke from the heart straight to mine.

Maybe I'm a terrible person, but I kiss her . . . *next to her mother's gravesite*. And she kisses me. Her fingers weaving into the hair at the back of my head, the tilt of her hips giving me an erection on contact, and the caress of her tongue against mine, and I have not one regret for showing up uninvited and unannounced.

I got up at three o'clock to get to the airport on time for a flight that took four and a half hours. Almost two hours after landing, I got to my parents'. A change of clothes into jeans, a tee, and boots, and I was fifteen minutes from her house. Add in the horse ride to finally see her again, and it was all fucking worth it.

But I will not let this go further until we find a new location. I pull back, which takes some effort. "Hey, we should go somewhere else. What do you say?"

"Probably." We're shadowed under a large rain cloud, and the sky rumbles, drawing us to both look up. "We're a long way from the house." She looks back at me. "Should we ride it out in the equipment barn?"

I'm onto her these days. The dirty little bird loves to tease. "Abso-fucking-lutely."

Her eyeing me like I'm ridiculous wasn't exactly what I was going for, but that's what I got. "Okay." She crawls off my lap and offers me a hand up. We both know she can't stabilize my weight, much less lift me like a dead weight. She acts tough, but she's still got that small frame.

I let her try by taking her offered hand.

Damn. It would not be too bad if I used my core to stand while pretending she was successful in her mission.

When thunder rolls across the sky, we need to get to shelter. Texas storms are not something to mess with. With no other option, we take off running. The first drops pelt us just before we reach the building. The warehouse garage doors are closed, and when I try the main door to enter, frustration sets in. "It's locked."

"We must have just missed Davey and the others." The rain falls harder, so we huddle under the small metal awning. "We're going to be soaked," she says, looking up at me from under my arm. Panic rises in her eyes. "I can call my dad, but I don't want him out in this mess. The sudden weather changes cause pain in his leg."

"I remember he never got knee surgery after that bad fall from a horse back in high school."

"It's getting worse."

His limp was definitely prevalent when I saw him. "We shouldn't bother him. Let's wait a few minutes to see if it lets up." Pulling out my phone, I check the weather app. *Welp.* There goes that plan.

When I show her the radar, her eyes flash to mine. "Five hours? It's not stopping for five hours?"

"And getting worse in the next hour." I tuck it away. "I think we need to head out. We'll get wet, but at least we'll be safe."

"Yeah, standing next to a metal building during a lightning storm probably isn't the wisest." She looks ahead at the makeshift gravel road that bends around a cabbage field. "It's only rain."

"It's only rain."

As if the words and a shared glance were enough of a plan, she takes off running.

This view—her running in her dress, hair wet and already sticking to her body—This view is all I ever want, and that smile she gives when she turns back to make sure I'm with her is all I need to dash after her.

Not just for fun or to hear her laughter, which I do, but because it feels like my heart is already with her, beating in her chest instead of mine. *Oh shit. This isn't just a visit.* I want to be with her more than a friend I kiss sometimes. I want her.

"Pris?"

Glancing over, she contorts her forehead in confusion. "What is it?"

I understand the emotion. I feel that way, too. I can't explain what's happening because it's so fast and out of the blue. I try to remind myself that she's the forbidden fruit and I should tread carefully. But I don't want to be careful anymore.

I want her.

Closing the gap between us, I take her hand and bring it to my mouth. I kiss the top and then her palm before setting one hand on her ribs and holding the other in my hand. If she asks me what I'm doing, I have no answer. Running for cover? Slow dancing in the rain? I don't know what's happening to me other than I'm a fool for this woman.

Lightning strikes too close for comfort, but what does it matter? I'm already a goner for her.

Capturing her face in my hands, I kiss her. And when our lips stop, I confess, "I'm falling for you, babe."

CHAPTER 20

Christine

I GAVE up caring about my appearance around half a mile back.

What was the point?

My hair is drenched, my dress soaked, and water has slid into my boots, but Tagger Grange kissed me in the rain and told me he's falling for me. I have not one complaint. And I practically floated into the barn, providing shelter from the storm.

We gravitate like the universe just yanked us together. His lips find mine while my hands graze over his back and grip his shoulders. He lifts me from behind, my skirt pushed up high on my thighs as I cross my ankles behind his back.

I could have never guessed that Tagger would become my haven. But now, I can't imagine it otherwise. I'm protected by his strong arms, adored when I look into his eyes, and victorious when I coax a smile from him.

Our tongues twist together as my body craves more—more of this and so much more of him. Breathless as I am, he asks, "Where can we go?"

No beating around the bush. I approve.

But it's at that moment I realize it's quiet, too quiet for a busy barn during a storm. The rain pummels the tin roof, and it's still thundering in the vicinity, but otherwise, a few chickens cluck, and I hear shuffling in one of the stalls.

I look right to see Nightfall safe inside, Bluebelly to the right of him, and her colt, Skyward, is tucked in his, but the stall to the left of Nightfall is empty. I lower my legs, but with Tagger holding me so tight, I can't reach the ground. "Set me down," I say, trying to sound calm, but I don't feel it inside.

"What is it?"

"Sunrise is missing."

He looks at the horses. "What do you mean missing?"

"She's skittish during storms. Most animals are, but she's been known to break out and run for cover elsewhere." I start for the utility truck, but he catches my arm.

"You can't go out in this. There's still lightning in the area."

I pull away. "I'm not leaving her out there. She got close to a cliff once. I'm not taking that chance again."

"She could be anywhere, Pris. It's not smart to go chasing her when you have no clue where she's gone."

"I guess we see things differently." I dash for the truck, tucking into the seat, and start the engine.

He comes after me, standing beside my seat as if he's going to block me. "The storm will pass, and I'll help you find her. We just need to wait."

"You can wait. Check on the other animals."

I shift into reverse, spewing mud from under the wheel, and turn the wheel before punching it.

"Pris? Wait," he calls. "I'll go—" His words are swallowed in the storm.

I hear the "fuck" before I look in the side mirror to see him boiling over in rage. Even through the thick rain pounding around us, the red of his face and fisted hands at his side are as clear as day.

The last time she ran, she headed to the lower pasture just inside the woods and brush closer to the river. I skid when I leave the gravel and cut through mud that splats over my boots and the bottom of my dress.

We spend most of the year in different stages of drought, so when the storms hit, we welcome them. But I probably should have looked at the forecast before deciding to wear white today.

It's bumpy, and the wet fabric under me slides against the vinyl seat. I hold the wheel tighter as I cover the rest of the acres. I shift into park and jump out. "Sunrise?" I call over and over as I weave between the trees. It's darker under the canopy of aspens, oaks, loblolly pines, and cedars. I stop, my intuition warning me not to go any farther. "Sunrise?"

I look back toward the UTV, not realizing I had gone so deep into the woods. After calling for her a few more times, I jog back with my senses on high alert.

Ducking beside the truck when lightning cracks too close for comfort, I hop in and drive the perimeter, hoping to avoid drawing attention from the angry sky. But I don't see her, and she doesn't tend to wander far if she's thinking clearly. But who knows with the storm rushing her veins.

The property is too vast to cover in a timely way. I'm drenched to the bone and cold from driving against the rain and winds. I'll have to trust she makes her way back because I'll be devastated if she doesn't.

I cut back in front of the equipment barn and keep on the gravel road, but I catch a flash of something out of the corner of my eye. Looking right, Sunrise is running through the cabbage patch and toward the taller cornfields. She must be turned around and lost. "Sunrise?" I call at the top of my lungs, but she's running too fast away from me.

I'll reach the cornfield faster by cutting through the other patches than going around. The truck doesn't go very fast anyway, not when I need it to, so I park and start on foot.

She moves too fast to keep up with, so there's no use in calling. I save my voice and just keep running. When I reach the edges of the tall field, I stop one row inside and look to my right and then left. Evening has fallen, and it makes it harder to see any distance. The rain makes it worse, so I pause to listen instead.

Closing my eyes, I listen for any change from the rustling of leaves to the sound of her hooves hitting the mud between the rows. I can't hear anything other than water pummeling the earth.

I push through some rows, weave down some aisles, and finally come out on the other side. The field is too big to search, and it's almost too dark to be out here. I drop my head, exhausted as frustration in my failure clouds my head.

This is pointless. I need to get back. Tagger was right. We need to just wait it out. Or hope she returns before then.

When I open my eyes, my breath chokes in my throat as tears swarm the corners of my eyes. There, on the edge of the field, under the wide canopy of an oak tree, Sunrise stands near the trunk.

"Sunrise." I walk toward her with my hand out, being

careful not to frighten her into running again. She stays, not seeming to want to run. I stroke her from the forehead to her muzzle, then lean my head against her. "Good girl."

I don't have a phone, so there's no way to contact Tagger. The leaves block a lot of the harsher raindrops, but they still trickle down. I stand beside her for a long while before eventually sitting at the base of the tree trunk. When Sunrise shifts closer, a little less rain reaches me. The bond we built over the years has only grown stronger. I searched for her because I was worried. Look at her now, protecting me.

The dress is ruined, but I've already given up on it surviving this harsh weather. No light reaches where we are except when lightning rips across the sky, and the clouds hide the moon and stars. I'm exhausted, so it's tempting to close my eyes. Maybe just for a minute. It's not like I can sleep in the middle of a storm when I'm wet and cold and covered in mud.

Wrapping my arms around my chest to keep warm, I rest my head against the rough bark and close my eyes. But I knew I wouldn't be able to do it for long. I shift to get as comfortable as a tree trunk can be, and stare into the distance to the east side of the field.

A flicker of light grabs my eyes, though it goes away just as quick. It's probably aliens coming down to abduct me and Sunrise. "It's okay, girl, I won't let them get you. Wait." I look up at her. "Did you hear that? Would aliens know my name? A nickname at that?"

I'm sure it's the winds taunting me, but I swear I heard my name . . . well, Pris, which means . . . I sit up and look ahead, finding the light through the rain again. Focused on the light, I listen. "There. Did you hear it?"

"Pris? Sunrise?"

Sunrise stomps her front legs, splashing more mud on me. I wipe my face and then attempt to stand, but the mud is so thick that I get stuck. I sit back down and wobble over a large root to clear the suction between my skirt and the ground. "Over here," I call as loud as I can while trying to keep from freaking the horse out.

Sunrise doesn't have a lead or reins, so if she takes off, there's no stopping her.

I continue to struggle to stand when the heel of my boot slips. "Tagger?"

"Pris?" The light grows, spreading wide over the area as it approaches and then blinds me when it's shined in my eyes. "Babe, are you okay?" He tucks the flashlight into his back pocket and reaches for me. "Oh fuck, you're covered in mud."

"I'm fine. I'm fine. But glad for the announcement." I can't help but laugh anymore. I'm too tired to try to be funny, so I'm forced to go with an old standby. "Otherwise, I wouldn't have known."

He takes my hand in his, and my upper arm in his other. "Let's get you out of here."

I'm pulled to my feet, then rest a hand on the horse to make sure she feels safe. "It's okay, girl."

"I brought a rope to lead her back."

I'm somewhat amazed, but more impressed, and feeling loved that he was searching for us in the first place. "How'd you know I'd find her?"

"I knew you wouldn't give up until you found her." He loops the rope around her head and hands me the lead. "She trusts you more."

I lean up and kiss him. "Thank you."

"You don't have to thank me." He runs his fingers along my cheekbone. "I'm glad you're okay."

As much as I would love to be buried in his arms, we have a long walk ahead. Maybe we can pick up where we left off if we have any energy left by the time we get back.

Most of the mud on my skin rolled off under the rain, which lightened as we approached the barn. *Of course it did . . .*

I put Sunrise in her stall, making sure she's set up with water and plenty of hay. Returning to Tagger, I stand there, unsure what to say. Hoping to find our way back to each other, I start over. "You're here."

"I couldn't stay away from you any longer." He gives me a wink, catching on quick.

I wrap my arms around him, hugging him tight. He has hard muscles and warm touches. "I'm glad you didn't." Resting my chin on his chest, I ask, "Do you want to go into the house to take a shower?"

He glances back as if debating his options. "No. As long as you don't mind me being a mess."

Laughing, I slip from his hold and give him a twirl. "I have no room to speak."

"Sorry about the dress getting ruined." As if his words cued the weather gods, the rain starts pouring down again. I'm glad we're under a roof and protected this time.

"Me too." I look down at the skirt of stained brown with some green grass streaks throughout. "It was my mother's. It's too far gone to save." I take his hand and lead him to a wooden ladder my eldest brother made years ago.

Tagger eyes the ladder leading up to the loft area. "What's up there?"

"I've been doing a renovation here and there. It's not much, and there are no walls, but I have bottled water and a place to wait out the storm."

The right side of his smile lifts first as if he knows I'm up to no good. It was never a plan to seduce someone in the loft of the barn, but now that the opportunity has arisen, I'm not opposed or beneath begging. At least not with Tagger. "Come on."

I climb up, with him waiting until I'm securely at the top. Probably best since the ladder wasn't made for durability or adults but instead for convenience and kids. When he gets to the top and steps off, he smiles. "You did all this?"

"My brothers and I used to play up here." I walk across the wooden planks as if to prove it's safe. "A few summers ago, I needed something to occupy my mind instead of the death of my mom."

"So you come here to read?"

His smile is small but sincere as he comes toward the far corner where I've set it up. He touches the soft pink bookcase and kneels to see the titles on the shelves. "There are only two shelves, but these are some of my favorite books." He glances up at me hovering over his shoulder. "A few of Mom's books are in there, too."

When he stands, he looks at the white wicker chair and then at the mattress covered in pillows. Some are in bags, and some I don't care about as much and left out. I rush around to pull some out of the protective bags, explaining, "I don't want them to get bugs."

"Makes sense." He takes one out of a bag, eyeing the shape. "This goes on the chair?"

"Yes." I don't know why I suddenly feel shy and embarrassed. But the feeling reaches my cheeks, heating them. I pull a sheet and blanket from the biggest bag and toss them on the bed.

He sets the pillow on the wicker and reaches for the sheet. "You do this every time you come up here?"

"I don't come up here often enough to keep the bed

made up. There's no heat in the cold months, and I can't bring a space heater up here. It would catch the barn on fire. In the dead of summer, I'd be sweating. No fan could save me."

He tucks the sheet's second corner around the mattress. "So spring, April and May, are the months you use it?" Every question is asked with such care and not one ounce of judgment.

I shrug. "Sometimes November and into December. You know how unpredictable those months can be weather-wise."

With the sheet on, he comes to stand next to me as I release the blanket in front of me and lay it in place. As if the conversation is a distraction to his purpose, he runs his hand along my neck while staring at my mouth. "Texas can never make up its mind if it wants to be fall or winter."

He's so close I can feel his breath coat my temple. The heat emanating through the wet shirt warms me, but it's the way his eyes are so focused on my mouth that I shiver under his touch. Bending down, he presses his lips to mine unhurried. And when he opens his eyes, he says, "Do you have a towel up here?"

I blink rapidly, trying to make sense of what in the world he's talking about. He must sense it because he grins. "To clean up so we don't dirty your pretty bed."

"Oh," I say, relieved, though I'm not sure why I was worried. It's not like he's a serial killer. At least, I doubt he is. I hope he's not . . . I eye him once more. Feeling confident he's not, I put that outrageous thought to bed, much like what he wants to do with me, which I'm all for. "I have a few napkins. I spill when I eat."

That makes his smile grow. "Huh. *Um*, I don't think that's

going to help in this situation." He looks me over. "We should get you out of that dress."

"I like that idea." There's been no pretense of my wanting to have sex with him. I've thrown myself at him, and the memory of how good he felt in the truck has gotten me off a few times on my own. We can just move forward with the understanding that it's clearly on the table.

So why do I suddenly feel insecurity clawing its way back up my throat?

Tagger's an experienced man. Not like I'm a virgin but I'm not sure whether the hole has closed up. It's been *that* long.

He pulls off his shirt first, like the gentleman he is. Looking around, he drapes it over one part of the loft with a railing. His boots come off next and the socks. Not exactly the sexy part of this strip show, but necessity beckons. I start to settle in, loose at the knees but straight back like my mom taught me. *Chest out.* "I hope I'm next."

"I'm going to take my sweet time with you."

Why does everything he says shoot right between my legs? I know this one by heart. *Tagger Grange.* Those two words say everything.

He peels his wet jeans off next and tosses them onto the railing before setting his sights on me and my dress. "You look so pretty it almost hurts to think about when I'm in New York."

"You keep saying things like that, and you'll have to pick me up off the floor."

"I don't mind picking you up, Pris. I only care what put you there." Reaching to touch my cheek, he kisses me. "I want to be with you."

"Me, too," I reply, running the tips of my fingers over his

abs. "All you need to do is help me with this dress and my boots and—"

"Not sexually." He shakes his head, clenching his eyes closed and rubbing his forehead. When he reopens them, he's more determined than ever. "No, I want you sexually, too, but I want us to date. It sounds so fucking old-fashioned, but I don't want to just be someone you fuck or mess around with when I'm in town. I want us to be together. I want us to be a couple."

I have to lift my jaw off the floor before I speak, but my mind hasn't fully processed what he's saying. Hope flourishes. "You want to be my boyfriend?"

Holding my hand, he flips it over and doodles on my palm with his finger. "Yeah, I want to be your boyfriend." There's an uncertainty in his tone that I can only interpret as him fearing rejection. "I didn't text because I didn't know how you'd take that or if I was assuming too much. You might have felt the same."

"I didn't want you to feel pressure from me."

"I was missing you the entire time."

My heart beats proudly in my chest, and five steps in front of my indecisive brain, and is ready to sign on the dotted line. "I've thought about you every day but tried so hard to let you go, to let you lead the life you've chosen elsewhere." It would be so easy to just jump in heart first, but then rationale kicks in. "You live in another state."

"We'll make it work. I promise. We'll visit each other. I can fly you up anytime you can get away. I'll fly here regularly."

I want to be with him. It's what I've wanted my whole life, but my judgment is as clouded as the sky is outside. Am I caught up in storms and distracted by incredible abs, aroused because we're finally standing on the verge of being fully together, and timid that beyond our bodies, we'll be exposing our souls? I'm wrapped so tight in a myriad of emotions that the weight is almost smothering.

As I look into his eyes, it's not about making him feel better. It's about making sure this is the right decision for both of us. It only takes a moment of swimming in his dreamy greens to know what I should do. For me. "I want to be with you, too. Sexually," I say, smirking. He sports his own roguish grin in reaction. "And dating. I'll be your girlfriend."

I'm embraced in his arms and kissed in a way that might not be legal in this state. They can take me away in handcuffs before I ever stop kissing this man. Except now to say, "Make love to me, cowboy."

CHAPTER 21

Christine

Poof!

My dress is gone under Tagger's deft fingers after a quick lift of my arms, the ruined garment draped next to his on the railing.

My bra follows, but a cool gust of wind blowing across my breasts has me reaching out to hold his shoulder to steady myself under a shiver. He places a kiss on each nipple, then runs the flat of his tongue over them. I knew he'd be smooth, but I didn't expect the seduction. It's better than any dream I ever had of him.

I appreciate his attention to detail.

Right here and now, nothing exists outside this connection—physical, emotional, intense. If we didn't go any further, it would still be a highlight in my memories forever.

Cherished in his care, beautiful under his gaze, and the slow pace makes me feel like I'm the only woman in the world who's ever mattered. He doesn't have to take his time with me. I'm not fragile in that way. But that he's choosing to savor every stage we enter only reaffirms that I can trust him. He wants to be with me, and I want him. I want to love him like he loves me.

I lean forward and kiss his shoulder, the muscles manipulating under my tongue as his hand slips to my lower back. I rub the peaks of my breasts across his skin to not only show what he does to me but so he can feel it too.

Sliding my hand down over his abs, I slip my hand inside the waistband of his briefs until I find his hardness needing attention. And now there's an ache between my legs that has me wanting to jump ten steps ahead—to feel him, his large erection, buried deep inside me.

Tagger's hold keeps me close as I rock against his leg, searching for relief that I don't want to rush. I also don't want the fabric barrier between us either. So I push back to take the cotton covering my hips and slide it over my boots to the floor.

He watches, drinking me in while he runs his tongue over his bottom lip. "It's criminal to look that good."

"Arrest me, then," I challenge. "I'm ready to do time with you in that bed."

A smirk quirks the left side of his mouth and reaches for my hand, pulling me against him again. "You'll be doing something in that bed alright, but it isn't going to be time." He kisses me, then adds, "It also might include some begging."

My eyes go wide while the desire between my legs builds. "Promise?" I grin, raising my brow.

"See?" He shakes his head, that smug smirk never leaving his stupidly handsome face. "It's already started."

I poke him in the abs, more to get a feel than to scold him. "That was pure trickery." I reach down, this time lacking a tentative touch as I rub over his erection on top of those bothersome boxer briefs. Instead, I take what feels rightfully mine. Glancing up to catch his eyes already on me, I ask, "How do you feel about getting rid of these?"

"They're all yours, babe."

"It's not the boxers I want." I grab the sides and drag them down, freeing what I've only felt through jeans and too briefly a few moments ago. Sliding them down to his ankles, I leave them for him to handle from there so I can take in his naked body for the first time. Broad shoulders lead to that pack of eight abs, which cut a sharp V to his prominent member. His cock is perfect—large, smooth, and temptingly straight for me—but I never doubted it wouldn't be.

I can't ignore his legs; the muscles are long, but the strength is held in the thighs. Running. Weights. Sports. I used to love watching him play basketball with my brother outside the barn and running to score touchdown after touchdown in high school at the four-counties stadium. I even remember the first time I saw him on TV playing for Michigan State. Though football was never what I was interested in, I missed as few games as I could get away with. Sometimes my rodeo days got in the way.

This is almost too good to be real. Manifesting really works, inviting me to manifest his mouth on me right now. *Down there . . .*

My chin is lifted, encouraging me to stand again. "What do you want, Pris?" There's no smirk and no humor. The question begs for a daring answer that has me suddenly nervous to utter. I shouldn't be, but— "What's going on in that pretty head of yours?"

"I . . ." Feeling exposed body and soul, I move against him, needing cover. With my arms around him, his arms encircle me, and he places a kiss on my head.

He whispers against my hair, "Talk to me."

With my cheek to his chest, I stare at the bed we made. I could kid myself and say it was for hanging out while this storm blows through, but I know we put the sheet and blanket on for having sex. And now that we're getting closer, I realize big talk did get my offer taken just like he said.

"I want this, Tagger. I want to be with you, but teasing you and saying things that I probably shouldn't, feels braver than I really am." I turn my head and look up into his eyes. Dropping my gaze to the bed again, I whisper, "It's been years."

"What's been years?" I hear the parting of his lips. I can feel the way his body tenses and that his arms have stilled. "Pris . . ."

I don't know what to say, so it doesn't surprise me that he doesn't either. "I really lived up to the nickname, didn't I?"

A breath leaves his chest, and he takes a deeper one in. "I'm sorry."

I laugh humorlessly to myself. "No one is more sorry than I am that I haven't had sex in years. Not with someone else anyway." I shrug, not having the good sense to shut my mouth. "Images of you have come in very handy over the years."

Stroking the back of my head, he rests his chin on the top of it. "I'm sorry for the name. I thought it was harmless."

"It was a curse."

He leans back. "This is bullshit."

There's no anger to worry about, but his clipped tone has me looking up at him again. "What is?"

"Guys are idiots for letting you slip through their fingers." He kisses my forehead and grabs my ass, giving it a squeeze. "If it's any consolation, I've had the dirtiest fucking thoughts about you and gotten off many times to those images. Watching you come while sitting on top of me had me so close to doing the same. If only the deputy wouldn't have shown up."

A smile works its way back onto my face. "That actually does make me feel a lot better." *It's the little things* . . . though his large and rock-hard cock is pressed against my middle. Sometimes the bigger things deserve the limelight, too.

He grins, and there's nothing but sincerity in the lines. Taking my hand, he rubs it over his dick. "This is what you do to me. And for the record, I was fucking hard before you even got naked. Now . . ." He twirls me out in front of him, giving me a solid once-over and then again. "I feel like the luckiest fucking bastard on the planet." When he pulls me back to him, he says, "Don't be nervous. I'll go slow."

"Unless I ask you to go faster, right?"

He chuckles. "Yes, unless you beg me to fuck you faster." Leaning down, he kisses me. "Now, where were we?"

"I think we were just about to get these boots off me."

Nodding toward the mattress, he commands, "Get on the bed, Pris. Years without sex is unacceptable. We'll have to make up for lost time."

"I'm all in." I love that he's not intimidated by my past, not relationships or activities. He makes me feel bolder than ever to be exactly who I am with him. I scurry over and climb on, situating myself toward the end and raising a leg in the air.

Tagger stands over me with a wry grin, his eyes locked on mine as he anchors the back of the boot on his palm and shimmies it off with the other. "So you touch yourself?" I've never heard his voice so deep and rugged and on the verge of a growl.

"No one is here to do it for me." I put my other leg in the air and throw my arms wide, readying myself for the taking.

"You might regret saying that."

"You'd have to make me." One thing he can't resist is a challenge. I'm just not sure if this is the subject to test him. *Too late now.* I rub my thighs together like a damn cricket.

"*Mmm*. Famous last words." He gets the other boot off and drops it with a thud to the floorboards. My socks are thrown over his shoulder before he bends down to rub his hands between my legs. "Thinking about you getting yourself off to images of me is quite the aphrodisiac, Ms. Greene."

"It's always done the trick."

"Fuck," he says, grinning with a shake of his head. "What do I do with you?"

I tilt my head to the side, admiring that Adonis body of his. "To be fair, I don't know what to do with myself sometimes either, so I get it."

He's still shaking his head when he climbs onto the mattress, appearing to genuinely try to figure me out and what he's going to do with me while I start manifesting his mouth on me again. *Maybe twice will produce results.*

We move up until our heads are cushioned on pillows, and we can slip our bodies under the covers. I stare at the ceiling for a few seconds before turning to confirm he's real. With the sides of our bodies pushed together, I can hear my breathing get louder. I tap his hand with my pinky finger. He obliges by wrapping his pinky around mine and then looks at me. I whisper, "Tagger Grange is in my bed." This is too good to be true.

"You're not the only one in awe, Christine Greene," he says, dragging out the syllables in his dulcet tone. Pulling my hand out from under the cover, he kisses it. "I've been dreaming about this." He sits up just enough to lift me by my hips to pull me on top of him.

Straddling him, I lift on his thighs with my hands and adjust over where I want to feel him most. His length is hard, his body already beginning a slow-moving dance against me. I maneuver down to kiss him once and then again before swiping my tongue over that sexy bottom lip of his like he does.

He chuckles. "Did you just lick me?"

"I did, and I might do it again."

His eyes travel from my mouth to my eyes and back again. "Your warning isn't a real threat. If you're going to do it again, I know where you can start."

Before I can move over his body, his hand captures the back of my head and guides me back to his mouth again. His lips brush against mine, and then he looks me in the eyes. "I can't wait to watch you come again."

My breathing slows, but my heart races under the darkening intensity of his eyes. "I'm ready." I slip out of his grasp with my eyes locked on his and start my descent under the sheet. "But I still owe you, and I always pay my debts."

I start with a slow tease of my hand around his length, sliding up and then down as I resituate myself between his legs. My eyes lock on his. Increasing the pace and gripping tighter, I watch as his head jerks once and then twice, and then his lips part. His lids start weighing down on him. A battle of wills has been waged.

Whispering, I say, "I'm going to make you feel so good that you're going to dream about this."

Tagger licks his lips, then shoves his hands behind his head as if he's ready for the show to begin. "I already do, so I can't wait for new material."

So naughty, but his thoughts inspire me to put on my game face. "You're starting to sound like me."

I've waited so long to pleasure him like this just to watch

him fall apart for me. I lean down and lick his tip just to watch it twitch in reaction. Inspired, I twirl my tongue around him several times before gripping the base and taking him into my mouth to slowly descend the full length. I only reach halfway before I pause for a breath and relax my throat to travel the rest of the distance to my hand.

With tight lips and hollowed cheeks, I slide back up.

"That's so good, babe."

Encouraged by his praise and the gentle pressure I feel on the back of my head, I take him again, this time with no break. The tips of his fingers tease through my hair while the sounds of our connection fill my ears. "Look at you," he breathes, slowly thrusting his length past my lips. My gaze travels up to meet the smolder in his eyes. "That mouth is always so beautiful, but wrapped around me like that? Such a good girl, aren't you?"

His tone—low with a gravelly growl—has me wanting to please him. I close my eyes and continue going down and sucking up. I take him in, to the sounds of his groans, and catch my breath at the tip. I move faster, his body bucking under me, forcing him to hit the back of my throat. But I love when he loses himself, loses control because of what I'm doing to him. I want all of him, so I take it over and over and over until his pleasure becomes mine. And selfishly, I find my body becoming needy for him. My thoughts scatter, and I go by desire, and pleasure, and act on instinct. "Mmm." It feels too good to stay quiet.

Reaching forward, he pinches my nipples, sending me spiraling while his hand then slips between my legs, sliding through the slickness he evoked. It's when he lands on my pulsing bud that I lose all senses and take him even deeper just to feel if he can reach inside to release me.

We're seeking those fireworks, so our bodies move in

tandem, erratic against the other, and then in sync again. His groans of pleasure. My moans of ecstasy. The first gratifying ribbon of his release covers my tongue.

It's carnal and raw, so fucking sexy that my body gives in in a thrust against his leg.

Just as he finishes, I hit my peak and then tumble into my release. The sweet relief strikes fast and leaves no prisoners as I fall to pieces on top of him, each tremor whispering, "You are his," as they rattle through my soul. I already knew, but now, I feel so attached that there's no denying it.

When my heart regulates and my breathing calms, I open my eyes and push myself off his stomach to climb higher until this dead-weight body of mine collapses on his chest. I'm not ready to return to reality. I'm not ready to be a functioning member of society. I just want to lie here all day or move this along to the next stage. The tingling begins again . . .

He chuckles while rubbing my back. "You going to live, Pris?"

"I don't think so," I mumble, my eyes closing. My body is worn out, and my mind pleasantly void of my usual troubles. "In fact, I think I've already reached the pearly gates."

He kisses my head. "You always give me hell, but this feels like heaven."

CHAPTER 22

Tagger

Pris is naked next to me, and I'm somehow supposed to keep my hands or, more importantly, my mouth to myself.

Tucked under my arm, she's been napping for almost an hour during the storm. But I'm patient. *Barely.*

It's a trait I've honed since working in finance. The markets move at the speed of light. Thinking quickly on my feet is a given, but studying and predicting what will hit next comes with patience.

It's peaceful, with the rain falling, the tapping on the roof, and the drops splashing in puddles outside the doors. The animals below don't even bother me, though the smell takes some acquiring. It's strange the things I'd forgotten about after being away.

As I look around the loft, it's kind of cute how she's made the most of the space. It's girly with frills and bows, the pink bookcase, and the little glass lamp with the flowers on it sitting on top. It's the perfect spot to get away since there's no way her dad can climb that ladder with his bad knee. I've never been in her bedroom, but I imagine this is one of the few spaces just for her. Since her mom passed, it's only Pris and men out here on the ranch.

That makes it even more impressive that she's the boss. But as I get to know her better, as the woman and not the kid sister, it doesn't surprise me.

Her nails gently scrape over my chest, and I hear her sleepyhead voice ask, "Did you stay awake the whole time?"

"I couldn't sleep." I glance down at her and smile. She's just as beautiful waking up as she always is.

"Too much on your mind?"

"No. Just didn't want to miss any of this."

Pushing up on her elbow, she widens her eyes as she stares at me in disbelief. "This? As in time with me?"

I tuck some of the wilder hair strands behind her ear. "Yes. I'm only here until Wednesday. I can sleep on the plane or at night when I'm back at my folk's place. With you, I want to remember everything, even how you look sleeping."

"You're very charming, Mr. Grange." She slides on top of me. There's no hiding that even being next to her gets me hard, much less when she's on top of me. Perky tits, curvy hips, and that smile that hasn't left her face since I showed up earlier today. It was even there when she was asleep. "And so ready for me."

She presses her hands to my chest and lifts. With our eyes fixed on each other, I adjust my dick to position the tip at her entrance. "Wait, we need birth control. I didn't come here thinking I was getting laid . . ."

Leaning down, she kisses me and then whispers against my lips, "I'm on the pill." She kisses me again, but instead of getting distracted by the soft plushness of her lips like I usually do, my mind ticks through what she said. The pressure grows along with parts of my body as if that were possible since I'm already as hard as steel for this woman, but I need to know. I carefully remove her from my mouth and tilt back to look her in the eyes. "Why are you on the pill if you haven't had sex in years?"

She shrugs. "I'm an optimist."

Unexpected.

Blunt.

Honest.

There's no one like her.

I grab her waist and flip her onto the mattress because I'm good with that. Wedging her knees farther apart, I settle between her legs and angle my cock until it's right where I want it. "Hey," I say, our lips just a breath away. "I'll go slow, but you tell me if it's too much. Okay?"

She wiggles just enough to put space between us, and then her fingertips press to my shoulders. "You're making me nervous, Tagger."

My chest tightens, and doubts start to creep in. She claims she's unbreakable. But resting my weight on my elbows, I look down at her. She's so much smaller when she's under my big frame. Careful needs to be my mantra, which is new for me. It's an act to get off. With her, it feels like more, more than myself and my heart are involved. Maybe this isn't sex.

Are we making love?

Yes. That's what I want with her instead of this solely being a physical act. It's all coming together. *Oh fuck, this is a first.*

Do I want to be connected to her with strings attached?

Yes.

Yeah, I fucking do, in ways I've never wanted with anyone else. It's got to be that mouth of hers that's caused this—snarky and self-assured, so fucking kissable, and the way she went down on me . . . it was the best blow job I've ever had. I'm surprised her killer skills didn't send me to an early grave.

I stare at her as the revelation clears any doubts I might have had. The features of her face are delicate—the bridge of her nose, the bow at the top of her lips, and even the chin that gives her a heart-shaped face. I kiss her cheek, then next to her eye, her forehead, and find her lips again. If I could kiss her heart, I would. Instead, I vow to protect it. "Don't be, babe. I'm going to make you feel so good." It's the minutest of nods, but her eyes are set on mine, and I can't find any hesitation inside when searching. I shift my hips, putting gentle pressure against her entrance. I kiss her, our tongues caressing, my hand stroking her face, and push in.

A gasp juts her head back into the pillow. Her eyes close, and her nails dig into my skin. I freeze in place, regretting not spending more time to prepare her.

She appears to catch her breath and is ready to go when she opens her eyes again. A hard swallow is followed by a sweet smile. Reaching up, she cups my cheek and runs her thumb back and forth as if soothing me when I know she's the one who could be hurt. "I'm okay, babe. Slow is good, but I want you to move. I *need* you to."

Relief washes through me, and I begin to relax. It's going to be okay. Inch by inch. *Slow. Steady.* I push in. She sucks in another breath, but this time, her eyes stay on mine, reassuring me when it's her I'm concerned about. She whispers, "You feel so good."

The heat of her body, the tightness of her pussy—it's so much all at once, too much—the feel of her begins to consume my thoughts, making me reckless as I push to my limit. Her knees squeeze, causing me to stop and drop my head down just to sink into this feeling even more. I take a breath and look up again. "God, you feel amazing."

"Yeah?" she asks, unsure. Uncertainty should never exist in her voice. I have to do better. Now is the time.

I nuzzle against her neck for her, but also for me. Her skin is soft, opposed to the roughness of mine. "It feels incredible to be inside you, to be bonded this way."

The feel of her cheek rising against mine has me shifting back to pull out almost entirely. Her arms wrap around my neck. She kisses my temple, and whispers, "You're going to be stuck with me if you keep that up."

"I want that so fucking much." Knowing she's acclimated to me, I push back in and force a moan right out of her. With each thrust, she becomes more confident and moves how it feels best for her. A gyrate of her hips, a buck when I touch her clit, and the tightening of her arms around me give her leverage to fuck me right back.

She takes every thrust I give, then scrapes her nails down my back as my name becomes one of praise and begging all at once. The embrace of her body around mine makes me want to go faster and then harder to reach that peak we're climbing.

"Oh God, yes, yes, yes. Tag, yes," she murmurs with her hair falling loosely around her shoulders. She's always such a stunning sight. Being inside her almost becomes too much to bear.

It's a fucking glorious sight—her tits bouncing on her chest, her mouth wide and ready for me to fuck again, the moans filling my ears, and the push of her pussy against the base of my dick.

Too much to hold back, I lose control of my better senses, giving in to the devil and the darkness when the light evades. I fuck and fuck and thrust until her body trembles around mine, squeezing my cock so tight that I come with her, my release exploding deep inside her heat. "Fuck," I start, pushing up on my hands and pumping in and out, though my breathing staggers in my throat. "So good, baby."

The rush has vanquished, leaving me empty of energy, so I collapse on top of her. Kissing her shoulder and neck and that curve between, I then drop my head to the mattress.

As I take a deep breath, it's cut short when I feel her hands pushing against me. "Babe, I can't breathe."

"Oh shit." Rushing to fall to the side of her, I land on my back. "Sorry."

"It's okay. I like the weight." She rolls onto her side, draping her arm over my midsection. "You're like a human weighted blanket. Comfort. That is, until I can't breathe."

"I lost myself in you." I chuckle with my arm under her, rubbing her back with my hand. "You drive me wild, woman."

"There are worse things that could happen." She releases a deep breath and closes her eyes. "It's wild that something that feels so good and so intense but only lasts a minute can wear you out so much."

My hand stills as her words sink in. *I'm not offended per se . . .* "It was longer than a minute."

She bursts out laughing, her back arching, and those beautiful tits of hers jiggling and becoming a major distraction to my argument. Patting my chest, she looks up at me. "Yes, it was longer than a minute."

It doesn't matter that I sense a hint of condescension because I won that battle. But she's winning me over. I angle toward her and scoot lower so I can appreciate these breasts of hers. I hold one and knead it before dipping down and flicking the nipple with my tongue.

Her hand settles on the back of my head and slides to my neck, holding me there. I kiss her pink tips until goose bumps populate, and she struggles not to wriggle her hips, seeking relief.

"My sweet girl." I could fuck her with my finger again, but I want to taste her this time. "You want more? I'll give you what you want, what you need."

I bend over her and put my mouth over those supple lower lips of hers. Swiping the tip of my tongue through the top of her folds, I tease her wanton bud and suck until she bucks against me.

Using my body, I still her. I don't take prisoners, and I want her too much to take my time. I go right for the prize and add another finger. She pulls my hair as her moans become more frequent. I fuck the bed beside her while pleasuring her to the extent of calling my name louder and louder. It's when she can't help jolting her hips off the bed that I French-kiss her clit and then nip.

The first tremor sends her quivering in bliss. And when she melts to the mattress, I'm pulled to go higher to be closer to her. I give her one more kiss on her lower lips before turning my attention to her mouth. Taking full possession, I kiss her and go deeper while her body squirms beneath me, moaning into my mouth.

When her body calms and her muscles ease, I pull back to see her tugging that swollen bottom lip of hers under her teeth. I fall to the side, lying next to her, allowing her to get the best of me before I even have a chance to release. It doesn't matter, only she does. Resting my arm over my head, I close my eyes, still tasting her on my lips.

"That was naughty," she says, and a gentle poke to my ribs makes me smile.

"Too far?" I ask, my eyes still closed as the adrenaline drains from my body.

Snuggling against my side, she kisses my pec. "No. I liked it more than I expected."

I spy on her through one open eye. "The sex?"

"The last part."

I curl her in my arm and kiss her forehead. "I like you, babe. A lot."

I score that grand prize smile of hers and laugh. "Who knew all I needed was a six-foot-three hunk of a man to make me come for my life to be sunshine and roses, even when it's rainy outside?"

"I could have told you that."

She snorts. "I'm sure you could've." Propping herself on my chest, she says, "This has been one of the best days of my life."

That hits deep and tightens my chest. I bring my other arm over so I'm holding all of her. "One of?" I tease with a smirk.

"Sorry, but winning the barrel races junior year gives it a solid run for the money."

I lean over, making sure her eyes are firmly on mine when I say, "I'm going to secure first place if it's the last thing I do before leaving Peachtree Pass."

"Promise?" She waggles her brows.

"Swear on my life."

CHAPTER 23

Christine

MANIFESTING WORKS.

I want Tagger Grange to fall in love with me.

"I think I already am."

I hadn't realized my whispers could be heard. My gaze darts to the right of me, where he's been sleeping or so I thought. Seeing him rub his eyes and look over at me with nothing but adoration has me feeling mushy inside. "You are?" Sure, he told me he was earlier, but a part of me just wondered if it was the appetizer before dinner started, wistful words before having sex.

"Yes, Pris." Taking hold of my hand between our bodies, he says, "I'm not sure after sex is the best time to discuss these things."

"True." He's right. My emotions are all over the place and spiraling from the activities. "We had sex." I smile. "Really good sex."

"Great sex." His warm hand glides over my stomach, and he rests it in the middle.

"The greatest."

"This isn't a competition, is it? Because if that's the case, it was spectacular sex. God's honest truth."

I cuddle to his side. "You win."

He rubs his hand over my hip. "I usually do." Redirecting his gaze upward, he asks, "What are your thoughts on long-distance relationships?"

"They're not great for most."

He turns to look at me again, and worry wrinkles his forehead. "What about us?"

I don't rush to answer, knowing this is a sensitive topic that can cause unnecessary concerns. Thinking about how this will work seems to be the biggest obstacle. "How will it work? For us, specifically?" I hate answering a question with another, but I'm curious how he sees this playing out.

"I come back here for visits," he says as if this is obvious. I feel like this needs to be stated, loud and clear. For me, at least, so it's good to hear. "You come to New York when you can."

"So traveling back and forth? Calls. Emails. Texts?"

An ember glows in the pupil of his eyes. "Video for when we want to get off." I love how hopeful he sounds.

"Okay."

"Yeah?"

"Yes." Rolling half on top of him, I kiss his chin. "I want to try this with you."

I feel his breathing stop as if he's holding his breath. His eyes study the ceiling, and then he looks at me again. "Do you hear that?"

Confused about what I'm supposed to be listening for, I ask, "Me saying I'll do a long-distance relationship with you?"

"No, though I love to hear it. No rain."

I stop to listen. He's right. "It's stopped. I didn't even notice when."

"We were preoccupied."

Sitting up, I'm both happy and disappointed at the same time. I look back at him still lying next to me. "I guess we should get dressed."

"Yeah." The ember dies out, and he sounds just as conflicted as I do. "Your dad will probably be looking for you."

I turn back around and silently nod, though I doubt he can see it. I climb off the mattress, needing a shower more than ever. But it was nice for a short moment in time for only us to exist in this little universe. After a few hours of hanging on the rail, my cotton dress is made of thin enough material to be dry most of the way. Unfortunately, the stains appear to be there to stay.

I don't bother with the bra, and I'm definitely not putting my underwear back on. I'll be tossing those anyway. The material of the dress is cool as it slips over my body, revealing my nipples pressing against it. "What if we don't work out?" I ask, gathering my socks and other garments together.

His head pops through the hole of the shirt, and he pulls it down. "No harm. No foul."

"We pretend nothing ever happened?" I pick up my boots in the other hand and return to where he's attempting to pull on jeans that are still wet, though not soaking anymore.

He stops, his eyes narrowing. "Does that mean you're thinking we keep this quiet?"

Kind of dumbfounded, I hadn't thought of that. "A secret relationship?" I hate the way shame creeps into the corners of my psyche.

"That's not what I had in mind, Pris," he says, coming closer and lowering his voice as if the tempered tone will make me feel better. "I don't want to hide you or what we have."

So many thoughts merry-go-round in my head, but two come to the forefront. "My dad—"

"And Baylor," he says, the same look of defeat dragging his expression down. "He'll kill me."

"He'd bury you alive somewhere on the property to never be found by me or anyone else ever again."

With a slack jaw, he stares at me. "Um, that's quite the visual. First time having that thought there, babe?"

"No. But it didn't involve you, if that makes it any less worrisome."

Seemingly shaking off that imagery, he says, "It does."

"But now we're back to hiding again."

He strokes my cheek with the back of his hand. "We don't have to hide. I'll face the music for you."

"The Death March." I look down between us at our bare feet, thinking how I felt like I was on cloud nine just five minutes ago. Now, I'm thinking it's best to keep things undercover. "Maybe we work through the kinks secretly? I mean, what if I discover you snore, and I murder you with a pillow in the middle of the night if I don't get rest?"

"I think we need to slow the roll on the different ways I can be murdered and get back on track to what will work best for us. You and me. That's all we should be considering right now."

"That's simple. We keep it a secret until we're ready to share with everyone."

He tugs his jeans on the rest of the way and secures the button. "How do you figure?"

"Whether we tell everyone or just show up together,

then the relationship becomes a thing—of gossip, scrutiny, and dealing with the fallout."

"Instead of enjoying what we have." He drops his socks and underwear in his boot, then grabs the other. "Dooms us from the start."

"Because it becomes about them instead of us." I rest my head on his arm, closing my eyes. I'm not quite ready to leave this little paradise we created. "I don't want that."

His arm comes around me, and he kisses my head. "Me either."

I shift in front of him, looking up and seeing how this isn't what he wants. He's agreeing to keep me out of the line of fire, knowing I'm the one who will have to deal with them here in Peachtree Pass. Though, it wouldn't be a walk in the park to break the news to my brother either. *So we're screwed.*

"One positive is I get you all to myself."

"You already had me. You just hadn't realized it yet." He heads toward the other side of the loft, tossing his boots to the ground before he takes a step down onto the first rung of the ladder. "I'll go down first."

"A girl can dream."

He shoots me a look that says I might get a tongue-lashing if I'm not careful. The thought makes me tingle. I decide to be reckless in hopes of receiving that reward, erm, I mean punishment.

At the bottom, he holds the ladder steady for me after I toss my boots to him, and asks, "Whatever happened to you and that guy in Denver? You never tried the long-distance thing?"

This time, I'm the one shooting the glare. "You sure you want to talk about exes?"

"I'm not threatened."

"Good." I step onto the ladder. "You shouldn't be." I take

a few steps and then say, "He dumped me as soon as I told him I was moving, so it was never a discussion. Guess I wasn't worth the effort."

I try to step off the ladder, but his arms hold me in place. When I turn to face him, his hands hold my hips, and he says, "He was a fucking idiot for not fighting for you. You're always worth the effort, Pris."

I try to play off the compliment by rolling my eyes, but he's just so swoony I can't resist him. "If you wanted to kiss me, all you had to do was ask."

"Can I kiss you?"

"Absolutely."

I'm given the kiss of all kisses—sweet with embracing pressure, gentle caress of our tongues, and he holds me in his arms like I might slip away if he doesn't. The one in the rain was pretty damn good as well. The man knows how to make me swoon. I'll give him that.

"You ready?" he asks as we approach the doors of the barn.

The night fell a while ago, but the light outside the barn shone bright enough to keep things visible through the dark. From here, I can see the lights on in the house and some movement in the kitchen.

I rub the muzzle of each of the horses, then catch up to him. "It's probably best if you head out from here. My dad will start with a whole line of questions. I can dodge them and go shower, but you could be stuck for the next hour trying to explain what we've been doing."

He scratches the back of his neck, eyeing the house. "You're probably right."

When I close the gap, standing next to him, I'm swept up in his arms and taken to a darker corner where no one can see us. Tagger kisses me once, and then again before whispering, "This was one of the best days of my life."

I grin. "It was winning at the rodeo for me. What am I competing with?"

"The birth of my son."

I surrender on the spot, throwing my hands up in front of me. "It's no competition, then."

"No. Two different events, important in different parts of my life." He sets me down on my bare feet, the hay both irritating and tickling. The mud can suck it. I'm sick of it after today.

"You're an amazing dad. Beckett's fortunate to have you."

"I'm fortunate to have him. He's changed my perspective on pretty much everything. I put importance on things that were never worthy in the big picture. Now I value things that really matter—my son, happiness, and living a life that feeds my soul." His gaze drops as if he needs a second to collect his thoughts. When he looks up, that determination he's always carried in his eyes is at the forefront. "Come to New York. I'll book you on a first-class ticket."

"When?" Clearly, it only takes hearing first class to get me to say yes. I'm not that bad. I can afford my own first-class ticket. The truth is, I'd go anywhere for him and sit in the cargo hold if I had to. *Desperate much?* I now know what dreams taste like, so I'll never get enough of him.

"When can you break free for a few days?"

I know I'll have to lie to my dad. Since I'm more transparent than glass, I'll have to come up with something good and a story that won't raise red flags. "Give me two weeks."

A smile splits his cheek wide open. "Two weeks it is."

We share one more kiss before I run for the house. I'm more than happy to distract my dad to help Tagger's quick getaway. I stop on the porch to drop my boots and look back at the barn, knowing it will always hold a special place in my heart.

I smile, then walk inside to find my dad at the stove. He glances at me. "You got caught out in it?"

"Yeah. Cats and dogs."

"Cows and horses," he says, smiling over a joke we've always shared to make storms less scary for me when I was growing up. Then he sees the dress. In my heart, I know he'd never be mad at me for wearing it, but I do hate seeing the pain it causes him to see it so dirty as if I didn't care at all. "Your mother's dress."

I look down as it sinks in again that it's ruined. "Sunrise was under a tree at the back of the cornfield. I waited with her." I don't say more because what is there to say? It was careless of me to wear it at all.

When he turns his attention back to the stove, he says, "You go clean up. I have some chicken noodle soup almost ready."

I stand there a second more, feeling his pain from across the room, and now feeling worse for wearing it in the first place. By the time I'm ready to go to sleep a few hours later, I look out the window, but there's too much cloud cover. I climb into bed, some new aches arising where I didn't know I had muscles. Or thought had long ago atrophied from lack of use and attention. Tagger cured me.

I giggle at my own joke. I must need sleep because I'm obviously delirious after the day I had. And that's when my phone lights up with a message on the nightstand as if it knew I needed saving from my ridiculous self.

Rolling over, I grab the phone and hold it above my head, instantly grinning like a loon when I see it's from Tagger, my boyfriend. Secret or not, we're the real deal, and one day, I just know in my heart I'm going to marry that man.

CHAPTER 24

Christine

Up before the chickens, I race outside, putting on my Wellington boots since my other ones are still covered in dried mud, and start the rounds. I'm feeling motivated and want to make sure if Tagger shows up, I'm free to mess around.

Whatever messing around entails . . . He's broken the seal, the curse, and cracked the dam. He doesn't stand a chance. I'm ready for that man.

"Morning," my dad calls when he drives the UTV up the side of the house and parks. "Why was this left out near the equipment barn?"

"Long story. Even longer storm."

"Listen, Chris," he says, angling his legs out the side of the vehicle while staying seated right where he is.

I cross the yard and jump over a few puddles that haven't dried up yet. "What is it?"

"We never talk about your brothers." He's not wrong. We reference them in funny stories or when something makes us think of them, but we don't talk about their absence or if they're ever coming home again.

"Why is that, Dad?" I ask. I didn't want to upset him. For me, I've held a lot of anger toward them for leaving me behind to deal with everything. I lean my hip against the front of the vehicle. It's practically sparkling after being clean in the rain yesterday.

"I was never supposed to be here on this earth alone."

"I'm here." I hate that my first reaction is offense because my dad would never hurt me on purpose. But even without intention, that stings.

His face falls. "I didn't mean like that. I meant, I never wanted to be in this universe without your mother. She was the glue that held us together, and with her gone, our family fell apart. I'm responsible for that."

"No, it's not our burden to carry alone. We're all guilty of letting things go. Griff and Baylor are responsible as well." I move closer and give him a hug. "They know they always have a home. They just have to make the trip."

When I step back again, he says, "I'm sure glad to have you in my life, dear daughter. It just wouldn't be the same without ya." He climbs out and heads for the toolbox in the back of the truck. "Best get on with your day. There are never enough hours."

I'm standing there as his words settle in. There aren't enough hours. Never enough. The work is never-ending. The rewards are further apart. I've turned this from a family-run business with two employees into a huge success with more than ten full-time employees and five others on rotation, all of whom earn shares as well. They have a stake in the ranch's success, and that basic concept has worked out well for everyone.

All four of us Greenes have millions in our accounts to

show for my hard work and business savvy. Looking across at the field where Bluebelly and Skyward graze, I realize I will work until I die here. I could drop in a field and not be found for days. Sleeping with Tagger should be a comfort, and him being officially my boyfriend used to be goals. But I want to achieve more than having a secret relationship with him.

I'll never know what I could have contributed to the world.

Bluebelly neighs, ready for me to feed her this morning. A whole beautiful field of the finest grass around isn't good enough, I guess. "Hold your horses, literally." I laugh because there's no point in crying, and then I get on with my day. "I'm coming. I'm coming."

"Hey, you," Tagger says, sauntering up just after eleven, looking like he had a hell of a fantastic sleep. Oh, to be living the life of a prince while visiting. I can't blame him. I just woke up on the sour side of the bed this morning. "Can you sneak away?"

He looks good, too good. Wearing a hard straw hat, the tips of his brown hair flip on the underside of the brim. His shirt isn't anything special, but it's great at highlighting his muscular frame. But those jeans and boots will do the trick for me every damn time. Fitted in all the right ways around the thighs and a good scuffing on the tips of the boots complete the fantasy. "What'd you have in mind, cowboy?"

"Lunch."

I pull the rope from my shoulder and hook it around a fence post before leaning against a rail and kicking my boot up. With my dad taking a midday break, I start for him. It's so tempting to give him a kiss, but I control myself and head for the truck instead. "I can sneak away for lunch."

He opens the door for me, and I climb in. When he gets in the cab, I say, "This feels like a date."

"It is, babe." Starting the engine, he glances over at me and gives me that winning smile. "We can't be showy, but we can make the best of it here in the Pass."

"You're quite the charmer, Mr. Grange."

Driving toward the exit of the ranch, he laughs. "Only for you, Ms. Greene."

"I'm sure some ladies in New York could argue against that statement."

Just a quick spike of his brow is seen before he rights it. "The storm cleared the skies for beautiful May weather."

Now I laugh. "Nice try, and I'll let it go. No need to get up in arms about something that doesn't affect me." Bringing my knees to my chest, I enjoy the pretty weather he mentioned by rolling down the window and letting the wind whip through my hair. "Soon, it will be too hot out here."

"To roll down the window?"

"For anything here in the hill country." I roll my head to the side to stare out at fields and scenery I have memorized by heart. When I turn to him, I used to feel I knew if he had a new freckle, but he's been gone so many years that I get to learn everything about him again.

His nose is straight but from the side it has the slightest bump on the bridge, like he might wear glasses sometimes. God, I'd love to see that. He'd look so sexy.

His jaw ticks when he's deep in thought and tightens when he's focused. He was very focused when he was making love to me. So hot.

But I'm still drawn to the lines beside his eyes that formed from laughter, sunshine, and through his concentration on everything he set his mind to. They matured his face from boy to man, reckless to established, dreams to achievement. He's done it all and deserves all the credit. He left the Pass to grow into his own man instead of following in the shadow of his dad or brother and returned with buckles of his own success, if they recognized life like they do at the rodeo.

I feel both flattered to be sitting next to him but also proud of who he's become.

He's humbled somehow, yet sexier than ever.

Cutting down a dirt road that I've traveled countless times, I smile. "We're going to the ridge?"

"It's always a great view, and I haven't been since I was in high school."

I look ahead at the swerve around the trees and over a rockier section that only a truck will get you over. "It never changes and never gets old."

It opens just around the bend to a flat field perfect for parking. It's always a popular spot for teenagers to come and make out. Maybe we can do the same after lunch. I'm too starving to sacrifice food for sex right now.

He shifts into park after situating the truck in the direction of the road so we can use the tailgate to sit on to enjoy the view. When he cuts the engine, we hop out and walk around to the back bed. With blankets and pillows under his arm, he opens the tailgate. He spreads the blanket and then tosses the pillow in. "I cleaned the bed this morning but wanted to make it a bit softer for you."

Tagger being a romantic wasn't really on my bingo card. It's something I never really thought about. Dream about dating him? *Sure.* Fantasize about him in bed? *Absolutely.* Wooing his girlfriend? *It's a welcome surprise.* Along with so many other aspects I never bothered to delve into. Dating him was an impossibility, but here we are, a couple secretly launching our relationship.

He lifts me up and wrangles my Wellies off, then sets them on the top of the truck. Wise man. The last thing I need to find in my boots are rattlesnakes or scorpions.

I get more comfortable while he climbs up next to me. We lie there holding hands and staring out over miles of trees and hills from this higher vantage point. He says, "We have the river running through our property, but no high points like this." Turning to me, he kisses my hand. "If you could have your house with views like this or of the river, which would you choose?"

"I hadn't thought about it. They both have their advantages. A house hidden in the trees near the river would be peaceful and cozy like a hug. A higher elevation would give views but also some protection, seeing things like wildfires before they reach the property. So security." I look over at him when he's silent. "What about you?"

"What if security was a given for both? Do you prefer one over the other?"

"You sound so serious. I feel like I might fail if I give the wrong answer."

He slips his arm around my shoulders. "No. There are no wrong answers. I've just been thinking about this a lot lately."

I sit up and angle toward him. "Are you thinking about moving back?" My heartbeat races for a response to a question I didn't think was at play.

He sits next to me, bending his knees and resting his arms over them. "I didn't mean to mislead you. I just want to get to know you, Pris."

"Right. Yeah, I figured. I just . . . I don't know why I jumped to conclusions like that." I shake my head and turn my gaze to the view again. "The river house." I take a calming breath. "I love the sound of water—rivers, oceans, even fountains."

I can feel his gaze still on me, but I don't look. I'm a bit embarrassed for sounding like a lovesick schoolgirl. If he moved here, it would give our relationship a solid chance because I'm still unsure how doing long distance with him will look.

"I'm sorry—"

"No. No need." I look at him, and ask, "Was lunch a euphemism, or is there going to be food involved?"

He grabs a box from the empty metal tool chest in the back of the truck and sets it in front of us. "I didn't know what you like, so I got a lot of everything from Sassy's over in Dover."

There's container after container of different foods, from cut fruit to pasta salad, burgers, fries, hot dogs, and a plethora of other things. I enjoy the tarragon chicken salad before eating grapes and cantaloupe, and sip on a can of Waterloo mixed berries sparkling water.

Because the sun is stronger today, he places his hat on my head to shade my face, which is basically the only physical contact we've had. I assume that he has as much on his mind as I do since we're eating in silence.

Being whisked away for lunch, I somehow imagined it being more couple-y. We're alone and free to kiss as much as we want. But we're not. I don't like the start of our secret relationship being heavy like this. "What's going on, Tagger? Please talk to me."

Rubbing his palm over my knee, he watches it instead of looking at me. "I have a flight tomorrow morning at six o'clock."

The fruit is suddenly unappealing. I set the fork and

bowl back in the box and turn to face him. "I thought you were here longer?"

"My flight was originally for Wednesday."

"Today is Sunday," I reply dumbly as if he doesn't already know.

"This was out of my control, babe." He finally dares to look into my eyes. "I had a meeting added to my schedule that I'm expected to attend at four o'clock tomorrow in the city."

Searching his greens, I can't find a lie to contradict him. "And if you miss it?"

"I won't."

"What if you do?"

"I'm not missing it," he says with such finality that I'm almost intimidated to continue questioning him. *Almost.* Few people intimidate me. *Even fewer men.* Yet he does, and I'm not sure why, other than it feels like we're on unequal footing. "I'll be cutting it close, but I'll be there."

"Okay," I say like I hold any power.

I do. I control how I react to bumps in the road. Anyway, he wasn't asking for my opinion. The decision was made regardless of how I felt. So what am I fighting against? Is his life in New York now the enemy? That's not going to change. He's already making it clear that it will win every time.

Either I adapt or there is no *we* anymore. It's that simple.

He tilts to the side to catch my eyes. When I look at him, I can't muster a smile, and I know he can tell. He says, "Like I said, I'm sorry. It's not something that was planned. I booked my ticket for Wednesday to spend more time here. But this meeting is important for my career."

"I wouldn't know what that's like. I'm just a ranch hand around these parts."

"You're more than that, but this isn't a reflection of my

life versus yours. Babe?" He takes my hands in his and holds them between us. "I'm just as disappointed. Yesterday meant a lot to me, and the time we spent together was incredible. But this is just a blip."

It just feels like this is bigger than it is, like some elaborate plan set in motion behind my back. "Is that why you brought me out here? To break the news and let me down easy?" *Don't do this, Chris.* I trust him. I have no reason not to. "You would stay if you could. I know that, babe."

"I brought you here to seduce you with pasta salad and me as dessert." He lies down, bringing me with him. I slide into his arms because that's where I want to be most right now, especially if we're on borrowed time. After placing a kiss on my collarbone and then on my neck, he asks, "How can I make it up to you?"

Manifesting really comes through for you when you need it most. Eyeing his mouth, I tap his bottom lip and grin. "I have an idea how you can make me feel better."

CHAPTER 25

Tagger

I LICK MY LIPS, wishing I could still taste her.

The moonlight shone over us as if we had all night. We didn't, but we sure made the most of it. When she rode me, a halo of stars hung over her head. My angel with a little devil inside. I grin, looking down in a failed attempt to rub it away before anyone notices.

"Tagger?"

I look up at Keith, free of any remaining grin. "Yes?" I ask, searching my boss's face for any clue as to what was asked of me. Nothing tips me off in the right direction, so I look across the table at the client. She smiles politely, but the tapping of her fingers gives away her impatience.

Kendra clears her throat, and whispers, "Risk."

"Critical separations of long- and short-term investments are partnered with your company's risk tolerance levels. The strategies I've developed under Keith's expertise have produced outstanding and trackable results . . ." I spout out the pitch I've been giving for years. "Our two-pronged approach to investor relations will cultivate a broader understanding of where you want to be in the market—seen, as well as driving innovations. This is my specialty. Putting your trust in managing your assets will grow the profitability of your financial sector, keeping your employees and your board of directors happy."

The client leans forward, resting her elbows on the table, and clasps her hands together. I've piqued her interest. I'll have her and the entire team she brought with her signing on the dotted line within the hour. She asks, "You can guarantee that?"

"It's investments," I reply with a wry grin. "There are no guarantees. Only reputations and I've built a formidable and client-first career that shows my track record in commercial asset management."

"He gives me too much credit," Keith adds. "I can tell you that Tagger is your guy. He's developed a tactic that's based on consistency, which we value, as well as profitable results." His faith in me early on allowed me to build my career to top-tier portfolio management. "He's the best we have, besides me." He chuckles. As if cued, so does everyone else.

The deal is signed thirty minutes later, and a celebration is planned in Midtown. After a quick discussion with the team, the room clears, and we disperse to our offices.

Kendra shuts the door just before I yell, "Fuck." Working my way to my desk, I drop the folio on top and move around to sit.

Crossing the room, she eases into a chair as if I might bite her head off. I wouldn't. I only have myself to blame for that shit show performance. "You did fine, Tagger."

"Fine? That's the goalpost now? Fine?" I take a breath.

Losing my shit isn't something I've done in a while. I briefly close my eyes and rub my temple.

"This meeting shouldn't have been added to your calendar. You've been up since what to be here?" Tapping her pen on a pad, she continues, "Two o'clock to catch the flight out of Austin? You're exhausted, boss."

As if it changes anything, I justify, "I stayed in bed until two thirty." I don't tell her that I was fucking Pris in a truck bed I parked just inside the entrance to the ranch. Our little plan to see each other one last time before I left had us sneaking around like horny teenagers.

"No wonder you're tired and short-fused." She smiles, though sympathy is shaping the corners. "On the bright side, the clients signed. So you may not be happy with your performance, but Keith is thrilled." She leans forward. "You should be proud, Tagger. You closed the deal."

"I closed it, but I wasn't on my A game. My mind was left in Texas."

"Is Texas something you're considering?"

I rock back in the chair and stare at the window. The view is so different from the one at the ridge. Buildings of chrome and mirrored windows, a slice of the avenue just down the right side of my office, and a touch of sky if I stand closer and look up—it all pales compared to the miles of trees and rivers, the endless skies, rock formations, and my girl next to me.

I exhale and think about Beckett. "No. Just visiting." My mood isn't going to improve. She's right. I'm tired and don't have the right mindset to play the part this evening. And still thinking about my girl back in the Pass . . . Pris in the back of a Chevy beats cocktails with wealthy clients any day or night. "Cancel the cocktails at The Polo Bar. Tell them whatever you need to get me out of it."

Surprise straightens her spine, and she moves to sit on the edge of the chair. "Are you sure? Keith will be there."

"Keith can handle it. We have a signed contract. If it falls apart because I didn't have a beer with them, then I lose the deal. I'm okay with that." I glance at my watch. Since it's just past six, I grab my phone and stand to go. "Don't stay long."

"I'm wrapping up." She stands to follow me out.

I head for the exit but call back, "Enjoy your night."

With a salute, she replies, "Yes, sir."

I trek to the street and take the subway. No train delays or waiting to find a car to squeeze into should put me in a better mood. Surprisingly, it doesn't. I reach the apartment building, and the doorman already has my suitcase beside the desk. I didn't want to drag it into the office, so I had it delivered here instead.

"Good trip?" Jeff asks, rolling the case around the counter to me.

"Too quick of a trip."

"I hear that. What dragged you back? I had you down for a Wednesday return."

Dragged is right. There might have been some mental kicking and screaming as well. "Work."

"Aw, man. No days off climbing that corporate ladder."

There sure the fuck isn't. He tips his hat. "Have a good night, Mr. Grange."

"Thanks." I drag the suitcase into the elevator and up to the twentieth floor. Down the hall, I loosen my tie before I reach the door and enter my apartment. My clothes are usually a source of pride, but today, they feel like they're strangling me for some reason.

Dropping my keys on the counter, I let the jacket slide from my shoulders and toss it on the arm of the couch as I cross the living room to the windows. Like the office, this is the view I used to aspire to have. Now, it's gray, flat, and has lost the shine it once had.

Besides the added suitcase, there's a ritual to my return each night. Predictable . . . I'm not sure when I became that guy, but it's not exactly how I imagined my life.

I walk to the fridge, open the door, and consider grabbing a beer. I need a reset, though, not to sink deeper into comparisons. That's what this is—Texas versus New York. Wide-open ranges versus a city that never sleeps. *Pris versus . . .* I close the fridge door. Unless I'm going to change the situation, it's best I don't continue down this path.

I should probably go for a run to burn off what I should be doing and get back to reality. Fifteen minutes later, I'm hitting the pavement. I don't miss the Texas heat and humidity. *Huh.* A con is found among all the pros on the list.

Hitting the High Line, I run faster, wanting to feel the burn, needing to clear my head of what is and what isn't my current situation. Wallowing was never in my blood. There wasn't time for it. If I failed, I moved on. I came back stronger, faster, better, and succeeded the second time.

So why'd I set myself up for failure in this relationship?

Why'd I do it to her when I know I can't be as present as she deserves?

Self-fucking-serving. She's captivated me.

I scratch the back of my neck, trying to figure out the exact moment I traded my balls in and decided to sound like an idiot from a Shakespearean play. I cut down a street heading west until I'm bent over, trying to catch my breath in front of my building.

Jeff stands with the door to the building open. "Do you want to come in or for me to call an ambulance?"

Sweat drops from my chin when I look up. I stand, staggering toward the door. "The man's got jokes," I say, entering the air-conditioned lobby and soaking in the cool air as it envelops my body.

"I try."

I punch the button in the elevator.

I crash on the couch, staring up at the ceiling. It's no rusted tin roof with rain splattering down to the sounds of our breathing, but I guess this one will do.

Glancing at the time, I grab my phone, hoping to catch Pris before she heads inside the house. Once there, her father will be hanging around, and she'll have to speak in code not to be busted.

Three rings and no answer have me doubting myself, but then there's a click. "Hey there, cowboy."

The tension in my shoulders subsides simply from hearing her voice over the speakerphone, peace finally finding me after the long day. "Hey there." I grin and try to wipe it away, failing this time, unlike earlier in the conference room. "Bad time?"

"Perfect timing. I was just wrapping up in the barn. How was your flight? Did you make your meeting?"

"Flight was fine. Meeting was made, but I don't want to discuss that."

"What do you want to talk about, Tagger?" I catch the rise in her tone. Worrying her was not my intention.

"I regret leaving you."

"I do too, but all day, I kept reminding myself that whether it was today or Wednesday, it was inevitable," she says, which has me picturing her raising her chin. *Protecting herself?* The thought that she's protecting herself from heartbreak guts me, though she's not unwise for doing so. "You're a busy guy with a whole life up there that I don't even know anything about."

Holding the phone on my chest, I lie there. What do I

say to that? I'm not sure there's a follow-up that feels right. "Pris?" I talk anyway, needing to get to what's wrong.

"Yes?" Her response comes reluctantly and softer in tone.

"I miss the barn," I confess. "I miss you."

"Tagger . . ." Her voice stumbles, and then she lowers it. "I've been trying to keep busy so as not to think about you being gone, but my mind was always on you and the barn and the truck . . . I miss you, too."

"I need you to know that just because I'm here doesn't mean my heart is. I left it in your care."

CHAPTER 26

Christine

Two weeks later . . .

Standing on the sidewalk in front of Tagger's building, I lift my sunglasses off so my gaze can follow the building until it disappears into the sky. I've always wondered what it would be like to live in the clouds. *I'm about to find out.* At least for the weekend.

Two nights to live the high life.

The doorman opens the door for me. "Good afternoon."

"Good afternoon," I reply, feeling fancy. If I said that to the guys on the ranch, I'd be laughed all the way back to New York City. It's a nice change hearing it while in the city. A little formal for my day-to-day, though.

He scoots around the tall marble counter. "How may I help you?"

"I'm here for Tagger Grange. Christine Greene. He's expect—"

"Yes, he is, Ms. Greene." He sets a key on the counter and

slides it to me. "Mr. Grange left this for you. He's running late and sent his apologies."

"Oh." I take the key and tuck it into my pocket. "So I just go on up?" And here, I was always under the impression that New Yorkers didn't trust strangers. *Happily proven wrong.* Of course, he did know my name, so there is that.

"Yes. Twentieth floor. Apartment A." He rests back on his heels and adjusts his hat. "The apartment is on the left."

I glance at the elevators. "Thank you."

The apartment is easy enough to find, but it feels weird to invade without him being home. It's like I'm an intruder in his life.

I open the door and am greeted with sunlight flooding the space from across the room. Stepping inside, I pull my suitcase in and walk down the short hallway. The hardwoods add warmth to the space, and the dark counter in the kitchen keeps it more masculine in style. Those windows, though. I leave my suitcase and hurry across the room to look out at the view.

I'm in the heart of the city, but the view over the surrounding buildings reaches all the way to the water in the distance. The blue sky and scattered clouds are so close I can almost touch them up here.

Turning back to the apartment, I find the kitchen is small, but I have a hunch it's not used much anyway. It's clean and looks high-end with matching stainless steel appliances and stone backsplash. I touch it just to feel the slick, natural surface.

My dad kept the sunny-colored appliances in our kitchen because they matched the flowers on the curtains, and yellow is my mom's favorite color. But they're so dated and starting to rust at the hinges.

I run my hands over the counter on the island, spreading them wide and resting my cheek on the cold surface. I'm no chef, but this nice kitchen would be inspiring. I remove myself from the counter before he catches me acting like a country bumpkin who has never been out of Small Town, Texas.

Two barstools are tucked under the counter overhang, and a wooden dining table for six is set up parallel to a wall of bookcases with few too many books and too much unused space. I walk closer to see a small collection of framed photos. One of Tagger and Beck on a beach with palm trees in the back and ice-blue waters washing over their toes. Another silver frame holds a photo of him back in high school with his parents flanking him. I remember that night. It was college night, and they had just announced he was going to Michigan State along with Baylor, who was next to him with my parents at his sides. It was a big night for Peachtree Pass.

I move closer to see a photo of Tagger solo in hiking gear standing on what looks to be the top of the world. I know he and Baylor traveled quite a bit after college, but I can't place where this might have been. I was in college by then, caught up in my own life, so not surprised. A kiss of a sunburn across his cheeks makes his smile blinding white, but the happiness can't be contained. I can even see it in his eyes. I'm not sure I've seen it at that level since we reconnected. I take a breath. He looks so handsome that it hurts to think some of the joy has been sucked away from his life.

Another photo of that cutie patootie Beckett makes me smile. When does he not? *Never.* His personality is so vivacious, and he's handsome like his dad. Dressed in a school uniform, he looks nice, but I think I prefer him playing at the farm to every hair being in place. He's a kid, not a little adult.

Shifting to the last frame on the shelf, I pick it up. Tagger and Baylor. It's how Tagger looks now, grown into his looks, harder jaw, those creases at the corners of his eyes I love to look at. Even his hair is similar.

Both are dressed in tuxedos in a crowded room with paintings on the wall and gilding everywhere. Best of friends since they were crawling on the floor. I'm glad they've always had each other. I have that with Lauralee.

It's been a while since I've seen my brother, even in photos. I'm not as familiar with this Baylor—the smile is the same, but he's all grown up with broader shoulders and his hair more styled than he used to wear it, and like Tagger, little lines are forming on the outside of his eyes.

There's no judgment, just noticing my brother grew up without me being aware. I'm sure it would surprise him to see how much I have changed as well.

I set the frame back in place and walk to the living room. Dragging my finger along the back of the structured leather couch, I notice the touches of hominess he's added—a fuzzy blanket draped over a chair and a few throw pillows that look expensive, judging by the design and size. The TV is big, but that doesn't surprise me. He and Baylor are huge sports fanatics.

It's then that I see the hallway leading to more. Do I snoop? Do I sit here patiently and wait for him to come home? Should I shower and freshen up after the day of travel?

I'm not sure, so I check my phone to see if he's sent a messages, but I don't have any. I set it down on the counter next to where I left the key and decide to snoop because that's what you do when someone leaves you unsupervised in their fancy apartment.

The first room on the left is unmistakably Beck's. Blue walls with Yankee pennants and a game ball that looks to be signed on display next to books on a shelf. It's a cute baseball-themed room. I close the door and walk to the next room on the right. The modern designed bathroom has a walk-in shower and a counter that matches the one in the kitchen. It's moodier in design when in a smaller space but still inviting.

Having a feeling Tag's room is the one on the right with a great view, I peek into the last room on the left first. It's not particularly exciting as an office setup with a treadmill. Looks like some junk lines the walls. *Thank God.* I was starting to think he wasn't human.

It's the last room I'm most anticipating. *Where does Tagger Grange lay his head?*

The door is cracked open, so I peek in before pushing it the rest of the way. I home in on the dress lying on the bed with a shopping bag next to it. It's out of place, and a knot of discomfort tightens in my stomach.

The room is brighter than the rest of the house, with lighter beiges and open curtains, a chair in the corner, and a king-sized bed as the showpiece. A darker rug anchors the bed over the hardwoods and leads to nightstands on either side of the mattress, which is covered in a down comforter and four pillows to rest your head. Who needs more than one?

I suppose someone who lives like a prince in a high-rise apartment or someone who is into foursomes. I'm not sure how I feel about either, so I go to personally inspect the dress situation to see what that's about instead.

Pris.

This is my kind of welcome.

I take the note and flip it open. There's an address and a time. Signed, Your Cowboy.

Okay, fine. I'm charmed right out of my underpants. He's so getting laid when we get back tonight.

The dress is pretty, though tighter than what I typically wear other than when I head out to Whiskey's in my good pair of jeans. I hold it to my body and turn to see myself in the mirror on the wall. "The man has excellent taste." Returning it to the bed, I look in the bag to find a shoebox and a tissue-wrapped handbag. "Gorgeous. Gorgeous."

I'm starting to feel like Pretty Woman without the bad stuff that happens. Two hours until I'm supposed to meet him. So mysterious and sexy and romantic. I'm liking this side of him. It's fun.

I pull my suitcase to his room and hop in the shower. It's when I'm drenched with soap running down my body that I start to wonder if he does this for all his women. *Way to ruin it, Chris.*

Refusing to dwell on the stuff that doesn't matter to the timeline our relationship is on, I finish up and get ready.

Thirty minutes to go, and I have no idea how long it will take me to get there. I'm not riding the subway. That's way too complicated to figure out when I'm running late.

Scraping my hands over the emerald-green silk dress, I look in the mirror, noticing how the color brings out the orange strands in my hair. I twirl to check it out on my body from all angles. It's a perfect fit, as if they had my measurements. Though I'm not sure if it's supposed to be this high on the thighs or it's just shorter on me, I give it a little tug from behind to make sure nothing important is showing. And I can appreciate the way my legs look a mile long, especially when I add the strappy black heels.

I send a prayer to Mary Bracelets to keep me from breaking my ankle. The patron saint of accessories has never failed me before.

Running short on time, I transfer my ID, lipstick, the key the doorman gave me, the note with the address, and my phone into the little black clutch. It's perfect for me, something I would have chosen myself. Understated but classic.

After one last glance in the mirror to make sure my makeup is flawless and the little black eyeliner wingtips are sharp at the ends, I tuck a section of hair behind my ears, impressed by how straight I got it. The most delicate curl curves the ends like a professional styled it. Lauralee would be proud of how far I've come with my skills.

If it were to ever work out, tonight is the night I would pick.

I rush downstairs after locking up, and before I can ask the doorman how to get to the address, he says, "Your car is waiting, Ms. Greene."

"My car?"

He laughs, but there's no mocking in it. He leads me to the door and opens it. "Yes, Mr. Grange ordered the car to deliver you to the restaurant."

First clue revealed. We're meeting at a restaurant. I approve of food. I'm starving.

He opens the back door of the Town Car, and when I'm tucked in the back, he taps the hood and then shuts it.

Leaning forward, I say, "Hello."

The driver nods, his eyes catching sight of mine in the rearview mirror. "Good evening."

"Good evening." *Fancy.*

I get the distinct feeling that he's not a conversationalist, so I sit back and watch the city at dusk go by. When the car stops, I check the time. Ten minutes late, but I assume that's to be expected here, considering the traffic.

The driver opens the door and assists me in getting out. Once I'm steady on my heels and standing on the sidewalk, I straighten the skirt of my dress with a little tug in the back and then walk into the crowded restaurant to find my cowboy.

CHAPTER 27

Tagger

HOLY FUCK!

Drop-dead gorgeous!

Makeup like I've never seen her wear makes her eyes look electric in the lighting of this room.

The dress hugs her curves, not only drawing my eyes but having every other asshole staring as well.

Stunning legs that seem to go on forever.

It's only been a couple of weeks since I last saw her, but I can't wait to kiss that plush and pink mouth of hers again. I leave the bar and work my way through the crowd to reach her. She doesn't see me at first, but when she does, her expression lifts as if I'm someone special. I am, if I scored her.

I cup her face, close my eyes, and kiss her. Her arm comes around me as she melts against me. When our lips part, I immediately catch the audience we attracted—the smiles and laughter, the looks of jealousy, and the joy in some people's eyes.

Pris slowly opens her arms and says, "That's quite the welcome."

"I missed you." I lean my head against hers, and whisper, "I missed you more than you'll ever know."

Straightening her shoulders, she looks me in the eyes with some help from those heels she's wearing. "You have all night to tell me about it, stud."

"I'm hoping there's less talking and more action on this trip."

"Glad to know we're on the same page."

My sexy girl is up for a good time in bed, whether that be a mattress or in the back of a truck. I don't know how I got so lucky.

I check in with the host stand to let them know we're here and then take Pris's hand. The man leads us into the next room, where the dining tables are. We're given a booth in the corner after I pulled some strings—not only for the reservation but also for the privacy of one of the corner tables.

After ordering drinks, she slides a little closer. "It's so good to see you."

I rub her bare thigh, so glad to be with her again. I kiss her because I can. "You look beautiful in that dress."

She glances down at the neckline and then at me again. "I don't know how you knew my size, but it's so pretty. Thank you for the shoes, the dress, and the bag. I didn't bring anything like this." Looking around, she adds, "I would have stood out like a sore thumb in this place."

"You would have stood out because you're breathtaking."

"You know you're getting laid, right? I feel like I made myself more than clear with the same-page comment and all that jazz."

Chuckling, I give her leg a gentle squeeze. "I'm not

telling you that to get laid, though I accept, but because you are beautiful. Whether on the ranch or at a restaurant, I can't take my eyes off you."

Her shoulders soften. She leans against me to put her head on my shoulder. Rubbing her hand over the front of my shirt, I have the slightest inkling she's copping a feel of my abs. Whether she's feeling sentimental or gets a good feel of me, I'm into it. I'm into her. So deep.

When she sits up, she plants her elbow on the table and chin on top of a balled-up fist. "Tell me the truth, Grange. Was the dress a setup? Were you trying to test me to see if I would snoop? Because I totally failed. I checked every room, though I didn't go into the closets." She pops upright. "I also used your shower and your expensive-smelling soaps and shampoos, the fluffiest towels to ever touch my body, and I wore the robe hanging in the bathroom while I got ready. A little makeup got on the collar. Hope you don't mind."

I stare at her, processing all that she just confessed. "All I heard is that being there felt like home." I grin, loving that she felt so comfortable to do that.

"It felt like you."

The smile falls, but not because I'm unhappy. I didn't expect to feel so strongly for her this soon into the relationship. It's never happened before to understand my emotions, but she's blindsided me into the deep end of the ocean without so much as a life jacket. I'm sunk when it comes to her and happy to drown in this love.

Love?

Holy shit . . .

While I'm staring into the ethos, figuring when the hell I fell in love—the first time she met Beck, slow dancing with her in the rain, and making love to her in the barn, her comfortable to use my apartment like her own because it feels like me to her— she says, "You look handsome in your suit. I don't think I've seen you all dressed up since prom your senior year."

Looking down, I see a few wrinkles from the day, but otherwise, the suit is holding up. And although I'm still distracted by the fact that I just admitted to myself that I'm in love with Christine Greene, I welcome the change in topic. "I was working late. Sorry I didn't get to greet you."

"So this is what you look like every day?" Her eyes widen, and I notice the pitch of her right brow. "For work?"

"Yes. This is what asset managers wear. A suit is expected in my line of work."

"I imagine this . . ." She swirls a finger in circles in front of me. "Is very distracting to women."

The right side of my mouth quirks up. I nuzzle the tip of my nose behind her ear, taking in the delicate floral perfume she's wearing and the softness of her skin. "You think so?" I place a kiss there and then another just on the underside of her jaw.

"Not cowboy hats and boots with those jeans that are fitted to that nice ass of yours, but I guess some would find this distracting."

I chuckle, sitting up. "What about you, Ms. Greene? I get that this is custom Italian, and you prefer a pair of old Levi's or worn-in Wranglers on me, but do you find me distracting?"

Our drinks are delivered, and we order our food. As soon as we're alone again, she replies, "You have me ready to skip to dessert." She leans so close that our noses touch. "Dessert being you and me in that giant bed of yours."

Fuck me.

The woman gives my lines a run for the money.

She kisses me, then settles back and takes a sip of her

cocktail like she didn't just cause an erection that I'll be fighting for the rest of the night. I scan the room for our server, and ask, "Wonder what's taking the food so long?"

I spend the next ten minutes making small talk in hopes of my boner going down. It takes three changes of topic and landing on the time I ate sea urchin and ended up in the hospital to do the trick.

The food is delivered, and as she cuts into her chicken, she asks, "Will I get to see Beckett while I'm here?"

"He's with his mother this week, so maybe next time."

She takes another bite of food but then sets her fork down again. "This meal is amazing. I'll be too spoiled to return to the ranch after this."

"I'm not seeing the problem." I take a bite of steak and watch a smile appear on her pretty face.

"I'm sure you don't." She takes another sip, finishing off her drink, then sets the napkin down on the leather bench. When she starts to slide out of the booth, she looks back at me. "I'm going to the ladies' room. Be right back," she singsongs.

I watch her walk away, checking out that fine ass of hers as she tugs her skirt down. I can't stop a laugh from escaping. Pris is exactly who she is—not pretending to be less or more and comfortable within her skin. It's so fucking attractive.

I cut another piece of my steak, but right when I take the bite, Baylor slides into the booth. "Imagine two best buds at the same restaurant at the same time. What a coincidence, man." He holds his hand out for me to shake, but the steak gets caught in my throat.

Hacking, I lean forward, more worried about him killing me for dating his sister than dying from choking on a piece of meat. *Wait* . . . that's not the headline I want announcing my death. He whacks my back just as I finally swallow it down. I take a large gulp of water, my gaze traveling to where Pris disappeared before shifting back to him. I clear my throat, and ask, "What the fuck are you doing here?" And now I'm pretending neither of us heard my voice raise two octaves higher than what's natural.

He sits back, spreading his arms wide across the back of the booth like he's settling in for a while. "Good score on the booth. We're stuck near the kitchen, but my date said I'll get laid if I score a reservation at this place."

"Apparently, she didn't know who she was messing with."

"Right?" He takes my glass and sips the bourbon, giving me a chance to look to make sure Pris isn't returning just yet. "That's good. You're spending the big bucks tonight. She must be special. I only caught a glimpse of the bombshell before she slipped behind the curtain to the bathrooms."

"Um." I rub my forehead, having no doubt I'm going to hell for this. Yet I do it anyway and lie, "It's a friend."

"A friend you fuck?"

"What the fuck, Baylor?"

"Sorry," he says, dropping his arms to his sides. "I don't know what's going on in your life because you're always working. Should have chosen personal finance over commercial. You'd get a lot more time off."

My eyes shift from him to the curtain and then to him again. "Listen, I have Beck this coming week. Come over and we'll have a guys' night in and watch the game."

"Yeah, sure." He slips out the booth, seemingly satisfied with the plan.

He's right. I've been avoiding him more and more frequently. The closer I get to Pris, the further I get from him. That's not fair to our friendship. Not wanting to make this all about me, I ask, "You still seeing that girl from the gym?"

"Yeah, that didn't work out." He stands tableside with his back to the curtained-off area that will produce his sister at any moment now. "I had to join a different gym downtown."

"Oh damn, that sucks."

He runs his hand over his head, not afraid to mess up his hair. "It got so bad that I considered a restraining order. Changing gyms was easier. A good lesson in not fucking women over."

"True."

He takes a step back just as she appears across the room. If I died right this moment, that smile on her face just for me would leave me a happy man.

Baylor says, "In the future, remind me not to date where I work out."

"Thought it was a given."

He leans forward, and we finally shake hands. "Yeah, you'd think." He turns east and disappears around the corner just as Pris slides into the booth.

She laughs. "I swear I thought that was Baylor from a distance. That would have caused a ruckus."

"Sure would have." I lean over and kiss her. "All good?"

"All good. There was a short line, so I had to wait." Thank fuck for trendy restaurants and their notorious shortage of bathrooms. Her eyebrows pinch, and she asks, "You okay? You look a little pale."

"Yeah, no." I shake my head, then nod like a lunatic. "I'm good. Happy to see you."

"Aw, I'm happy to see you, too." She glances at my plate. "You're not hungry?"

"No." I set the napkin on the plate. "How about you?"

"I'm already stuffed." Sitting back, she rubs her stomach. "I'm full of gummy bears and had lunch on the plane."

Just what I wanted to hear. "Let's get out of here, then." I catch our server's attention. "Check?"

We needed to get out of there. I was starting to sweat waiting for the check. Pris is convinced I have a touch of food poisoning and is concerned about whether we should stop for something over the counter to settle a sour stomach.

After telling her I'm fine fifty times, she's relieved to see color return to my face. My heart starts to regulate, and by the time we reach the lobby, I'm breathing so much easier.

We say hello to the overnight doorman on the way to the elevator. As soon as that door closes, she's on me—leg hiked up on my thigh, arms around my neck pulling me to her, and her lips crashing into mine.

She only had one cocktail. If this is the result, I can only imagine if she were drunk.

The elevator dings, and the doors open. I don't bother peeling her off me. I just pick her up, the skirt of her dress hiked to reveal her ass, and carry her down the hall. Pinning her back to the wall, I keep kissing her while I struggle to get the key in the lock.

The latch clicks, and I push the door open.

Pris rubs against my cock like I'm a man on fire, and she's the one to put it out. Ironic since she's to blame for starting the fire in the first place. I kick the door closed, then attack her neck, nipping and kissing, sucking and licking, as I carry her down the hall to the bedroom.

"I missed your mouth on me so much." Is that a compliment to the current state of affairs, or is she making a wish? Either way, I'm granting it.

I toss her on the bed and yank my jacket off, dropping it

on the floor. I work on my belt, then start on my pants. "Take off your panties."

"What about the dress?"

"Doesn't matter. I want you too much for us to fuck with the clothes."

She scrunches her nose. "Do you mean fuck with the clothes on, or you want me too much to fuck without taking them off?"

My pants fall to my ankles, and I grin. Not because they dropped, but because she's so fucking cute. "What do you want to do?"

Lifting onto her elbows, she replies, "I like where this was leading. Surprise me."

The levity slowed things down but also put it in perspective. I run my thumb over my bottom lip, looking her up and down, and spying the little cotton panties between her legs. I take a heavy breath, then bend before her to take them off myself. I get a glimpse of the pussy I've missed so fucking much I can already taste her sweet nectar.

Taking them off one foot and then the other, I stand back up. "Move up the bed and turn over."

Emotions filter through her expression before she challenges me with a glare. I don't give in and neither does she. "Take those off," she demands, her eyes dipping to my dick and back up at me to resume the will of power between us.

I take off the boxer briefs. *I was going to anyway.*

She grins like she won, then moves higher before turning over. Pressing her head, her tits, and her torso on the bed, she digs her knees into the mattress, advertising her bare ass in the air. I could come from the sight of her, but there's no way I'm not getting her off first.

I loosen my tie, taking my time to study each angle of my attack. I strip my shirt off and finish getting completely naked. With a plan to execute, I climb on and slip onto my back before sliding between her legs.

She lifts onto her forearms and looks down at me. "What are we doing, Grange?"

"I'm going to enjoy my dessert." I take her hips and pull her pussy to my lips. The first kiss leaves her gasping. The second deepens, and I'm rewarded with a moan. The third has me nipping at that sweet little bud of hers, causing her to buck against my mouth several times.

Grabbing her hips, I hold her down on top of me and start fucking her entrance with my tongue. I can almost taste the peaches that run through our veins at the Pass, the juice that has me licking my lips and going back for more, and when her body tightens and fucks my tongue right back, I fall for her all over again.

She bounces on top of me, her body becoming more erratic as she nears her release. I don't want to slow the momentum, but she needs to be fucked properly. I sit up, flipping her beside me. Her face is flushed, her breathing heavy, her body squirms with need for me. "Tagger," she begs.

"I'll take care of you, babe. Such good care." I tug the straps of her dress down, revealing her tits and those perfect hard nipples to me. I suck one and then the other as her legs rub together beneath me, seeking the relief I denied her earlier.

"Tagger, please."

"Don't worry, my good girl." I place my cock at her entrance, then pin her wrists on either side of her head. "I'm going to fuck you so hard that you'll remember this in every step you take for the next week. Is that what you want?"

"God, yes—"

I thrust inside her. Her mouth opens, and her head

pushes back. A breath is sucked in and then I lean forward to kiss her. I pull back out and thrust back in. The tightness, the embrace, the heaven, the hell, her wet pussy taking me, all of me as I chase my release to catch up.

Her eyes are closed, and her tongue running along the corner of her mouth keeps my rapt attention. When she starts fucking faster and begs me for harder, I oblige, giving her all of my fucking body and soul.

"Yes. Yes. God. Yes," she moans as I dip to kiss her neck and lick across her mouth. She frees a hand to dig her nails into my back. "I'm coming."

The first squeeze of my dick sends me into my own blissful abyss. I sink lower and lower, fuck harder and harder until I hit that one place that has her trembling under me and teases my release out of me.

"Fuck, yes. So good, babe." I'm left a hollow shell of the man I was, my girl taking every part of me she could. I gave it freely. I'll give her anything she could ever dream of.

I only lie on top of her for a few breaths as I catch them and then fall to my back on the bed. Throwing my arm out wide while she's on the other side is paradise. I finally can breathe normally, so I look over at her next to me.

She's smiling and rolls to face me. "I'm really liking New York."

"Now that's what I want to hear."

CHAPTER 28

Christine

I'M in Tagger Grange's bed.

In New York City.

On a secret trip that only we know about.

Oh, how I wish I could text Lauralee. She'd be dying inside with me right now.

Would he kill me if I took a picture?

He's just so freaking handsome, even sleeping. It would just be a little keepsake for me to have once I leave.

Although I could stare at him all day, as I have for the past approximately fifty-three minutes, my heart has become his in the short time we've been together. That can't be captured in a photograph. So I don't reach for my phone because it also might be interpreted as creepy. I don't want to freak him out, especially since I once casually mentioned ways to murder him in his sleep.

I blink a few times, thinking I should probably get more rest. I sound absurd, even to myself. I close my eyes, but I already know it will be futile. Sleeping in isn't typically something I get to do too often. My body is trained to wake before the roosters. I wonder if there are any roosters in this city. Hidden in a penthouse somewhere or a pied-à-terre in Brooklyn? What is a pied-à-terre anyway? I heard it on *House Hunters* recently, and it's been lodged in my brain ever since.

Do they make rooster clocks? I bet Tagger would like one. It would remind him of home and maybe even of me. Yeah, I can't sleep with my thoughts bouncing off the walls of my brain.

It's been nice to stare at him, but I need something to occupy my brain.

Very slowly, I reach over to the nightstand and grab the remote. Praying the volume isn't going to blast the room, I click it on, ready to watch a cooking show. Or a murder documentary because duh. Whatever will tickle my fancy this morning. I can do as I please. I'm on vacation, after all. In Tagger's perfect-fit-for-me-and-him bed.

I stare at the TV, but the screen is still solid black. And then the blinds start sliding up the windows . . . *Crap!* I sit straight up, aiming the remote at the three windows and punching buttons, desperate to make them stop and, even better, close.

The remote is swiped from my hand. Tagger pushes one button, and the blinds begin lowering to the sill again.

Blinding light is a terrible way to wake up when you're not ready. I feel awful. "I'm sorry," I say just barely above a whisper.

"It's okay." Grabbing me by the middle, he pulls me into his arms. "I'm just not ready to get out of bed yet. Not when I have you here with me." He kisses my head. His patience and sweet words, and the way he makes me feel like his queen make me fall even more for him. Though I'm already head over heels for the man.

I snuggle in with him spooning me from behind and close my eyes. That's when I realize there's no rush to hide and no sneaking around when we're here. It's a short trip, but we can spend the time however we want. Right now, his arms are a good place to start.

He kisses the back of my bare shoulder. "This feels right. You feel right, babe."

I'm not a crier. I had to learn to be tougher than any boy out on the ranch to avoid mistreatment, to hide my softer side to earn respect, and move on after my mom's death like it didn't hurt me. It destroyed me inside, but I held my chin high like she taught me and carried on doing what needed to get done.

Here, cuddled in Tagger's warmth, I can be soft and vulnerable. I can cry because tears are for joy as much as they are for pain.

He presses his lips to my skin again, then takes a breath. "Are you okay?"

"More than okay. Happy." I turn to look into his eyes, wanting to see the sage the morning brings before the jewel tone comes out in the sunshine. Touching his cheek, I reply, "I'm so happy with you."

Lifting, he kisses my head, then rolls on top of me, anchoring his knees between my legs and spreading them. With our eyes locked together, I open myself up to him, and he pushes inside me. I lift to wrap my legs around his middle as he slowly moves in and out, deliberately easing in before teasing me by slowly pulling back.

The fullness is there, and so is the feeling that I'll be left empty without him when we're done. I hate it, but I love this so much more. His eyes study me like he's memorizing everything that makes me tick. It's not only making love, it's the physical art of learning about each other.

I take a breath, briefly closing my eyes, and feel—experience instead of thinking so much.

He leans down and kisses me, our tongues dancing just as slowly as our bodies. The sensation deep in my belly always blooms too soon, the spark of electricity picking up speed as it travels my veins and pushes me closer to finishing. It's all I want, yet it's all I want to delay as well.

This is what I want for the rest of my life—this beautifully torturous purgatory—staring into eyes that reflect love back into mine, the gradual build, my desire taking on a life of its own, his hard length, unbending and driving into me over and over again. It's too much all at once and never enough.

I will never get enough of him.

When Tagger shifts, he hits deeper, forcing me to breathe through the pain to reach the pleasure. He already knows what I need before I crave it. Wrapping my arms around him tighter, I hold on while he picks up speed, taking every thrust and pummel, tease and withdrawal, and then beg him for more. "Please don't stop. Please."

This feels too good.

He feels too much.

But I don't want this to end, not ever. This physical connection gets under my skin and reaches into my heart, binding us together in pure bliss. *Happiness.*

"So good," I purr, still holding on to him as if he can save me. "Oh God. Yes. Tagger."

And when the spring uncoils, my breath is stolen by a kiss. As he swallows my moans, his body feels everywhere and all at once. A hand on my hip and another between my legs coax me to the edge. But it's the brush of legs against mine, that divot in the sides of his ass, and his hard shoulders that have me feeling both turned on and protected at the same time.

I love our size difference. I don't have to be strong with him, emotionally or physically. He'll take care of all my needs. He's already proven to be a man I can depend on—in and out of the bedroom.

My mind, body, and soul embrace this feeling, all of them. *Wholly.*

This is love in its purest form.

My head spins from the emotional strings attached to this man, my body spiraling toward a sensual end . . . *and then darkness comes too fast and shrouds my thoughts.* I sink into the mattress, lying still other than the rise and lowering of my chest. I just want to feel, to live here in this moment for a bit longer.

When I exhale, my breathing evens with his as he moves to my side and kisses my shoulder, back to how it all began. "I'm so in—" He stops himself, and the heaviness of the exhale has me turning to look at him. With his eyes still closed, he rubs his fingers across his forehead. A deal gone wrong. His puppy was stolen. Got a late notice from the electric company? Those reasons seem more fitting for his reaction than the aftermath of having sex with me.

"You're so *in what*?"

His eyes are closed, his troubles clenching them shut. He finally opens them to see me watching him. "Nothing, babe. I'm just tired."

I keep staring at him until I realize he's not going to say more. If he wanted to tell me, he would. "I'm going to the bathroom," I announce as if I must. Flipping the covers back, I climb out to slink into the en suite. I use the toilet, then wash my hands while catching a glimpse of my appearance in the mirror.

My skin looks washed out and in need of reviving. I'm used to the humidity and heat of Texas. It feels slightly drier here. It's kind of BS that I'm not all glowy after having the best sex of my life with the man of my dreams multiple times over the past twelve hours, and the day has barely gotten started.

When I turn, my muscles ache between my legs. *No surprise.* He's discovering new unchartered territory every time he goes exploring. Cracking the door open, I poke my head out. "Do you mind if I take a bath?"

He peeks his eyes open. "You don't have to ask."

I smile, though it feels more fake than genuine, and I don't know why. "Thanks." I close the door and run the water. After twisting my hair up, I take the soap from the shower because I like the smell. It's not feminine or masculine. It's just clean and fresh. Perks of being in a building—instant hot water. I wait forever for it to heat up at home. I'm going to be so spoiled I won't be able to stand myself after this trip.

I pour the liquid shower wash under the running water, letting it bubble in the bath before I dip one foot and then the other. As soon as the water touches my inner thighs, I flinch, holding myself by the sides of the tub until I get used to it. I slowly lower my body under the water and lean my head back against the porcelain.

Running my hand over my body, I take careful inventory of each muscle that aches. I shouldn't be so happy about something like pain, but I do find myself amused with the soreness I'm discovering, and I wouldn't trade the activities that created the issue for anything.

A light knock on the door has me look over my shoulder.

"Come in." When Tagger enters, I smile at the sight of him. Sleep still shapes his expression; his eyelids hang a bit lower and broodier, his lips freshly licked, which I get to enjoy at the tail end, and his hair a reckless mess on top of his head. It's grown out a little since I last saw him. It's not so tamed these days. I approve of this look on him. Very much. "It's your apartment, you know?"

"I didn't want to intrude if you wanted time alone." Dressed in boxer briefs, he sits on the floor next to me.

I rest my arm over the side of the tub. He takes it as the offering it's meant to be and holds my hand between both of his. "I can ride a horse all day long, and nothing is tender. I ride a cowboy, and I'm sore for days. Make it make sense."

"I think we're using different muscles."

"I think you're right." I roll to the side, resting my arm on the edge of the tub to pillow my chin as a heaviness comes over me. Exhaustion? The lying to everyone back home weighing on me? *Or . . .*

He runs his hand over my neck to my shoulder and massages. It feels so good that I close my eyes, enjoying the distraction from the aches and pains, but it doesn't clear my head. "How are you feeling, babe?" His voice is lower, befitting the early morning hour.

He calls me babe like it's my name. And I gobble it right up every time, savoring the sound of it for when I'm not here.

"Everything is picture-perfect, and that's not how life works. I'm on top of the world, but the clouds still threaten." I glance away, searching for clarity on how to explain it. I'm not sure I find it, but I'll still try. "I'm treating this like a vacation, and you're acting like this is our home." I look at him, hoping I don't hurt his feelings. He's a tough guy, but words can sting sometimes, even if unintentional. "It's confusing.

I'm wearing silky dresses and high heels, eating at fancy restaurants, and acting like this is normal for me because I want to fit into your world so badly."

"You already do," he says, grazing the tips of his fingers over my cheek. "You don't need to change for anyone, especially not for me. I love you, Christine."

CHAPTER 29

Christine

"WHY DID YOU SAY THAT?" I ask, sitting upright and staring at him.

"I love you? Because I do." Tagger is unshakable and not a regret is heard.

My emotions are twisted. I'm not sure what to think about this. "No. The Christine part."

He chuckles. "So let me get this straight," he says. "I tell you I love you for the first time, but that's overshadowed because I used your real name?"

"Yes. It's Pris. That's who I am with you."

With a gentle smile creasing his cheeks, he kneels beside the tub and leans over to cup my face. A kiss to the head is followed by one placed gently beside my eye, then he kisses my cheek and ends the tour on my lips. This one lingers as I lean my head against his. He says, "I love you, Pris. I'm so in love with you."

Words I never believed I'd hear are said with such

fervency that I have no doubt they're real. Cupping his neck and sliding over the scruff of his face, I pull back to see his eyes so brilliantly alive with color and honesty. "I love you, too, Tagger. So much it hurts."

"I'll be gentler then."

I smile. "No, don't change a thing." I kiss him and then sink back into the water to soak in his love, which I'm bathing in. "I love who we are together."

"Me too." He breathes a sigh of relief as he gets to his feet. "Hungry?"

"Famished."

"I'll take you out to breakfast. No rush, though. We'll leave when you're ready." Walking to the door, he says, "I'll shower in the other bathroom so you can have some privacy."

"I don't need privacy from you, babe. I mean," I say, wobbling my head back and forth, "you've kind of seen everything. Well, not everything, but you've been inside me, so I think it's okay if you see me putting on makeup or doing my hair, drying, and whatever else I'd get up to in here."

"I love listening to how your mind works," he says. "You talked me into showering here."

"Not going to lie." I start cleaning my body, wanting food sooner than later. "It was for purely selfish reasons."

"I'm good with that." He strips off his boxers, freeing his dick from the confines. I'm pretty certain his body part shouldn't be that attractive. It doesn't surprise me since it's him.

Just over an hour later, I'm wearing one of my favorite sundresses and a pair of sandals while walking the streets of New York holding hands with my boyfriend on a beautiful Saturday morning. It's early, but restaurants overflow with the brunch crowds, and the lines to get a table already extend longer than we're willing to wait.

"How about we go to the deli and eat in the park?"

"I think that would be better than any crowded restaurant."

We stop for coffee and pick up bagels, muffins, and some fruit before entering a smaller park surrounded by skyscrapers.

He walks down a path to an empty bench. "Is this good?"

As I look around the park, the leaves are blowing in the wind and the grass appears recently cut and softer than the St. Augustine a lot of us have in our yards. "We could sit in the grass?"

"I didn't bring a blanket. The grass could stain your dress."

I look down, wondering if I'm willing to sacrifice another dress to nature. I glance once more at the park bench. I'd rather be in the grass than sitting away from it. "I'll be careful."

"My lap is also available." He scans the area. "There's a spot over here," he says, signaling to a patch with no one else around. He sets the bag of food down, then offers me a hand.

Although I had one short-lived ballet class on my preschool résumé, I didn't remain graceful and sit down without regard for etiquette. While we dig in, I ask, "What do you do in your free time?"

"Every other week, when I don't have Beck, I play basketball on Thursday with your brother at some courts near our buildings. He lives five blocks from me."

My brother . . . I don't know what to think about him. Some days, I feel abandoned. Others, I'm relieved I get the final say with Dad instead of having to run it by a committee. But I know what the issue really is. "I miss him."

Tagger sets his bagel down and lifts me onto his lap. Hugging me, he says, "I'm sorry. Maybe we should stop by and see him while you're here?"

I lean back. "And blow our cover by telling him I'm here to see my boyfriend? How do you think it will go over?"

His chest deflates from a heavy breath. "Not well." His gaze lengthens in the distance. "We can't be a secret forever."

"You already want to blow our cover? You're the worst secret keeper that ever existed, Grange." I giggle because, being honest with myself, I'm not opposed to the idea. But damn, we're weak. *For each other.*

Chuckling, he says, "I have no interest in hiding you away from the world." The laughter disappears quickly, though the way he looks at me like I'm solid gold—or in his industry, my stock just took off—has me cuddling to him. "I want to show you off to everyone, Pris, and I know when they meet you, they'll know exactly why I fell in love with you."

My gulp is embarrassingly loud as I squeeze him tighter. The floodgates of his heart have opened, and now his emotions are on full display. I know the feeling. "We need to decide whether this is the way to continue for now or if we want to face the consequences to be together openly."

"It's wild that we have consequences to handle because we fell in love."

"Really only one . . ." I let that float around in the fresh air, curious if he'll take the bait.

His lips twitch to restrain the corners I can see want to go up. He could have scrutinized me for setting him up, but I think he's onto my wily ways. "I see what you're doing, but you don't have to. I agree that I need to talk to your brother soon." He kisses me. "Remember this kiss, though. It may be the last one you ever get from me since he's going to kill me as soon as I mention your name."

My thoughts are still ticking through options. "If that's the case, maybe you tell him with me around. I can protect you."

He laughs. "I have no doubt, but I think you need to be reconnecting with him without this baggage around."

"There's no rush. Let's think about it." I slip off his lap and lie on the grass with my arms spread. "Because right now, I don't want to think about anything but us staring up at this stunning blue sky and the clouds." I point. "That looks like a cactus."

He lies beside me with our heads bumped together. "I can see that. What about that one?"

Out of the corner of my eye, I see the smile that makes me happiest—the carefree cowboy he is when he's home on the ranch. "I'm thinking of a pagoda."

"That's a good one." His hand finds mine, and our fingers weave together.

"I've lost hours to this game growing up. It was a big ranch with not a lot of people my age to play with." I glance over at him. "Lauralee was my saving grace."

"Let me be that for you now."

The words momentarily stun me, and my stomach squeezes. "What makes you think I need saving?"

"I don't think you do, but I do think you need someone to lean on more than you admit." The sincerity in his eyes captivates me. "It's okay not to be strong all the time, so let me be there for you when you need to rest."

My heartbeats pick up their pace, and tears fill my eyes. I shouldn't be as affected by the sentiment as I am, but it feels like I finally have a place to rest my head. I don't need expensive dinners or beautiful clothes I'll only wear once. This right here—Tagger. He's all I need to be happy.

We spend the rest of the day not doing much of anything. We stroll, do a little window-shopping, and daydream of when we can see each other next. Sitting on the couch with Thai takeout and a movie that happens to be on the TV that neither of us is much interested in, I say, "Come back for the Peach Festival and Rodeo."

"When is it?" He sets his plate on the coffee table and drinks from a bottle of beer.

I laugh, marveling that someone could forget details ingrained in us Peachtree Passers our whole lives. "Second weekend in June when the peach season is in full swing."

He grins as if the memory returns. "Peach season." Setting his eyes back on me, he says, "I miss the simplicity of being excited about fruit ripening in summer."

"Us hokeys live for it—"

"That's not what I was going to say or mean. You know me better than that." He has a point. I've never heard him mock where he came from.

I drop my defenses and lay down my fork. "I shouldn't have snapped at you. I'm sure you remember how some tourists looked down on us."

"I don't think they were looking down on us. I think they were envious that life could be that down-to-earth. I think most people want that in their lives more than we know." He glances out the windows to dots of lights outside his window instead of stars. "Maybe not New Yorkers."

I laugh, loving how down-to-earth it is to be with him, even in the city that never sleeps.

The more I sleep in this bed, the more I never want to leave it. I roll over and hug it the best I can. "I'm going to miss you."

He wraps himself around my back. "Did you just tell my bed you're going to miss it?"

"I did," I reply, feeling a little self-conscious about being busted. But what I wouldn't give to have this bed in my room on the ranch. Or even better, my own place altogether. With Tagger there with me. That would be heaven on earth.

"Will you miss me or the bed more?"

"Tough call. Let me get back to you." I giggle and turn in his arms. With the morning barely peeking in, I cup his face and kiss him. "You. Always you."

He pushes up on his forearm. "Hate being the bearer of bad news, but you have just about two hours until you need to leave for the airport."

I pout, sticking my bottom lip out. "This weekend flew by too fast."

"We have the festival to look forward to. Beck is going to love it."

Tapping his nose, I ask, "And you?"

Popping his lip out from under his top teeth, he smirks. "I'm going to love it so hard that it's going to reawaken all those aches that have started to fade."

Oh my! "I like the sound of this very much."

"Get the barn ready for us."

"It will be ready, alright."

To my dismay, he gets out of bed and clicks the remote to open the blinds. "I'll go grab coffee and muffins for us and let you pack." Pulling on his jeans, he adds, "I'll ride with you to the airport."

"That could be two hours round trip." Sitting up, I add, "It's not necessary. You can spend that time with Beck since you pick him up today."

He's watching me as he pulls on a T-shirt. It's not the same style of jeans or shirt he'd wear back in Texas, but he looks good. "You sure? This isn't something we need to decide right now."

"No, it's fine. You can plan your day."

Coming around the bed, he leans over it to kiss me. "I'll be back soon."

Flopping back on the mattress, I grin. "I'll be here waiting."

"You don't know how much I fucking love that." He gives me a wink before disappearing down the hall. I hear the door open and then close, the sound reaching all the way down the hall.

I reluctantly get up and steal one of Tagger's Michigan State college shirts. Slipping it over my head, it drapes down to my mid-thighs. It's soft, and the faintest scent of him is embedded in the fabric. I take a deep inhale.

Then I get to business and refold my clothes and organize my suitcase before laying the dress on top of it. I'm not sure how to travel with it, so I wonder if I should leave it here for when I visit. Where would I wear it there anyway?

Basically done, I spread-eagle over the top of this glorious bed to take advantage of it while I can.

The sound of the door opening and then the louder closing of it makes me smile. "In the bedroom," I call out, thinking coffee and muffins in bed sounds divine.

"Hello." Startled by the feminine voice, I pop my head

off the pillow to find a woman standing in the doorway. "Shouldn't you be cleaning?"

"What?" I sit up and watch her eyes dip to my chest. *The shirt.* I don't feel like I'm in danger and could probably take her if I had to if she doesn't have a weapon. "I'm a guest—"

"Of Tagger's." Disappointment coats her throat, and she looks toward the windows letting the sunshine in. "I thought you were the cleaning crew."

"No." I push up, dipping my legs under the covers as if they'll protect me and hold them to my chest. "I'm his girlfriend. You?" Please don't say his girlfriend, too. It's not like I think he'd ever do that to me in a million years, but I've seen enough movies that play out like that with pilots having families in different cities and— "Who are you?"

"I'm the mother of Tagger's son," she replies like she's birthed the heir to the throne. I guess she did, technically. It's not a title that can ever be taken away. I exhale a breath, somehow relieved she's not breaking in and defeated that I had to meet Anna this way—a bird's nest for hair, no makeup to hide my freckle-covered face and dark circles, and naked under this Spartans shirt.

I'm not sure what I'm supposed to say. "Beckett is an incredible kid."

She crosses her arms over her chest, looking horrified, judging by the lines she's trying so hard to form between her brows on her already tight face. "How do you know my son?"

"Um . . ." I have a strong suspicion that I just screwed up. Do I lie to her? It would be easy to get to the truth. All she would have to do is ask Beck or Tagger, for that matter. Go with the truth. It's always best. "He came to the ranch when Tagger and he were visiting Peachtree Pass."

The sneer vanishes instantly, and she laughs. "You're from his hometown in Texas?"

"Yes. We've known each other a long time."

"Tagger has a girlfriend from his hometown in Texas?" she asks, but it's not really sounding like she wants an answer, especially since she already got it. Her gaze goes to my suitcase, and then returns to me. "What is your name?"

"Christine."

"Christine." She stares at me as if it's the first time she's heard it. Not exactly an original name but it's not as sour as she makes it sound. "Miss Christine."

It was at that moment I realized I'm a dead woman walking in her eyes. "Beck calls me Miss Christine."

"I know he does. He's mentioned you before." Her arms lower to her sides, and she says, "I had an image of some sweet little old lady who was baking pies and feeding her pigs the leftover scraps from dinner."

"Well, I'm not old, but the other part isn't so foreign. Beck fed the horses—"

I go silent when her palm flies up. "The name fits where you're from."

My head juts back on my neck. "Did you just insult me?"

"Is it an insult to reference your town?" Dumb is the last thing I believe Anna is, though she's feigning it.

I lower the covers, the fear long gone. "I'm proud of where I'm from."

"It's so cute. Tagger used to say the same thing until he realized how it made him look like a foolish cowboy to everyone."

"Only assholes," I bite back. She laughs, though I don't.

Nodding, she says, "I can't even argue because it's probably true." She points at the dress lying across my suitcase. "It's really brave of you to wear a piece from three seasons ago. I could never do it, but it suits you." She turns and starts down the hall. "I stopped by for Beckett's navy-blue cardigan. We have lunch down at the pier with friends."

I sit there, more astounded than upset. I don't give a crap what she says about that pretty dress, and who cares how she feels about my name. But the jab about the Pass pisses me off. I get out of bed and wait in the room, debating if I'd love for Tagger to walk in to defend me or hoping he's never the wiser she was here.

None the wiser wouldn't ruin our final hour together. So I hope he doesn't run into her.

When I hear the door close, I tiptoe into the hallway and down to the living room. She's gone, but the damage of her presence still lingers, like her perfume. It's not strong and actually smells really good. *Damn her.*

I get my jeans on and put on a bra under the shirt I'm stealing. When I slip a sweater over my arms, I don't bother buttoning it up. That's when I hear the door open. "Hey babe, sorry. The fucking crowds of this city are relentless."

"It's okay." I come to the kitchen, where he's laid out what he's hunted and gathered for me. Sliding my fingers into the hair at the back of his head, I kiss him—long and deep and filled with the passion he's shown me all weekend. When I pull back, I lick the corners of my lips, and say, "I'm going to miss you so much."

Am I marking my territory? *Maybe.*

Am I making sure he knows exactly what he'll be missing? *Absolutely.*

His arms come around my waist, and he's so handsome when he grins that I consider changing my flight so I never leave his arms again. "Nice shirt."

"You like it?"

"So fucking sexy, babe."

We kiss once more, but this time when our lips separate, the inevitable sinks in. I'm leaving, and he's staying. "We have the Peach Festival to look forward to."

"Three weeks. That's all." Caressing my face, he wipes under my eyes with his thumb, catching the sadness before it falls. "It will fly by. I promise."

Light laughter escapes me. "I hear you're not the best at keeping promises."

"I've broken one promise," he exclaims through laughter. "One." Kissing my head, he then hands me a blueberry muffin. "And it was worth it."

The winds were with my flight, so we landed early. *Thankfully.*

I'm so ready to be out of my head thinking about that encounter with Anna. I'm not sure how I feel—both irritated and small. I hate that I allowed someone to affect me that way. I had no clever comeback, but that wouldn't have been the right thing to do. Starting a war with her will never end for me when they share a son. And I care about Beckett and his well-being enough to tolerate a little insult.

I'm still conflicted about whether I did the right thing by not mentioning it to Tagger. Everything comes out in the wash, they say. Do I want to control the narrative by pleading my case first, or is staying silent the right thing to do? I don't know. It's given me a lot to think about, though.

The earlier arrival time allows me to stop by Peaches before they close on my way home. I swing the door open, and sing, "I'm baaaack."

Lauralee comes from the kitchen and greets me with a huge smile on her face. "Hey, you. How was the conference?" I meet her at the counter, and we stretch over it to hug.

"What conference?" *Oh crap!* It dawns on me too late. This is why I should never lie.

"The Farmers of Central Texas conference you just attended all weekend in Dallas."

A humorless laugh rattles my throat. "Oh, that. *Right.* It was a convention, not a conference." I inwardly roll my eyes at how ridiculous that sounds.

Grimacing, she says, "I didn't know there was a difference."

"Oh yeah." I try to leave it at that and add, "The place looks good."

"What's the difference?"

I reach for a cup and head for the fountain machine. "One serves coffee. Was it busy this weekend with the peaches starting to ripen?"

She replies, "It's picking up."

Coming to the counter, I dig a bill out of my wallet, thinking it's in my best interest to hightail it home because I know I'll fail a Lauralee Knot interrogation. "Keep the change," I say, already heading for the door.

"It's a twenty."

Oops. I wave it off like I'm Ms. Moneypants, then shoulder the door open. "Keep it. See you soon."

Really not wanting a repeat of what happened at Peaches, I'm more careful and have the story straight by the time I reach the ranch. I open the door and drag in my suitcase. Seeing the back of his head in the living room, I say, "Hi, Dad, I'm home."

He gets up from his recliner and comes to give me a big

hug. “Christine, how is my daughter?”

“I’m good. How about you? Have you had dinner?”

“I’ve eaten and saved you a plate.” He moves into the kitchen and pulls a plate out of the oven. “I kept it warm for you.”

Even a liar like me would change their ways over that kindness. “Thanks, Dad.”

“How was the conference?”

I sigh, knowing I can’t keep this up for long. “Enlightening.”

CHAPTER 30

Tagger

THE AIR in the apartment has changed. It's stagnant, losing the life it carried when Pris was here. I miss her. *Plain and simple.*

She made the bed, but I lie on it, messing it up all over again by bunching the covers with the pillow she slept on and burying my face to smell if her scent remains. It does. The sweetest cotton candy and the lightest of florals. *That's my girl.*

I roll over onto the remote and grin as I pull it out from under my back. It's still funny that she mistakenly thought it was the TV remote. Not so much being blinded by the morning light, though. I find so many little things about her fucking adorable, so this one gets added to the list.

Setting it on the nightstand, I get up, ready to go pick up Beckett from his mom's. We have a little daylight left to go to the park if he's up for it. When is he not? I don't think he gets there much during his weeks with Anna, so we make up for it when he's with me. Of course, he could be playing us both. I wouldn't put it past him. He's a lot like his dad was around that same age.

A great weekend with my girlfriend has me grinning as I lock up the apartment. It's only made better that it leads into time with my son this week. I'm winning in this game of life.

The car pulls up in front of Anna's place. "Thanks." I get out and take the steps by two before ringing the doorbell. The heavy wooden door swings open like it's light as air, the breeze floating against my ex's hair and gusting the loose dress behind her. In a flurry, Anna waves me in. "Come in. Come in. We're running behind." She leans against the railing with one foot in the air behind her, and calls upstairs, "Beckett, your dad is here."

She shuts the door behind me, then returns to the stairs to rest her hands on the top of the spindle. Smiling like we're old friends is the dead giveaway that she's up to something.

"What?" I ask, smart enough to learn from past mistakes. We may have settled the custody battle, but that doesn't make us best friends.

"What?" she retorts, genuinely perplexed by the confusion written in her features. "I'm just being social. Can't I be friendly without an accusation accompanying it?"

Not judging by our history, but maybe she's changed. She huffs in annoyance. "I wanted to share that I got offered a promotion."

Although this is none of my business, I know she works hard. It's paid off in her success. "Congratulations. I'm sure it's well-deserved."

"In Paris."

My heart halts in my chest. My breathing stalls in my throat. I don't respond quick enough for her, so she adds,

"Marcel thinks this is it. If I don't take it, I'll never be offered another."

Staring at her, I cinch my brow together. "Who's Marcel?"

"The gentleman I've been seeing." Her expression portrays calm, but I can see her searching my eyes for a reaction. "It's . . ." She looks at the floor between us as if the words are there before her eyes return to me. "Serious."

Serious? Her dating life is of no interest to me. Her boyfriends being involved in our son's life is, though. "Beckett hasn't mentioned him."

"He hasn't met him," she replies casually.

"How is it serious if your son hasn't met him?"

She takes a breath and glances up the stairs. "I didn't know it was serious, and then it was."

The puzzle pieces come together. "So this Marcel is French?"

"He is and lives in Paris, where the company is headquartered."

"So this promotion—"

"Came without his influence though I know that's what you thought. He does make the offer more intriguing. And the money would be hard to turn down." She toes the floor with her flat dress shoe. I've never seen her . . . *softer*.

But my chest tightens when it becomes clear what she's really saying. "You want to take Beck to live in Paris?"

"I don't know what I want. It's all happening very quickly, but they've given me time to think about it."

"This isn't a decision you make alone."

"I'm well aware of that, so I'll keep you updated on how things progress or don't." She's allowed to have job offers, promotions, hell, to even move if she wants. But locally, where I can still see my son per our agreement. "Things are so complicated. I'm sure nothing will come of it."

"Something to drink?" She turns to weave through the living room of the brownstone and into the back where the kitchen is located.

"No. Thanks." He's taking too long, so I glance up the stairs. "Hey, Beck? Come on, buddy."

She returns with two glasses of cold water and hands one to me. "Do you have any plans for the week?" she asks like we didn't just have a conversation that might rip my kid away from me, making small talk like we do it all the time. Beck is supposed to be ready so we don't have to speak at all.

"No big plans. The park today—"

"Keep him off the merry-go-round." The park always sets her off. It's like she never had fun as a kid. "Remember how he almost fractured his elbow."

"I remember how he *didn't* fracture his elbow." She hates being challenged, but a chance of breaking a bone is not the same as breaking a bone. I don't want him living secured in bubble wrap. I let him play but am right there to keep him safe when needed.

"Funny," she replies, not laughing at all and smoothing her hair along the side of her head. "It was a close call." She sips her water like she has the final say.

For me, it's not worth the argument.

Eyeing the glass in my hand, she asks, "You're not drinking? Don't trust me not to poison you?" She laughs again.

What is it with women always talking about ways to kill me? "It wasn't something I was worried about until now." I'm still not going to drink it. Pretending that hanging out is normal is outside the boundaries that I'd like to keep in place. "Hey, Beck? Hurry up."

"I don't know what he's doing up there. Probably playing

with those plastic horses he wanted. Anyway, why are you so moody?"

"You got him horses?" Finally, something worth talking about.

"Yes. I said he could pick out a toy at the store last week, and he chose a set of two horses." She's sipping her water like she's been stuck in the desert for days. I'm starting to wonder if she's nervous or needs to see a doctor. One thing I don't like is when she acts out of character. That means there's more going on that I know will affect me. "He named them Bluebelly and Skyward. What strange names." *Another sip.* "Don't you think, Tagger?"

Oh shit . . . It was a trap, and I fell right into it.

My throat thickens. I don't want to reignite a battle. "I think they're perfectly fine for horses."

She sighs and rolls her eyes like that was not the answer she was looking for. But there was never pleasing her anyway, so I gave up that notion a long time ago. "Let's not do this. Part of the deal we made was that our son wouldn't be exposed to any lasciviousness."

I balk. "What the hell are you talking about, Anna?" Glancing up the stairs, it pisses me off that I let her get to me. I lower my voice to whisper, "What lasciviousness has he been exposed to?"

"Miss Christine is someone you're having sex with?"

I swear to fucking hell and back, my eyes practically bug out from my skull. My heart starts racing like I'm in trouble with the principal for fucking his wife. I just really hope this isn't something Beckett told her, or he and I are going to need to have a heart-to-heart. "What are you talking about?"

"I thought it was some gray-haired lady out in that godforsaken town you're from. Only to find out she's younger than I am and pretty." She'll have to spell it out because I'm not leading her down this path. She glances up the stairs and deems the coast clear enough to lean in and whisper, "I found her in your bed."

Fuck.

What I have with Pris is none of Anna's business. "When would you have found her in my bed?"

"So you're not denying it?"

I balk again, too astonished to control it, but I need to regulate my reactions. She loves to get a rise out of me. Keeping my voice low, I reply, "Not sure if you don't understand how this works, but we're not together. That means I don't have to confirm or deny anything to you. Just like you don't owe me any explanation about Marcel or any part of your life outside of what concerns our son." *Fuck me, what's taking so long.* "Beckett?" I shout.

Anna moves to the door and opens it, signaling me to step outside. I follow her but leave the door cracked. As soon as we're outside, she crosses her arms over her chest like she still believes she has a say in the matter. "She's rustic at best. Simply put, she's pedestrian, and I don't think she's the kind of woman who should be around my son."

"*Our* son." My blood boils. I step down a couple of steps, needing air to cool me down. "She's not fucking French, but she has a heart of gold, so don't you dare—"

"Our son needs to be surrounded by people who lift him in society and give him the connections to elevate his opportunities—"

I start laughing because what the fuck am I listening to right now.

"It's not funny, Tagger."

"Well, it's a good fucking thing he's not dating her, then. But I am, so I'm going to warn you, Anna. You don't say another fucking thing about her, or you'll need to lawyer up again. Sounds like we're heading in that direction anyway if you take that promotion."

"Don't turn this into something it's not."

I'm not getting caught in her games. I turn my back to her and take a deep breath. And then another. When I turn around, I exhale long and slow. "How did you get into my apartment?" It dawns on me a second too late. "The key for Beck." *Fuck.* "It's for him, not you. You are not allowed to enter my apartment without him with you, or I'll have security lock you out completely. You understand?"

The door finally opens, and my son barrels out into my arms. "Daddy!"

I pick him up and hug him tightly. Over his shoulder, my eyes are still on his mother. "It's good to see you, buddy." I keep him anchored on my side with his little backpack on his shoulders and a toy horse in each hand.

"Look what I got. Just like Bluebelly and Skyward."

Seeing him so happy is contagious despite what happened between Anna and me. This is what matters. *Our son.* "So cool. Can't wait to play with you." I set him down and scoot him toward Anna. "Give your mom a hug goodbye."

Her demeanor mollifies, and she kneels to hug him. Kissing him on the side of the head, she says, "I love you. See you next Sunday."

"Love you, too. See you soon."

He trots down the steps, neighing. *I'm sure she loves that . . .* Marcel doesn't stand a chance against the roots anchoring Beck to Texas. I follow him, but I stop when she says, "Thank you for doing that."

I give her half a nod and walk away from her, scooping Beck onto my back. "Guess what?" I ask, peering over my shoulder at him.

His smile changes my entire mood. "What?"

"We're going to the Peach Festival and Rodeo in Texas during our next visit." I look back once to catch Anna rolling her eyes, then turning to go inside the brownstone. "And there's this event that little kids can participate in called Mutton Bustin'."

"What's mutton busting, Daddy?"

I grin because he's going to love this. "It's an event I won when I was seven."

"But I'm only six."

"Eh, you're a Grange." I turn the corner to head to Central Park. "You'll do great."

"Yeah, I'm a Grange," he states matter-of-factly. "Just like you."

"Just like me, buddy."

That kid wore me out. We were both in bed by eight o'clock. I also have big intentions of running on the treadmill at five in the morning to get back on track. Gotta stay fit for Pris since I realized she has a slight obsession with my abs.

I keep my promise.

After getting Beck ready for school and feeding him, we head out. It's a quick drop-off because he loves going there. He has friends and great teachers, and according to him, they don't give much homework, which is the biggest selling point. I don't blame him. I went to school for the social aspect. I was just lucky enough to have some natural intelligence since I never cracked a book in high school and skills on the field to get me recruited on a full ride to be able to go to college.

Just before lunch at my desk is over, I get a text from Pris.

I'll never look at the barn the same.

I text:

Wait until you see what I can do to you in a peach orchard.

Three dots roll across the screen and then disappear. I'll assume I've left her speechless, in a good way, and probably turned on since my girl likes getting it on with me.

A text appears:

Peach juice just ran down my chin and hit the rounds of my breasts. See?

A photo appears of her cleavage with a shiny trail of juice vanishing between her tits. *Fuck me.* I'll be jerking off to this later, but right now is not the time to get a hard-on.

I reply:

My naughty girl. You just wait. I'm going to lick that juice from every inch of your body.

"Tagger?" A knock on the door startles me, causing me to fumble my phone and drop it on the floor. Kendra says, "Sorry, I didn't mean to sneak up on you. Am I interrupting anything?"

"No. It's fine. Come in." I retrieve the phone and then slide the chair forward to make sure I'm covered. The screen lights up, so I flip it to face downward.

"I need to confirm something." She pulls a sticky note off her pad and shows me. "I found Peaches Sundries & More in Peachtree Pass, Texas. I called, and they said they can take the order over the phone. But you didn't give me a name, so I couldn't place it."

Speak of the devil . . . "*Pri*—Christine Greene."

"From you, sir?"

Oh. *Hmm.* This is tricky. "Send it from a secret admirer."

I catch the smile tickling her cheeks. "I take it those are her favorite?"

"Yes, but please don't make a big deal of it. The only reason I'm not leaving my name is because they know me there. Small-town gossip travels fast."

"Well," she says, sitting down. "It's a very romantic gesture. Thoughtful."

I shouldn't be embarrassed, but I typically keep the women in my life out of the workplace to steer clear of being office fodder as entertainment. Tapping a pen on the desktop, I lower my voice. "Please keep this between us."

"You have my word. But I did want to mention the credit charge will be attached to your name. So they'll see it."

"Oh, right. Good point." I swivel to face the windows to figure this out.

But then she says, "I could pay for it on my card, and you can just send me the money."

Turning back to her, I ask, "You'd do that for me?"

She beams a smile so bright the light reflects in her eyes. "I'm all for love and gestures from the heart." Walking toward the door, she adds, "Glad I can help. I'll let you know when the order is placed."

"Thank you. I owe you one, Kendra."

She stops in the doorway, and says, "You don't owe me anything unless it works out. And then I want an invite to the wedding."

Wedding? "I think we're getting ahead of ourselves."

She shrugs and lifts an eyebrow. "Are we?"

Gone before I can answer, I ponder that thought. It's not as far-fetched as the idea of marriage used to be. We just have to break it to the world that we're a couple first.

CHAPTER 31

Christine

"What's this mysterious package?" I ask as soon as I open the door to Peaches.

Lauralee dips down, pulls a box from the pastry case, and sets it on the counter in front of me. "Here you go."

I know what it is by smell and weight alone. "A dozen cheddar biscuits?" I hold the box to my chest. "Aw, you shouldn't have."

"I didn't." She laughs. "There's a note inside if you're curious."

"Darn tootin', I'm curious." I set the goodies in front of me and wedge the box open. "So mysterious." I glance up when I see the note. "Did my dad do this?"

"Nope."

Joking, I ask, "Did Deputy—"

"Just read the note, Chris."

"Okay. Okay. Someone is short on patience per usual." I take the paper, flip it open, and silently start reading.

"Say it out loud."

"Good God, Edward Cullen. Settle yourself." She starts laughing at the reference, but I drop my head to the side, entirely suspicious now. "Didn't you write it?"

Hopping up on the counter to sit, she leans against the brass and glass case and bats her eyelashes. "No. I still want to enjoy this, though."

"I was starting to believe it was from you."

"It's not." Holding her hand up in a Girl Scout promise, she says, "I swear."

"Alright." I glance back at the paper and read aloud, "You're better than any biscuit could ever be. Your Secret Admirer." I pull the note to my chest, holding it over my heart, wishing I could hug the real thing instead of a piece of paper. It's a poor substitute for Tagger Grange, but since this is all I have right now, I'll treasure it always.

"Who's the secret admirer, Greene?"

Tucking the note into my back pocket, I ask, "Have you always been this nosy?"

"You should know."

"So the answer is yes." I pick out a biscuit and take a big bite. "They're literally orgasmic."

"Speaking of orgasms with Tagger Grange . . ." I spew biscuit everywhere and then start choking on the bread. Resting my hands on the counter, I cough up what feels like a piece of cheese just as she sets a bottle of water on the counter in front of me. "Drink up, buttercup, and settle in. It's going to be a long afternoon. I need all the details of when you and Tagger started having sex, and I want to hear all about your trip to the Big Apple."

I drink the water, soothing my throat as well as biding some time. I lower it to take a breath, but when I see her sitting idly by waiting on me, I drink some more.

How does she know about Tagger and me?

The trip to New York and about us having sex?

What am I supposed to tell her?

She knows I lied. What else does she already know that she's ready to call me out on?

She laughs with a quick roll of her eyes. "The water can't save you, sister."

I lower the bottle and set it down, ready to drink more if this interrogation gets too heated. "First off, I can explain."

"Mm-hmm."

"Second, how do you know all that?"

"It's not exactly trade secrets." She holds out her finger and ticks it once. "You're the worst liar." Ticking off another finger, she adds, "There is no Farmers of Central Texas conference or convention in Dallas because it doesn't exist." Flipping out a third finger, she grins. "This secret admirer order was paid by a Kendra Donovan out of New York City. She works for Delaney Financials. Do you know who else works there?"

It's a trick. "Two months ago, I didn't."

"Nice try, Greene." She shoots her eyebrow straight up and glares at me.

I cave because I'm weak, and honestly, I just want to share this happiness with my best friend. "Tagger Grange."

"Ding. Ding. Ding. Mr. Tagger Grange works there. Do you know who his assistant is?"

"Technically, no. But I'll take a wild guess and say Kendra Donovan?"

"Right-O again!"

She's ridiculous, but she does have a way of making everything more fun. Laughing, I ask, "What do I win?"

Her smile softens. "I think you already won your all-time crush."

She's right. "I don't know how it happened."

"I do." She hops off the counter. "It was love at first sight. It just took him seeing you at Peaches. I saw the sparks flying, the connection you two had, and the chemistry was out of this world."

"I felt it. I was too scared to admit it, though. But when he came out to the ranch the next day, and then the day after that, I knew in my heart that he was my soulmate."

She comes around and hugs me. I'm not sure if it's for me or her, but it's nice to have the support. We embrace, and then she sits on a stool beside me, pulling my hand until I'm seated on the other. "Does Baylor know?"

"No. But how is it his business anyway? He's forgotten he has a sister, that I even exist. So I'm not going to ask his permission or to free Tagger from a promise he made when they were so much younger."

"I hear what you're saying, but I want you to consider something." She pauses, looking between our knees that just about touch. When she looks back up, she says, "Baylor lost his mother as well. Was it right that he and Griffin took off? No. But were they grieving in their own way? They were, Chris." Taking my hands, she says, "I'm sorry you feel you had to give up your dreams to run the ranch with your dad. But you know what I see?"

"What do you see?" I'm already tearing up, touched so deeply. I didn't know I needed to hear this. I didn't know how much bitterness I was carrying around. Until now. With every word, my burden lightens.

She takes my hand in hers, and replies, "The strongest woman I know taking her responsibilities and creating a new dream. I know you. That ranch has become part of you. You love it, but you need to let go of the blame on others to truly appreciate your accomplishments."

I reach forward and hug her like the sister she's always

been to me. "You're right," I whisper over her shoulder, trying to keep the tears from falling. But who am I kidding? This girl has wiped more of my tears away than anyone. I've done the same for her. We don't need to hide behind lies or pretend we're stronger than we are with each other. I drop my head. "I've been having sex with Tagger Grange."

She bursts out laughing, then spins my stool around. "About time you admitted it."

Breathing comes easier, so I ask, "How did you know I went to New York?"

She reaches behind her and pulls out her phone. "Did you forget we have tracking for each other just in case anything ever happens?"

Smiling, I have to give her credit. She's a regular Sherlock Holmes. "Well played. I totally forgot."

Flipping her hair over her shoulders, she asks, "So are you going to tell me everything or keep me guessing?"

I spin myself around, dipping my head back, and feel giddy. "I've been *dyyyying* to tell you." I plant my foot on the floor to still me, and say, "He kissed me in the rain. That's when I knew I would marry that man one day."

CHAPTER 32

Tagger

BECK JUMPS out of the rental car before I have time to put it in park, practically giving me a heart attack. I'm fast on the brake, so no damage is done. I'll need to remind him how cars work before he starts pulling some stupid shit like I did when I was a teen.

Jumping from one truck bed to another while flying down the highway.

Playing chicken at the top of The Ridge and hoping your brakes work.

Drinking too much after winning the State championship and thinking it wise to do donuts in a Dover County shopping mall parking lot.

Real dumb shit.

I'm glad my dad never found out, or surviving a string of bad decisions would have been the least of my concerns. He wasn't hard on my brother and me, but he was strict. I've tried to find more balance with my son . . . that is, until he jumps out of a car that's stopped for less than a second. At least it's a soft landing on the lawn if he did tumble.

Anna would still kill me, but I have a feeling my little daredevil would wear a cast with pride.

My parents come out of the house and down to greet us. Beck throws himself into my mom's arms, so excited to be back in the Pass. "Grammy!" My dad gets a hold of that wiggly kid before he can escape to see the chickens. He's been talking about that since we left Manhattan. "Will you take me to see them, Grandpa?"

"Sure will, rascal. Let me go say hi to your dad first."

It's not only my parents who love the bond they share with my son.

My mom greets me with a hug. "Happy to have you home again."

"Me too."

She hooks her arm around mine, and we take a few steps back away from the car. "You said you were coming back for the festival. It's always such fun. Beck's going to love it."

"Biggest event of the year. I didn't want to miss it."

"Was that the only thing you were missing?" I look to my side to find her eyes ready to search mine.

Maybe I'm reading too much into the question, but it feels like there's an agenda behind it. I want to share more with them, to tell them I've fallen for Pris. My mom's not one to start rumors. I'm her son, so I know I can trust her. Pris and I have an agreement in place. Until we decide otherwise, together, not even my parents are privy to the information.

Although dancing around topics only makes people more suspicious, I keep it vague but honest. "Not only that."

She hums with a huff at the end. "You're a tough nut,

Tagger." She pats my arm. "I'm here when you're ready to share. But no matter what, I'm happy to have you home again."

Leaving me to stand near my dad, she calls, "Hey, Beck?" He jumps off the porch steps, nailing the landing, and looks up. "You're here at the best time of year. Peach season." When she reaches him, they climb up the steps to the porch together. "I'm going to teach you how to make my blue-ribbon-winning peach cobbler. Want to know what the secret ingredient is?"

"Yes?" he asks, enraptured by her storytelling. She makes everyone feel like they're the most important person in the world, or in this case, you've been chosen to get in on her secrets.

I know the secret ingredient before she even reveals it. "Love."

She stops at the door and turns back. Giving me a smile, she nods. "That's right. Love."

Beck asks, "What does love taste like?"

"It's different for everyone, but you'll know the moment you find it." It's been a long time since I learned her secret to great cooking—a dash of love, a pinch of kindness, and putting your heart into everything you do. She even has it stitched and hanging on the wall in the kitchen. I've heard it a million times and read it even more, but it never hit until now. That's what she meant. *When you find it, you'll know.*

There's no denying I've found it with Pris.

What am I going to do with this knowledge? I know that's the next question my mom would ask. Pris would, too. They're not so different. *Unlike my ex.*

Pulling me in for a solid pat on the back, my dad says, "I hear we're getting you and the little guy for five days."

"Five *whole* days," I emphasize with a chuckle. I'm not

sure he knows what he's taking on, considering he loves to "fish," a.k.a. nap, during the day. "Is that alright?"

"This is your home, Tag."

I catch the tail end of Beck telling my mom, ". . .for the whole summer."

"I hope you get to spend more time in Peachtree Pass with us, then."

I was already trying to make some extended visit plans, but it's good to know we're welcome, especially because it's not easy to take on a six and thirty-year-old when you're used to quiet in the house.

Popping the trunk, I get our suitcases out and set them down. My dad takes Beck by the hand, and says, "It's also rodeo time this weekend. Beck would make a fine mutton buster."

I'm undecided if that's a good or bad thing. Anna would kill me, but Beck would probably have the time of his life. "I told him Rollingwood Ranch has a few sheep I can show him up close. I won't pressure him, so we'll see if he's up for it."

"You've mentioned he's a pro at riding the subway with you. It'll be good to see him trying to ride a sheep." He chuckles, glancing at the door just before it shuts behind them. "Once he gets a taste, he might want to ride in the rodeo after that."

Picking up my suitcase, I reply, "That would be hard to pursue living in New York."

I'm met with a side stare. "You couldn't live in New York. You'd need a home base to raise him with some acreage and have some animals."

My dad has never understood the appeal of the city. I don't think it's worth trying to change his mind at this age.

But he has a good point. I doubt Beck is ever joining the rodeo, not if his mother has her way, but giving him a home base where he can open the door and run outside is what every kid needs. Earth under their feet instead of concrete. Waiting at a cattle crossing instead of being a part of the herd at a crosswalk when the light turns green.

We have one drive-thru in the county and no stoplight. It would be a major change for him. Although I know he likes to visit Texas, is it somewhere he'd like to live? And more importantly, is it the best decision for him?

I turned out alright, if you ask my closest friends. Enemies will always say shit.

This is not the first time I've thought about moving back, but I'm the closest I've ever been to seriously considering it. Pris and I have a lot to discuss, which I hope to do if I can sneak away for a bit.

Setting the small case down at his side, he asks, "Got any other plans? Going to see some friends?"

Since neither of us is rushing inside, I set my case down as well. We stand side by side, crossing our arms over our chest, looking more like each other every day. "Thought I'd look at painting the house."

His gaze travels over to the house and studies it as if he hadn't noticed the peeling paint. I know he has, but his pride won't let him admit he's no longer up for the task. Or shouldn't be if I can keep him off ladders. "Looking at it isn't going to get the job done."

Chuckling, I say, "I plan on getting it done if you're up for being a foreman over the site." Justin Grange is an old-time cowboy. Fifth generation that we can account for. Just like his dad did for him, he taught us three things to live by: Talk is cheap and should be kept to a minimum, putting in the work is required whether working hard on a farm or on your marriage, and feeling useful gives us a purpose. I also just want to spend time with my dad.

Without making a big deal about it, he says, "I suppose I can fit that into my schedule. When are you starting?"

"Tomorrow. I want to take Mom to pick out a color, and I'll get the supplies to bring back with me. Power wash it and then start the day after that."

"It will look good with a fresh coat." Reaching over, he squeezes my shoulder. "I reckon that will work for my schedule."

Picking up the cases, we start for the house. I peek over at him, seeing the smile he can't wipe from his face, and ask, "Are the fish biting?"

"They have been the past few naps." He laughs and heads to the house. "We're good with watching Beckett and getting him to bed if you want to go see those friends tonight."

My mom knows. She's good but subtle and probably knew how I felt about Pris before I did. She's in tune with her family. She also told my dad. He's not as subtle. "I think I'll take you up on that offer."

"Sounds good. Let's get inside. I got Beckett his first cowboy hat. Thought it was time." His sentimental side is showing. Being a grandpa looks good on him.

"He'll love it." I follow him inside, glad I don't have to hide my girlfriend anymore. As for Beck, I still need to have that conversation with him.

I take Dad's truck because it beats driving the rental and pull onto Greene property. Pris knew I was coming in today, yet she didn't pressure me to come see her. She knows time with my parents is important and doesn't want to take that away from me. But I've waited weeks to see her again and hold her in my arms. Waiting another hour wasn't going to happen.

The sun has decided it's tired, hanging lower in the sky and showering the fields in a golden hue. Other than my girl, no prettier sight in the world tops it.

Mr. Greene stands from his chair on the porch and moves to the railing to rest his weight against it. "I'm seeing ya enough to think you have business out here other than ranching."

I walk closer, keeping my feet on the ground and giving him the upper hand in perspective. Not sure this charade is going to work much longer. Most people have too much time on their hands to miss the connections others make. My gut tells me he has suspicions. "I was looking for Pris."

"Figured as much." He shields his eyes and scans as far as he can see. "No sign of her yet for the night. Horses are in the stable, or you can take the UTV. Can't give you more than that. She could be anywhere."

I'm not dressed for riding since I didn't change clothes before I left. Wearing my clothes from New York makes no sense anymore when I'm slowly building the wardrobe here. I'm not having a business meeting, so maybe I need to start dressing more comfortably when I travel here.

I choose the UTV to find her. Before I start it up, Mr. Greene says, "Not sure what your intentions are, Tagger, but my daughter deserves a good man in her life."

I don't know if he's warning me or I just got his stamp of approval, but he's already returned to the rocking chair he was previously occupying, so I can't ask. Would I accept the answer if it wasn't what I wanted to hear? I may be uncertain about a few things in my life, but Pris isn't one of them. I want her dad's approval, but I'm not walking away if he doesn't give it.

Taking the corner, I cut across behind the cornfield and in front of the equipment barn before scoping out the lower pasture. It's not until I take the long way around to the far end on the southeast side of the property heading toward the peach orchard that I see her and Sunrise.

Walking on foot, she leads Sunrise by the reins across the front of acres of blooming fruit trees. I cut the engine so I don't disturb them. But having a moment to watch her in these surroundings she calls home makes me realize I can't ask her to leave. It's not a deciding factor for me, and I would never want her to leave a place she loves so much.

I start to walk along a path worn through the grass toward her. Catching the rays of the golden hour shining through strands of her hair makes it as vibrant as the sun. It's so much redder than I ever thought. Wearing boots on her denim-clad legs, a black tank that hugs her curves, and a black hat that I recognize instantly, she's spectacular like her surroundings.

When she catches me, she stops and puts a hand on her hip. She's not annoyed, but she sure does love to give me a hard time. I love it, too. I love her mouthiness and strength, her killer body, and the quirky way her mind works sometimes.

I fucking love everything about her.

I stop about ten feet back or so. "Nice hat."

She laughs and pushes it up on her forehead. "This old thing?"

As much as I love it when she runs into my arms, a sense of peace comes with the slower pace of this hello. "Heard you were out here somewhere on the ranch."

She moves closer as her smile blooms like the peaches

for me—perfect, ripe for kissing, and so beautiful. "Thousands of acres and you still found me. Intuition or—?"

I close the gap, cupping her face and kissing her like I've wanted to since the moment she left my place. When our lips pull apart, I lean my head against hers, feeling whole with her in my arms again, and whisper, "Destiny."

CHAPTER 33

Tagger

"You sure on the sage green?" I hold the swatch out in front of us.

Nodding, my mom appears confident in her decision. "The sage."

There are a million colors, but she picks the same color already on the house. "Sage it is, then."

I buy all the supplies, and we head over to Sassy's to grab lunch since we're out. I've been waiting for the topic of Pris to come up since we left the Pass this morning, but she's not said a word. She picks up a french fry and points it at me. "You were out late last night. Did you have fun?"

Images of Pris on the mattress with that fine ass of hers in the air while fucking her from behind come to mind. The sexy sounds of her moans I worried would reach the house if she wasn't careful still fill my ears. The hot, slick embrace of that sweet pussy milking me has me shifting on my side of the booth.

I glance outside to rid the memories before I have to

leave to handle the situation in my jeans. I turn back to look at my mom, and that does it. "Yeah, a lot of fun."

"That's good. Who did you spend time with?"

I push my plate away since I'm done eating and rest my arms on the table, keeping my voice down. "You know who, don't you?"

A mischievous grin teeters onto her face after a good little laugh. "I can hope."

"Mom, just say it."

"Chrissy Greene." Leaning forward, she says, "You two had such a connection at dinner during your last visit. She has the loveliest personality and what a beautiful young woman she is." Placing one hand on the other, she leans back again. "I know I've said it before, but she reminds me so much of her mother."

"I'm sure she loves to hear it."

"How serious is it, Tagger?" *Goes in for the kill . . .*

No hiding anything from her. Never could. "Serious."

"Marriage serious?"

I'm not sure if it's right to talk about things when they haven't come up between Pris and me, but I'm not going to lie about us anymore. "There's no proposal planned at this time."

The gentle upturn of her lips has me feeling I'm on the right track. I've thought about the relationship a lot, but I don't know where Pris stands on the topic. Something else for us to talk about.

I pay the check, and we drive home—no more talk of marriage, and an ounce of pressure was never applied. It was nice to have the time with her and even more to hear how she feels about my girl.

When we return to the house, I recruit Beck to help his ole dad out. While I get the ladder out of the barn and set it up against the house, he's happy to jump in and play with the power washer. I had no doubt that would be his favorite part.

I pull my shirt off and grab the straw cowboy hat from the hook inside and get to work. Beckett does the same. I want to laugh, but I don't want him to think I'm making fun of him. I'm touched that he wants to be like me.

An hour later, we successfully power washed two sides with the third to go. I'll tackle the porch last since it will need more attention.

The machine is too loud to hear cars pulling up, but when Pris walks around the corner, visoring her hands over her eyes, a smirk dances across her lips as she looks me up and down. "Looks like I'm missing all the fun."

I chuckle. "What are you talking about? Looks like the fun just arrived."

"You flatter me so." She smiles at Beckett. "Hi, buddy. I like your hat."

"Grandpa said it makes me a real cowboy now."

"Sure does." She giggles lightly and then looks back at me. "Like father, like son, I see."

She's so comfortable around my kid that it allows me to see a bigger picture of how it might be some day if we are together in a more permanent fashion. He steadies his hands on the ladder with a tighter grip. "Hi." *Is he showing off for her?* I have a future Romeo on my hands.

Before I get back to washing the awnings and knocking some wasp nests down, I ask, "What brings you by?"

"Had a little time on my hands. Need any help?" The woman starts work before dawn and past dusk most days, so putting her to work over at my folk's house is the last thing I want to do.

She goes to Beck and leans down to look in his eyes

under the brim of his new hat. "You're doing a good job holding the ladder for your daddy." Sometimes I wonder if she calls me daddy on purpose. Whatever she's trying to do to me, it's working. *So fucking naughty.*

"Safety first," he says, kicking his legs out like the ladder is only steady if he uses all his strength. I appreciate the effort.

"Always," she says. "Are you coming out to the ranch to visit the horses?"

He looks up at me. "Can I, Dad?"

"You bet."

When I look at Pris again, she says, "I don't mean to keep you—"

"Do you have time to stick around?"

She doesn't hesitate. "I do." The response hits different after the conversation I had with my mom, but I wouldn't mind hearing those words again to try them on for size.

"Sorry, I missed that. The power washer is loud."

She cups the side of her mouth, and calls out, "I have time. I'll go hang out on the porch and wait for you." *Blocked.* I was never good about missing a touchdown.

After Beck and I finish the area above the porch, we do what we need to clean up. Beck runs to the garden where my mom is picking something, so I take the opportunity to see Pris.

I come up the steps and look around one last time to make sure there are no eyes on us before bending down to kiss her. Her hands slide over my shoulders, and she says, "I sure do like this look on you."

"Shirtless and a cowboy hat?"

"And jeans making that ass look too good not to appreciate getting a big handful, babe."

Chuckling, I can't argue that I like that my girl finds me

so attractive. "If you're a good girl, I'll let you squeeze it later."

"I'd rather be bad."

"Be careful what you wish for."

"I'm not afraid. Bring it on, cowboy."

That mouth of hers is going to be the death of me. Considering how reactive my body is to her, a change of subject is needed about now. "I'm glad you stopped by."

"I wanted to see you." When I sit next to her on the porch swing, she says, "You could have paid someone to do the work."

"I like using my hands."

"I like that, too." Reaching over, she slips hers into mine, and our fingers weave together. "It also is beginning to sound like you might be missing Texas."

"That's not what I'm missing most."

She genuinely looks like she's waiting for the answer. *How is that possible?* I clearly need to do a better job of making sure she knows exactly what she means to me.

"You, babe," I say, bringing our conjoined hands to my mouth and kissing hers. "I miss you most."

"I was tempering my hopes just in—"

"You don't have to, not with me." I lean over and kiss her once more. "My parents know I'm seeing you."

"Ah." She looks out past the porch. "Lauralee knows."

"I think your dad does as well." Her mouth is hanging wide open, implanting thoughts inappropriate for the situation.

"He hasn't said anything to me."

"He hinted at it when I came by yesterday."

She takes a sobering breath and angles toward me on the swing. "So what you're saying is that everyone knows, but we're still pretending they don't?"

“Seems that way. So what if we were a couple like any other instead of hiding?”

I see the joy in the blue of her eyes as potential fills them, but she bites her bottom lip and gnaws before licking it. “How do you feel about a hard launch at the Peach Festival?”

“Two days? That will give me time to talk to Beckett.” I look up at the corners of the cream-painted ceiling, analyzing the work required for this part of the house. When I look at her, I say, “And to get this house painted. Can I pick you up on Thursday at five?”

“I’d like that. The three of us can go together.”

“It’s a date.” A hard launch is the same as a soft launch when it comes to small towns. Go big or go home, as they say. *I’m ready.*

Shortly after she takes off, I get my son to help me clear off the porch of all the junk that’s collected over the years: an old bike tire that never got patched that might be from my brother’s bike back in high school, two stacks of cracked clay and ceramic pots never glued back together, and even an old stove that outdates me turned into another dumping spot. My dad helps me move that to a pile of garbage we need to deliver to the dump.

When it’s just me and the kid again, I spray the ceiling and upper corners and let him power wash the lower parts. “Hey buddy, I wanted to talk to you about Miss Christine.”

He only glances at me before aiming at a hole where a lizard just disappeared. “She said I can name the next colt that’s born on the farm.”

“Oh yeah? That’s a big responsibility.”

“She said I’m old enough.”

“You are. Almost seven in July.” I try for casual. I don’t need to make this bigger than it is. She is my girlfriend. I could just say it or do it the hard way, which is what I'm leaning toward right now. "I know you like her a lot." He nods but pays no real mind to me as I nervously stumble through this awkward conversation. What am I looking to get from it? His approval like her dad's? I could disregard Thomas Greene's opinion, then work on winning him over in time. That's not the case with Beckett. If he doesn't want her in my life on a larger level, that will be a problem I'm not sure we'll be able to solve.

Will I give up Pris if my son wants me to?

I don't owe my happiness in exchange for his well-being. It's not one or the other. They can exist in the same universe. But it will make it more challenging and probably put an end to moving to Texas. Not that I'm moving here only for her, but she's a big part of the pull I've been feeling to be back here.

When he messes around with the washer, I say, "Let's take a walk and dry off."

He drops the wand like a hot potato. I shut it down, and we start for the pasture to lean against the rails under a big tree-shaded spot. He squats and draws in the dirt with a stick. "She's nice to you."

The stick stops, and he looks back up at me as if he knows where this is leading before continuing his art. He's six. No way he knows. I'm not even sure he'll understand after we discuss it.

He says, "She's nice to you, too."

"She is."

Looking at me once more, he squints with the sun in his eyes. "She likes you." He stands and drags the stick around on the ground a few times, causing a mini dust storm. "You like her."

I try to tamp down the surprise in my tone when I ask, "Why do you say that?"

"Because of how you look at her."

"How's that, buddy?"

"She's your secret ingredient."

Damn. The kid has a way with words and gets straight to the point.

He comes to lean against my leg and looks up at me. "It's okay if you want to marry her." I'm glad he can't feel the way my heart beats harder, but I wish he knew how he eased the clenching in my chest, the tightness with something newer. *The secret ingredient.*

Two days of painting, while covered in sweat, leaves me barely any time to finish the last side of the house before I need to shower to get to Rollingwood on time to pick up Pris. Add in the paint Beck sprayed on me—twice—and that shower took longer.

I'm plenty moody. My arms and back are sore. I swear that the hard spot at the back of my head is paint the shampoo did not remove. I haven't had any updates from Anna on the promotion or Paris, for that matter.

Add in that Pris and I haven't had time to reconnect in the loft since I've been here, and it makes me wonder why I took on this job. She was right. I could have paid someone to do this while I did what I really wanted to do. *Her.*

A fun night is what's needed to get my mind off things with a guaranteed good time afterward. I practically warned her already when I told her not to wear underwear under the dress tonight. She likes to tease and bonus, she likes sex with me, so I wouldn't have been surprised if that's how she showed up anyway.

Seeing her look so goddamn beautiful helps.

We reach the fairgrounds just after six. Beck wants out,

so Pris opens the door to free him. "Stay close," she says like he's already one of her own. She leaves the door propped open, but when she looks at me, she smiles. "You owe me a proper hello, cowboy."

I reach over and rub her leg, then kiss her. "If by hello you mean fuck, I'm down."

Under a lifted brow, she smirks. "Well, you're not actually down, but I'm happy to let you go down later."

"Promise?"

She starts laughing. "Promises. Promises." She hops out of the truck, then leans over the seat, and says, "Ready to go break the one who's holding you back?"

"Thank fuck your brother isn't here."

"He's going to find out. You ready to face that music?"

I open my door, but before I get out, I take her in once more. Together for more than a month, and we're ready to blow our cover. Seeing that angelic smile of hers, the one that shines only when she sees me, has me feeling invincible. "I'm ready to be with you, so I'll do whatever it takes, babe."

Walking around the back of the truck, Pris holds Beckett's hand, so I take his other. "Ready to have some fun?"

CHAPTER 34

Christine

"OH. MY. GOD." Lauralee's mouth falls open as soon as she sees us. She lowers her cotton candy, and says, "Way to start a rumor."

"No rumors. Pure facts," Tagger says with his arm draped over my shoulders. He's dressed to impress me, wearing his best Levi's, a pair of spiffed-up black boots with a shirt to match. I loaned him the black hat since it goes best with it, but only after he swore to give it back later tonight.

Beck runs circles around us after too much cotton candy, as evidenced by his blue tongue and matching lips. I try to catch him, but the squirmy worm hasn't run out of sugar yet. He's going to crash so hard.

Holding my boyfriend around the back, I dip my hand lower and shove my hand in his back pocket. It gives me a great grasp of that firm ass, so I give it a squeeze. That earns me a lopsided grin. I say, "We decided a hard launch was best."

"It's hard alright." Her eyes dart around, then return to

mine. “I don’t think this town will recover once this gets out.” Moving closer, she says, “Everybody’s watching.”

“Let ’em.” Tagger shrugs. “This relationship doesn’t involve them. At least this way, they can gossip and get it out of their systems.”

“What are you talking about, Tag?” She laughs. “They still gossip about Ashton Kramer sleeping with the phone book salesman from 1982. They’re not going to let this fade away anytime soon.”

Beck tugs on Tagger’s belt loop. “Can we ride the Ferris wheel?”

“Sure, buddy.” He glances at Lauralee. “Want to join us?”

My heart squeezes from the heartfelt gesture.

“If you’re looking to spread some real rumors, this will do it.”

“Lauralee,” I playfully caution. I shouldn’t worry. If Tagger gets my humor, he’ll get hers.

The line has grown, so we get in line with our tickets to wait it out. “I’m hot,” Beck whines, kicking the grass. He pushes his hat so it’s anchored on his crown, revealing his red cheeks.

“It is quite warm,” I say, glancing at Tagger. “We should get water after this ride.”

He nods, appearing to analyze how much longer we’ll be waiting by counting the people ahead of us. “Are we interested in the rodeo?” He squats to talk to Beck directly. “Painting the house kept us busy, so you didn’t get a chance to see the sheep over at Miss Christine’s. How are you feeling about the Mutton Bustin’?”

Shaking his head is enough for his dad to respect his decision. Tagger says, “It’s okay. There’s always next year.”

As cute as it would have been to see, Beckett isn’t living this life every day. It’s still a vacation to him. I appreciate

Tagger not pressuring him to do something he knows nothing about.

I rub Tagger's shoulder when the line moves up. "The barrel racing and bucking broncos is tomorrow night. We could take off after the Ferris wheel if you think he's ready to leave."

We shift up to the front of the line. I think Beck is hitting a wall after two hours of being here in the heat, eating a hot dog, downing a blue raspberry slushie, devouring cotton candy, and riding four vomit-inducing rides. *The joys of being a kid.*

I'm certain Anna would be losing her mind if she saw her kid right now. I'm not sure if we need to get him in the shower or toss him in the river to clean up. One thing I know is that his sticky hand was enough for me to wish I brought hand sanitizer.

We finally get in a cart, but as soon as the door is closed, Beck says, "I feel sick."

"Stop the ride," Lauralee yells from beside him, then waves her arm out the open air above the door.

I move over to scrunch in next to them and rub his back. "It's okay. Try breathing in through your nose and blowing out through your mouth."

Tagger pulled the truck over three times on the way back to his parents' house. Beck fell asleep fifteen minutes ago, so it's a bummer to wake him up so soon. We barely beat the sun setting, so I get a view of the freshly painted house when we pull out front. When Tagger cuts the engine, I look out the window. "The house looks great."

I get out quietly, wondering if we can get him cleaned up and to bed without upsetting him too much.

Tagger comes around and gives me a peck on the lips. "Thanks. I'm popping ibuprofen like candy."

"Welcome to the club. That's what I do after I spend the night with you."

I don't get any sympathy, but I do see a full-on smirk like he just won best in show. He shows up ready to perform alright. Every time.

Mary and Justin come out. She has her hands clasped in front of her chest. "Upset tummy?"

"Yeah." I move so that Tagger can get him out of the truck.

She slips her arm around my back and gives me a quick hug. "Chicken broth might help. It always did with my boys."

Tagger situates him on his shoulder. "If he's up and wants some, we can do that. He might just want to sleep, though." They walk to the house, and I'm left standing there not sure what to do.

They know we're dating, but I'm not Beck's mom, so I'm not sure I have a place where he's concerned.

The four of them reach the porch. As his parents shuffle inside and hold the door open, Tagger turns back. Our gazes connect, and he says, "Join us."

Closing the truck door, I go not only because he wants me there but also because it feels wrong not to be with them, not to be by Beck's side while he's not feeling well. I hurry in behind them before the screen door closes.

The shower is running, letting me know Tagger chose option one when it comes to cleaning up the sticky mess that is his son. Beck comes out ten minutes later dressed for bed in his cotton pj's with little hats, books, and lassos on them. The cutest.

Beck pads barefoot through the living room and straight to me, climbing up on my lap like he intends to camp out here for a while. I don't mind. *I adore it.* Sitting back, he rests against me as an animated show with talking squirrels plays on TV.

Slowly rubbing the side of his head, I can feel his body trying to give in to sleep. I've never held a kid like this. I've had friends who have babies and held them but not little munchkins like Beckett.

It doesn't feel as foreign as I would have thought. I relax along with Beck, but over his head I catch Tagger's eyes, feeling a soft smile forming as if my heart has taken charge.

While Mary and Justin fuss in the kitchen, Tagger sits in a chair next to his dad's recliner. He swipes two hands through his hair, looking exhausted. Selfishly, I hope he gets a second wind. If he doesn't, that's okay, too. Even though this week is slipping away from us, we always have tomorrow.

It's that look in his eyes, the one of awe and adoration that makes the butterflies come to life in my tummy, that just about does me in. The gentle smile, the mussed-up hair, and the peace he carries in his shoulders could send me to an early grave if I'm not careful.

Can life be more perfect than this right here?

Mary comes in with a mug of broth that Beck happily sips on, which pleases her and all of us. It's good to help counteract all the junk he apparently doesn't get back in the city. I almost feel guilty for not trying to find a vegetable to sneak in there. And we never even made it to the Peach Fest tent to try all the yummies in there.

After drinking half the broth, Beck finds sleep by the third commercial break. Tagger comes over and lifts him from my arms to carry him into the bedroom. No one bothers to change the station, which makes me think his parents want to chat.

I go first. "No entry in the dessert contest this year?"

Mary leans back, kicking her feet up on an ottoman with a contented smile on her face. “Not this year.”

“She decided to give someone else a chance,” her husband says with pride. “Her five-year streak is going to be hard to beat.”

Tagger stands at the opening of the hallway with his hands on his sides. “Better to go out on top, right, Mom?”

She looks over her shoulder at him. “It really came down to me wanting to spend time with my son and grandson more than days prepping a dish and standing at the festival all day after that.”

He comes around and gives her a hug from behind the chair. “Beck should be fine. He’s so sleepy. I told him I was going to take Pris home, though, so if he gets up . . .”

“We’ve raised two outstanding young men. We’ll take good care of him, so don’t rush home.”

“Thanks. I appreciate it.” He comes to me and offers a hand to pull me to my feet. “You ready?”

With a slight nod, I move around him to thank his parents before we’re quick to the truck. “If you need to stay—”

“He’s doing okay. He was a new kid in the bedroom when I was tucking him in. Tired from the day, but full color in his face and happy. Though, I’m not sure he’ll ever have another blue raspberry slushie again.”

“I don’t blame him. I haven’t had one since eighth grade when I vomited on the way home. My dad had me sit in the bed of the truck with my brothers and Lauralee so he didn’t have to stop.”

“That’s rough. And not sexy in the least.” I start to laugh when he reaches over to hold my hand, and asks, “But you still are. How about spending some time together back at the barn?”

"Are you asking me to have sex with you, Mr. Grange?"

"I'm asking if I can make love to you, Ms. Greene."

We're still talking about sex, so it's not the most romantic thing I've ever heard him say, but a lump still forms in my throat from the change in how we usually talk about it. "I'd like that. I like being with you, always."

He doesn't say much else on the drive over to mine. Not sure if it's the day holding on to his muscles, the physical labor wearing him out, or that he's still concerned about his son, but there seems to be a lot on that mind, leaving me to only guess what it might be.

Before we pull onto the property, he pulls over, shifts the truck into park, and says, "Anna might take a promotion in Paris." I'm still not sure how to react to this shocking news. No wonder he's been preoccupied. I reach over to hold his hand. He lowers his head, and says, "I don't want him in Paris. I want him with me."

Angling closer, I lean over to kiss his shoulder. "I'll be here to support you however you need me."

He looks over and strokes hair that has fallen loose from the ponytail away from my face. "I love you."

"I love you, too."

His shoulders relax, and the vibrancy returns to his eyes. "Let's get you to bed."

I grin, knowing exactly what that means. I also know what he's doing when he parks a little way from the side of the house. Easier to go unnoticed once my dad heads to bed and drive away without lights shining in the windows. This isn't my first rodeo, either.

We're not sneaking around, but we don't need to make a production that we're aiming for the barn to go have sex. Excuse me, make love. I swoon a little more over that.

The horses have a garbled neigh, their way of telling me

it's time for them to rest, and the chickens are in their coop for the night. We climb up the ladder and light the little lamp on the bookcase to break up the dark.

When I turn back, he's watching me, not with hunger, but that reverence I saw in his eyes earlier has returned. It's just an old dress and boots with a ribbon around my ponytail, but he makes me feel like the most beautiful woman in the world.

"Want to dance?"

I move across the room, ready to melt into his arms. Slipping my hand in his and resting the other on his shoulder, I've seen this scenario in movies before and know my line by heart. "There's no music playing."

"Who needs music when we have the moonlight shining in? And a little lamp." He starts to sway. Finding rhythm with him is easy when we fit together so well. Pulling me close, he kisses the side of my head, and says, "I love you."

With such heavy emotion wrapped in those three little words, I lean back to look into his eyes. "I love you, too." I'm not sure what's come over him, but maybe some things are on his mind while driving. "Is everything okay?"

He spins me out and pulls me gently back in against him. "I think we need to talk, Pris."

That's not good. Every breakup in history started with those very words. I stop dancing, feeling sick to my stomach. Although our hands are still attached, I take a step back. "That statement never ends well for the receiver."

"No, it's not like that. It's the opposite. I don't want to be apart from you anymore."

I move back in, closing the space so as much of us can touch as possible. I don't even mean to bat my eyelashes, but they flutter for this man. "I like that. Go on."

He chuckles, but it's caught in the thoughts warring to slip off his tongue. "I can't move without Beckett."

"I would never ask you to."

"I know, but I want you to ask me. I want you to need me as much as I do you."

Oblivious to how much I had fallen into pretending we weren't a thing, I'd forgotten to make sure he knew we were. I reach up to caress his cheek, and whisper, "I don't just want you. I need you, Tagger. I don't want to be sneaking around in barns to be with you. I want to share a bed with you every night and wake in your arms in the morning." Holding a finger in the air, I add, "An aside, but preferably in that amazing bed of yours."

"I can get a bed of our own, but where will we put it?"

Wrapping my arms around his middle, I rest my cheek on his chest. "I have no idea, but . . ." I look up again. "This stuff can be worked out. Just know, I want you so much, not the fantasy of you that I had in my head. I want you, the man who's made me fall madly in love with him. And I adore your son, so however we need to work this out, we'll do what's best for him."

Cupping my face, he kisses me long and slow, and says, "I didn't know I needed an angel until you came along. Now there's no living without you." I'm kissed again, and as we walk our way to the mattress with tongues dancing and our heartbeats racing, we fall like we fell in love—together and all at once.

We make love, then we kiss and love each other all over again. It's just gone ten when we kiss goodbye at the opening of the barn doors. His arms are strong and hold me so tight I'm not sure I'm getting away tonight. I freaking love it, just like him.

I lift on my bare toes with my boots in one hand and kiss

him once more before he leaves. His arm comes around me, and he rubs my back while the other hand finds my ass and gives it a good squeeze.

"What the fuck?"

Our lips part before I realize what's happening. I lower back down and look over my shoulder. The little remaining air I had in my lungs is ripped from them. "Baylor?"

CHAPTER 35

Tagger

Pris stands in front of me like she'll be able to stop the power of a charging bull, also known as her brother. She throws her hands in front just as he reaches me. My girl is braver than most.

Baylor shows no sign of slowing and pushes against her. "Move it, Pris," he yells in her face when she pushes back. That's enough incentive to beat his ass.

Fuck that. "Don't you fucking yell or touch her!"

Grabbing her arms, he shifts in one quick move to the side and is in my face. "What are you gonna do about it?" He shoves his chest against me, out of fucking control and taking this bullshit too far.

I shove his ass back, not intimidated in the least. I don't want to kick my best friend's ass, but I won't hesitate to throw the first punch. "You're such a fucking asshole, Baylor. She's a grown woman."

He recovers from the push and stupidly comes back for more. The veins in his neck start protruding, and I can tell he's going to take this too far. "She's my baby sister, you fucker."

"Oh my God, Baylor!" She entangles herself between us. Shooting me a dirty look over her shoulder, she then pokes him in the chest. That's going to leave a mark. "I can have sex with whoever I please, and it pleases me very much to have sex with Tagger."

Fairly certain that's not helping the situation.

His ire reaches his eyes, turning his blue eyes dark with anger. Staring at me from over her shoulder, he says, "I'm going to fucking kill you, Grange."

A call to arms, adrenaline races through my veins, and I strengthen my stance, ready to land the first punch if forced to do so. "No, you're not."

"The fuck?" He tries to reach over her to land a half-assed jab, but I duck too fast for that loser.

"Stop it, Baylor," she shouts, still between us. "Calm down."

"No fucking way, sis. I look away for one minute, and this asshole starts fucking my sister." He throws his head back. "Good God, out of line and so fucking gross."

She whacks his chest. "Hey! That's me you're talking about." She pushes him back a few feet, and says, "And that minute was four years."

"Blink of an eye," he snaps at her.

I'll fight him if he wants. Not sure what that will accomplish, but he apparently needs a lesson in not fucking with the wrong guy. I weave around her. "I'm not proud of kicking your ass—"

"Wha—" My fist lands right where I want it—on this upper cheek.

Pris gasps, holding her hand over her mouth. "Oh my God." On the receiving end of a dirty look, she throws her arm out and points at the barn. "Go over there." *Shit.* Now she's upset with me? *Damned if you do . . .*

I throw my hands up like I'm innocent in all this. "He was threatening me." I'd be lying if I said this was the first physical fight we'd been in, but we competed for everything growing up. We could be happy for the other, but we also came to blows a few times.

She huffs, her anger getting the better of her. "Just go." Going to her brother, she says, "Why are you doing this? You disappear for years of my life, then come back like you have a say in who I date?" Holding his face, she forces him to look at her. "You don't. You don't have a say anymore."

Her words hit harder than I ever could, and they change him. The tension in his face lessens, the veins in his neck not as obvious, but the pain in his eyes has me wondering where we go from here. Redirecting his anger, he scoffs. "What the fuck, Tagger?"

"What's going on out here?" Their dad comes stomping across the porch and leans on the railing to figure out what he's missing. "Baylor?"

"Surprise." The friend I have, the one who cracks jokes and gets a little too close to the sun sometimes in some of his decision-making, doesn't back down from much. Except when his dad gets involved.

Mr. Greene comes down the steps and around the house. His eyes latch onto me first, then volleys to his daughter and back. When he sees Baylor, he releases a heavy breath from his chest. "Good to see you, son." He taps his temple. "You got some blood to clean up." Shooting me the next judgment, he asks, "Did you do that, Tagger?"

Why do I suddenly feel fifteen again?

Mr. Greene's always been a fair man, a good dad, and devoted husband. I don't want to anger him more than I have, especially when it involves Pris and me dating, or moving in together, or whatever else we decide to do together.

Considering my knuckles are beginning to swell, I don't think lying is the direction to go in. "Yes, sir. I did."

A scowl wrinkles his forehead. "You sure do sound proud about punching your best friend in the face."

I catch Pris rolling her eyes. She glances my way but maintains the distance between us. Nobody wants the heat of Thomas Greene on them. I say bring it on. I'll go down in infamy for her, be Clyde to her Bonnie any old time. "Not proud, sir, but also not backing down because of someone's demands."

He eyes his daughter again. "Did those demands involve you?"

She pauses from the storm brewing in his voice, but then stiffens her spine like the woman I know her to be. "Yes."

"And Tagger here?"

Raising her chin, she replies, "Yes."

He looks at Baylor again and nods toward the house. "Go clean yourself up so you can say hello with respect."

Baylor seems to have forgotten how things work on his father's ranch. He and Pris have the final say since Baylor walked away.

Regret starts to set inside, not for loving my girl, not even for making love to her in the barn, but I never wanted to cause problems between her family. I can't claim I didn't know better, no matter how much I regret this conclusion.

Baylor glares at me once more before leaving to go inside the house.

It's that look on his face, the one of anger and betrayal, that tells me where we stand in our friendship. It's over, which fucking sucks. It didn't have to be this way, but I'm sure he sees it the same.

Her dad approaches to stand in front of us, though the five feet remain between Pris and me. "You aren't that clever. I don't know why you were sneaking around. And I don't think I want to, but the man in the moon could see what's happening between you two. So let's cut the shit and figure out how to deal with the unnecessary mess you found yourself in."

"I love her, Mr. Greene." I was pleading my case to him, but the look of surprise I catch in my periphery draws my gaze to her. "I love you. I've said it before, but I'm not hiding it anymore." Turning back to face her dad, I say, "I'm in love with your daughter."

"I know." He sighs. "So what are you going to do about it with you up north in New York City and my daughter running our family ranch down here in Texas?"

"Dad." Pris steps forward. "We're—"

"I want to hear from him, Christine." His eyes never leave mine. "What are your intentions for my daughter?"

Seeing her worry her lip in concern, I reach out to hold her hand. When she slips it in mine, I whisper, "It's okay. I don't mind answering his question." I don't either, but I say, "We may not have it all figured out, but I'm confident in the direction we're heading."

"Jesus," Baylor exclaims from the porch, tossing his head back in exasperation.

Her dad ignores him and pivots his gaze to her. "Is that how you feel?"

"I love him." She glances at me quickly, then says, "With all my heart."

Finally turning his attention to his son, he says, "It sounds like it's settled then. Right, Baylor?"

He pushes off the railing and silently retreats into the house.

Mr. Greene chuckles. "It will take a few of us a little more time to get used to the idea." Coming over to me, he pats me on the arm. "Seems you have another mess to clean up, but it's best if you do it another day. Say your good night and head on home, son."

His gaze passes over my shoulder and then narrows. "There's a light on in the barn."

Shit.

CHAPTER 36

Tagger

WITH TEARS WOBBLING on her lower lids, threatening to fall, Pris says, "I don't want you to go."

I look into her pretty blue eyes and smile despite the pain in my hand and her dad telling me to go home like we're star-crossed teenagers. I'm fucking thirty, but I'll still respect his wishes because I'm standing on his property.

With my back against the driver's side of the truck and an ice pack taped to my hand, I hold her around her waist and kiss her. "It's only tonight."

"Tonight." She throws her arm out in frustration. "You only have two left, and then you're back in New York. You might as well be in Bali because they feel the same distance to me. My heart doesn't know the miles. It only knows that when you're here, my life is complete."

"I feel the same, but you have your family to deal with, and I need to get off the ranch before someone comes out with a shotgun."

Her gaze drops to my chest, where she fiddles with a button. "No one's shooting anyone."

"You sure about that?" That gets me a hard-earned smile. I lift her chin to get a better look at her just in case I'm not allowed on Greene property in Greene County again anytime soon. The tears have fallen, but no others are in line. "It's going to be okay, babe. We'll take the night and let everyone cool down. Tomorrow, we'll reconvene."

"I know that's what we should do to smooth things over, but what about us? Don't the two in the eye of the hurricane matter at all?"

I'd love to give her some words of wisdom and leave her to chew on a tidbit of positivity, but I can't. I'm struggling to make sense of this as well. We're adults, but we're being treated like kids. Fuck that. "Come with me. Come stay with me for the night."

The appeal of the idea curls the sides of her mouth up. "I *could*, but what about your parents? Will they mind if I'm there? I could sleep on the couch or—"

"You're going to stay with me." I push off the truck, adjusting her back so I can stand. I glance at the house, and say, "Go inside and get your stuff. I'll wait here for you."

She lifts on her toes to steal a kiss, then takes off. "Give me five minutes."

I can't believe it's come to us sneaking off together for the night. *Wait . . .* It's literally no different than what we've already been doing. "I'll be here."

Stopping, she looks back and whisper-yells, "No. Meet me closer to the gate so we don't get caught."

I rub the back of my neck and get in the truck. We're really doing this. Skipping out in the middle of the night so we don't get caught. I think I've seen this movie before, but no music was allowed in the small town either. *Or dancing.*

Releasing the brake, I start the engine but am quick to hit the radio to make sure there's no noise. Since I have no plans to dance, I think we're safe. Though I shut the headlights off just in case. I start a slow roll backward, trying to make as little noise as possible, and finally reach a safe distance from the house. This is good. I'm not going to have her running a half mile to catch up to me.

I wait.

And wait even longer.

I check my watch to see that fifteen minutes have passed. I don't remember the ending of that movie, but I have a strong suspicion that he got the girl. At least, I hope so.

Then, an angel appears in the moonlight. Her hair catches in the breeze, her dress flowing behind her, a bag in her hands, and a smile that beats any sunrise set on her face. I reach over and pop the door open for her.

"Did you miss me?" she asks, tossing her bag in the back seat and climbing in.

"I always do." I lean over and kiss her. "Buckle up, and let's get out of here."

We're not far from the ranch when I can tell the excitement begins to wear off—she's gone quiet, the smile that she had has smoothed to a more even line, and her attention has remained out her window since crossing the cattle guard.

I reach over to rub her shoulder, which brings her eyes back to me. "Are you doing okay?"

"I'm fine." I'm tempted to believe she is by her voice holding steady. There's no shake or uncertainty heard. She says, "What are we doing?"'

"Staying together?"

"No, I mean with our relationship. Our love for each other shouldn't hurt the people we care about."

"It doesn't."

"Tell that to my family." She waves her hand out in the cab. "We're still sneaking around even though we went public. Help me understand, Tagger, because I'm starting to lose faith that this will work out and keep my family intact."

I pull off to the side of the road. It's not a conversation we can have in my boyhood bedroom with my son sleeping in the room below it and my parents across the hall from him. Voices travel in that house. I learned that early on.

And right there is how fucking ridiculous this situation has become.

Gripping the steering wheel, I stare out at the two-lane road ahead, not another car in sight. I don't want to say it, but this is the line we always knew we'd have to cross one day. "You're right." I keep my eyes steady ahead, needing to say it, to get it out there so we can't avoid it anymore. "We can't keep doing this."

Even in the dimly lit cab of the truck, I can see her staring at me in the periphery. I don't look, not straight on. We should have already had this conversation. "What are you saying?"

"We need to make the hard decisions."

I know damn well most of those decisions fall on my shoulders, and they're not being made yet because I'm in limbo with my son's mom.

With her elbow secured on the door, she rests her head on her fisted hand and stares at me. "Do you care to elaborate?"

"I made your brother a promise when I was barely a man. I guess he planned to hold me to it until the day I died."

"It was a ridiculous promise that you guys should have never made in the first place. If he's going to make you choose between me and him, well . . ." Her gaze flows through the windshield into the dark road ahead. She sits up and looks right at me. "You don't have to choose for me. You don't even have to choose me over your best friend. You need to do what's right for you and for Beckett. I'll understand if I'm not what's best for your lives. I won't like it, but one day, I'll look back and remember how great it was to love you. Even if only for a short time in our lives."

How did we end up talking about a life without each other when we should be planning our futures? I reach over and rub the back of her neck. Watching her eyes close and her giving in to my touch doesn't help me decide. I already knew who I'd choose.

"Baylor can call me a traitor all he wants. I'm not willing to lose you, babe. I just need time to figure out how to do this better because seeing you once a month isn't enough."

Blue and red lights surround the truck and, "Pull over," is blasted over a speaker. Pris and my eyes connect. She rolls hers right after, and I roll down my window.

I can see him in the rearview mirror, taking inventory of the truck and tags, the registration stickers and the tires. When he reaches the window, I sit up. "How are you this fine evening, Deputy McCall?"

He tilts his head to make eye contact with Pris before me. When he looks at me, he says, "We're well past evening time, Mr. Grange." Shining a flashlight in my eyes forces me to squint. "You broken down?"

"No, sir."

"You're obstructing traffic."

I check the rearview mirror and then swing my gaze forward. "There is no traffic."

Pris leans over. "Can we go?" I have a feeling he won't appreciate her direct approach.

"Ms. Greene, you've been pulled over—"

"We weren't pulled over, Dirk. We were having a conversation that we thought was best, safest to have on the side of the road so we wouldn't obstruct traffic." She throws her arms up, and yells, "We can't win."

Ten minutes later, the cuffs are removed from my wrists, and he says, "All clear. You can get back in the vehicle, Mr. Grange."

It's not the first time I've tangoed with the law, but this is the first time I haven't broken it. I rub my wrists and get back in the truck. I know he tightened the cuffs because I'm sitting with the woman he can only dream about being with.

As soon as I shut the door, I shoot a glare in her direction. "Happy?"

Sympathy lies in every feature of her face, and she says, "I'm sorry. I didn't know he was going to search you . . . and the truck . . . and my bag."

"He didn't search you, though, the mouthy one who got me frisked and cuffed in the first place."

"He was never going to take you in."

"Let's not push our luck. Getting booked into county jail isn't something I want to do. So zip those lips, and I'll handle it from here."

In the side mirror, I watch Dirk returning by walking close to my side of the truck again.

She says, "I think he's just lonely and jealous of you, Tagger." She spies him one second too late. "Oops."

"Step out of the vehicle, Mr. Grange." He opens the door wide for me. "And put your hands behind your head."

"Fuck," I mutter under my breath and glower in her direction. *You have got to be fucking kidding me. Don't miss these small-town cops. Not one fucking bit.*

He starts into the spiel, "You have a right to remain—"

Pris says, "Hold your horses, Dirk." Hopping out of her

side of the truck, she comes around. "Put the cuffs away. You're not arresting him."

"I am, too, Christine," he says indignantly while cuffing one of my wrists, "so stick to your business."

"He is my business." Her voice is firm, but I think she's playing with fire. "And my boyfriend." *This is really not going to go over well.*

Trying to calm tempers, I say, "It's okay, babe. Take the truck and—"

"No," she replies with a stamp of her boot, giving me the sass that's getting me arrested. She marches right up to him and pokes him in the chest. "Release him now."

Four minutes later . . .

"First time here?"

She bursts out laughing. "Don't make me laugh. It hurts with my arms twisted like this in the back."

"You'll get used to it."

"I don't want to get used to being arrested and shoved in the back of cop cars."

Leaning my head against the seat in front of me, I try to keep her mind off being arrested for the first time. I don't want her scared. "What's your dad going to say when he finds out you've been arrested?"

"He's going to kill me." She's grinning, a good sign, but then shrugs. "Kidding. What can he really say to me?" She leans forward, mimicking me.

"Fair."

McCall gets in the driver's seat and buckles in. "You both

struggle to keep your traps shut, but I expect silence out of the two of you."

Pris and I exchange looks and then laugh.

The car pulls out, grinding gravel under the tires. The laughter fades as does her smile. She sits up and looks around once before taking a deep breath.

I sit back up but inch closer to her. "It's going to be okay."

She sighs. "I'm not worried about being arrested. My boss is tough, but since it's me, I'm okay hiring a hardened criminal." Angling in my direction, she bumps her knees against mine and looks into my eyes. "What about us?"

"We're going to be okay as well."

With a playful grin, she asks, "Promise?"

"I promise, but I'm thinking this is the last one I should ever give. They tend to get me in trouble."

"Keep it down," McCall says, banging on the mesh separating us from him.

You know what? *Fuck that.* "I'm not going to keep it down. I've been hiding too long." Turning to my girl, I say, "When I get back to the city, I'm going to figure out a way to make this work. I don't want you sleeping alone in our bed, and I'm tired of missing you so much. I promise you the whole fucking universe, Pris, because you deserve nothing less."

A sniffle fills the air, but it's not Pris.

"That was beautiful, Tagger." McCall is pulling a tissue from a box in the front seat.

"Thanks, man." I look at the woman beside me, caring more about what she thinks, though. "What do you say?"

"I do love that bed." She falls to the side and rests her head on my arm. "So is that bed in Texas or New York?"

CHAPTER 37

Tagger

THREE WEEKS LATER . . .

"THANKS FOR MEETING ME, TAGGER." Anna takes a sip of wine, our eyes meeting in the mirror over her glass.

I've wanted to talk to her for so long about the promotion and Paris, but voicing it gave it life I wasn't prepared to face yet. I'm on a mission, but I need to respect that there are two parents to consider. "What's this about?"

She turns to face me, spinning the stem of the wineglass and resting her other hand on the wooden bar top. My gaze is drawn to her finger. "Oh . . ." It's all I can muster.

"That's all?" she says with a trickle of a laugh. "I almost expected something snarky."

"It's a beautiful ring. Quite the statement piece."

"Five point five carats and the only statement it's meant to make is that I'm engaged."

"Congratulations. Marcel?" I don't purposely rub her

wrong. It just works out that way. Another reason we're not together any longer.

"*Funny.* Of course, it's Marcel. He popped the question last week when you had Beckett."

"Have you told him?"

Her eyes travel to the solitaire on her finger, a wistfulness coming over her as she sighs quietly. "I have."

I imagine it's a difficult conversation to have and one I've been thinking about a lot lately. "How did he react?"

Righting her shoulders, she sits straighter. "Marcel adores Beckett, but it's not necessarily mutual. But these things take time."

It didn't for Pris. He took right to her. Not having met Marcel myself, I'll assume our son has a good judge of character.

She says, "The wedding will be next spring."

Hate stating the obvious, but I'm unclear how the pieces are falling together. "Beck will be in school."

"I think it's best. It's going to be a large affair in the French countryside. Royals will be in attendance."

"Sounds like all your dreams are coming true."

She moves the diamond back and forth on her finger, then sets her hands in her lap. "We'll do a smaller celebration with Beckett and some family when he can visit in the summer."

"Visit?" My chest tightens for my son. "What are you saying?"

"I took the promotion, and I'm moving to Paris. I'm engaged and starting a life there. Marcel wants children."

I stare at her, waiting to see where she's heading with this. "Of his own."

"Doesn't every man?" She turns to her wine and takes another sip.

"I don't know about every other man. You're allowed to start a new life, but I'm wondering how Beckett will fit into it. That's my only concern."

She seems to be at a loss, but when tears fill her eyes, she says, "I love him more than anything, but I can't compete against what you're offering him."

"What are you talking about, Anna?"

"He doesn't want escargot or the Louvre. I could tempt with chocolate croissants because he loves those." She smiles as if a memory has returned. Her eyes shift back to mine, and she says, "He loves horses, Peachtree Pass, the ranch and being a cowboy, painting the house with you, and . . ."

I can see the pain she's fighting through, but she still carries her smile bravely. I need to know, though, so I ask, "And?"

Taking a deep breath that has her leaning back, she exhales slowly. "Your Christine." My Pris. There's a pause where her lips twist as if she doesn't want to admit defeat. But it was never a contest. "He adores her. He's told me so much about her that I think I adore her." Dropping her hand, she shakes it under a humorless laugh. "I was so rude to her, too, and to you. I'm sorry. I don't know why I was jealous, but I've thought so much about it and I'm happy you've found someone who not only loves you but also our son like her own. Though I don't want him calling her mom. Okay?"

"Okay. Same goes for Marcel."

"Do you love her?"

"I love her."

Her smile is genuine, which gives hope for some reason. She says, "We're moving in different directions, across continents, and he needs to live with one of us. Although it will shatter my heart to pieces, he's happiest with you, and his happiness is more important than my sadness of missing him."

I breathe. For the first time in weeks, I feel my lungs pumping air freely through my system. "Do you mean that?"

She nods, the confidence in her eyes and the smile that sits firmly in place underneath have me believing her. She says, "School starts at the end of August. I've already done research, and there are no private schools in the surrounding eight counties. But you have time to enroll him in Peachtree Elementary before the start of the year."

"I'll take care of it," I say, not minding the to-do list she's giving me because it's more than errands and tasks. She's giving me our son to raise where there's room to spread his wings and run without cars threatening to hit him.

After taking another sip, she sets her heels back down on the floor. "I need to go. Marcel has never had a hot dog, and I told him Beck and I can take him to the best stand in the city."

"Minelli's on Fourth?"

She laughs. "You know I don't care for street meat because yuck, but for Beck and I guess for Marcel, I'll be hot dogging it for dinner."

"I like this side of you."

"The one risking my gastrointestinal tract?"

"The one that believes she deserves happiness as well."

She playfully points a finger in my face. "I still get him during breaks."

"And anytime in between. You'll always be his mother, Anna, and as such, you have a place to stay in Peachtree Pass. Or if it's too boring for you out there in the middle of nowhere, there's a Four Seasons Resort near Fredericksburg."

"I like the sound of that."

"I'll bring him to see you."

"You've got yourself a deal. Tell your attorney to contact mine, and we'll get everything sorted legally." Leaning in, she kisses my cheek. Not quick to leave, she whispers, "You deserve happiness as well." Straightening her back, she takes her purse from the bar and tucks it under her arm. "She's a very lucky woman."

I knew the moment I saw Pris in that sundries shop that I was the lucky one. She starts walking but turns back to say, "Oh, you got the tab, right?"

"I got you covered."

"Thanks." There's a lightness to her steps. Happiness that I haven't seen in her in years. It looks good on her. But I'm glad it's not because it's me. I wish her and Marcel the best. "We always made a good team like that."

I hold up my bourbon. With that conversation out of the way, I'm finally able to take a sip. "Drinking and eating, and me paying the check?"

"You're the best, Tagger. Toodle-oo." Details need to be worked out, but the obstacles have been cleared from my path. I can work from anywhere or retire from asset management. But I also have more money than I can spend in a lifetime, so why not spend it with the two people I care about most?

One down.

My best friend to go . . .

THREE DAYS LATER . . .

. . .

I'VE BEEN SECRETLY TRYING to wrap up some of my accounts. The others will shift to Keith for him to keep or reassign. Nothing too obvious until I'm ready to announce.

Coming to sit in front of me, no notepad or e-pad, pen, or phone in sight, Kendra says, "Deloitte has been processed and shifted to the accounting team. Baer needs signed paperwork that I had delivered earlier today. But Mastrioni said they are happy with the work you're doing and look forward to continuing when they paid their invoice on Tuesday."

"That's great. I suspect there will be another hefty bonus for us at the end of the year."

"But you won't be here?"

"I'll still be—fuck." I release a heavy sigh, knowing I can't hide it from her.

She gets up to close the door. When she returns, she asks, "So you *are* leaving?"

Sitting back, I steeple my fingers. "I'm not walking out the door tomorrow. But I plan on giving notice before the end of July. I'm hoping that's enough time to wrap up what I can and reorganize the team for the clients."

"It was the biscuits, wasn't it?"

I chuckle. "The biscuits helped, but I was already in love."

"Oh Tagger, that's so romantic. You deserve this. You work hard, you're a great father, but you also need a life. If that's what she gives you, then I couldn't be happier."

"She makes me want to change my life. She makes me want to be a part of hers, to use my hands again, to work the land, and get back to my roots." I'd already shared that Anna was moving to Paris, so she knows Beck will be with me.

"I forgot to mention you're a great boss."

"It's been great to work with you. I've been thinking about consulting and working freelance. If that's something you'd be interested in—"

"I'm interested."

I rest my hands on the desk. "I'll keep you in the loop with what's going on, then."

She stands. "Remember to invite me to the wedding."

Chuckling, I reply, "You're on the list."

I rush home to change into basketball shorts and a tee before racing out the door in my sneakers. It's later than I intended, but there's so much to do lately that time is lost if I'm not paying attention.

Walking onto the courts, I scan the players before finding Baylor playing on the back third. They're short a player since it's usually me, but I don't jump in. That's not how pickup games of basketball work around here. I lean against the fence and wait for someone to score.

Baylor sees me out of the corner of his eye but keeps playing. He's not been responding to my texts or calls. I even sent him an email to see if he'd reply. *He didn't.*

One team scores points, and they scatter to take a water break. Baylor walks by me and says, "Find another team, asshole."

"Fuck you, Baylor."

"*Ohhhh,*" the other players caught that and start to laugh.

Holding the water bottle at his side, he says, "Fuck you, man. Go find another court."

He flips me off, then squirts water in his mouth.

"No. We will either take this out on the court or take it off the courts and get it all out. Your choice."

He comes closer, looking me up and down like the sight

of me pisses him off. "You don't get to make the rules. You're the one who fucked up by fucking my sister."

"*Dammmnnnn*," another player says, holding his fist to his mouth. "That's dark, man."

I don't even know who this dude is. "I don't need the commentary. Thanks." Baylor is tossed a basketball, which he starts dribbling in beside him. That he's even listening is progress. "We've invested thirty years into this friendship. You ready to let it go? Because it's in your hands." Crossing my arms over my chest, I ask, "What's it going to be, Greene?"

He eyes me over his chin, then tosses the basketball to another player. "Fine, we'll talk outside the courts." He grabs his stuff and heads for the exit.

I follow, giving him the space I think he needs. He takes a left and heads for some benches where spectators sit. Sitting on opposite ends, we still take up most of the bench. I rest my forearms on my knees and watch the games being played before us. "I should have talked to you."

He looks over at me. "And say what? You want to sleep with my sister? Not sure that approach would be any better." He returns his gaze to the courts. But then he sits back and says, "I heard what you told my dad." He looks at me. When I look at him, I nod. "You love her?"

"I'm in love with her."

"Why?"

"What do you mean why?"

"What is it about her that you fell in love with?"

"Oh, um." I glance at the sky. I know the answers, but I just don't know if he wants to hear them. He's asking for a reason, so I'll respect him enough to honestly respond. "She's funny and smart. She knows who she is and doesn't hide it." I close my eyes and see her face in my head, her sitting in the wildflowers, staying with her horse during the storm, her hair splayed over the pillows of our place in the barn. "She knows how to fix an irrigation system and make a killer peach pie." I look over at him, lowering my voice. "She's beautiful inside and out."

"She's just like my mother. It's like looking at Mom sometimes."

"She has her strength and determination, her dad's easy-going nature, and her brother's charisma."

"That's all I get? Charisma." He rolls his eyes and chuckles. "It's a start, so I'll take it."

"She rolls her eyes like you just did." I glance between the game on the court in front of us and then at him again. "You guys are more alike than you realize. She's got your sense of humor—"

"My humor is in the gutter."

I shrug. "Point proven."

"Jesus. I don't want to know that shit about my sister." But the smile on his face tells me he's not too bothered. He looks over at me once more, and asks, "Have you told her all that?"

"Give or take." I take a few seconds to breathe, then add, "She loves hard and gives all of herself to the people she cares about, but let me tell you what opened my eyes to the woman she's become." He's staring at me, but a lump forms in my throat. I push through and swallow it down. "Seeing her with my son. That changed everything for me."

"And made you break your promise."

"I'm sorry about that."

"We were stupid kids. Twelve years was a good run, but I never should have made you agree to it. It was about then. I never thought about the future. But I have had a lot of thoughts about that lately. My best friend marrying my sister might not be the worst-case scenario. I mean, we're already like brothers." He stands up and holds out his hand. I stand while shaking it. Bringing me in for a shoulder bump, he says, "Promise me you'll never hurt her."

I chuckle, feeling we've come full circle. "I promise. I love her so much that it hurts to be apart."

I'm given another eye roll. "Fine, we're friends again even if you did take a cheap shot and punch me in the face."

"Sorry about that, but it was either you or me and—"

"I'm in a different headspace now, but I do owe you one."

He's not going to do it, but I can go with the flow on this one. "Sure, if it will make you feel better."

"Not sure if it will, but we'll find out." Backing up, he laughs. Crossing his arms over his chest, he stares ahead, seemingly caught in his thoughts. But then he says, "Be truthful. If you had to choose . . ."

"I choose her. Every time."

"You're such an asshole." Grabbing me into a headlock, he scrapes his knuckles over my head. That's my asshole best friend. It's good to have him back. "Come on. Let's go play some basketball."

The rest of the week has flown by with all the things I need to put in place. By Sunday evening, I sit with Beckett, eating ice cream at a shop around the corner from my building. Anna and I sat down with him when I came to pick him up. We discussed the plan we've put in place, then asked for his input.

It will be hard not seeing his mom every other week, but we showed him how they'll video call and talked about visiting. He's a resilient kid. He'll go through some adjusting, but he's happy to be going to Texas. Not so happy about leaving his friends at school.

That's when I promised him his own horse . . . Promises just fly off my tongue, but these I'll keep.

"I told Seraphina I was going to marry her, but she has to like horses."

Chuckling, I say, "Wise words, kid."

"But now I'm moving."

I lick my ice cream and think about Pris. "If it's meant to be, it will be."

"Like you and Miss Christine?" Bending his head to the side, he's quick to lick a spot on the cone before it drips.

"Yes. What do you think about me marrying her?"

He's determined to retrieve a gumball from the ice cream with his tongue, so he's momentarily distracted. But then he says, "I thought you were. I thought when you found the secret ingredient, that meant you were together forever."

Grinning like a fool, he's teaching me as much as I am him. "Yeah, that's how it works. I'm just going to make it official when we go back."

He lowers his cone and tilts his head. "By giving her a house?"

I tap his nose and rub his head. "That's not a bad idea, kid."

CHAPTER 38

Christine

"I MISS YOU." Wedging the phone between my shoulder and ear, I lean against Skyward's stall, where I just added fresh bedding to the ground. "When will I see you again?"

The positivity I've held on to for the past three weeks is waning. I need a hit of Tagger in my life again. Just a little one will keep me going long enough until he can visit at the end of July.

If I close my eyes, the sound of his breath travels the distance like he's here by my side again. The way it would breeze against the back of my neck when he cuddled around me in sleep. If I let myself go further, I remember how the tips of his fingers pushed into my hips as he took me and the slightest of smile he wore right after while he slept.

"I miss you more than those gorgeous Texas sunsets."

"That's saying something because the sky is on fire this evening, and it's just getting started. I wish you were here to see it."

"Soon, my love." His voice is low and comforting like his arms when wrapped around me. "Are you taking care of yourself?" He asks me this often because I once mentioned that no one does and I'm just expected to always be strong.

When he's here, he makes sure I'm taken care of. When he's not, it makes me feel loved in his absence. I smile to myself, kicking up a little hay that had fallen when I carried it in earlier. "I'm getting by. How about you? How's the little guy?"

"Excited to be down there again."

Beckett makes me smile even more. He's pure joy, enthusiasm, and raw energy wrapped up in that little frame of his. "A full week this time?" There's a pause in the conversation that has me adjusting the phone against my ear. "Tagger?"

"I'm here, babe, but I really can't wait to be there with you."

The little delays in responses make me wonder if I called at a bad time. "I can let you go if you're busy."

"I'm sorry. I have a meeting."

My brain always shifts to the East Coast time zone when we talk. I know what time it is for him more than my own sometimes. "At eight o'clock at night?"

"My days have been busy, so I've taken care of stuff after hours."

A chorus of crickets have gotten louder, so I plug my other ear. "Sounds like you're ready to work a ranch. No days off, from sunrise to sunset, and no food delivery, which might be one of the saddest parts."

"Tell me you ate today, Pris."

"I ate today."

"But did you really?"

Honestly, I haven't been thinking about food much since he's been gone. Sure, I make dinner with my dad, but it's nothing special or noteworthy. "I'm about to. That counts, right?"

"I don't know how you're fueling yourself, but you need to. That's hard work you're doing day in and day out. Why aren't you eating?"

"I like to stay busy so my mind doesn't wander as much."

The pause is long enough for me to walk out the back of the barn to catch the last of the sunset. I don't fill in the space. I don't have interesting things going on in my life. I'm just living day-to-day, trying not to focus on the hole left in my heart.

"Babe?" he says, his voice quieter as someone else might hear. "I'll be there soon. You be ready for me, okay?"

"I'm ready," I reply, more than ready to see him again.

"I love you."

"I love you, too." I tuck the phone in my back pocket and return to my final duties to wrap up for the night. When I walk toward the house, I see my brother over on the pasture's fence. His eyes are aimed at the sunset, so he doesn't see me coming.

I have stopped anyway, not sure if I'm ready to approach him. I dust my hands off and shove them in my front pockets. Better to go straight through the pain than linger around the edges. I mosey up next to him, setting my foot on the lower rail and resting my arms on the upper.

The sun dips just below the trees, but there's still enough to expose the fissures in our relationship. "Visiting twice in a month?" I ask like it's normal to see Baylor on the ranch. "What brings you by?"

Tilting his head down, he angles it sideways to look at me. "I've been a shitty brother to you, Pris." Hearing that name feels wrong from his mouth, which is ironic since he's the one who dubbed me Pristine to begin with. I don't correct him, but moving forward, we need to agree on leaving it for only my boyfriend to say.

"I deserved better." I can hear Lauralee's words about giving him space and time to share his truths. I know he has some buried in there. Though it doesn't mean I can't still be mad at him for abandoning me.

"You did." He turns to face me. "Did Tagger talk to you?"

"About?"

"We talked."

I find relief that their relationship is intact. I know they both need their friendship. "He hasn't mentioned it, but I'm glad to hear it."

He nods and looks across the property. As if he has something he wants to get off his chest, he takes a breath, then exhales slowly. "I'm sorry." I straighten my back, gobsmacked by those two little words. I try to close my mouth from catching flies when his eyes find mine again. "I'm sorry I left you to deal with the mess."

"Why did you leave? You didn't even say goodbye. You didn't respond to my texts." The buildup of years of frustration and hurt floats to the surface now that he's brought up this topic. "Did you think the occasional text or photo of you living your best life was serving anything other than what you selfishly needed? You didn't ask about me? You didn't care."

"I cared. I care about you."

I hate that it's so easy to make me cry. This conversation should have been had years ago instead of being repressed. My emotions were put on hold, waiting for him and Griff to act like I existed. Although a big part of my heart is waiting for Tagger to fill, hearing those four words seems to be all it takes to start feeling whole again.

When a tear slips down, he pulls me into his arms.

Closing my eyes, I realize I never needed much, but shaking off the burden of holding this grudge already has me feeling so much better. I lean back and use the inside of my T-shirt to wipe my face.

We start to walk side by side. The pace is slow, but it gives us time to talk. I say, "I needed to hear that, Baylor." I glance up. "I care about you and Griffin so much, but it's felt like I don't even have brothers anymore."

"I want to make it up to you."

I playfully bump into him on purpose, breaking up our stride. "You don't have to. Just don't disappear on me twice."

Pulling me in for a side hug, he says, "I won't. You're stuck with me now, kid."

When we separate again, I ask, "Why did you leave?"

"Truth?"

"Of course."

"I didn't get to tell her how much I loved her."

It's tempting to roll my eyes as annoyance sets in, but he's opening up, which is something I've wanted since he left. "None of us did. It was a car accident."

"She had called, but I didn't answer. She tried over several days. I was so busy living my big, important life in New York that I couldn't be bothered." I stay quiet, giving him the freedom to lighten his burden as well. "You look just like her, even the coloring of your hair and your smile . . . I looked at you, and I felt worse." I'm told this all the time. It's a source of pride for me and makes me feel closer to her for some reason. But I also catch the reactions people try to hide—the pity she died so young, the sympathy for her family, and me carrying her around so prevalently makes them miss her as well.

I've learned to embrace the similarities instead of pushing against them.

He shakes his head, and says, "That sounds terrible to admit, but you have to know it wasn't you, never you, Pris. The guilt was eating me alive, so I avoided it. I avoided comforting you and being there for Dad. Sadness and devastation, that's what this place had become."

I can't argue with him. I've never been able to put it into words like that before, but they fit—sad and devastating. "It's true. Everything suffered until one day I woke up and knew I had to change it. I had to be present instead of letting my head be sucked into the memories. I had to fix the part of the farm Dad was no longer tending. I used the money from insurance to hire a crew to help me, and then I put my business degree to work as well as learning everything I could to improve the ranch."

"You did it. You're kind of small," he says, nudging me with his elbow. I pretend to blow over before returning to his side under my own amusement. "But you're so much stronger than either of your older brothers. You did all of this, Sis."

I laugh, though I'm not sure I'm entertained. "You guys are reaping the rewards."

"I can't speak for Griff, but I want to sign over my share of the ranch to you."

I stop so fast that I topple a little, then right myself. "What do you mean?"

"Dad set it up so all four of us have equal shares."

"He did that on purpose."

"He did that when he thought I would be contributing. I'm not. I'm only taking. It doesn't seem fair when you're out here working day in and day out. You took an old farm barely above red on the financials and turned it into a multi-million-dollar business. You've done so much for our family but deserve more."

"I want all of us to be listed."

"Tagger said you'd say that."

The name has me smiling. I shrug because I'm guilty as charged. "He knows me well."

With his eyes on me, he says, "How about this? You own the majority share and have final say. Instead of twenty-five percent, we'll cut it in half, and I'll retain ten."

I laugh because that makes no sense. "That's not half. Also, aren't you a financial adviser?"

"Take the deal, Sis."

I study his face, his eyes, and his tone. *He's serious.* When he holds out his hand, I look at it, and ask, "Are you sure?"

"I'm sure."

We shake on it, setting me up as majority owner and controlling partner. I grin, feeling this is the reward for all my hard work. "Deal."

He leans down and hugs me. "I'm proud of you and all you've accomplished."

Why does this mean so much more simply because he's my brother? "Thanks, Bay."

"As for my best friend . . ."

"Here it comes. Go on, get it out of your system."

Since it's dark, we turn around and start back for the house. "I couldn't be happier that you two found each other. You guys make a great couple."

"You really mean that?"

"Yeah, but he's been threatened to stay in line or else."

"I had no doubt." I burst out laughing. "You are my brother, after all."

Just shy of the front porch, he says, "I love you, little sis."

I rest my head on his arm and smile. "I love you, big brother." Standing in the light of the first stars and the floodlight on the barn, I ask, "What do you think it will take to get Griffin to come for a visit?"

"I don't know." Looking around the property, he appears to be taking everything in. "Some things never change." He looks at me, and says, "But maybe we just ask."

Walking up the steps, I start to toe my boots off on the porch. A few things are still on my mind. I can't change how I look, but I'm still curious about his thoughts. "Is it still hard to look at me when I look so much like Mom?"

His smile grows, and a chuckle escapes his chest. "I'm glad we talked. That helped. Now I see you, Christine, the woman you've grown into."

Standing in my socked feet, I go to him and hug him so tight. "Glad to have you back in my life."

HANGING out at Whiskey's is not where I wanted to be tonight. I was really looking forward to falling asleep before *Saturday Night Live* started and waking up in time to see the musical guest perform so I could trick myself into believing I could stay up that late. But Baylor insisted on it for the sixth and last night of his visit.

Since he's leaving tomorrow, I cave, which sends Lauralee into overdrive to dress me for some reason.

"You're pretty in dresses, but I think you have an incredible body and should show it off."

"To whom, may I ask?" I turn as far as I can to look over my shoulder and still be able to check out my ass in the mirror. "My boyfriend is halfway across the country."

Our eyes connect in the mirror. "For you, that's who. And stop being so formal with your whom."

I start to laugh but stop when she hands me mascara to

apply, and lord knows, I need to hang my mouth wide open to coat my lashes for some reason. After applying a candy apple lip oil, I slip my painted-on jeans into my taller black dress boots. "Hat?"

"No." After applying her gloss, she taps her lips together several times. "This face and bod deserve all the attention."

I tuck my phone in my back pocket and make sure I have my ID and money in my front pocket. Standing behind and off to the side of Lauralee, I give one more look over in the mirror, happy with the sweetheart neckline of the fitted red tank top. The material is soft, and I won't sweat so much since it's July in Texas.

Stepping back, I look at my friend and whistle. "Wowsa." I almost do a double take. My friend is gorgeous, but this is a whole new level of sexy as well. "New jeans?"

"Got them in the mail today." She tugs the hem of her purple satin spaghetti strap shirt and then smiles. "I'm ready."

Baylor waits by the truck and pushes off the bumper when he sees us. I hear him mutter, "Jesus," from the porch and see him shaking his head as he heads for the driver's seat. But he stops before he opens the door, and says, "You know I'm going to have a good time. I'll be fending fuckers off you two all night looking like that."

Got to love that his night is ruined because we look good. Lauralee turns to high-five me as we head to the truck. I climb in first because I won't force my best friend to squeeze in next to my brother on the cushioned bench. *I mean, ew.*

Regret sets in not ten miles down the road with a good twenty left to travel. I can't pinpoint the exact moment the tension between them fills the cab, but it's smothering me in the middle, an innocent bystander. But now I find myself silently trying to have an exchange with my friend through glares and widening them. I only get a pop of her shoulders in return.

I don't bother with my brother. I just hit him with a glare for making this awkward.

As soon as we arrive, I practically push Lauralee out of the truck, ready to breathe freely again. But before he comes around to her, I whisper, "You're not interested in my brother, are you?"

"It's Baylor."

"Exactly." I start walking toward the door, raising my hand in the air. "Let's have some fun."

Two hours and two beers in, I pool-sharked another victim out of a twenty. "Easy money, baby." I grab my beer and tip it back until it's empty.

As soon as I set it down, someone whispers, "You still owe me a rematch," in my ear. Hands come around me, and I'd know the voice and feel of him anywhere. The goose bumps popping up all over my arms are the only confirmation I need. My heart knows who it belongs to. My body could recognize him in the dark.

I cover Tagger's hand, rubbing the tips of my fingers over the veins and firm hold he has over my stomach. Tilting my head to the side, I grin. "Sorry. It's one and done."

"I can live with that." His voice is smooth, his entrance back into my life even more so.

I spin in his arms, wrapping mine around his neck, and stare into those green eyes like he'll disappear if I blink. "Giving up that easy, cowboy?"

"Don't you worry, pretty girl, one and done is all I need."

Cocking an eyebrow, I finally blink. "Is that a sexual reference? Because I'm going to need more than once with you."

"No," he says with a light chuckle. "It's a reference to finding my forever."

I tighten my hold on him because he's here, finally, back in my arms again, and I can. "I'm not following."

"Let me be a little clearer." He slips a box from his back pocket, causing my heart to stop, and places it on the edge of the pool table. "One game. Winner takes all."

"I'm not afraid to kick your ass in a game of pool. But what's on the line?"

His laugh is heartier, a smirk well in place. "My heart and a ring."

Speaking of hearts, mine is already beating out of my chest, but I try to shake the nerves of what this really means and play it cool. "And if you win?"

"I get you." He leans down and kisses me. His lips caress mine, and then he whispers against my lips, "It's a win-win. Are you in?"

I lick my lips and chalk the tip of my stick. "All in, baby."

I break since I've been owning the table before he showed up. My heart is still racing because he's here, but I do my best to take him out quickly. "The girl's got skills," Baylor says, keeping track of all the balls I sank. "Dude, you're going to lose."

"There is no losing when it comes to her." He leans over the table and sets up. Tagger can't stand to lose, so he's not afraid to fight for the win, even when it comes to me. I respect that.

Of course, judging by that turn, I've got this and him in the bag.

Lauralee has parked next to Baylor at a tall table with two chairs. She's guarding the ring, and probably like me, dying to see what he picked out. "Come on, Chris. You got this."

It only takes three more turns for me to sink the final eight ball. I receive a round of applause from the gathered crowd, but it's not their reaction I'm looking for. It's Tagger's.

He hands his stick to Baylor and grins with pride in his eyes as he takes the box from Lauralee. "You want your prize?"

This is really happening. The Prince Charming I dreamed about my entire life is mine. So I won't force him to concede into giving me a ring over a lost game of pool. Hooking my fingers into his belt loops, I tug him forward. Cupping his face, I lift on my toes and kiss him again. "You are all I want, babe. You're here, so I have everything I need."

His eyes search mine before he kisses me again. And then he drops to one knee. "I never thought I'd be doing this in Whiskey's, but here we are, and I always keep a promise."

Baylor clears his throat.

I roll my eyes, but Tagger shoots him a look that I wouldn't want to be on the receiving end of. "It was one time, dude." Turning back to me, he steadies himself again, and says, "Will you marry me, Pris?"

I'm a simple country girl. I don't need the big to-do. I need him. And when he lifts the lid on the box, I also need that gorgeous ring on my finger. "Yes. Every day with you for the rest of my life, yes." I throw myself into his arms and almost knock him over. "I can't wait to wife you up, cowboy."

"We don't have to wait."

Sometimes the brightest stars burn out the fastest. *Not us.* We're just getting started.

CHAPTER 39

Pris

"This came for you." My dad drops the letter on the desk in front of me. "Are you going again this year?"

"Going where?" I pick it up to see The Farmers of Central Texas Membership Committee on the return address. I burst out laughing, covering my mouth with the back of my hand. *My sweet ole dad.* "I don't think it's necessary."

He sits on the end of my bed with his hands resting in his lap. He doesn't hang out for no reason, so I ask, "Something on your mind, Dad?"

Taking his time as he always does, he looks out the window at the leaves blowing in the gentle breeze. When he redirects his gaze to me, he says, "I wish your mom could be here to help you with all this wedding planning and hullabaloo."

"I do, too." My heart pings over it from figuring out the flavor of the cake Peaches is making for us or shopping for a dress, which has been done online before bed since that's the only real time I have to dedicate to it. "But you're here, and I'm so grateful for all you do to help with the property."

He takes a breath and looks down. "You deserved a mom to be here. I'm sorry she's gone, and you're stuck with me."

I get up to sit next to him. Wrapping my arm around his back, I lean my head against his shoulder. "You're enough, Dad. You're not a consolation prize. I'd love for Mom to be here, but I'm at peace with how things are. I need you to find it in this life as well."

He covers the hand I rest on his shoulder and pats it. "I can find joy in these special occasions. I'll celebrate every family milestone on this earth that I'm given. I will do my best to be all you need, but you have to tell me if I'm failing. I'm not good with this stuff, but I'll keep trying."

"That's good enough." I kiss his cheek, then return to the desk to finish putting on my makeup. Lauralee has insisted we go all out with all the occasions. I'm not sure what to expect at a bachelorette party, but I'm worried it will be like what I've seen in the movies.

He stands and goes to the door. "So you and Tagger Grange, huh?"

I waggle my finger, unable to stop the epic smile taking over my face. I've smiled so much recently that my cheeks hurt. "Seems that way."

"You'll make a good wife and a good bonus mom to his son, but make sure he understands that you're your own woman and he needs to be a good husband. Or else he'll have to deal with me."

"And Baylor." I laugh.

He opens the door, and adds, "You make a fine pair." When he ducks out, I hear crinkling in the hallway. "And since this seems to be a done deal, I wanted to give you something."

I stand, having no idea what it could be. We've always had modest birthdays and Christmas gift exchanges, so a present out of the blue is new for us. "Is this a wedding gift?"

"Two gifts." He comes back into the room and hands me a little store bag. "This one is from your mother."

My breath deepens as a swarm of emotion overcomes me. I don't know why I'm afraid to open it. I look at him, and ask, "What is it?"

"Just open it, Christine."

I do, the crinkling of the bag connecting to the sound he made outside my room. I pull out a little velvet bag, then pour the contents into my palm. He says, "I know you can buy your own, but I thought you might like to have Mom's sapphire earrings. I had them cleaned and polished. They look new."

A tear falls on top of one of them. Glancing up at him, I take a staggered breath. "I forgot about these. She used to wear them on her birthday—"

"And our anniversary."

"She once wore them to the grocery store and whispered we don't have to save our special things for only special occasions." The memory makes me sob. "I don't think I'd ever seen her smile and laugh so much while shopping for pantry staples. It was like she had discovered the secret to happiness." I turn them over in my hand. "Enjoy life and every day you're given." I put one on and then the other. "How do I look?"

He nods and clears his throat, but I see the tears in his eyes so I can only imagine the size of the frog in his throat. "You look beautiful, dear daughter."

I hug him. "Thank you. I'll treasure them forever."

"Good. Now," he says, standing and going into the hallway again. "I have something from me. Well, your mom and I, but you'll understand." Pushing open the door, he holds her white dress on a hanger in front of him.

My makeup is ruined, so I don't worry about it and rush to the dress. Holding it between my fingertips, I pull it out in front of me. "How?" I look at him, smiling proudly. "It's perfect, not a stain on it. I thought it was ruined. How did you get it so clean?"

"Your brother set me up on the computer and introduced me to YouTube. I must've tried ten techniques that strangers on the screen recommended. But then I went to the laundry, trying to remember how your mom got everything so clean. Baking soda, Borax, and a lot of elbow grease did the trick."

To say my dad loves me is an understatement. Taking the dress from him, I hold it to me as I hug him with my other arm. "Thank you. It's perfect."

"Perfectly clean?"

"Yes, but also perfect for the wedding."

My head might hurt from drinking too much last night at a mildly wild bachelorette party that involved me drinking too many Blow Job shots without using my hands and having Deputy McCall driving most of us home—I sat in the front seat this time and was on siren duty— last night, but I arrive to the transfer of ownership meeting with our attorney on time. The meeting is being held at our kitchen table, but I'm still here along with my dad and Baylor. *Barely.*

I'm handed a pen before the lawyer goes through the paperwork to explain. The percentages don't add up. "It's supposed to be thirty-eight percent in my name, correct?"

I tap the numbers on the page. "This says fifty-one percent."

The door opens. "Sorry, I'm late."

"Griffin." I jump from my seat and run into his arms. "What are you doing here?" I cry into his shoulder. Getting married sure does bring out the emotions.

"Hey, baby sis." When I step back to give him access to my dad and brother, he says, "You're getting married. I wouldn't miss it for the world."

I'm so tempted to text Tagger and share the good news, but he's at the elementary school signing Beckett up for school and taking a tour to get him more comfortable before it starts in the fall.

As soon as they take their seats again, I hug him. "I've missed you so much." Even though I've grown up since last seeing him, he's bigger than I remember. Dark hair like my dad once had, and Baylor's mop top. His eyes are blue like mine, and the spark I remember so vividly being in his eyes has returned to be a part of the festivities.

Griffin Greene is not someone we can keep up with. His life has led him all over this earth and back again. He left like Baylor after my mom's death, but we didn't get many texts after that, and fewer calls came through. I have no idea what he's been up to.

And due to all that needs to get done, I'm not sure we'll have time to catch up.

The attorney calls us over and goes through the numbers again to show me how it got to fifty-one. "Baylor is transferring thirteen shares. Griffin is doing the same. That puts it at fifty-one."

My head swivels so fast on my neck to look at Griffin that I think I twinged it. Rubbing it, I ask, "You did that?"

"It only makes sense. Like Baylor has said, you've earned

it. We keep some of it in our family name, but you deserve it, Christine." He nods toward the document. "Go ahead and sign, and let's make this official."

I take the pen and sign my name. I don't think it sinks in that this ranch is mine like it is my dad's. I gave up a lot to be here, to pick up the pieces when no one could. I never imagined I'd get this kind of payoff.

When I walk the lawyer to his car, he stops and looks around like he wants to make sure we're alone. "I have one more thing for you." He digs into the pocket of his briefcase and pulls out more documents.

"What is it?"

"A prenuptial agreement from Mr. Grange."

The words strike like a slap across the face. "We're getting married tomorrow."

"Time is of the essence, but I think he was wise to protect the assets."

I cross my arms over my chest. "What asset are we specifically talking about?"

"The ranch, the business, the farm, the orchards, and the houses on the property."

"There's only one house."

He replies, "For now."

I find the statement as confusing as this whole surprise prenuptial agreement. There was never a mention of anything or protecting ourselves from the other. So to say this feels like a blindside . . . a Mack truck hitting me and coming back for a second round is more fitting.

Taking the papers, I say goodbye and march straight into the house and up to my bedroom, ready to give Tagger a piece of my mind. If he doesn't want to share, fine, we won't share a damn thing, including that bed I was promised.

I flop on the bed, my head still pounding from too much

alcohol last night and pull the papers from the envelope. Holding them above my head, I start to flip through pages but land on one—the division of assets. Should I have seen this coming? He's in finance, so it would have been a stretch. Otherwise, it's not in his character to surprise me with last-minute betrayal-nuptial agreements.

Scanning the page, I stop when I see what's included and what's very much not listed. I sit up to reread just in case I didn't read it correctly the first time. But there it is, plain as day. "There shall be no claims to Rollingwood Ranch or any associated businesses, properties, financials, or incomes." *No claim?*

Why do we need a contract to state he has no claim to my family's property?

And then it occurs to me . . . He has no claim to my money and assets, but I have full rights to his. *Oh my God.* Tagger, what have you done?

He's getting so lucky for this.

"YOU'RE PRETTY," Beck says, standing in front of me in his spiffiest jeans, button-up, boots, and hat. *He's acclimating.*

"Thanks, buddy." I squat to adjust the little lariat around his neck. "You look very handsome yourself."

"Wait until you see Daddy. He said he looks handsome for you."

"Oh yeah?" Standing back up, I add, "I can't wait."

He pulls something from his pocket and holds it in his hand. "I have something for you."

"What is that?"

"I made you a friendship bracelet." He holds up the satin ribbon with beads on it. "It has my name."

I can't handle his cuteness. Taking it, I hug him. "Thank you so much." When I sit back on my heels, I ask, "Can I wear it now?" He nods. "Will you help me?" He takes the bracelet and slides it on my wrist. I twirl it back and forth several times to admire it. It really is perfect for the occasion. I manage to get one hug out of him before he dashes because he heard there were the good kind of gummy bears on a table somewhere.

A kid after my own heart.

WITH A RING of flowers wrapped around my head and my hair flowing over my shoulders, Sunrise brings me across the fields to where our friends and family have gathered.

It's the perfect spot to see the sunset explode in stunning oranges and pinks with blues mixed in. The sky will be on fire before we seal our nuptials with a kiss.

In the shade of the orchard with the fragrance of peaches floating in the air, my soon to be betrothed is waiting for me. My cowboy looks as handsome as ever in his pale gray felt cowboy hat and his shined-up boots. He went with dark denim and a white shirt for the occasion. His incredible smile wins me over as if he hadn't all those years prior.

Lauralee holds the bouquet of wildflowers I picked this morning near the ridge of where my mom is buried. A gentle breeze welcomed me with dew still shining on the leaves as the sun rose over the greener pasture. I only had a few minutes, but it was good to share the peaceful moment with her.

There is no music, but who needs music when love is in the air? Tagger isn't an overly emotional kind of man. But the sunset shines in his eyes, and I can see the tears forming while he watches me.

The sun beats down, so I don't want to keep everyone waiting in the heat. Griffin helps me off the horse, and Baylor guides me to where my dad will walk me down the makeshift aisle to my handsome soon-to-be-husband.

After a quick embrace of my best friend, I take the bouquet in one hand, and the tissue she sneaks with it, and hook my arm around my Dad's arm. I catch the tears in his eyes as he looks me over as if it's the last time.

We know it's not, but this is the end of one chapter and the beginning of a whole new adventure. "You've made me unbelievably proud, Christine. I love you."

"I love you, too, Dad."

I turn to take Tagger's offered hands, his heart, and give him mine in exchange because the way we look at it, it's a win-win.

Dabbing the inner corners of my eyes with the tissue, I laugh from the happiness escaping me. I always thought I had a crush on Tagger Grange. It wasn't. It was love. I knew he was my soul mate. The universe took us in different directions but destiny brought us together in the end.

And now, standing with our boots touching and our hands held together, the man I dreamed about my whole life is ready to marry *me* as if I'm his dream come true as well.

EPILOGUE 1

Pris

As I hold my favorite black hat on my head, Tagger carries me onto the dance floor outside the barn and sets me down. He's quick to take my hand and spin me around, out from him, and then bring me back to him again. He captures me in his arms, and we slow it down and sway together.

My love overflows for him like the champagne at the reception. "I'm afraid I might love you too much," I say loudly, the music stopping before I finish talking.

Tagger smirks just eating up the attention when a few gazes find their way over. But most people are having too much fun themselves to pay attention to the newly married couple. Though he has my attention on lockdown. "Nothing to fear from loving someone as much as I love you, babe." I'm dipped, the hat falling right off my head, and then my neck is kissed . . . and licked . . . and nipped, causing my body to stir for more of this. Hovering over me, he whispers, "How long do we have to stay, dear wife?"

He has me wanting to rub my legs together. Too obvious

to others? Too late. I clench my thighs in anticipation. "As long as we want, dear husband."

"I want to dance," Beckett asks, staring me in the eyes.

Tagger rights me and then looks at me for the answer. An unspoken agreement is shared that we'll be picking up where we left off later. I bend down, and say, "I'd love to, Mr. Beckett."

Holding his hands, we come together and then back again. My grade school lessons of square dancing are coming back mixed with a little hokeypokey. But he's swept up by Baylor and set on his shoulders. "Want to help Lauralee and me put the horses up for the night?"

"Yes."

And then I'm on the dance floor alone.

My dad saves my pride, and we catch the next slow dance. "I wanted to give you something for your wedding."

"You already gave me so much—my something blue, the sapphire earrings, and the borrowed dress I took from her closet."

"Those were always meant to be yours. As a minority owner of Rollingwood Ranch but a major decision maker, I had a plot of land mapped out." He stops and pulls an envelope from his back pocket. "This is for you and Tagger to get your own home started."

"Dad, you didn't have to do that."

"I know. It's the place your mom always wanted to build her retirement home."

This is news. "You have a house. Right there."

"She wanted a cottage for just the two of us one day. We were going to keep this one for when family visits or we had the grandkids for the summer." He taps the envelope. "But this right here was the place she called most magical."

I take the envelope, feeling a stupid lump in my throat.

My emotions are running the gamut this wedding season. Before I can ask, he adds, "I buried her where the sun could shine on her. She was always looking for a sweater. But the spot where she lies is where I found her most mornings picking wildflowers. For several years, she spread the seeds. Now, they grow in her memory."

I move into my dad's arms, feeling closer than ever and knowing my mom is with us right now. "Thank you, Dad."

"No getting sappy. Go and get on with your night, Christine, and enjoy it."

I turn to see Tagger smiling at me. There are no signs of impatience or rushing me, but I still run right into his arms. He lifts me off the ground and twirls me around. I kiss his temple and whisper, "Where are you taking me for our honeymoon?"

He sets me down, leaving his hands heavy on my hips. "To heaven, baby, and back again."

"Promise?"

"I just made a vow before our friends and family and the skies above—"

"Fine," I say, playfully rolling my eyes. "I believe you."

While others are filing through the buffet of barbecue and homemade cheddar biscuits, we start dancing in the dirt because why not? But then I remember something and reach down to swap one contract for the plans my dad just gave us. Handing it to him, I say, "Here's your prenup."

"Are you mad?"

"Hell-bent with fire." When he flips open the paperwork, his eyes return to mine. "You didn't sign them."

"I'm not going to. We're in this together forever. What's yours is mine, and what's mine is yours."

With the papers in his hand, he lowers it to my hip while holding the other in the air. We start a slow dance that will only end up with us in bed, judging by the look in his eyes. *Sexy devil.*

He leans down and kisses me. "Tell me, Pris, was it worth the wait?"

"The wait was worth the while, cowboy."

. . . And they lassoed their way right into their own fairytale ending. But there's more *winks* So keep reading!

EPILOGUE 2

Tagger

Two years later . . .

Beck is running up ahead, Pris not far behind, though she looks back twice, crossing her eyes and pretending she's about to die from being run ragged by him, and somehow looks just as beautiful as she did at the sundries store. It's like not a day has passed, and my love only grows for her. She waves him forward. "Go on without me, Beck. Take care of your chickens, and I'll be there when I catch my breath."

From her encouragement, he's gotten into running to burn off all that energy he keeps stored up all day in school. The kid never tires, so now he outruns us all. He's taking after me and growing like a weed at his age. I just know I'm going to blink, and he's going to be in high school. But I guess that's how it works. We look up, and they're grown.

She's still too far ahead for my liking but turns around and starts walking backward. "He told me he's going to run around the Eiffel Tower this summer when he visits Anna." She laughs. "Hope she enjoys running."

"She enjoys yoga and shopping, if that counts."

"We all have our skill sets." She stops to wait for us.

When I reach her, she kisses the baby strapped to my chest on the head. Daisy Grange giggles and coos, kicking her legs wildly for her mom. She utterly adores her. *We all do.* She loves my son as if he's one of Pris's brood. I can't think of anything better than for him to be loved by so many parents and extended family.

As for my gorgeous wife, it's not just our lives that revolve around her. She's our entire universe, and I wouldn't have it any other way.

Pris lifts on her toes and kisses me next, still holding her side to release the cramp she got from running. Climbing up the hill from where our house sits on the edge of the woods in the lower pasture, we've worn a path up to Grandpa's house.

Sunday dinners are the family tradition we put in place, but Thomas eats with us most nights and then sits with us on the porch, listening to the flow of the nearby river. But tonight, Uncle Baylor is in town. Beck couldn't wait. Pris can't either. It's not been that long since he's been here, but it's always good to see him.

I'm hoping to rope him into a game of basketball. We built a half court last year that I get a lot of use out of. Sometimes, I even get her dad out there with Beck and me. He has a decent free throw for someone who claimed he never played.

Pris swings her arm out dramatically, bringing Daisy's and my attention to her. "I don't know when I got so out of shape. I used to run this place practically by myself. Now I can't even keep up with an eight-year-old."

"He's very fast."

"I'll give him that." We keep walking.

"And you still do run this place. It's a success because of you. It's okay to have a baby and recover at a pace that feels right for you." I catch her hand before she escapes again. "And you're so fucking sexy I can't keep my hands off you."

"No swearing while carrying Daisy. As for the last part, it's not your hands you struggle keeping off me." I chuckle. No lie is detected. "Since you brought it up, I wanted to give this to you."

I'm not even sure what we're talking about, but I'm curious. "What is it?" I look down and see a pregnancy test in her hand. My eyes flash from the test to her eyes and back again. "It's positive?" I ask with hope filling my chest.

Swinging her finger in the air, she says, "This is the part that loops back to you finding me utterly irresistible—"

I pull her to my side and kiss her forehead. "I do. I find you irrevocably irresistible."

She tears up and then laughs. "I thought I could play this off like it's no big deal, but it's a big deal, babe."

With the baby still between us, I say, "I can't think of anything better than having more babies with you." I hold her under my arm and kiss her head again until she tilts her chin to kiss me back. "I didn't know life could be this good."

"I did." Her confidence has always been such a fucking turn-on, but it was her heart that loved me enough to wait for me to catch up to her. Now that I am, I'm never letting her go. "This is the good life."

When she smiles and her cheeks pinken from the emotions coming to the surface, I fall in love with her like I do every morning when we wake up together in the fancy bed she never wants to leave and again at night before we turn off the lights and fall asleep in each other's arms.

I reach down and get a good grab of her ass. "Careful, cowboy, or you might get more than you bargained for."

I fucking love when she threatens me with a good time, but if she's not careful, I'm going for baby number three with her soon. *Who am I kidding?* I'm going to do that anyway. Three babies with her and their awesome big brother sounds good to me.

Four was always the perfect number.

Make sure to check out, *Lead Me Knot,* the next book in the Peachtree Pass Series.

YOU MIGHT ALSO ENJOY

Recommendations - These are books you'll enjoy reading after *Long Time Coming in addition to other Peachtree Pass series books.* These books will grab your heart and have you falling in love along with the characters.

Read in Kindle Unlimited and Listen in Audio

Never Got Over You - You met Harbor in Forgot to Say Goodbye. Now read the captivating and emotional journey that will break and heal your heart. Free in Kindle Unlimited.

Read in Kindle Unlimited and Listen in Audio

Along Came Charlie - You met Loch in Forgot to Say Goodbye. Now is the time to jump into this unexpected amnesia journey that will have them discovering who they want to while figuring out the mysteries that surround them. Free in Kindle Unlimited.

Read in Kindle Unlimited and Listen in Audio

Forgot to Say Goodbye - You met Marina's brother Noah in When I Had You. Now you get to follow his journey from playboy to the journey that leads him where he never expected - right into being a dad. *Surprise!* And how the life you thought you needed isn't the one you're destined for. Free in Kindle Unlimited.

ACKNOWLEDGMENTS

Thank you so much to this incredible team:

Kenna Rey, Content Editor
Jenny Sims, Copy Editing, Editing4Indies
Kristen Johnson, Proofreader
Andrea Johnston, Beta Reading
Cover Design: RBA Designs
Front Photo: Britt & Bean Photography
Back Image: Depositphotos
Audio Producer: Erin Spencer, One Night Stand Studios.
Narrators: Samantha Summers & Ryan Hudson

Thank you to my amazing Super Stars and my awesome SL Scott Books group members. To those who are not only peers but also friends. I adore our friendship, support, and you! *To my husband & sons, I love you more than the universe! Thank you for your forever support and love. Love you always. XOXOX*

ABOUT THE AUTHOR

New York Times and *USA Today* Bestselling Author, S.L. Scott, writes character driven, heart-racing, and swoony romances that will leave you glued to the page. Her stories are highly regarded as emotional, relatable, and captivating. They are journeys of the heart that always come with a happily ever after reward at the end.

Find her at: www.slscottauthor.com

Printed in Great Britain
by Amazon